Thirteen Stops

SANDRA HARRIS

POOLBEG

This book is a work of fiction. The names, characters, places, businesses, organisations and incidents portrayed in it are either the product of the author's imagination or are used fictitiously. Any resemblance to actual persons, living or dead, events or locales is entirely coincidental.

Published 2020
by Poolbeg Press Ltd.
123 Grange Hill, Baldoyle,
Dublin 13, Ireland
Email: poolbeg@poolbeg.com

© Sandra Harris 2020

The moral right of the author has been asserted.

© Poolbeg Press Ltd. 2020, copyright for editing, typesetting, layout, design, ebook

A catalogue record for this book is available from the British Library.

ISBN 978178199-748-2

All rights reserved. No part of this publication may be reproduced or transmitted in any form or by any means, electronic or mechanical, including photography, recording, or any information storage or retrieval system, without permission in writing from the publisher. The book is sold subject to the condition that it shall not, by way of trade or otherwise, be lent, resold or otherwise circulated without the publisher's prior consent in any form of binding or cover other than that in which it is published and without a similar condition, including this condition, being imposed on the subsequent purchaser.

www.poolbeg.com

About the author

Sandra Harris is a Dublin writer, poet, film-blogger, autism mom, animal lover, serial eavesdropper, horror fan, history buff and self-confessed bookworm. She always knew she was going to be a writer, having made various mad Viking-style dashes at it over the years before settling down to it properly in 2009.

She lives with her two children, her favourite books and the unassailable notion that, somehow, everything is still going to work out fine.

Thirteen Stops is her debut novel.

Acknowledgements

Thanks to Lisa for all the cups of tea and technical assistance, and to Reuben for the pats of encouragement on the shoulder.

Thanks to Orla and the Kevin Street Writers' Group for giving me my start.

Thanks to my wonderful agent Jonathan Williams, a gentleman to his fingertips and meticulous in his edits, for believing in me and the book.

Thanks to Paula Campbell of Poolbeg Press, the original Superwoman (I've seen how much she accomplishes in a day!), for taking a chance on me, and to my editor Gaye Shortland, a cool customer who's seen it all and who professed herself only *mildly* bemused when it transpired I was unfamiliar, to say the least, with the concept of track editing.

And last, but definitely not least, thanks to my fantastic Facebook friends who, over the years, have read my stories, my poems, my reviews and my blog posts and unstintingly dispensed encouragement, consolation (after the many rejections!), advice, suggestions for improvement, technical help and praise in equal measures.

I literally couldn't have done this without you all.

To Lisa and Reuben, my greatest achievements, and the gang of twelve

Autumn 2016

STOP 1: SANDYFORD

Laura

Laura Brennan stepped off the Luas at the Sandyford stop, as she did every morning, Monday to Friday. She quivered with excitement at the thought of seeing *him* again shortly. It was a cool clear day, so she would arrive in work with no damage to her long blonde hair, lovingly blow-dried poker-straight that morning. That was the trouble with straightening your hair. The least little upset in the weather and it all went to shite. Still, there was a price to be paid for beauty and sometimes the price was not being able to go out in the rain. Or the heat. Or when the sun was shining but it had just been raining and the air was still chock-full of sneaky old precipitation. That was the real killer. That gave you hair like Monica from *Friends* in 'The One in Barbados'.

Laura flipped her hair back over her shoulders and bent down to adjust her skirt, conscious as she did so that some perv was watching her, a dark-haired sleazebag with a wedding ring you could spot a mile off. *Spoken for, so you can't have me, but always up for some no-strings-attached sex*, it seemed to scream. Christ Almighty. Guys were such assholes. Laura shot him a filthy look and then clip-clopped off down the platform and out onto the road, pleased with the nice tappy noise her new black-velvet high heels were making.

Most of the other girls didn't put on their fancy high-heeled shoes until they reached the office, but Laura believed in making an impression and starting as she meant to go on, so she usually slipped into her good office shoes on the Luas. There was always some disapproving old biddy to scrunch up her nose in distaste at the sight of someone taking off their shoes publicly, but sod 'em, Laura always said. She'd bloody well change her shoes on the Luas, *and* put on her make-up and perfume as well, if it suited her. Everyone else could bloody well bugger off.

With her feet pinching only a little (later they'd be pinching a lot), Laura reached Phelan & Co. Warehousing Ltd with a few minutes to spare. His car, the nearly new 2015 Peugeot, was in its usual parking space in the big yard.

She went straight to the Ladies', as she always did first thing, to check her appearance, even though she was sure it was perfect. A quick selfie wouldn't go amiss either. No point wasting all this effort unless there was someone to see it, preferably a couple of hundred someones like the followers she had painstakingly amassed on her Instagram account. She expertly added another coat of mascara to her lashes and an extra dab of lip gloss to her mouth. It wouldn't do to look too tarty, so she didn't bother with any more powder over her foundation. The other girls disliked her enough as it was, for fussing so much about her looks. She did fuss – but you didn't catch a man with sweatpants and a shiny face.

Laura knew this full well. It was practically her mantra. She wasn't the most beautiful girl in the world, but she made the most of what she had and that was how she'd bagged Him-with-a-capital-H. Maybe the other girls should take note, instead of constantly bitching about her behind her back like she knew they did. They'd be laughing on the other side of their faces when they found out the identity of the man she was dating. She wished they could know now but telling anyone was strictly off-limits. Paul would have a fit if he thought anyone knew about their 'little fling', as he'd made the mistake of calling it once. He hadn't made it a second time – Laura had seen to that.

As it happened, she didn't get near him until quarter past eleven, by which time she was all agitated and hot under the collar. From her own desk, she had an unimpeded view of his office. All the junior managers in Phelan's had glass offices, not much bigger than toilet cubicles, which you could see into, and today the three or four junior managers were in and out of one another's offices for some reason, like the bloody cuckoo in a cuckoo clock gone haywire. It was always the same when she was desperate to see him. It was as if Fate was laughing at her. No, openly taking the piss out of her.

"I've missed you," she whispered, when she eventually got to enter his office on the pretext of needing his signature for something. She leaned over his desk, pretending to look at the papers she'd brought in with her but making sure he got a good look down her silky top and that her long, naturally blonde hair (one up on the bottle blondes anyway) brushed against his face.

"I've missed you too, Miss Brennan," he whispered back as he squeezed her thigh, making sure to keep his hand out of sight of anyone who might be watching.

The other junior managers had dispersed for now and the girls in the outer office, or the 'typing pool' as they still jokingly called it, were all clustered around the water cooler looking at something on someone's phone and laughing uproariously.

"I love that you take the time and trouble to wear these to work," Paul said, running his fingers up over her stocking tops and the bit of soft flesh between them and her high-cut lacy knickers.

Laura smirked at his praise. She well knew that he hated what he referred to as "those god-awful black woolly tights women wear the minute the weather turns a bit nippy". He had told her often enough. To have to wear sheer stockings and sexy undies to work was a pain in the backside – pun definitely intended. They cost more than regular underwear and were not designed for comfort by any stretch of the imagination, but the extra effort certainly paid off. Laura prided herself on the effect she had on Paul. He had an erection already under his pricey pinstripe trousers as he groaned and cursed the fact that they wouldn't be alone together until later on that evening, when he would come to her flat off St. Stephen's Green after work.

"Don't worry," she giggled, turning her head so that anyone looking in from outside wouldn't see her laughing. "I'll take good care of you tonight, my sweet."

"I wish you could take care of me now," he grumbled, indicating his tumescence. "What the fuck am I supposed to do about *this?*"

"You could always slip into the lads' loo and do-it-yourself," Laura sniggered before picking up her papers and swanning out of his office, making sure to give her backside in the tight skirt a little wiggle as she did so because she knew he'd be watching her.

Back behind her own desk, she shifted and fidgeted in her chair for the rest of the day, impatient for the evening to come so that she and Paul could be together. From where she sat, she was able to watch him at work. She was glad that he was spending most of the day at his desk under her watchful eye, although she frowned a little when he was taking phone calls, in case any of them were from Barbara. Barbara called him constantly, the needy cow. *Paul, the electricity's gone off. Paul, the school rang to say that Jessie has a stomach-ache – can you go and pick her up? Paul, I need money for shopping. Paul, your mother wants you to call out to the house after work today – your dad's had a fall and there's nobody to bring the coal in from the shed. Paul this, Paul that, Paul Paul Paul all day long.*

It drove Paul nuts. He told her so every time they met up. He always made a big show of putting his phone on silent whenever he arrived at Laura's flat. He never quite managed to turn it off though, she noticed, and she frequently caught him sneaking a glance at it during the evening, especially when they'd finished having sex and he was trying to leave without seeming to be rushing. That was an art few men had ever bothered to perfect, or even managed to carry off with any degree of panache. Laura tried her absolute hardest not to comment on it, because then she'd have been no better than Barbara the nag, Barbara the ball-and-chain, Barbara the big fat pain in the bloody arse, but sometimes she couldn't help it. She'd say something and then he'd get all defensive and claim that he was only checking what time his first meeting was in the morning. It might even end up in a row, and then Laura would blame herself for the rest of the week until she saw him privately again. Seeing him at work didn't really count. And she couldn't always manage to get to see him on his own.

They couldn't afford to have any more rows, Laura thought as she typed up a boring old invoice for a customer while keeping what she hoped was a discreet eye on Paul from her desk. He was so good-looking, with that strong jaw and the dark-brown Hugh-Grant-style hair that was always falling over his forehead. Laura loved to sit on his lap and push it out of his eyes, only to have it immediately flop straight back down again. But they'd fought a lot lately, argued quite bitterly, in fact, and mostly about that bitch Barbara. *When will you tell her? When are you going to talk to her? Are you just stringing me along, Paul, keeping me as your bit on the side while the whole time you're playing Happy Families with her? Why should I stay home alone all the time while you've got Barbara and Jessie and Lucy? You must take me for all kinds of a fool, Paul! Answer me, Paul!*

Laura hadn't really known before that it was possible to feel such black, all-consuming hatred towards another human being, especially another woman, a woman who had done nothing to harm her except marry the man that she, Laura, loved, and long before Laura had met him too, which made her hatred all the more unreasonable. For the thousandth time, Laura wished that she'd met Paul before his wife had. Paul was always saying stuff like that too. *If I'd only met you first, my love, my Laura,* he'd comment sadly with a beautifully mournful smile, *there would have been no contest. I would've married you and we'd have been together for always. We wouldn't have had to sneak around behind people's backs. We could have shown our love for each other openly.*

Laura always felt like her heart would break when he talked like this. It was nice to hear it, sure, but didn't he realise how hurtful it was, hearing him say stuff like that just before he went home, as happy as Larry after all their sex, to climb into bed beside Barbara? She, Laura, had feelings too, hadn't she? At least he wasn't sleeping with Barbara, that was one good thing about the situation. He slept *beside* her all right, but it was like sleeping next to a sibling or a mate, he'd assured Laura numerous times. There was nothing remotely *sexual* about it, if that was what was worrying Laura. Of *course* that was what was worrying her; what else would be? *That side of things has been over between us for a long time now,* he said every time Laura brought it up, which was more often than she should, she knew, but she couldn't help it. *We haven't had sex since Lucy was born. Any time I went near her, she freaked out and went all frosty on me, so I just left it and it sort of died a natural death, that side of things.* Laura wanted to believe him, she really did. And it was such a believable story as well. Women *did* go off sex during and after pregnancy, everyone knew that. But little Lucy was two years old now. How likely was it that Barbara was really still off sex? Never having been pregnant herself, thanks mainly to blind luck (blind *drunk* luck, more like, she thought wryly) and a sweet little invention called the morning-after pill, Laura wished she knew. According to Paul, Barbara was still playing the Ice Queen towards him a full two years after Lucy's birth. He was so sincere when he said it too. Laura always felt like a total heel for not fully believing him.

Just then her phone vibrated in the desk drawer with a text from him.

Can't wait to see you later, he'd typed in. **What colour are your knickers?** with a smiley face attached.

Cheeky! Laura immediately texted back, before relenting and adding the words, **Pink, if you must know.**

Oh, I must, I must! he texted back, with a huge smiley face attached. **Are you touching yourself under the desk and thinking of me? Are those little pink knickers nice and wet yet?**

You'll get me sacked, Laura texted back, adding a smiley face to take the sting out of her words. He must be out of his mind if he thought she found their distinctly unsexy workplace a turn-on.

Will you touch yourself for me later?

Maybe, if you're a good boy, Laura replied, conscious now that she was getting nosey looks from some of the other girls, who'd seen her texting and smiling like a simpleton at her phone. **But now get back to work, okay?**

Yes, ma'am, whatever you say!

Laura sighed and dragged her attention back to her work, putting her phone firmly back in her desk drawer. Paul had a sexually submissive side to him which she hated. He liked a woman to take charge of him in bed, be assertive, put him in his place. *It's something all powerful men like to do, so that they can switch off in their personal lives*, he'd say in explanation and, even besotted with him as she was, Laura always had to suppress a giggle at the thought of one of the junior managers in their piddly little warehousing company referring to himself as a 'powerful man'! Who the hell did he think he was – Richard Branson or Bill Gates or someone like that?

At first, two years before when they'd started their affair, this side of Paul had been something new, something exciting and kinky to look forward to, but now Laura was sick and tired of having to wear high heels and suspenders whenever he called to her flat and 'dominating' him in bed the way he liked. This could mean slapping his face or his backside, calling him names like 'a bad boy' or 'a dirty little gurrier' or 'a filthy maggot', sitting astride him during sex and being verbally or physically assertive, walloping him across the face or pinching and tweaking his nipples, which always made him yowl like a cat whose tail had just been trodden on and put Laura off her stride. *Not so hard, Jesus!* he'd whinge at her while she rolled her eyes. *I'll be deformed!*

Then he'd brought over a cane with him which folded up in his briefcase like a blind person's stick and asked her to hit him on the arse with it.

"Good and hard now. Don't be afraid. I won't break, you know."

She'd felt ridiculous doing it, but he'd enjoyed it so much that she hadn't had the heart to tell him how much she'd hated it and how degraded and silly she'd felt while doing it.

"Where'd you get this?" she'd asked him curiously.

"On the Internet," he'd replied with a shrug that seemed to imply, where else? "Isn't it great? It folds up neatly for discretion purposes. It says so on the box. That's what swung it for me."

"Yes, it's, *erm*, great." She'd tried her hardest to appear interested and excited and not to let her face show that her stomach was sinking all the way to her feet.

Once, she'd asked him if they could just have sex 'the

normal way,' with no slapping or name-calling or kinky stuff, and if he could just lie on top of *her* for a change, instead of the other way round. He'd done as she asked, but with such a bad grace and a sulky puss on him that she hadn't dared to ask him again. Now she was stuck in her role as Paul's private, unpaid dominatrix. She couldn't possibly say now, after all this time had elapsed, that she hated dominating him and that she just wanted to have ordinary sex with him, where they kissed, cuddled, made love and whispered sweet nothings to each other, just like normal couples.

Barbara wasn't into any kinky stuff, Paul had once confided to Laura. She wouldn't wear the sexy lingerie or be naked in front of him because she felt self-conscious about her body after two pregnancies, and she'd refused point-blank to dominate him in bed. That kind of thing made her feel physically sick, she'd said. She'd made him feel like a bleedin' pervert, he'd told Laura. He'd sounded genuinely surprised when he'd said it, too. So now Laura was stuck doing it, because she'd pretended to be fine with it in the beginning and now she couldn't possibly tell him that she loathed it with all her being. It would make her look stupid, or as if she'd lied about it at first. But if it gave her the edge over Barbara, if it meant that Paul kept coming to her for the things he couldn't get at home, then she'd bloody well keep doing it for as long as it took. She'd just have to put up with his weird fetishes for now and, once she was married to him and Barbara was history, she'd wean him off it somehow and they'd slip back into being a normal loving couple in no time. That was the plan anyway. It was the only plan she had.

In the meantime, though, he'd be calling to her flat

later on tonight and she had a surprise for him from Victoria's Secret, paid for with the money he'd given her himself for that exact purpose. He'd love the kinky little purply basque thing, that left her boobs and backside hanging out – the box called it 'tantalisingly uncovered' but it really meant just plain old hanging out – while sucking in her stomach and pushing up her boobs to an unnatural but exciting degree. Worn with the obligatory stockings, high heels and suspenders, the whole get-up would give him the hard-on of his life. After they'd had sex and she'd slapped his face and butt and called him every bad name she could think of (sometimes it was hard to think up new ones to thrill and excite him and he often had to tell her what to say, but he preferred it when she came up with them herself – he said it felt more natural like that. Natural! As if anything about a man begging a woman to belt him one in the kisser could ever be termed 'natural'!) – well, after all that she intended to ask him again when he was thinking of leaving Barbara. *Soon, my love, soon*, he always said, but then time passed, and yet more time passed, and nothing ever changed. Before she knew it, she was twenty-eight-going-on-twenty-nine, a whole two years of her life had vanished in a puff of smoke and they were no further forward, not so much as an iota.

Yes, tonight she was going to ask him again and, this time, she would attempt to pin him down to an actual time and date. When she'd first started seeing him on the sly, Barbara had been pregnant with Lucy and, of course, he couldn't have upset her then by announcing that he'd just met the love of his life at the office. The new girl, in fact, a girl called Laura, with silky blonde hair and blue eyes and a soft red mouth just made for kissing, which was how he always described her.

But Baby Lucy was over two years old now and it was time to stop tiptoeing around Barbara like she was some delicate flower, a fragile little woman who needed protection from the real world. Barbara Sheridan was thirty-four to Laura's twenty-eight. She was more than old enough to hear the painful home truths that Laura had been living with for so long – home truths about how Paul had found someone else and he didn't love her, Barbara, any more. He'd see her right, of course, her and the kids, during the big break-up, but then he had to be free to live his own life, with Laura, the woman he now loved and wanted to be with.

Tonight, Laura promised herself as she tap-tapped away on her computer for the afternoon, dealing with boring customer invoices and stupid customer queries with only half a heart. Tonight she'd ask Paul where she really stood with him, and she'd get it out of him as well, even if she had to threaten him with telling Barbara. She'd only do that as a last resort, of course. Something so drastic would be tried only in the event of a dire emergency, such as Paul trying to leave her (God forbid!), or Paul absolutely refusing to give her a straight answer about where she stood with him. She'd love for Barbara to know about their affair but, since Paul didn't want that under any circumstances, she'd have to go along with it for now. But not for much longer. There was a limit to even her patience, and God knows she'd been patient enough with him these last two years.

At the end of the seemingly endless day, she shut down her machine, chanced a quick glance across at Paul, who was deep in conversation with one of the other junior managers, grabbed her coat, phone and bag and headed out of the office to catch the Luas back to town.

There were thirteen stops on the part of the green Luas line that ran between Sandyford, where she worked, and St. Stephen's Green, near where she lived, and she usually counted them off in her mind while she gazed out the window at the passing landscape: *Sandyford, Stillorgan, Kilmacud, Balally, Dundrum, Windy Arbour, Milltown, Cowper, Beechwood, Ranelagh, Charlemont, Harcourt Street* and finally, home, *St. Stephen's Green*. Such lovely, dreamy *wispy* names. The automated female voice that intermittently requested passengers over the public address system to '*please move down the tram*' counted the stops off too, in English *and* in Irish for good measure ('*Next stop, Windy Arbour. An chéad stad eile, Na Glasáin*') for the benefit of commuters, and Laura never failed to find the woman's modulated, impersonal tones comforting, even soporific, as the tram chugged on its rhythmic way. Today, as always, her thoughts on the journey were full of Paul and, when she reached the Stephen's Green stop, she alighted briskly and hurried home to get ready for the night ahead.

Just as Laura was coming in the door of her flat, her mother phoned. She dearly wanted to ignore the call but her mother would only keep ringing and ringing until she answered. It was easier just to answer the damn thing straightaway and be done with it than to risk her phoning later, when Paul would be in the flat with her.

"Hi, Mum," she said, dreading whatever was coming next. "What's up?"

"I feel strange," her mother whined. "I have new tablets and they're making me feel dizzy and light-headed."

"Are these the ones for the depression or the ones for the anxiety? Or for the insomnia?"

"How should I know? Her at the chemist just gives them to me from the prescription and I take them."

"Can't you talk to her about them then? Or to Dr. Lee?"

Laura sat down on her bed and eased off her shoes with an enormous sense of relief. They looked fabulous but were extremely hard to walk in and even to sit at her desk in, and her feet were sore now. She really should have changed back into her flat-heeled pumps on the Luas but she'd enjoyed so much the way her legs looked in the high heels that she hadn't bothered. She'd even taken a few photos for her social-media accounts. Her poor feet were crippled now though. She rubbed them with one hand while holding her mobile in the other.

"I can't talk to Dr. Lee," her mother complained. "I can't understand a word she says and she can't understand me."

Laura sighed. Her mother was always complaining about poor Dr. Lee, a Chinese woman Laura had met a couple of times when she'd accompanied her mother to the surgery. Dr. Lee's grasp of English had seemed to Laura to be perfectly adequate but there was no pleasing Eleanor Brennan.

"Her English is fine, Mum." Laura, exasperated, began fantasising about the bath she planned to run the minute her mother was off the phone.

"All right then, she's an old bitch!" Eleanor burst out. "Are you happy now? She keeps telling me not to drink while I'm on the medication. The bloody cheek of her!"

"You *are* staying off the drink though, aren't you, Mum? And she has to do that. That's her job."

The silence was all the answer Laura needed. She sighed heavily again, closed her eyes and wished for the umpteenth time that her father, who she had never known, hadn't dumped Eleanor when he'd found out she was pregnant with Laura at the tender age of seventeen. Things might have been so different then. Laura would have had a father as she grew up, like all the other girls in school – might still have one – and the fragile Eleanor wouldn't have had a load of nervous breakdowns and become an alcoholic, leaving Laura to be mostly brought up by a succession of aunts and uncles who all had kids of their own to mind, and to whom Laura was just a nuisance and an extra expense they didn't need. Some men just didn't know, or care, about the damage they caused when they walked away from the women they had impregnated. Laura had lived with this depressing certainty her whole life.

"Can I come over?" Her mother was still wheedling. "Or can you pop round here?"

Laura thought frantically for a moment. Then the lies came bursting forth. "No, Mum. I'm sorry but I've got a friend coming over in a minute to stay the night. She's just broken up with her boyfriend and . . . *um*, she thinks she might be pregnant, so we've got a lot to talk about and I really just need to be there for her right now. You – you do understand that, don't you, Mum?"

"Fine, leave me here on my own to rot, why don't you?" Eleanor was in full sulk mode and snapping all around her like an alligator with a toothache.

"Look, I'll come over tomorrow, okay?" Laura was racked with guilt as she always was when she couldn't (or wouldn't) immediately comply with her mother's frequent demands. "I'll bring food and I'll cook you a lovely dinner, and I'll – I'll bring you over a nice bottle of wine to wash it down with." She hated herself for encouraging, even enabling, Eleanor's alcoholism but tonight she really had to see Paul. Nothing, not even her mother, would be allowed to interfere with that.

"You won't forget, will you, love?" The pitiful neediness in Eleanor's voice cut her to the quick.

"I won't forget, Mum. I promise."

After Eleanor had finally been persuaded to hang up, Laura sat on her bed for a long time, motionless, just staring into space.

Laura wouldn't have wanted Paul to know this, but she had a history of this kind of thing. Married men, attached men, men with girlfriends and children, men with baggage. They had to have baggage. She always went for the same kind of guy. Guys who were single meant less than nothing to Laura. They had to have wives or girlfriends, so that she could work hard to lure them away from their significant others. This made her feel good about herself. It made her inordinately happy to have a man prefer her to the woman he'd promised to love, honour and cherish until death did them part. If she thought about the psychology of it at all, she would have said that because she hadn't had a father of her own, she felt the need to be close to men who were husbands and fathers themselves. She didn't think that she was trying to deprive other kids of *their* fathers just because she hadn't had one herself. That would have been horrible. It was more that she was attracted only to older men with families and responsibilities and that was just the way it was. Who the feck cared about the psychology of the thing?

In her last job, she'd had an affair with the company's managing director. That wasn't as grand as it sounded because the company had been a small freight one with only a handful of employees. The affair had ended in disaster when Harry's wife found out about her husband's relationship with his new receptionist. She'd come charging round to the office and had screamed at Laura in front of everyone. It had been a truly demoralising experience. Harry had given her her notice then. She'd lost both her job and her lover on the same day – a new low – but nobody in that office had had any sympathy for her. No one had talked to her, not a single murmured word of encouragement or empathy, while she was clearing out her desk and doing the walk of shame out the front door with her arms full of her cardboard box, her potted plant and other small effects.

The time before that hadn't ended quite so publicly, but it had ended nonetheless, leaving Laura feeling unwanted, unloved and unlovable. It was bad enough that her own father hadn't wanted her, and that he'd left her mother the instant he'd found out about the pregnancy. The feelings of being unloved were hard to bear. Laura hoped and prayed that, this time, she'd really found *The One* in Paul Sheridan. It had to be Paul. She'd put so much time and effort into making him want her and love her. It just *had* to be Paul.

When Paul came over that night around six-thirty, they went straight to bed as usual. Much to Laura's gratification, he practically salivated at the sight of her in the stockings and suspenders, and the tight purply basque thing that made her waist look waspishly tiny and her boobs round and full. The thing was as uncomfortable to wear as a bloody whalebone corset from the Victorian era and she felt utterly ridiculous answering the door of her flat while wearing it, but Paul's reaction was all the reward she needed. Madly fluttering her heavily mascara'd eyelashes, she led him to the bed and helped him undress as if he were an emperor and she were his concubine. She went straight into her usual spiel when he was lying there expectantly, naked as a jaybird and semi-erect, waiting for her to start their regular procedure.

"Have you been a naughty boy this week, Paul?" she asked him as she stroked his pale, hairy body. She could recite the words by heart at this stage, she'd said them to him so often over the course of their relationship. "Have you been thinking naughty thoughts, Paul? Maybe doing naughty things like touching yourself? Have you been touching yourself, you wicked, wicked boy?"

"Oh yes, mistress!" he panted, taking her hand and moving it with his own over his engorged penis. "I need to be punished, mistress! You will punish me, won't you?"

"Oh yes, of course I will, you wicked boy!" Laura sneaked a glance at the clock on the bedside table. If she wrapped this up pretty sharpish, she'd still have time to talk to him about the very important matter of Their Joint Future. She wasn't spending all night walloping his flabby arse and pretending to give out stink to him for thinking about naked women while he wanked. Trying to disguise the boredom she felt, she continued: "Yes, you're certainly going to be punished, you disgusting boy! I'll teach you to touch your filthy – *thing* without my permission!"

She slapped him smartly across the face three or four times in quick succession.

"*Now will you learn?*" she shouted at him as he frantically pulled at his willy. "*Now will you learn to do as I say, you filthy little maggot?*"

"*Oh yes, mistress! I'll learn, I'll learn, I swear!*" he gasped, the sweat breaking out all over his forehead. "*Hop on,*" he added, frantically indicating his swollen member. "*Hop on fast while it's hard! Come on, come on, hop on, will you, before it goes down!*"

Hop on? thought Laura irritably. What is this, a stiff willy or the 46-fucking-A bus? She had a sudden mad vision of herself tapping her Leap card against something bendy and fleshy and had to turn a stray hysterical giggle into a cough. She hated when he talked like that. It was about as romantic as a bout of diarrhoea or a heavy period. Suppressing a sigh, she dutifully climbed aboard and rode the bus into the station, thinking about other things the whole time, like a new fashion website she'd seen that had some gorgeous boots for sale. She might go online after Paul had left and order a pair. She could justify the expense if she was going to be the official girlfriend of a junior manager soon.

After the sex, Paul lay on his back panting, bright red in the face, scratching at his armpits. "That was amazing, love!" he said when he'd got his breath back.

"You're not going home already, are you?" she said in dismay, when she saw him heaving himself into a sitting position on the edge of the bed, prior to scrabbling about for his trousers. He always left a load of loose change on her bedroom floor after sex, when the contents of the pockets of his carelessly discarded trousers spewed out and scattered everywhere in his haste to get her into bed. It made her feel like a hooker, picking his money up off the floor after he'd left.

"*Um*, no, of course not."

Liar, liar, pants on fire, thought Laura.

He fished about for his socks. "I'm just getting dressed so that you can make me a nice cup of coffee before I head off, that's all."

"Good," said Laura firmly, "because I need to talk to you before you go. It's about time you told me where I stand with you, with this relationship. I mean, after two years I'm still your bit on the side? Like, what's all that about?"

She hadn't meant to bring this stuff up while they were still basking in the afterglow of sex but, what harm, it was out now. And what difference did it make whether they talked about it here and now, in the bedroom, post-coitally, or when they were sitting down at her kitchen table over a cup of coffee? The questions to which she wanted answers, would *demand* answers, would still be the same, regardless of the venue or how careful she was about the timing. Anyway, she knew there was never really a good time for this kind of thing.

"You know you've always been so much more to me than just a bit on the side," Paul said.

He was crouched down tying his shoelaces so she couldn't see his face, but it sounded as if he was uncomfortable with the topic of conversation. It was always the same whenever she tried to bring up the subject of Their Relationship, or Their Future. Well, this time she was going to push it and she didn't care how uncomfortable Mr. Paul Sheridan became. He was just going to have to man up and grow a pair and that was all there was to it. She *hoped*.

"When are you going to tell Barbara about me?" she persisted.

When he straightened up, his colour was high and he

was running his fingers through his dark hair, making it stand on end, a thing he did every time he was stressed.

"Babes . . ."

She gritted her teeth. She hated when he called her that because it invariably meant that a big fat fobbing-off was coming.

"Babes," he said again, placatingly, "that's not the kind of thing you casually drop into conversation over breakfast, you know. '*Oh, by the way, Barbara, I've met someone new and I'm leaving you and the kids for her, and could you please pass the butter, dear?*' Oh yes, I can just see that going down really well at the breakfast table, can't you?"

Laura was in no mood to let him away with any of his usual mealy-mouthed sarcastic excuses or bullshit, or that thing he did where he put everything back on her, making *her* look unreasonable for bringing up the subject, the way he'd just done.

"But you've had *two years* to do it in." She was challenging him now and she knew it. "Two fucking years, and you still haven't told her about us?"

"It's not that simple, Laura." He sounded mutinous. "People can't just go around dropping bombshells on people like that willy-nilly."

"*Willy-nilly?*" Laura was practically yelling now. "*Willy-nilly? Paul, you've had two fucking years! How much longer could you possibly need?*"

"There's no need to shout. You'll have the neighbours in here in a minute." Typical Paul, trying to deflect any negative attention away from himself, if only for a minute. It gave him time to regroup, get his story straight.

"I'm not shouting." Laura took a deep breath and tried hard to compose herself. "But what, for argument's sake, would stop you from going home and telling her about us tonight, after you leave here?"

"I told you, Laura, it's not that fucking simple."

"*Why not?*" She knew her voice was rising to dangerously shrill levels once more but she couldn't help herself.

"Because," he said, looking her straight in the face for once, "because Barbara's fucking *pregnant,* that's why."

Laura gasped in shock.

"Pregnant? *Pregnant?* By whom, might I ask?"

"By me, of course." He looked genuinely puzzled. "Who else would knock her up?"

"*You fucking bastard!* You swore you weren't sleeping with her. You even swore it on your grandmother's grave! Her actual *grave!*"

"It only happened the once." He sounded sullen now. "I had no idea that *this* was going to happen."

"It only takes the once, you idiot!" Laura snapped back. She felt angrier than she'd ever felt in her life before. "What are you going to do about it?"

She jumped out of bed and tore the stupid purply basque thing off her body, replacing it with her long woolly brown dressing-gown, the belt of which she tied tightly around herself. *There.* That made her feel more armoured, ready for the fray.

"And were you ever going to tell me about it?" She narrowed her eyes and gave him her coldest, hardest stare.

He said nothing, just looked down at his feet in their stupid novelty socks, a pair with happy reindeer on them which his kids had given him for Christmas the year before. (It always annoyed her when he wore them. She knew it was unreasonable of her, but she couldn't help it.

And, anyway, you'd think he'd have the wit not to wear them when he went to bed with his mistress.)

When the penny dropped, Laura's blue eyes widened.

"You fucking little shit," she said softly. "You were never going to tell me, were you? What *were* you going to do? Just crawl back to that bitch Barbara and pretend that I never existed?"

"Something like that." He shrugged. "And don't call her names, will you? She doesn't deserve that. She doesn't deserve *any* of this shit. I feel terrible about what we've – what *I've* –" he amended when he saw her furious face, "been doing to her these last couple of years. She may not know about this – this affair we've been having, but she certainly knows that things haven't been right between us now for a long time. Our sex life is completely fucked and we haven't communicated properly in months now. She's been trying to talk to me about it, but I've been giving her the run-around because of you, us. I'm actually kind of surprised she hasn't left me before now. How she puts up with me, well, I just don't know. She must be a fucking saint."

He stood up after this little speech and began pulling on his shirt and jacket, seemingly unaware that everything he'd just said had only served to light Laura's blue touchpaper.

"Oh, *Saint* fucking Barbara!" she sneered. "Of course, we mustn't say a word against the precious *Saint* Barbara the fucking Great! And just exactly when were you planning on leaving me?" A note of hysteria had crept into her voice.

"I don't know." He ran his hands through his hair again so that it stood up like a chicken's feathers all over his head. "Some time in the next few weeks, maybe. Barbara only found out about the baby a few weeks ago.

We were hoping it might, you know, help to glue us back together as a family if we all rally round. Me, Barbara, Jessie, Lucy and the new baby. We were hoping it might be a boy this time," he finished hopefully.

The horrible realisation that she was being dumped, that she didn't figure anywhere in Paul's plans for his cosy family future, hit Laura like a swinging brick to the face.

"But I've . . . I've spent the last two fucking years waiting for you to leave her!"

"I never asked you to, not in so many words." He was patting himself down now, checking for phone, wallet and keys.

"You implied that we'd be together if I was prepared to wait for you!"

"Well, you must have misinterpreted what I said. I can't be held responsible for that, can I?"

He actually had the nerve to sound bored now.

Her voice rose ever higher as she said, "*And I've done all that kinky stuff you wanted me to do. I've been your own personal fucking dominatrix and sex-slave for two fucking years now, for Christ's sake! I even shaved my whatsit for you! I bloody-well nicked myself doing that!*"

"You got as much out of all that as I did, surely?" he said piously.

"*I fucking hated it, you sick pervy bastard!*" she screamed across the bed at him.

He looked at her as if he couldn't quite make her out. "Well, you should have said so, then."

She should have *said*? *She should have fucking said?* She wanted to kill him. Instead, what came out was: "*I straightened my hair for you every single day! For two whole years, I lived in fear of a bloody drop of rain!*"

He stared back at her uncomprehendingly, as if she'd gone off her rocker altogether. It enraged her, especially when she thought of all the agonies of effort and inconvenience she'd endured to straighten her naturally wavy tresses, just because he'd once commented that he loved her straight hair. The absolute fucking *bastard*.

"If you leave me, I'll tell Barbara!" she said wildly then. "You're forgetting I know your home phone number!"

"No, you won't, Laura," Paul retorted wearily, pulling on his tie. "You're not that much of a bitch. You wouldn't go around deliberately causing that kind of havoc, ruining my kids' lives as well as mine and Barbara's and the new baby's. You're better than that."

If he was trying to use reverse psychology on her, Laura thought, then he was bloody well barking up the wrong bloody tree.

She took a step closer to him and said quietly, "I'll tell her, Paul. I swear to God I will."

His face hardened into stone. "That's *your* choice, Laura. It's entirely up to you what you do. It's got nothing to do with me any more. Now, *goodbye*, Laura. I'll see you at work tomorrow, although it's probably better if you look for a new job. There might be some – *awkwardness* between us for a while." And, with that, he walked out of the flat, closing the door behind him.

"*Fuck you, Paul Sheridan, fuck you! I hate you, you fucking bastard, I hate you!*" she screamed. She picked up the little bedside clock and flung it with all her strength at the wall, where it smashed, and then she grabbed up her phone. She hesitated for a moment, then dialled a number she knew by heart and waited.

"Hello?" she said.

STOP 2: STILLORGAN

Suzanne

Suzanne Carragher got on the Luas at Stillorgan. It wasn't her usual stop but she'd been spending the night at her sister's house. She'd received a garbled call from Barbara late the night before. Barbara had sounded almost incoherent with grief and rage, something about Paul and another woman. Once she'd established that nobody was sick or had died, and that Barbara's kids Jessie and Lucy were okay, Suzanne had asked her sister to slow down and start from the beginning. Apparently a strange woman had phoned Barbara on her house phone, claiming to have had a sexual relationship with Paul, and even saying she was pregnant by him, if you please.

Barbara had gone into hysterics, screaming abuse at Paul when he got home from working late (if that's what he *was* doing) and not allowing him to get a word in edgeways, it seemed, which was typical of her. When he was finally allowed to speak, Paul had point-blank denied the whole thing. Barbara, not believing a word out of his mouth – this was not the first time she'd had reason to doubt him – had ordered him out of the house, and Paul, obviously unwilling to go too far away from the family home in case he couldn't get back in again, had spent the night in their garage, on the back seat of his car, wrapped in a slightly mouldy sleeping bag left over from their one attempt at camping. From the state of him at breakfast time, Suzanne reflected wryly, he'd had a miserable night. Well, it bloody well served him right.

Barbara had called Suzanne, the older sister to whom she'd always been close, once she'd banished Paul from the house. After establishing the basic facts of the matter and stopping off at a supermarket to buy wine (before their off-licence shut at ten) and big family-sized bars of emergency chocolate for comfort, Suzanne had jumped on the Luas and gone straight to her sister's house in Stillorgan.

"Who is she, Barb?" she'd asked when they were both installed on high stools at the breakfast bar in the kitchen, knocking back the wine and breaking up the chocolate bars into bite-sized chunks. There was no situation that couldn't be improved upon with wine and chocolate, the sisters had long since discovered.

"Some absolute *slut* from his work." Barbara chugged back the ends of a glass of wine and immediately poured herself a refill. "One of the tramps from the typing pool, I think. *Laura!*" She'd spat out the name with venom.

"And you believe her, do you?" Suzanne asked tactfully. "I mean, she's not just some young one trying to stir up trouble for Paul for some reason? Or maybe she tried it on with him, he rebuffed her and now she's out for revenge? It happens sometimes, you know."

Barbara shook her head grimly, her long dark hair swinging in time with her movement, and lit a cigarette. She normally didn't smoke in the house (smokers had to congregate in the back yard), but this was clearly an exceptional circumstance. "Too many of the things she said made sense, Suze. She told me what nights he'd been round at her place, *fucking* her. They were the nights he said he'd had extra work on at the office or nights he was pretending to see his mates to watch the football. I *knew* he was lying, the sneaky little fuck! All this wagon did was confirm it for me."

"And you really believe her when she says she's pregnant?" Suzanne's mouth was full of chocolate but Barbara got the gist.

"Well, why not? It'd be just like him to be so fucking irresponsible. Knock up me *and* some slut as well at the same time. I'm going to have myself tested for venereal disease, and so is he if he ever wants to come anywhere near me or the kids again. I could *kill* him. Bringing all this down on us just when we've got a third kid on the way. He's ruined everything, the spineless prick. Just because he couldn't keep it in his fucking pants. Yet again."

Barbara's brown eyes were bright with tears and Suzanne's heart went out to her.

"It doesn't have to be the end of everything, Barb. Plenty of couples eventually put this kind of thing behind them, especially where there are kids involved. It'll take time, but why should your marriage be destroyed by some little trollop from his office who's just out for what she can get?"

"She's welcome to him," Barbara said but there was a note of uncertainty in her voice, as if she didn't really mean it.

"You don't mean that, Barb." Suzanne warmed to her theme. "What are you going to do, just hand your husband meekly over to this little gold-digger in a gift-wrapped package? Tell her what time he likes a cup of tea in the evening and how he likes his eggs done? Why should she get the benefit of all the years you've spent training him to be your ideal husband?"

"Much good it did me. Sure, I taught him to put the bins out on the right night and how to do the weekly shop on his own, but where did it get me? The second my back's turned, he's sticking it to some little hussy from his office. I can just picture her, this *Laura*, all glossy and perfect and blonde and petite. In other words, everything I'm not."

"Don't you dare say that!" Suzanne was fierce in her sister's defence. "You're beautiful and you know you are. You're just tired and you have no time to doll yourself up because you've got two small kids to look after and now you're pregnant again. This Laura has obviously got all the time in the world to put on false fucking eyelashes and a stupid fake tan. Let's see how much time *she* has left for prettying herself up when she's as big as a house and puking her guts up into the toilet every morning."

Suzanne realised her mistake when Barbara burst into loud howls.

"She's having his baby, Suze! Oh Christ, his *baby!* I can't bear it, I can't!"

Shit shit shit, Suzanne berated herself. Why on earth did she have to open her big mouth like that? Hurriedly she said, "Look, Barb, do we know for a fact that she's pregnant? She could be lying. Women do that, you know, to hold on to a guy who's trying to shake them off."

"Do you really think she could be lying?" Barbara whispered, her eyes huge and tear-filled.

"Why not?" Suzanne hoped against hope that she was right. "A woman who's low enough and nasty enough to sleep with another woman's man would certainly be capable of lying her scrawny little arse off to get what she wants."

Damn Paul to hell, Suzanne thought angrily, causing all this hurt to his wife just because some tramp in a tight skirt and a low-cut top made goo-goo eyes at him and his stupid thoughtless willy responded in kind.

"How can we find out?" Barbara said, sniffling.

"Well, that's up to Paul, I guess. He needs to find out whether this woman is genuinely pregnant or not, or if this baby is even his. It might be someone else's kid, and she might be trying to palm it off on Paul. In which case," she went on, glad to see that Barbara's face had brightened, "he'd have to wait until the baby was born to get a DNA test to find out for certain."

"But that takes the full nine months!" Barbara sounded disconsolate again. "Do I have to wait *nine fucking months* to find out if some little slapper is going to wreck my marriage?"

"It might not be as long as that," Suzanne said in what she hoped were comforting tones. "I mean, it depends on how far gone she is now. That's if there even *is* a baby. We shouldn't be talking about it as if it's a done deal. There might not even *be* a baby to worry about!"

"Do you really think so?" Barbara whimpered.

"I think we should wait to find out for sure before we start fretting about it," Suzanne said firmly. "And now you should definitely go on up to bed. You're exhausted and you've still got to get the kids up for school in the morning."

Barbara looked at the clock with eyes that were red and bleary from crying. It was twenty to one in the morning. The phone call had come about five hours earlier.

"Will you sleep in with me?" she asked her sister.

"Of course I will. But come on up now before you fall asleep down here."

"You won't let Paul back into the house, will you?"

"Just let him dare try," Suzanne replied grimly. "He'll get a taste of this if he does," she added, picking up the nearest thing that could pass muster as a weapon.

At the sight of her older sister standing in the kitchen brandishing one of Jessie's Barbies, a tennis-playing one with a tiny electric-pink skirt and baseball cap on her ridiculously disproportionate frame, Barbara burst out laughing.

"Hey, I can stick these in some pretty small places, you know." Suzanne made menacing jabbing movements with her weapon of choice.

"Try Paul's pea-brain, then. It's the smallest part of him by miles," Barbara said drily, and both sisters laughed.

Before the laughing could turn into sniffling again, Suzanne determinedly propelled her exhausted sister out the kitchen door and up the stairs to bed.

"Tickets please, love," said the Luas ticket-checker, a big smiley-faced fella with a beard. All the Luas staff were lovely lads, Suzanne thought. And the ladies were lovely too, of course.

"Sorry – I was miles away there," she said, fumbling in her bag for her ticket.

"Somewhere nice, was it?" he said, punching a hole in her ticket.

"Not exactly." Suzanne laughed wryly.

"Then it's no good for you, love." The man grinned before moving on to the next passenger. "Keep out of there."

I wish I could, Suzanne answered him in her mind. But it wasn't that simple. As the gentle motion of the Luas lulled her into a state of near-relaxation, she deliberately repressed the thoughts she'd been having when the ticket-checker had interrupted her reverie. Instead, she forced her mind to drift back to earlier that morning at Barbara's house.

She'd woken up the kids herself so that her distraught and hungover sister could have a lie-in. Poor Barbara, Suzanne had thought when she'd seen her in the bed, lying on her back with her mouth open, snoring lightly. Let her have this bit of oblivion. There'll be time enough to face all the heartache and bullshit later, plus the big fat wine hangover.

While she'd been decanting cereal into the girls' bowls from the plastic cereal tub Barbara insisted on (Why not just leave it all in the boxes, she always wanted to ask her but never did — Barbara had her particular little ways), Paul had crept into the kitchen from the garage, shamefaced and unshaven.

"I need to get ready for work," he mumbled as Jessie rushed at him, delightedly crying, "*Daddy! Daddy!*"

"I'm not stopping you," said Suzanne coolly.

"*Pooh*, Daddy, you smell stinky!" Jessie recoiled from him, wrinkling her tiny button-nose in distaste.

"That's because I need a shower and a change of clothes," Paul said ruefully as he patted his daughters' curly heads and headed for the kitchen door.

"You can use the bathroom in the guest bedroom," Suzanne cut in when she realised that he intended to go upstairs and probably disturb Barbara with his morning ablutions.

"But all my stuff is in the master bedroom. All my shaving things and the clothes I need for work!"

His protests sounded to Suzanne's irritated ears like those of a whingy schoolboy. "I'll get your things for you. Barbara needs to sleep."

"I don't see why," Paul said sulkily. "She's not the one who's spent the night freezing her fucking hole off out in the garage. It's like the fucking Arctic Circle out there."

"*Daddy said a swear, Daddy said a swear!*" Jessie cried gleefully.

Not wanting to be left out of any fun, Lucy in her highchair promptly upturned her cereal bowl, leaving a soggy mess for Suzanne to clear up.

Suzanne shot Paul a look that she hoped conveyed the words: *Listen, you whingy little prick, do you really want to talk about why you were sent to sleep in the fucking garage last night?*

He shut his mouth, obviously thinking better of that tactic, and said not another word as she ushered him upstairs to the guest bedroom and made him wait while she quietly fetched his clothes and shaving things from the master bedroom.

Later, as he was waiting for Suzanne to do the girls' hair and get them into their coats for school (Jessie) and crèche (Lucy), he said, "Will you talk to Barbara for me, Suze?"

"What about?" she said coldly, attempting to coax Jessie's long brown curls into an elaborate series of slides and hair ribbons.

"Well, all this, of course." He shrugged and threw his arms wide to indicate that he meant the general situation in which he found himself.

Not through any fault of his own, of course, Suzanne thought sourly. That was so typical of Paul. He never took responsibility for bloody anything if he could help it. Every time he got Barbara pregnant, he went round for weeks afterwards wringing his hands and saying how could this have happened? She and Barbara laughed about it together every time as they mock-explained: *Well, Paul, you see, it's like this. When a Mammy Rabbit and a Daddy Rabbit love each other very much . . .*

"All what?" She was determined not to make it easy for him.

"You *know* what," said Paul. He turned to the children. "Jessie, be a good girl and take Lucy out to the car and wait for me there, will you? It's open. Be careful now."

"Are you in trouble, Daddy?" Jessie asked, before skipping off to the garage, trailing her toddler sister in her busy wake.

"You could say that," muttered her father glumly.

He turned to Suzanne when the kids were gone. "Look, I know what this looks like but I swear to God I was breaking it off with this girl and that's when she decided to go all Glenn-Close-in-*Fatal Attraction* on me and squeal on me to Barbara."

Squeal on you? thought Suzanne, disgusted. What are you, a fucking schoolboy who's been caught cheating on a spelling test?

Aloud, she said: "Spare me the sordid details, please. All I care about is that Barb and the kids don't get dragged down as well just because *you've* fucked up."

"I care about that too!" He took a step closer and held his hands out to her, palms up, in the traditional gesture of openness and honesty, neither of which qualities he possessed. "I swear to God, Suze. Just help me out this once, please, will you? For Barb's sake, and the kids'. Just talk to her for me, would you? Persuade her to give me another chance? I swear on the kids' lives I won't fuck up again."

"*Don't say that!* Swearing on the kids' lives like that. I hate it when people do that. What if you're lying, or if for some reason you can't keep your promise? It's sick, saying things like that."

"Okay, okay – but you'll do it, won't you?" He was pleading now. "You'll talk to Barb for me?"

He looked so pathetically eager, like a puppy begging to be let in out of the rain, that Suzanne felt herself weaken. Making a clicking noise of disgust with her tongue that was as much for herself as for him, she nodded. "All right, Paul, all *right*. I'll do it. For Barbara and the kids, not for you. As long as we're clear on that. But, for now, I think it's best that you go to work and keep out of her way for a while. Give her a bit of space to think and don't be bombarding her with any texts and phone calls. I'll talk to her later, when she wakes up, but only if she's ready to talk about it, okay?"

"Whatever you say, Auntie Suze." The little weasel was all smiles now that he'd got his own way. He hurried away through the door that led to the garage. A minute later, she heard his car pulling off down the driveway.

After clearing away the kids' breakfast things, she went quietly up the stairs and into the master bedroom to see if Barbara was awake yet and ready to have that talk.

They'd had their talk, during which Barbara had raged and sworn blind that she never wanted to see that cheating, lying scumbag again, then reversed her position and declared that she couldn't live without him and would do anything to keep him, even if he wanted to bring that knocked-up strumpet to live with them both in their very own house. (Barbara had apparently read in a magazine about something like that happening once and she'd never forgotten it. Some woman in England had taken her husband's pregnant, much younger mistress into her home, because it was the only way she could hold on to her man. There'd been a group photo of the three of them. None of them had looked even slightly happy.)

After persuading Barbara that no such drastic action would be necessary, and that all she needed to do to keep Paul was simply to agree to give him a chance to talk things through with her that evening when he got in from work, Suzanne had managed to get away, promising faithfully that she'd be back again by dinnertime at the latest to keep Barbara and the kids company, and even to stay over with them again if necessary.

"*Please move down the tram*," said the automated female voice now over the tannoy, but nobody moved. Nobody ever moved or took a blind bit of notice of the announcement. Which way was down, anyway? Suzanne had always wondered. Was it going *away* from the driver, or was it going *towards* him? Did anyone know or ever bother to find out? The posh automated woman was pretty much wasting her breath, but she was just doing her job.

Now the tram was passing through Ranelagh on its way into town and Suzanne tearfully craned her neck out of the window to see if she could spot their house. She could and did. There was a white blob in the garden which might have been Ida hanging out the washing on this breezy autumn day. She chose to believe that the white blob had indeed been Ida. Suzanne wanted nothing more at that moment than to be at home in the dinky little two-bedroomed house with Ida, coming up on her from behind and enfolding her in a big cuddly bear-hug, there amongst the sheets, towels and pillowcases billowing in the breeze. Instead, she was going into town, to one of those big old Georgian buildings that encircled St. Stephen's Green, the tall imposing buildings with four or five storeys and the servants' quarters at the very top, which had once housed the rich families of Dublin but that now mostly served as boring old office space. Suzanne had been there before, and she was dreading the thought of going there again.

She tried to distract herself with the passenger-watching that she normally enjoyed. There was an attractive young couple sitting across from her who were having one of those muted, passive-aggressive arguments that people have when they're in public, when they don't want to be seen fighting but they nonetheless can't help it because the matter is so pressing. Suzanne watched the lad (they both looked like college students) try to take the girl's hand in a gesture of affection, but she snatched it away.

"What's the matter with you?" he asked, holding up his hands as if he genuinely didn't have a clue why she was upset.

To Suzanne's amusement, the girl, sounding upset and annoyed, replied, "If you don't know, then I'm not telling you!"

Suzanne would have sworn that women never really said that outside of books or films, but here was living proof that they did.

To which the lad answered, perplexed, "But if you don't tell me, then how the fuck am I supposed to know what's wrong with you?"

"You should already know," persisted the girl.

"Ah, fuck this." The young man glowered, turning away from her and folding his arms to indicate that he was now closed for business and he wouldn't be extending the hand of peace or friendship again.

Tears were now forming in the girl's eyes, but it was obvious that she was going to continue to let the boy stew in his own juices, that she wasn't going to tell him what it was that was upsetting her because she'd rather bite off her own tongue than be the one to back down.

Thank God I'm done with all that teenage angst, Suzanne told herself as she allowed her glance to drift away from the squabbling couple to a young mother across the aisle who was having trouble comforting her crying baby. Everyone else was scrolling frantically on their phones or listening to music, their earbuds firmly in place. *Don't disturb me,* they were saying without words. *I'm not amenable to any social overtures today, thanks.* The chubby little baby boy didn't want to sit in his buggy and he didn't want to be lifted out and hugged. He didn't want his dummy, his rattle or his bottle. He just wanted to kick and scream and lash out at his embarrassed mother, much to the annoyance of some of the passengers nearest to them, who were shooting the poor mother filthy why-can't-you-control-your-own-child looks.

Suzanne dug around in her bag until she found what she was looking for – an orange lollipop, still in its wrapper, that she'd bought for Jessie but had forgotten to give her. Barbara was very Sergeant-Majorish about sugary sweets and drinks, so the treat would probably have found its way into the bin at some stage anyway. It might as well go where it would do someone some good.

"Is he allowed to have this?" she said, extending the lollipop across the aisle to the harassed mother. "I know it's sugary but . . ."

"Thank you!" the mother cried gratefully, taking the treat from Suzanne and proffering it to the fractious, red-faced toddler, who was already holding out his grubby little paw for it. "He's teething at the minute, you see, and everything makes him cranky. He normally loves going on the Luas but not when he's like this. Anyway, thank you. You're a life-saver."

"No worries." Suzanne settled back in her seat and closed her eyes, enjoying the blissful silence.

The sight of the vociferous little baby boy reminded her of the conversations she and Ida had had lately about maybe one day having a child of their own and the different ways that that could be achieved. They had just about hit on the idea of asking a woman they both knew, who had been a surrogate mother once before for someone else, to have their baby for them (they felt it would be fairer to have a surrogate – that way, the baby would 'belong' to neither and yet both of them) when Suzanne had suddenly found the lump, the stupid fucking lump that had her haring over to St. Stephen's Green in the middle of the day in a mad panic, when she should have been at home with Ida. Was this lump going to snatch everything away from her, just when she was the happiest she'd ever been in her life? She had Ida, she had her painting, she was living as her true self for the first time ever, a gay woman who loved and lived with another woman. Life had never before been so rich, so fruitful.

She wasn't without her problems though. Her father had stopped talking to her when she'd come out to her parents two years before. Her mother she still saw from time to time, but it had to be in secret so that Suzanne's father wouldn't find out. They'd meet in coffee shops and restaurants and exchange bits of gossip on *'safe'* topics (nothing whatsoever to do with the *'g'* word), then maybe do a bit of shopping on Grafton Street, but the meetings were strained and overshadowed by the fact that Suzanne's father seemingly wanted nothing more to do with her, simply because she'd come out as gay. It hurt Suzanne more than she ever would have thought possible. He'd been her father for thirty-six years by that stage but suddenly he wasn't any more, and just because he'd found out that she preferred women to men in the romantic and sexual sense. "It's just his way – he's from a different generation," her mother said, but it still hurt. Her mother was from the same generation as her father, but *she* hadn't cut off all contact with their first-born child over Suzanne's being gay. It was obvious that she was still very uncomfortable about her daughter's sexuality, but at least she made the effort to keep seeing her. Suzanne longed for the day when she would be able to take Ida to meet both her parents, but that day was still a long way off. Barbara had been fine about the whole thing, had even laughed and said teasingly that she'd always known Suzanne was gay, that she was just waiting for Suzanne herself to find out. Barbara had met Ida and loved her, and so had Paul and the two little girls. Paul hadn't even disgraced himself, as Suzanne had half-expected, by making sly, sleazy remarks about what lesbians did in bed and the so-called 'girl-on-girl action' he probably watched on his computer when no one else was around. He'd behaved like the perfect gentleman and welcomed Ida into the family in a genuinely friendly manner that had gladdened Suzanne's heart. He wasn't all bad, even if he could be a total moron at times and lose the run of himself. The two little girls had adored Ida on sight. Ida was brilliant with children. She never patronised them or talked down to them. She treated them with respect, as if they were individuals in their own right with opinions and important things to say. Barbara had told Jessie and Lucy that Ida was their Aunty Suzanne's 'special friend' and that was exactly how they saw her.

Barbara didn't know about the lump, though. Nobody did, not even Ida. Suzanne hadn't told a soul. Her reasoning, she'd decided, was sound. If the biopsy came back negative, then there would have been no need to alarm everyone with tales of insidious lumps found by chance in the shower – and she would have been right to keep things to herself. If it came back positive, however, well, she'd make her plans then and tell the people who needed to know. Barbara first, of course, and then Ida. And then Ida . . .

The poetry reading where they had met had been a crashing bore. Suzanne, who'd had the event recommended to her by a friend who worked in the library where the reading was taking place, nearly dozed off while the female poet droned on endlessly about a cat she'd had in her childhood. He'd died, this poor unfortunate moggy, and been replaced by a succession of other cats who had all kicked the bucket as well. Suzanne liked cats, even loved them and was thinking of getting one of her own, but this never-ending dirge was almost more than she could bear, and nowhere near as funny as when Lisa Simpson had talked about her own bad luck with felines in *The Simpsons*. Suzanne felt herself nodding off. It had been a long day for her, working non-stop on a recalcitrant painting that just wouldn't come right, and then correcting some essays on art theory from the students at her college night classes. Her head sank lower and lower onto her jumper, until a gentle nudge in her side caused her to jerk upright, her eyes suddenly wide open.

"Sorry," whispered the woman who'd been sitting beside her, a woman with a wide smile and glasses. "I didn't want to wake you, but I was afraid for you – you know, that you might start snoring . . ."

She spoke with a slight accent that Suzanne immediately warmed to.

"Thanks," Suzanne whispered back. "That would have been embarrassing."

"Yes, wouldn't it?" The woman grinned mischievously. "Still, it might have livened up this place a bit. I'm only just managing to keep awake myself."

Suzanne giggled, earning herself a stern glance from the reader of the interminable poem about cats.

Suzanne didn't know why she said what she said next. She only knew that her mouth opened and she said it. "Would you like to get out of here? I mean, *um*, go and grab a coffee somewhere?"

Suzanne felt her face blush a fiery red. She would just die if the woman said no or recoiled and looked at her as though she had two heads or something, but she just smiled and said yes, she'd love to. They gathered up their coats and bags and left the room, much to the disapproval of the poet, who *tsk-tsk*ed audibly before going back to her poem. It seemed there were plenty of deceased moggies remaining to be mourned publicly in iambic pentameter.

Coffee had certainly been interesting. They sat in the café beside the library for nearly two hours, drinking coffee and eating Danish pastries, chatting non-stop with virtually no awkward silences. Suzanne learned that the other woman's name was Ida Mueller and she was thirty-eight, the same age as Suzanne. She was a computer programmer from a part of Switzerland where they spoke mostly German (the accent, Suzanne thought, was out of this world – she could listen to it for ever) and was working with a Swiss company based in Dublin, and she loved to ski but had broken both arms and one leg at one point or another in different skiing accidents. The accident in which she had broken her leg had left her with a slight limp, which was noticeably worse when the weather was cold and wet, or when she was tired.

"Why did you keep doing it, if it's so dangerous?" Suzanne asked.

"Life is better with a little risk, you know," Ida said, her eyes gleaming behind her glasses. "You cannot always play it safe."

Suzanne wondered if there was a double meaning behind those words. How she would love it if there was, although the thought was nerve-racking too. They continued talking, and Suzanne told her new friend that she was busy making a small name for herself as a painter who had just had her first exhibition, at which she had even sold a couple of paintings, rather miraculously, or so she'd thought at the time. She was hoping to have another exhibition sometime next year. To pay the bills in the meantime, she taught art classes three nights a week at a local college and sometimes gave grinds to art students who were working on their portfolios for art college.

"You must be very creative," Ida said.

"Well, *um*, I suppose so." Suzanne blushed and laughed self-deprecatingly.

"Then do not play it down. You must own it and be proud of it."

"Well, we weren't brought up to be proud of ourselves." Suzanne remembered how her parents had always been offhand and dismissive whenever she'd brought home good marks on a test, or a drawing the teacher had particularly praised. They'd been the same with Barbara. "We were seen as showing off or boasting if we tried to make ourselves look good in any way. It's the Irish way. You mustn't make yourself out to be special or talented or better than anyone else at something, or you're asking for a fall. Don't stick your head up over the parapet or you'll get it shot off type of thing."

"That is the wrong way to bring up children, surely," Ida said firmly, her eyes shining earnestly. "If a child does well, you tell the child. Why not?"

Suzanne was warming more and more to this plain-spoken, slight-of-stature Swiss woman with the winning smile. They chatted until nearly half-ten, at which point the café was closing and the woman behind the till was starting to look decidedly grouchy. She was passive-aggressively clearing up all around them, putting chairs up on tables and turning the *Open* sign on the door to *Closed*.

"I have a rented house in Ranelagh," Ida said simply, gathering up her coat and bag under the bleary-eyed gaze of the waitress. "It is only a short taxi ride. Will you come and drink a glass of white wine with me?"

It was getting late, and Suzanne knew she should be at home painting, working on the recalcitrant project that wouldn't oblige her by coming right, or up in bed sipping a nice soporific camomile tea and reading the latest Karin Slaughter thriller, even if the gory nature of the book did tend to cancel out the tea's calming benefits somewhat. And there were always classes to prepare for, and those essays on art theory to correct. Instead, she found herself agreeing to share a taxi to Ida's charming little house.

"I rent this house because it has a garden with a good long clothesline," Ida told her as they hung up their coats and bags in the tiny cramped hallway. "In Switzerland, we hang out washing on the line and mountain breezes dry it, so always I like to have somewhere outside to hang washing."

Suzanne pictured that Swiss clothesline full of spotlessly clean white sheets billowing away in the fresh Alpine air, just like in an ad for washing powder. "It sounds lovely," she said wistfully.

They drank the wine and talked some more, and then they went up to bed together.

"Tonight, we just sleep," Ida said sensibly as she pulled back the bedcovers, and that was exactly what they did – two tired women sleeping deeply side by side, their arms wrapped lightly round each other.

They didn't have any other contact until the following morning, when Ida woke Suzanne with a kiss that made Suzanne think of blue Alpine skies she'd never seen, and a mountainside dotted with little white flowers she couldn't name that looked like snowdrops.

Afterwards, they lay together and cuddled and chatted.

"Am I making you late for work?" Suzanne asked Ida at one point.

"I mostly work from home," Ida said with a broad grin. "So, if we want to stay here in bed all day, who is there to stop us?"

And that was exactly what they did. Now, of course, they lived openly together as a gay couple in Ida's little house. Suzanne painted and marked essays while Ida wrote her computer programs and they hung their washing out on the clothesline no matter what the weather. (Suzanne loved that Ida didn't rush out into the garden, shrieking like a dervish, like every Irishwoman ever when a drop of rain threatened to fall. She simply let the clothes get wet and waited until they were dry again to bring them in.) They owned a big fat ginger cat called Rembrandt, and in their spare time they listened to music and went to symphony concerts and poetry readings. Barbara had a close-knit circle of female friends, all either artists like herself or writers or musicians, who welcomed Ida unhesitatingly into their midst, all genuinely thrilled for Suzanne for having found her soulmate at last. It was the happiest Suzanne had ever been in all her thirty-eight years and Ida said the same.

But Ida didn't know yet about the lump, the stupid fucking lump that Suzanne had found one day in the shower, the lump that was probably going to ruin everything. It was under her arm, perilously near her left breast. In secret, she'd gone to have the biopsy, not telling Ida or Barbara, and within a very short time, less than an hour probably, she would have the results.

Isn't it weird? she thought as she alighted from the Luas at St. Stephen's Green and began to make her way to Dr. Cross's office nearby. *In less than an hour, I'll know whether life goes on for me or not, whether I'm to carry on living and painting and being with Ida and being truly alive in the best sense of the word, or whether I'll be six feet under in a year or even less, pushing up daisies in an overcrowded fucking graveyard.* And did she even want to be buried, she wondered, or was cremation the best way to do it? It struck her that she didn't even know. *I can't die yet,* she thought frantically, slowing her walk so that she wouldn't show up too early at the doctor's office and have to sit twiddling her thumbs or, worse, flicking idly through an old edition of *Hello!* magazine. Suzanne didn't give a flying fuck about so-called 'celebrities' at the best of times, never mind their complicated love lives, and she certainly didn't today. No, she couldn't die yet. What about her sister Barbara and her two little nieces, who she loved as if they were her own? They'd all need her more than ever now, especially if Paul was acting the maggot again. There was Barbara's new baby to consider too. And what about the baby that she and Ida were talking about having together some day? And what about Ida herself, the first person Suzanne had ever known with whom she could be her real, true self? How cruel it would be to have her first bit of real happiness snatched away from her, and after they'd been together for such a short time!

They'd been talking about going to Switzerland for a good long holiday once Ida's contract in Ireland was up. Ida was going to introduce Suzanne to her parents and all her aunties and uncles and even her grandparents, all of whom were apparently perfectly okay with Ida's sexuality, even though gay marriage hadn't yet come to Switzerland. Suzanne had been envious when she'd heard about Ida's loving, liberal relatives. Although Ireland had recently voted for same-sex marriage, there nonetheless still existed a smattering of decidedly unenlightened folks who weren't happy about it (as there would in any country in the world, Suzanne supposed), any more than they were okay with divorce or cohabitation or any of the other things that it was perfectly all right to do nowadays because this was the twenty-first century and no longer the Dark Ages. Suzanne's parents definitely belonged to that handful of people who disapproved of pretty much everything that smacked of liberalness and wouldn't hold with chats about feelings, or sexuality, or bodily urges or even bodily functions that everyone has and that people therefore shouldn't be ashamed of or embarrassed about. Even if Suzanne was able to tell her mother about Ida, it would have to be kept a secret from her father, and Suzanne didn't want Ida, her lovely Alpine Ida, to be a sordid little secret that had to be kept from people. If she couldn't talk openly to her parents about Ida and their love, then she wouldn't talk about the subject at all. It made her sad, though. She missed her dad and sometimes wondered if he missed her too. If he could only get over this mental block about his daughter's sexuality, they could be friends again and play chess together once more in the front room of the family home, while Suzanne's mother knitted and watched television in the background. The comforting click-clicking sound of those needles while Suzanne pondered her next chess move had formed part of the soundtrack to her childhood *and* adult years, and she missed it more now than she would ever have thought possible.

"You can go on in now, Ms. Carragher – you're the last client of the day," said Dr. Cross's receptionist, a good-looking, chatty young woman called Fauve whose bright dyed-red hair was a welcome splash of colour in the cream-and-beige waiting room. There were no copies of *Hello!* on the table, only well-thumbed old medical journals and a few broadsheet copies of that day's *Irish Times*.

Suzanne found that her mouth had gone dry. She wished she'd had the foresight to drink a cup of ice-cold water from the water cooler when she'd arrived, but she hadn't thought of it and it was too late now.

Dr. Cross, a specialist in cancer, in her mid-fifties, got up from her seat and held out her hand to Suzanne with a warm smile.

"Right, now," she said when they were both seated. She reached for a brown folder on the desk in front of her and opened it. Taking out a few sheets of paper, she studied them intently with her glasses halfway down her nose. "Let's see what we've got here."

Suzanne swallowed hard and dug her fingernails into the palms of her hands.

Stop 3: KILMACUD

Fauve

Fauve Delahunty was dog-tired when she got off the Luas at the Kilmacud stop and started to walk home to Ashley Crescent. She had managed to get a seat for once on her normally jam-packed homebound tram from St. Stephen's Green, and she had nearly fallen asleep to its rhythmic movements and the sleep-inducing tones of the automated female who said things that passengers mostly ignored, like "*Please move down the tram*". Dr. Marcia Cross was one of the top cancer consultants in the country and her outer office was always crowded with people seeking her expertise, so Fauve as the receptionist was always busy. Today hadn't been too manic, though, but she was still knackered. And sometimes watching all those people troop in and out of Dr. Cross's office to receive their (mostly) bad news could really get you down. Fauve could always tell when someone had been given bad news, even before she got to peep at the files. They would come out pale-faced, looking shell-shocked. Sometimes they'd be crying. Mind you, some people cried buckets when they were given *good* news. Take today, for example.

The last patient of the day, a dark-haired woman in her

late thirties who had been so wound up when she'd gone into Dr. Cross's inner sanctum that Fauve was worried for her, had practically danced back out into the reception area after her appointment, beaming from ear to ear while crying tears of sheer happiness. Another one of those patients whose cyst or lump had thankfully turned out to be benign. Fauve loved when that happened, but unfortunately it didn't happen nearly often enough. The dancing woman, however, a Suzanne Somebody, Carragher maybe, or Farragher, had been a sight for sore eyes and Fauve had smiled at her warmly before saying goodbye. No follow-up appointments for this patient – just a clean bill of health and off you go now to live a full and happy life.

Fauve sometimes wondered if the patients who had been given the all-clear did, in fact, make the most of their remaining time like they'd surely promised God they would when they made their frantic bargains. *Oh, please God, if you'll only give me some more time, I swear I'll never waste another minute!* How long, she wondered, did it take them to slip back into their old ways? Or did they keep their long-dark-night-of-the-soul promises and become useful, productive and compassionate members of society who, like Good Samaritans, always had a moment to spare for their fellow human beings?

Fauve sighed heavily as she trudged up the road. She herself had lived rather too full a life recently, which was how she came to be in her present predicament. She thought now about the contents of her handbag. *Oh Jesus.* Well, she'd put it off long enough. She'd do it tonight or she'd bloody well die trying. It had been so embarrassing in the chemist's, though. She'd felt like everyone was looking at her and judging her, even though they were all probably fully preoccupied buying their own cough-and-cold remedies and having their prescriptions filled. Cough-and-cold season had come in with a bang the minute the summer slipped away, allowing autumn (and the flu) to make her debut for another year.

No. 16 Ashley Crescent was lit up like a Christmas tree when Fauve walked through the gate and up the path. It wasn't even properly dark yet. Just let them wait till the electricity bill comes, she thought crossly. Let's see if they'll be so bloody free and easy then, with their lights and their immersion for the hot water on round the clock, as if we're all made of money.

"Coffee, my love?" Doireann offered the minute Fauve set foot in the brightly lit kitchen.

Fauve immediately felt guilty for having just been thinking bad thoughts about her three housemates, and Doireann in particular, who switched on the light every time she entered a room, even during the day, if it was just the teensiest bit overcast. Doireann's family were super-rich and so she was unfamiliar with the concept of scrimping and scraping. Not that Fauve was particularly *au fait* with the concept herself – her own parents were far from poor – but at least she'd been brought up to have some common sense about it, unlike Doireann.

"Yes, please," she said gratefully. "I'm bloody gagging for one. Are the others home?"

"Sasha's not back yet, and Orla's upstairs hogging the bathroom for her date with Nathan. So if you need the loo, you're going to have to hold it in. Or nip out the back and wee up agin' the wall!" she finished with a laugh.

Doireann, filling up the kettle, had made a face when she said 'Nathan'. None of the other three girls in the house liked Orla's loud, obnoxious boyfriend. He was always boasting about his big fat salary as a Mercedes salesman and holding forth on the subject of women saying 'no' when what they really meant was '*Oh yes, of course, please fuck me now, I've been waiting my whole life for this very moment, you virile stud-muffin, you!*'

Fauve couldn't stand Nathan. He was constantly trying to grope her tits when Orla's back was turned and asking her what her original hair colour was under the bright red dye. Ever since she'd once answered, rather sourly, "Mousy Brown," he'd made a point of calling her his Little Brown Mouse and feeling her arse to see if she had a tail back there, the odious creep.

"What does she see in him?" she said. She was seated now at the kitchen table. She felt completely done in. A nice hot strong cup of coffee would surely revive her, and Doireann made the best coffee out of the four of them. Orla's in particular was revolting, tasting like burnt hair for some reason, and Sasha's was always as weak as piss.

"His big fat wallet?" Doireann said cynically as she poured the hot coffee into the two mugs. "It can't be his big fat prick anyway, because that simply doesn't exist."

"You've seen his knob?" said Fauve, her eyebrows shooting upwards.

"Oh yes." Doireann nodded sagely. "One morning when he'd been staying over and he must've forgotten that he wasn't at home or something, because he went to the toilet in the nip. I was coming out of my room and I saw it then. It looked just like a slug stuck to his inner thigh, and not a very big slug either. I nearly puked at the sight of it."

"*Eurgh!*"

Both women shuddered and then laughed.

"Imagine being Orla, though," said Fauve, "and having to, you know . . ."

"What, suck it? I'd rather eat nettles stewed with my own pubes, thanks very much." More laughter, then: "Have you heard from *him* yet, sweetie?" Doireann's tone was serious.

"Who?" said Fauve, feigning surprise.

"You know. *Him.*"

Fauve shook her head miserably, willing the tears not to fall.

It sounded clichéd to say it, but she had really, *really* thought that this one was *The One*. She'd been so happy to think that she might just have met the love of her life at the tender-ish age of twenty-six, but it was looking less and less likely now that she'd ever even hear from him again. One morning recently, Doireann had come down early to breakfast to find Fauve in floods of tears at the kitchen table, clutching her phone. Over copious amounts of Doireann's (decent) coffee, Fauve had confided the whole sorry story to her friend.

A few weeks ago, she'd gone out to Copper Face Jacks nightclub on Harcourt Street with another girl from the medical practice where they both worked. They had drinks together after work, on the strict understanding that if either of them pulled, the other would fade graciously into the background and not be a problem by springing a guilt-trip on the other. Both girls pulled early on in the evening. But, from the moment the tall, dark *and* handsome stranger had wandered over with the two blue cocktails in his hands and offered Fauve both of them because he'd observed that she'd been drinking blue cocktails, she'd had the feeling that this wasn't going to be just another rubbish Copper's shag, best forgotten. His name was Jack and he was over six feet tall and almost criminally good-looking.

"You're called Jack, and we're in Copper Face Jacks," she marvelled in tipsy wonder once he'd introduced himself. Then she kicked herself mentally for saying something so moronic.

"It must be Fate, so." He reached out to gently touch one of the many stray tendrils that had come loose from the messy bun into which she had carelessly piled her tresses that morning. "I love your hair colour. It's just so damn vibrant."

"It's not, *um*, it's not real," Fauve said, wishing she'd been able to come out with something a bit more cutting-edge. Mind you, witty repartee wasn't usually called for in Copper's, just a Wonderbra that pushed your tits out and up balcony-style and a packet of condoms from the machines in the jacks.

Jack smiled, anyway, at her remark, and said, "It doesn't matter. It's gorgeous. Can you let it down?"

"Like Rapunzel," giggled Fauve, on whom the cocktails were already working their sultry magic.

"Like Rapunzel," Jack agreed solemnly.

He'd watched while she unpinned her hair, which fell in a lustrous coil to halfway down her back. She shook it out self-consciously and then chanced a look at him from beneath the fake eyelashes she'd glued on after work.

"It's beautiful. *You're* beautiful."

"Ah, g'wan out of that!" Fauve slurred in mock-modesty. "Would you ever feck off!"

"No, you *are*, and, what's more, you *know* you are."

"Well, maybe," slinked back Fauve, who knew no such thing, but who was she to argue with this drop-dead sexy Adonis who was easily the best-looking guy she'd pulled in, like, a bazillion years?

"Another cocktail? These are going down like water, aren't they? I'm done with mine already."

Fauve nodded in what she hoped was a coquettish manner but which she feared merely said about her: "*Yes, Attractive Stranger, you're quite right! I'm an old soak who'll put out for booze, so can you liquor me up on the double, please, you delicious sex-bomb, you?*"

They drank more cocktails. She'd told Jack quite a lot about herself by this stage, not just the usual stuff about what she did for a living and where she lived and about her housemates, but silly stuff from her past too, like how she'd had braces on her teeth until she was nearly twenty-one because her father was a dentist and had a big hard-on for straight teeth. She told him about how she'd once had a dog called Nellie, named after Nellie Oleson from *Little House on the Prairie*. Nellie, a feisty Jack Russell, bit the neighbours, the postman and anyone who came within an ass's roar of the house. In the end, it became so bad that Fauve's dad had to take Nellie to live on a farm somewhere 'down the country'. When Fauve grew up and discovered what the words '*a farm down the country*' really meant, she'd been traumatised beyond words. It still made her cry buckets to think about it. Poor, *poor* Nellie.

She'd even told him something she didn't usually talk about to other people: the fact that her parents were disappointed with her for only working as a doctor's receptionist instead of going to medical school, or to dental college as they'd wanted her to. Or even law school, like her solicitor mother. That was the trouble with having professional people for parents. They always bloody well wanted you to follow in their boring bloody footsteps.

"But I didn't *want* to spend another six or seven years of my life in fucking college," she'd slurred at Jack, who'd nodded gravely. "I bloody hated school and I couldn't bear the thought of a load more years spent swotting my arse off over a bunch of dry old textbooks that I couldn't make head-or-tail of, d'you know what I mean? I couldn't stand all that stuff in school, so why would I want to sign up for years and years more of the same?"

Jack had nodded in sympathy again while signalling to the overworked barman to bring two more drinks over to their seats. He let Fauve talk and talk and talk, all the while stroking her hair or putting his hands lightly but proprietorially on her arm or on her knee or even on her bare thigh in the short skirt she was wearing. Fauve adored that he seemed to be listening so attentively to her bemoaning her situation. She was tickled pink by his close attention. As for any sleuthing on Fauve's end, all she had managed to get out of Jack was that he was twenty-eight, that he lived in Dublin and worked in marketing. He didn't specify what aspect of marketing, he didn't say where in Dublin he lived or even if he was single, but he wasn't wearing a wedding ring or sporting the tell-tale tan lines that indicated that he'd taken one off and slipped it into his pocket for the night – the mark of a true sleazebag, as Fauve and her friends well knew. Still, it was the least amount of information that she'd ever managed to wheedle out of a guy she was thinking of going to bed with. He was definitely very close-mouthed on the subject of himself. If she'd been sober, she might have done a bit better but, as it was, the cocktails had done *their* work magnificently and she was utterly plastered when she staggered out of the club on Jack's arm, waving royally to her friend Molly as she passed. Molly had pulled a portly, pinstriped wanker-banker, not unlike Orla's Nathan, and was as pleased as Punch with herself.

They'd got a taxi to Fauve's place in Kilmacud.

The sex with Jack had been fan-fucking-tastic. He had been much more in control of his drinking than Fauve – thank Christ! – and he'd managed perfectly serviceable intercourse twice (condomless – the subject of protection never even came up, much to Fauve's later shame) before they both fell asleep in Fauve's bed. Fauve had thoroughly enjoyed gazing up uninterrupted at Jack's handsome face during the sex, the face that looked as if it should be gracing a billboard ad for designer aftershave or some celebrity's brand of underwear. He was gorgeous in a totally swoonsome way. Even while blind drunk (enough to completely forget to take her pill, anyway), Fauve could appreciate this fact. How easily she could fall in love with a guy like this!

The following morning she'd been gutted when he'd said he had to go to work. But it was, after all, a workday – Wednesday, or 'Hump Day', after which you'd be freewheeling down to the weekend again. But he'd left her his mobile number, at her request admittedly, on a piece of paper she'd hurriedly torn from a notebook. She'd snuggled back under the covers with his phone number under her pillow after he'd left, too hungover to go to work and wanting nothing more than just to lie there in her warm toasty bed, congratulating herself on her good fortune in meeting someone as attractive and special as Handsome Jack.

After begging Doireann to phone in sick for her – not for the first time – she'd slept like a log until nearly the close of business for the day. She'd hauled herself out of bed then, showered and made herself a light meal of an omelette with some salady remains from the fridge which were rapidly nearing their sell-by date. There was no name pasted onto the salad bowl, which meant that anyone who wanted could fill their boots. A name pasted onto the bowl meant *Piss Off And Get Your Own Food, You Scabby Git*. Over her meal, she'd sent a text to Jack on the number he'd left her that morning. After agonising over the wording for a full quarter of an hour, she'd finally settled on: **Hey you, how was your day? Loved last night, must do it again soon. Rapunzel here, aka Fauve.** Absolutely no kisses yet – it was much too soon. She wasn't a fool. She knew how easy it was to scare blokes off with all that soppy stuff. She thought her text was bright and breezy enough to more than pass the acceptability test.

To Fauve's distress, Jack didn't reply to the text, even though she'd received a delivery report for the message and so she knew it was a real number and that she hadn't been fake-numbered, something that had happened to her in the past. That had really pissed her off. How could a man be so immature and childish as to give a woman a fake number? She couldn't understand the mentality of someone like that. What was the big deal about giving a woman your real phone number? Why were guys so precious about their bloody phone numbers, anyway? Afraid of their lives that some woman might get a hold, however tenuous, on them? *Meh*. Screw that, seriously.

She'd spent a miserable evening moping about the house, jumping every time her phone beeped with a text. As was always the way when she was waiting – hoping – for a text from a special someone, Fate mocked her with a succession of texts from the wrong people. (Clearly not the same sympathetic Fate that had brought them together in the first place, *harrumph harrumph!* An underling, maybe, filling in for the real Fate, an underling who hadn't read any of the notes on Fauve and Jack left out for him or her to peruse. You just couldn't get the staff these days. Again, *harrumph*.)

First her mother Elaine, saying she hoped Fauve was planning on wearing something nice when she came over to the house for Sunday Lunch-With-A-Capital-L, as Granny Helene and Granddad Joseph, both professional people (though not still practising) and from whom Fauve's mother had inherited her terrifying ambition, would be there. *Oh, joy unconfined,* Fauve wanted to text back but of course she didn't dare, just told her mother what she wanted to hear. Next came a text from her hairdresser's. They wanted her to know that they were having a twenty-per-cent-off sale on all their bottled shampoos and conditioners. Fauve was fine for hair products at the moment and she deleted the text with a huge sigh. By the time she'd had the text from Orla, asking her to put on the immersion heater so she could jump in the bath the minute she came home because she was going out with Nathan later on, and the text from the local takeaway place, urging her to buy a poxy chicken snackbox on a Wednesday in order to avail of one free poxy mini-snackbox and a free can of orange soda on the same day, Fauve was ready to throw the phone at the wall the way she'd seen people in films do it. She'd seen a guy in a film chuck his phone in the ocean once. She didn't throw it, though, because what they never show you in these films is the bit where the hasty phone-thrower has to slink sheepishly over to where they've flung their phone to gather up the pieces and try to glue them back together. Because everyone needs a bloody phone, right? Worst-case scenario, they have to eventually present themselves shamefaced at the New Phone Emporium to buy a new phone because the old one was, basically, fucked from being flung at walls. People in films were so stupid sometimes.

Fauve kept the phone beside her when she slept, though, and left it on 'loud' and on 'vibrate' so that she could hear it if – *when* – it beeped in the night. When she woke the next morning, the first thing she did was check her phone. Only one text, from her bloody service provider. It was time to top up by twenty quid again if she wanted to keep availing herself of free text messages for the month ahead. For *fuck's* sake. She was gutted, but she'd still had to drag herself out of bed and practically force herself to go to work and be nice and smiley to the clients who came in for their biopsy or ultrasound results, because none of this was their fault.

There began then a long, bleak horrible period of Waiting-For-Jack-To-Call-Or-Text, but he never did, no matter how many texts or voice messages Fauve sent him, and she sent him a *lot* of messages. It wasn't very satisfactory leaving him voice messages, because it meant listening to that annoying automated bloody woman's voice starting in with her "*You have reached the voice mailbox of 087-blah blah blah, please leave your blah after the blah.*"

Blaaaaaaaaah! It wasn't even Jack's own voice on the message. She could imagine him casually saying: "*Hi, you've reached Jack, leave me a message and I'll get back to you as soon as I can, especially if you're Fauve, the beautiful girl I met a few nights ago in Copper's and who I've been thinking about every minute of every day since. Please call, Fauve, I desperately want you. I'm nothing without you. I need you to make me whole again.*"

She confided in Doireann about the whole sorry affair, on the morning her housemate had come downstairs to find her bawling her eyes out and holding her phone like it was a photo of someone dear to her who'd gone off to fight in World War II or something. Doireann made large amounts of coffee and agreed with Fauve that Handsome Jack was clearly the kind of shit who slept with women he didn't know and then buggered off without any intention of seeing them again. Doireann was kind and tactful enough not to say stuff like, 'Well, what did you expect, Fauve? You slept with a total stranger who got you blind drunk at Copper's?' Fauve was immensely grateful for her tact. She didn't need judging – she had already judged herself plenty. She knew that it was a bit sluttish (well, a *lot* sluttish really) to have irresponsible one-night-stands with blokes you met in pubs and clubs, but what guys didn't understand was that the women who did that weren't really looking for sex at all – they were really just looking for love, like most women were, and they shouldn't be dismissed as slags because of the way they went about it. Like, where the hell else were they meant to meet fellas? Fauve wasn't about to sign up for a night class in basic motorbike mechanics. She *had* a life, thanks very much. Anyway, everyone knew that those classes were mainly attended by grim-faced single women looking for a man in the Last Chance Saloon, so there. You had about as much chance of meeting a man there as you did of ever convincing your mother that you were a worthwhile human being deserving of her respect.

But Jack obviously viewed Fauve as just another notch on his bedpost, a structure that was probably so riddled with notches by now that it likely couldn't even take its owner's weight any longer. Fauve thought it was terribly unfair that *she* was the one who'd be classed as the slut, while Jack was just doing what came naturally to guys and no blame would attach to him whatsoever. No consequences either. But there would be consequences for Fauve, might already *be* consequences. At the very least, and she'd be lucky if she got off so lightly, there was the whole thing of feeling shame and remorse for her impulsive behaviour, and mainly there was the fact that she felt like a giant twat for letting some smooth-talking Casanova chat her into bed for just the price of a few blue cocktails. Why had she priced herself so low? And had she always done that? She was deeply ashamed of her own answer.

"Will we have a biscuit?" Doireann said now, breaking into Fauve's reverie. "I'm feeling reckless. I've stuck to my diet all week and I deserve a break. Chocolate or plain?"

"What does it matter?" said Fauve glumly, wrapping her hands around her coffee cup and taking a grim pleasure from the fact that it was burning her hands. "I'll be the size of an elephant soon enough anyway, so who cares what I eat?"

"Now stop it. You don't know that," Doireann said firmly, sitting down across the kitchen table from Fauve and putting the biscuit tin between them. "Think of all the times in your life you've done a pregnancy test and they've all been negative. Every single one of them. Think of all the times *I've* done tests, and Sasha and Orla too. We're . . ." she thought for a minute, "we're the *Uncatchables!*" she finished with a flourish.

There was even that one legendary time that all four of them had been convinced at the same time that they'd been caught and were pregnant, even though all four of them were on the pill and (mostly) carried condoms around with them on a night out. (The 'mostly' nights were the nights you had to worry about, especially if you forgot to take your pill on the same night, or accidentally puked up your pill when you had a stomach bug. These things had all happened to girls they knew at one time or another.) It was about a year earlier, not long after they'd all started living together. They'd stocked up on booze, bought four pregnancy tests and had a 'test' party at the house. They had done their tests one after the other while nearly blotto on the gin and vodka they'd bought, and every one of them had had their tests come back negative, much to their collective relief and surprise. They'd celebrated by grabbing a taxi into town and getting even more shit-faced at Copper's. Every one of them, bar Orla, who was already seeing the awful Nathan by that time, had got the ride that night, and the following day saw a mad scramble to find places that dispensed the beautiful, ever-blessed morning-after pill. Life goes on. Sasha, in particular, had been certain once more that she'd been knocked up and there was no consoling her until enough time had elapsed for her to do another test, which had come back negative. She had been so relieved she'd sworn blind to never, *ever* have unsafe sex again but of course she'd broken her promise the next time she went out. They'd *all* broken their promises to behave more cautiously and sensibly a dozen or more times. It was hard to be good all the time, goddamit, reflected Fauve as she disconsolately dipped a chocolate digestive into her coffee, not even caring when half of it broke off and fell in her cup. Fauve sighed heavily. It was no more than she deserved, after what she'd done. A soggy biscuit was surely the least of what she deserved, for her rank stupidity in getting *'caught'*, and by such an obvious player too!

It was inevitable that one of the four women would get caught one day. You can't continuously play with fire and not get burnt. So now, Fauve thought, she'd be pregnant and her parents (and grandparents) would be even more disappointed in her than they already were, and her sister Brianne, the perfect sister, would shake her head in disbelief and say, "C'mon, Fauve, honestly, a baby?" in that snooty fucking voice of hers, as if getting pregnant was the worst sin you could commit. Well, it probably was, thought Fauve sadly, but she still wasn't relishing the thought of Brianne gloating at her misfortune which, let's face it, was what she'd do. Of course, Little Miss Perfect Sister Brianne had a degree in Economics and an important position in a fancy company perched at the very cutting edge of mobile-phone technology, and she was engaged to the equally perfect but dull-as-dishwater Eamonn who worked in the same company. Their wedding next summer would be the Wedding of the Year and it would make Posh and Becks' nuptials look like a cup of char and a fag in a greasy spoon somewhere, that was how big a deal it was.

Whereas she, Fauve, was *only* a receptionist. It didn't matter that her boss was one of the most eminent and highly esteemed cancer specialists in the country – the way her parents treated Fauve's job, you'd swear she was only the fucking cleaner in the place and now, probably, a knocked-up receptionist/cleaner to boot. She'd have to quit her job and go and live in a council flat somewhere with her snotty brat who'd cry all day and all night until Fauve went insane and flung herself, or the brat, out the window of their high-rise tower block. Okay, so there weren't any high-rise tower blocks any more to which single mothers could be exiled as punishment for their crime of committing the ultimate sin against decent society, but the whole situation was still a steaming, stinking pile of horse doo-doo. Guys would never look twice at her again. Everyone knew that no fella in his right mind wanted to be saddled with a single mother and her offspring. They came with too much baggage for the average guy to cope with. She'd have to give up fags and booze and lovely smoky nights out and all the things that made life worth living. And for what? So that she could get fatter and fatter until one day she found it was just easier to wear horrible elasticated sweatpants than attempt to fit into something that gave her a waist. She'd even have to give up dyeing her hair for now because she'd read somewhere that hair-dye was bad for the baby. Nearly everything she liked to do would be Bad For The Baby. Probably even having sex was bad for the baby, not that she was currently having any. And who'd ever want to have sex with her again, after she'd lost her figure and her boobs drooped down to her knees because of all the breastfeeding the booby-feeding Nazis would shame her into doing? She'd have to devote the rest of her miserable, sexless saggy-boobed life to a baby she didn't want, a baby whose father wouldn't even know of his or her existence.

Jack never answered when she rang the phone number he'd given her. He never replied to her texts either, even though she received delivery reports for every single one she sent. He never acknowledged her many phone messages. Was he disgusted, she wondered, at how desperate she seemed to be to contact him? Did her pathetic eagerness and persistence make him want to puke? Or did he just get some sick buzz out of the whole thing? Earlier that day she'd sent him a text saying that she thought she might be pregnant. She'd wanted to shock him into ending his communication silence, but she'd waited all day and nothing whatsoever had come back from his end. How could a man be so cold? Fauve asked herself this question constantly. How could he be so unfeeling? She herself felt much too *feeling* these days. She felt as fragile as a flower whose petals were in danger of being plucked off by the wind or the sticky fingers of children. She was exhausted and emotional all the time. She was so emotional she wanted to cry every time she saw a sad ad about road-traffic accidents on TV, or when someone on the news had had a child on a medical-treatment waiting list for years and they still weren't any closer to getting that life-saving operation, and meanwhile the parents were nearly half-dead from stress and worry. And don't even get her started on the flippin' Angelus, the one minute of reflection time on RTÉ One every evening before the *Six O'Clock News* came on, when the dings donged and the bongs binged. The sight of all those dear old geriatrics or special needs children and adults working together on their sweet little craft projects, smiling happily all the while, had her bawling like a baby before the fourth or fifth dong had dinged. Like, what were they trying to *do* to her anyway, twisting her poor tormented heartstrings into such agonising knots like that? It was a form of legalised torture, that's what it was. And to think that the government condoned it!

Also – and this was the real proof – the reason that Fauve was absolutely convinced that she was pregnant was that, a couple of times in the past week, she hadn't wanted to go to Copper's or Flannery's after work, hadn't wanted a drink even. If that wasn't an indisputable sign of pregnancy, Fauve honestly didn't know what was. She who was tired of Copper's was obviously pregnant. She wanted to cry. She loved Copper's. It was practically her favourite place in the world. She loved watching the Guards, the Lady Guards and the nurses getting off shamelessly with the teachers and the social workers and the civil servants, and she adored bitching with her friends about the state of such-and-such a person, who was going to get herself A Reputation For Being An Easy Lay if she wasn't careful. Would she ever again fall onto her Luas or into a taxi while stinking drunk, clutching her chips and batter burger and only just making it to Kilmacud before she puked her guts up all over the pavement? Would she ever have those carefree, happy times again? Fauve could feel them slipping through her fingers like shite through a goose.

"I think he must have fake-numbered me after all," Fauve told Doireann now, her lower lip wobbling and the tears threatening to spill over in earnest. "No one ever answers."

"The slimy prick!" Doireann exclaimed with such conviction that Fauve felt momentarily comforted. "Like that time with me and Ronnie. Remember Ronnie? He had the Porsche and the kind of mole thing on his face. I was gutted about not seeing the Porsche again when he fake-numbered me but quite honestly, Fauve, I could never have brought myself to kiss him on his mole thing."

Both women giggled guiltily. The thought of Ronnie the Mole was just too funny.

"You have the test, right?" Doireann said then, draining the last of her coffee and licking the biscuit crumbs off her lips.

Fauve nodded dully. "In my bag."

"Right, well, what are we waiting for, then? Let's just get it over with, why don't we?"

"You promise you won't tell the others, no matter what the result is?" Fauve felt really anxious now. This didn't feel like those other times, when they'd all done pregnancy tests together and cackled with booze-fuelled laughter and relief when the tests had come back negative. This time felt different, which was what really worried her. This time felt real.

"I swear to God I won't say a word," Doireann promised. "Cross my heart and hope to die. May I never get off with another grease-monkey again if I tell a lie."

Fauve grinned in spite of herself. Doireann was a posh bird from Dublin 4 who loved a bit of rough. She was drawn inexorably to mechanics, construction workers, plumbers and electricians. She fancied anyone in overalls and big dusty boots, carrying a greasy rag and a breakfast roll from the local Spar shop. Whenever a workman was called to the house, Doireann always tried to make sure she was in to give him the once-over, like the cheeky young plumber who'd come to unblock the kitchen sink recently but who'd stayed, as Doireann put it with a filthy grin and an elegant quirk of her perfectly shaped eyebrows, to give her own pipes a bit of a flushing-out as well. And very good at it he'd been too, according to her.

"See, now you know I really mean it." Doireann held out a hand to Fauve in encouragement.

Fauve smiled weakly and took the proffered hand. "Okay then, let's do it," she said.

STOP 4: BALALLY

Orla and Nathan

Orla Dunlop stormed off the Luas at Balally and began charging up the road as fast as her strappy high heels would permit, not caring if Nathan was behind her or not, although she knew he was. She couldn't believe he was being so obnoxious about the whole pregnancy-test thing. Was he really such a prick, she wondered? Was he really as much of a prick as her friends thought he was? They tried to hide it from her, to give them their due – they were all decent, kind-hearted girls – but Orla knew just the same.

"Slow down, for fuck's sake," Nathan whined from behind her. "I'll get a fucking heart attack if I have to keep up this pace."

If you do get a heart attack, Orla thought uncharitably, it'll be because of all the steak dinners you eat with your clients and your friends and all the booze you swill down like a hippopotamus with dehydration, and not because of me, you big ape. Immediately she felt guilty for thinking it.

Aloud she said, "Well, we're already late, aren't we?"

"It's a *party,* Orla. We're *supposed* to be late."

"Well, that's good then, because we *are.*" Her voice was all high and shrill, the way it got when she was angry with him, which had been happening a lot lately. Too often for her liking.

"I said I was sorry, didn't I?"

To Orla it just sounded like more whining. "I don't care. Let's just find this place and get it over with, will we?"

"You're meant to enjoy a party," he grumbled, sweating already in his pinstripe suit. "Not just endure it like it's some kind of torture devised by the Waffen SS or something. I knew we should have taken a taxi instead of getting the bloody Luas. A taxi would have brought us right to the door. And that bloody robot woman with her '*Please move down the fucking tram*' really gets on my wick. She's not the boss of me. Have you got a tissue on you?"

Wordlessly she handed him a mini-packet of hankies from her handbag. He pulled one out awkwardly with his stubby fingers and used it to mop the sweat from his neck and forehead. His neck was bulging over the collar of his shirt as if he'd tied his bloody tie too tight. No wonder he felt uncomfortable.

"Jesus, it's hot tonight!" He stuffed the sweat-soaked tissue into his suit pocket.

Well, good. She wouldn't have put it past him to try and hand it back to her to dispose of.

"It's not hot, it's cool. You're just sweating," Orla said coldly.

"You're a hard woman to apologise to." Nathan checked again on his phone for the location of No. 19, Mornington Crescent. "The bastarding street should be around here somewhere," he said, looking around.

"Oh, an apology?" Orla said sarcastically. "Was that what that was meant to be?"

"What do you want, Orla? For me to go down on my

hands and knees and grovel around in the dirt and the muck, is that it? Of course," he went on pompously, "I could do that here if you really want me to, but the knees of my trousers won't be any the better for it."

"Oh, for Christ's sake, stop being such a drama queen and get up," Orla said irritably as he made as if to actually get down on his hands and knees on the wet ground, much to the surprise of an elderly lady who was trundling past with her shopping in one of those check trolleys favoured by old dears. Am I forgiven then?"

He consulted his fob watch on the fancy watch chain, a new gimmick that drove Orla nuts. The watch-and-chain combination was expensive and the real deal all right, but it was so fucking hipsterish it annoyed her. She knew she was being unreasonable but she couldn't help it. Everything about Nathan was annoying her lately, from his loud, hectoring voice to the Brylcreem he slathered on his hair which, when he kissed her, somehow managed to get itself all over her clothes. It was sticky and disgusting and hard to get off. But Brylcreem was back in fashion again, worse luck. It fitted with the image of the successful businessman Nathan was trying to project, and it went with his pricey pinstripe suits ("All bespoke, I'll have you know," he said when people were misguided enough to bring up the subject) and the stupid show-offish fob watch that made him look like a twat. He was only a Mercedes salesman who worked in a showroom and took people out for test drives in the cars he sold, and he occasionally treated favoured clients of the showroom's to slap-up meals on the company's credit card, but the way he acted, always lording it over people, you'd think he owned the whole bloody company, the Mercedes brand itself. Talk about full of himself!

"Well," he reiterated when she hadn't replied, just stood fiddling with the strap of her bag, "am I forgiven or what?" He looked at her expectantly.

She slid her gaze away from his and mumbled, "Okay, fine, whatever. Now can we just get to this stupid party, please?" But she hadn't really forgiven him. And his thinking that the test was hers was only the least of his misdemeanours. It was the other, more insidious, ones that were bugging Orla.

"What the *fuck* is this?" he'd demanded suddenly, holding it up for her to see.

They were in the bathroom of the house in Kilmacud that Orla shared with her three friends. They were getting ready for the party in Balally, just one Luas stop away, which was being held in the home of one of Nathan's old rugby-club pals. They were leaving Nathan's car, the Mercedes he was hire-purchasing from his work with his staff discount and of which he was inordinately proud, outside Orla's house and taking the Luas, so that he could have a few drinks at the party and not have to worry about being done by the Guards for drink-driving on the way home. He'd chanced it plenty of times before but not since he'd bought the Merc. The Merc was his pride and joy in life. He loved that Merc more than he loved Orla, she was starting to think.

Nathan no longer played rugby himself because of what he called his 'trick knee', but he still kept in touch with all his old rugby mates, who Orla couldn't stand because they were all nearly as loud and vulgar as Nathan. They treated women like commodities, like objects to be used and abused and then cast aside when they had fulfilled their purpose. Orla was dreading this party for that self-same reason. Nathan's friends acted like they knew all about what she got up to in bed with him, which they probably did because Nathan was most likely telling them, the blabbermouth. He put his pals ahead of her, Orla sometimes felt. Then she'd feel guilty for thinking that way. Nathan was perfectly fine when they were on their own together. He was loving and even considerate and thoughtful at times (when she reminded him to be), but when he was with his friends he turned instantly into a foul-mouthed lout. It was clearly just a guy thing. She'd known other blokes who were exactly the same. Grand until you saw them around their mates.

"Where'd you find that?" Orla said, her eyes wide.

"In the bin, when I went to put a tissue in." He glared at her accusingly. "Can you tell me what exactly it's supposed to be?"

"Well, it's obviously a pregnancy test." Orla took the little object from his hand and peered at it curiously. "And . . . and it's *positive*!"

"Well?" he demanded.

"Well, what?" echoed Orla, still not getting what he was driving at. When the penny dropped, her eyes widened further and she squeaked, "You don't think this test is *mine*, do you?"

"Well, who else's could it be?" His face was shiny with sweat and looming alarmingly close to hers.

"*Who else's?* What do you mean? I live with three other women! Fauve, Sasha and Doireann, remember, my housemates? This could belong to any one of them!"

"So what are you saying? Are you saying that this isn't yours?"

"Of *course* that's what I'm saying!" She dropped the test

back into the wastepaper basket and covered it over with some clean toilet paper she'd pulled from the roll. "I'm *not* pregnant, Nathan. I take the Pill. You already know that!"

"Well, I hope for your sake that you're telling me the truth, Orla," he said grimly.

"What do you mean, you hope for *my* sake?" She was shaking now.

"Well, I'm as sure as fuck not getting tied down with some snotty brat at *my* age. So if that's what your little game is, you can think again, missy!"

"*Missy?*" she shrieked. "*Who are you calling 'missy'?* I told you that this test isn't mine! Don't you believe me? What do you want me to do? Do you want me to go out and buy another test and wee on it right in front of you to show you that I'm not actually pregnant?"

"There's no need to get hysterical." Nathan sounded sulky now. "What was I supposed to think, Orla?"

"Well, you could have just *asked* me if it was mine, instead of jumping to all the wrong conclusions." She was starting to cry now.

"All right, all right." He was using the wheedling voice he brought out when he was trying to make it up with her after a row. "There's no need for tears, okay? I believe you."

"Okay," she gulped, turning away from him and dabbing at her eyeliner, which was starting to run. That was all Nathan's fault, damn him.

"We're perfect just as we are, aren't we?" he went on, coming to stand behind her so that they could each see the other's reflection in the bathroom mirror. "A baby would just screw up how perfect everything is for us right now, wouldn't it? Well, wouldn't it?"

She nodded because he expected it. His hands went up to

cup her breasts in the lacy top and bra she was wearing. In the mirror she watched him kiss her neck hungrily. She could smell the Brylcreem on his dark hair (so much for her lovely new top, anyway) and the heavy, expensive designer cologne he had on. Everything he wore had to be designer, from his shoes to his underpants. She closed her eyes, not in passion but to block out the sight of him. His breathing grew heavier as his hands moved lower. She felt herself being pushed forward over the sink and her suede skirt being hiked up over her hips. Then her little lacy knickers were coming down and Orla felt herself tense up between her legs.

As he entered her, hurting her because she wasn't even remotely turned on, he grunted and said, "You're so beautiful, Orla. You're so fucking beautiful, I can't resist you!"

She didn't answer, just gritted her teeth and waited until he was done.

Now they stood outside the house on Mornington Crescent. It was a house in which a party was clearly being held. Balloons were tied to the trees in the garden, the place was all lit up as if for Christmas and loud rock music was pumping from the open windows.

"*Nate, ya fat bastard, how are ya keeping?*" bellowed the very large bearded man who opened the door. He was so big he even dwarfed Nathan, who was solid enough himself.

"Grand, Mattie, grand! Yourself? You remember Orla, don't you?"

"I certainly will after tonight," Mattie said suggestively, allowing his gaze to roam over Orla's breasts in her tight top.

"Did you see that?" Orla whispered after Mattie had

gone off to find them drinks and their host, a guy called Ronan. "He was practically raping me with his eyes!"

"Ah relax, would you, Orla love! It's a party."

After he'd necked a few beers himself, Nathan was slobbery and horny, pawing Orla openly in front of his mates. Orla tried to relax with a few drinks too, but she couldn't seem to stop herself from being all tense and uptight.

"I'm going to the bathroom," she said at one point, desperate to get away for a few minutes.

"Don't be long, sweetheart," Nathan slurred, having a quick feel of her backside as she passed him.

He was deep in a conversation with his mate Ronan, whose birthday it was, and another man called Georgie, about the current state of Irish rugby. Orla had been bored to death sitting there with them in the battered-looking armchairs, but Nathan didn't like her to mingle when they were out together. He preferred her to stay by his side. "Where I can keep an eye on you," he always said jokingly, but it was no joke when he got her home and started accusing her of flirting with other men or even just of eyeing them up. He'd given her a couple of digs on occasion simply because he hadn't believed her when she'd sworn blind that she hadn't been flirting. She was much too afraid to even talk to other men any more when she was out with him, so his accusations were nearly always unfounded and born out of his jealous and paranoid mind.

She weaved her way carefully up the stairs in her high heels. Couples were sitting on nearly every step kissing and groping one another, and the sounds of sex came vigorously from behind one closed bedroom door. The loo was mercifully free, though, even if the person who had last used the toilet hadn't bothered to flush it. Grimacing at the unsavoury sight (and the smell), Orla flushed the toilet and then parked herself on the edge of the bath and lit a cigarette. Nathan didn't like her smoking but, fuck it, she needed one now and anyway she always carried a breath-freshening spray with her. She heaved a huge sigh of relief when she took those first few wonderful puffs. She was still upset that Nathan had thought the pregnancy test was hers, but she was even more upset about his violent reaction to the notion of pregnancy in general. He had more or less implied that she'd be left on her own, a single mother, if she ever found herself knocked up, a loathsome phrase she'd heard Nathan use before in connection with his mates' wives or girlfriends. He always laughed his head off when he heard that another of his pals had been 'caught' by an unexpected pregnancy.

"Poor bastard," he always used to say scornfully. "That's *his* life over now anyway."

He had a very cynical view of the whole love and babies thing, Orla reflected now as she puffed away furiously on her cigarette and ignored the bangs on the bathroom door and the impatient cries of "*Come on, hurry the fuck up, will ya? I really need to go!*". Nathan seemed to think that women were always out to trap men with their bodies and their uteruses, or should that be uteri, Orla wondered idly, not really caring. She was starting to relax now that she had a fag in her hand and some time away from Nathan and his nauseating friends.

She knew that Nathan's father had left his mother when he had been around seven or eight, and that his mother, Deirdre, had for ever after bemoaned the fact that she'd been 'saddled' with Nathan on her own. Stuck with him, as she put it, she'd brought him up, but it had been grudging. Orla had met her and she still talked frequently about all the things she could have done with her life if she hadn't had Nathan 'dumped' on her the way he had been. Orla had felt desperately sorry for Nathan, for his having been brought up by someone who had resented his presence, his very existence, even though she had carried him in her own body for nine months and given birth to him. How could you not love someone who was a part of you? Orla wouldn't treat any baby of theirs like that. She'd love it to bits and smother it with love, the love that Nathan never got when he was a child and the love that she'd never got herself. Their baby would be the most loved baby in the world. Orla would see to that.

Her own parents hadn't been anything to write home about either. When Orla was about seven years old, her father had died and her mother had remarried shortly afterwards to a man named Colin. Colin was a good deal older than Orla's mum, Yvonne. He'd been wealthy enough for her not to have to go out to work – she'd been able to stay home with, first, Orla, and then the twin boys who'd arrived about a year after the wedding. From the moment that Yvonne and Colin had found out that she was expecting twins, Orla might as well have not existed. Oh, she'd been well fed, clothed, housed and educated like Noah and Christopher, her new little twin brothers (the word 'half' as applied to the twins was never used in their house – they were Orla's full brothers and that was that), but she'd never felt loved. It was the younger siblings who now got all the cuddles and kisses and whispered endearments, all the loving tuckings-in and bedtime stories. Yvonne worshipped her two new little blond-haired, blue-eyed sons and Colin was proud of his pretty, younger wife and his adorable twin boys. They were the perfect family. Orla was left on the outside, wistfully looking in. Sometimes she even felt her mother resented her presence in the household, as if Orla were part of her past and had no place in her present cosy and comfortable present existence.

In the spirit of 'if you can't beat 'em, join 'em', Orla had thrown herself into the care of her new little brothers while still a child herself. That had pleased Colin and Yvonne no end and Orla, young as she was, felt like she'd found her true vocation. From then on, her role in the family was redefined as willing minder, baby-sitter, nursemaid, nanny and chief-cook-and-bottle-washer to Noah and Christopher. Her parents noticed her only in the context of what she did for the twins, but it was better than nothing. She loved the twins to bits, of course she did. Who could resist such cuddly little golden-haired cherubs? But sometimes she resented them too, for taking up all the room there was in her mother's heart and leaving her with virtually nothing.

Orla had gone to a vocational college after school instead of to university, but her mother and Colin didn't care where she was studying as long as she was home in time to make the boys' dinners every evening, the way only she could (they preferred Orla's cooking to anyone else's), and see to their school clothes. She did a course in childcare since it seemed like the obvious choice, the *only* choice. Now, at twenty-seven, she worked in a crèche in Stillorgan and she loved it. She especially loved working with babies. She adored babies and they loved her. When she was holding a baby in her arms, she felt complete in a way that she seemed unable to achieve under any other circumstances. Her twin brothers were grown-up now and they didn't need her any more, at least not in the same way (though they still counted on her for the occasional hand-out of money and advice on their complex love lives), but the babies in the crèche did need her, at least from eight in the morning until six at night, and she loved that. It was nice to be needed. It made her feel better about herself.

Nathan needed her too. He'd told her so often enough. Although he didn't bring it up, she knew it was because of his (mostly) loveless childhood that he liked having her around so much. She was kind and sweet and loving towards him and that was what he needed after the cold horrible way he'd been brought up. She would cry herself to sleep some nights thinking of Nathan as a fat little unloved schoolboy, fatherless and unwanted by his mother. It broke her heart to think about it. It was true that she found Nathan annoying at times, but it didn't mean she didn't still love him because, if anything, she loved him even more now than she had in the heady early months of their relationship. And he still needed her. She knew he did. Yes, he lost his temper with her sometimes and lashed out and did things that he would regret afterwards, but then he'd be so apologetic and loving that it would nearly be worth it. He'd bring her apology roses or chocolates and perfume and be so very gentle with her for ages after an 'incident'. Orla liked to think that they'd been drawn together initially because they had something major in common: the fact that they'd each been brought up without the comforting cushion of parental love. They didn't need anyone else now that they had each other.

She let her mind slide back to the events of earlier that

day. Whose pregnancy test had Nathan fished out of the bathroom bin anyway? Orla thought about it as she stubbed out her cigarette in the ashtray on the side of the bath and used a generous amount of her breath-freshener spray. Her money was on poor Fauve, who'd seemed in the past few weeks to be what mothers everywhere tended to call 'a bit peaky-looking'. She'd caught Fauve deep in a major pow-wow with Doireann a couple of times lately too, and they hadn't looked as if they were talking about the *X Factor* auditions or who was to be sent home next in *Strictly Come Dancing*. And the weirdest thing had happened, now that she came to think about it. She'd come down to breakfast one Saturday morning recently to find Fauve in floods of tears in front of the television, which was just then showing an advertisement for the yearly fundraiser, Children in Need.

"Fauve, what on earth's the matter?" Orla had said, rushing to kneel down beside her friend's armchair and put her arms around the shuddering figure.

"The b-b-b-bear – P-P-P-Pudsey!' Fauve managed. 'He's wearing a little p-p-p-patch over his – over his – over his – his *eye!*"

The last word came out on a howl and no more sense was to be had out of Fauve. Doireann had come down then and taken over the care of the sobbing Fauve, telling Orla it was all grand and she could go on back up to Nathan, who'd been staying over. That had been the end of it.

Oh well, thought Orla as she came downstairs now in Ronan's house, weaving her way once more through the amorous couples – had the crowd thinned out a bit, she wondered? – let Fauve and Doireann have their little secrets. She didn't care. She was only sorry that Fauve hadn't felt she could confide in her. She had been so wrapped up in Nathan lately, though. He was her everything now, and she knew that she was his. The occasional bust-up between them didn't matter a damn in the scheme of things. They wouldn't be a normal couple if they didn't sometimes argue and squabble like a pair of kids.

"Where've you been?" Nathan said when she returned to where he and his three mates were sitting. The four of them were lounging behind a giant potted palm that hid them from the rest of the big sitting-room.

"I was in the loo," said Orla, shrugging.

"Must have been some big shite," said Nathan nastily in a tone she hated because it nearly always meant that he was pissed off about something and spoiling for a fight. What was wrong now? His three friends, Mattie, Ronan the Birthday Boy and Georgie, each laughed at Nathan's crude remark.

Orla, flushed with embarrassment, sat down beside Nathan, crossing her legs and then uncrossing them immediately when she realised that Nathan's pals were staring at them. Nathan pulled her onto his lap and began to kiss her neck in a slobbery way and paw her thigh in the sheer tights she was wearing. Orla removed his hand from her thigh, but he just put it back and moved it a little higher up on her leg.

"Knock it off, Nathan," she whispered angrily but he just laughed.

"What's the matter, babes? We're among friends here, aren't we?"

He moved his hand from her thigh to her breast. He undid the first few buttons of her little lacy top and now her bra was visible. His friends, the friends she'd assumed were all as bad as Nathan, were starting to look awkward and uncomfortable, to their credit. One of them got up and wandered away to the drinks table. Another took out his phone and began scrolling.

"Stop it, Nathan, please." Her eyes were brimming with tears. "I want to go home now. *Please.*"

"Ah, lighten up, will ya?" he said, squeezing her breast over her lacy bra. His breath reeked of beer. "It's a party. We're all having a good time, aren't we?"

As his hand moved over her back, looking for the clasp of her bra to unhook it, Orla jumped up off his lap. Deliberately, to cool his ardour, she tipped her drink over his crotch and then, grabbing up her bag, with her phone, her purse and her return ticket for the Luas in it, she made a run for it through the crowded sitting-room. Out into the hall she ran, then out the front door with her top still undone like Jodie Foster's in *The Accused*. She'd have to forfeit her jacket, which she'd left on her chair, for the time being. It wasn't her favourite jacket anyway. She belted down the garden path and out through the little gate as fast as her spindly high heels would allow her (which wasn't very fast).

"*Orla! Orla! Wait! Stop, babes, please!*"

She whirled round, her hands flying to her top to do up the buttons he'd opened. "*Fuck off, Nathan!*" she screeched. "*I don't want to see you! In fact, I don't want to see you ever again. Just fuck off, will you?*"

"Look, I'm sorry for inside, okay?" he said, running his hand through his hair and cursing when it came away all covered in Brylcreem. He must have been super-agitated, thought Orla in wonder, because he wiped his hand absentmindedly off the trousers of his suit and he didn't even seem to care that he was ruining the expensive material. "But you're the one that's made me look as though I've fucking pissed myself," he added, indicating his drenched crotch with distaste.

"*You're sorry for inside?*" she shrieked, drawing curious looks from the middle-aged couple across the road who were unpacking their groceries from the boot of their car. "You're saying that as if you've just forgotten to buy teabags or something! You're saying that as if what happened *inside* just now was nothing at all!"

"Look, of course it wasn't nothing," said Nathan, edging a bit closer to Orla while glowering across at the nosey couple across the street. The couple were still looking over at them while pretending to be busy with their bags and boxes of shopping. "But let's not get it all out of proportion either. It was just a stupid notion of mine that went tits-up, if you'll excuse the pun. Feeling you up in front of everyone, I mean. *That* stupid notion. It was just meant to be a bit of fun. A bit of a turn-on, you know? Getting frisky in front of my mates." Seeing Orla stiffen with disgust and disbelief, he added hastily, "And of course it goes without saying that I shouldn't have done it and obviously, I'll never, *um*, I'll never do it again. I swear, babes."

"*Don't call me 'babes'!*" she shouted. "My name is Orla! *Orla!* Is that so hard for you to say?"

"Of course it's not, babes, I mean, *um*, Orla. Look, please come back inside with me and we'll talk. We're not achieving much out here anyway." He had another hard look at the couple across the road.

"Do you need a hand, love?" the man of the couple said to Orla, coming a little of the way across the road. He was huge in build, and well over six feet in height. His wife, or whoever the woman was, stood by the car, smiling encouragingly at Orla who shook her head.

"No, it's okay, thank you," she said to the man, although her voice was trembling. "I can handle this on my own."

"Well, if you're sure, love," said the man.

"You heard her. Fuck off," Nathan said nastily.

The big man from across the road raised his eyebrows. "There's no need for that kind of talk," he said. In contrast to Nathan's, his tone was pleasantly moderate.

"Why don't you just do as you're told, mate, and fuck off out of here before I deck you one?" Nathan retorted, full of beer and bravado.

"Shut up, Nathan! Don't be so fucking stupid. You're pissed and he's bigger than you are!" Orla said, before turning and apologising to the man. "I'm sorry about that. Please don't mind him. He's locked and he doesn't mean it."

"Yes, I bloody do." Nathan swaggered nearer to where Orla and the man were standing, his chest all puffed up like a peacock's. "I'm – I'm gonna knock his fucking block off."

"*No, you're not, you idiot!*" screamed Orla. From where she was standing, she could see that he was sweating profusely. "*Get back inside, will you, you pillock, or I'll never talk to you again, I swear!*" To the helpful man she said, "Please, just go in home, will you? I'll be all right, honestly I will."

The big man hesitated, then said: "All right, love, if you're sure." He turned to go back to the woman who must have been his wife.

She called over to Orla with a smile: "You know where we are, love!"

Orla flashed the pair a grateful smile and a nod, then

turned to Nathan and said quietly, "I'm not coming back in with you. I just want to go home now."

"I'll take you," he offered immediately. "Just let me go in and get our jackets."

"You're just not getting it, are you, what I'm saying?" Orla was suddenly aware that the couple who'd been unpacking their groceries had gone inside their house and she and Nathan were alone once more on the wet darkened street.

A few of the party people were watching the little scene delightedly from the windows of the party house, but they seemed to have no intention of getting involved or of coming to Orla's aid. Watching the dispute was infinitely more fun. Would they still just stand and watch if she were being beaten to a pulp, Orla wondered, or would they finally intervene? Somehow she doubted they would.

"Getting what?" joked Nathan. "Our jackets? I told you I was going back in for them now." Seeing her expression, he backtracked immediately. "Okay, okay." His voice was placatory now. "What is it that I'm not getting?" It was the voice of a man who would have preferred not to ask, but who has no choice if he wants to move forward and end a deadlock.

"That I'm breaking up with you, Nathan!" She wiped an unwanted tear from her eye with the back of her hand, not giving a toss about her mascara and eyeshadow. What did it matter? What did anything matter now, if she was losing Nathan?

It was crucial not to cry while she was doing the breaking-up, though, or Nathan would think she didn't mean a word of it. He always thought that way when she was crying. Whinging, he called it. *What are you whinging about now, Orla babes? Time of the month again, is it?* He was always saying things like that to her. It pissed her off and she felt belittled by it, but it was just Nathan's way. He couldn't change the way he was any more than autumn could prevent itself from turning into winter. Could he?

"We just don't want the same things," she said now sadly.

"That's bullshit," said Nathan confidently. "What same things don't we want? That's just an excuse people make up when they don't want to be with someone any more. Of *course* we want the same things. Nice car, nice clothes, a nice house in a good area, decent holidays, a good night out with a few quid to spend, all that kind of thing, all that stuff that people usually want. *I* want it, and I know you do too."

"*I want a baby!*" screamed Orla, not caring who heard her.

There was a silence, so deep and intense that Orla could almost hear the sound of something clicking neatly into place in her brain. With a stunning clarity, she realised that she *did* want a baby of her own to love and cherish. It was the *only* thing she'd really ever wanted, now she thought about it. How could she not have copped on to this sooner? She'd minded her twin baby brothers as if they were her own. At first, she'd been doing it mainly to earn the approval and attention of her mother and stepfather, but she'd grown to love the twins as if she herself had given life to them. She worked in a crèche because she wanted to be around babies. There was one baby there, a little boy of about eighteen months called Seb, who was her particular favourite, her pet. With his golden curly hair and huge trusting blue eyes, he was a precious little good-natured cherub who all the staff loved. Orla spent as much time minding him as she could, changing his nappies, settling him with his bottle and helping him to play with the building blocks, loving the way he chuckled when he knocked down the blocks. She pretended she was his mother and he her darling baby boy. She spent so much time with Baby Seb, who was always dressed in such gorgeous blue romper suits with ducks and sheep and teddy bears on them, that her supervisor had given her some funny looks and reminded her that the other babies in the crèche needed attention too. One day Orla was so lost in her lovely warm fuzzy fantasy that she was Seb's mummy that she'd been shocked and almost angry when his mother had come to the crèche to collect him at five-thirty. If she was to be unflinchingly honest with herself, she'd have to admit that she'd fantasised more than once about somehow sneaking Baby Seb home with her one night and keeping him with her for ever. She'd even worked out where in her bedroom his cot would go. Of course, she knew that this type of thinking was very wrong and so she'd never breathed a word of it to Nathan. He'd have been horrified and probably called the Guards or had her committed. She wouldn't have blamed him. She wasn't insane, though. She knew perfectly well that stealing someone else's baby was wrong, a terrible crime, and she'd never have gone through with it. It was just nice to fantasise sometimes. That was all it was. A fantasy, nothing else. Something nice to think about sometimes.

Now, some of the party people had come outside with their drinks and were laughing and eyeballing the drama unfolding in front of them, as if it were a particularly absorbing play or a television soap opera that they were watching.

Nathan, on the other hand, was standing stock-still. His face was white and sweaty. He looked shell-shocked, as if he'd been struck dumb or something. It was cold and damp on Mornington Crescent.

Orla shivered. "See? I told you we didn't want the same things," she told him quietly. "I'm going now. Goodbye. Don't follow me."

She turned to leave. It was pissing down heavily now, to add insult to injury. She had no coat, no boyfriend and she'd probably never again meet anyone she loved enough to have a baby with, a baby and a cosy little family whose members always had time for one another and were always there for each other. Yes, she knew it sounded like a soppy American television sitcom, but that was what she wanted. She was only surprised that it had taken so long for the thought to really crystallise in her brain the way it had tonight at this shitty party. She knew what she wanted now and, if she couldn't have it, well, then she didn't want anything.

"Orla, no – don't go, love! We need to talk about this. Can't you see that?"

She began to walk, albeit a bit unsteadily in her party heels, throwing words back over her shoulder at him. "What's the point? There's nothing to talk about. I want a baby and you don't." Then she swung around again and stood stock-still, staring at him. "You don't *ever* want one because your parents split up and your mum was awful to you and you don't ever want that to happen to a child of yours. I don't blame you for that. Really I don't." Her voice broke on a sob.

"What if I *do* want a baby, though, same as you?"

Nathan said, stepping close to her and lightly taking hold of her arm.

"But you don't," said Orla, doubtfully. "Do you?"

"Maybe I do. Maybe I *do* want the same things as you. Can't we go back to your house where it's nice and warm and at least talk about it?"

The heavens opened properly now. There might even have been a clap of thunder. Orla wavered.

STOP 5: DUNDRUM

Mick and Donna

Donna McKenna walked to the Luas stop at Balally by herself. She'd be taking the tram as far as Dundrum, where Mick would meet her with the car and they'd drive on together to Avondale Road. It was a damp, drizzly day, which didn't help her humour.

"Good luck, Mum," Livvy had said before she'd left for school, enveloping Donna in a giant bear-hug.

"I'll be fine," said Donna, more cheerfully than she felt. "It's your dad I'm bothered about."

"Dad's fine, Mum." Livvy's voice held all the optimism of youth. "He's strong. He can handle anything."

Which is exactly what fathers *want* their daughters to think about them, Donna reflected as she watched her youngest child, seventeen now, head off down the garden path with her giant schoolbag bumping off her sturdy frame.

"I thought that schools were all computerised nowadays," Donna was always saying to her when she saw Olivia trying to lift the heavy backpack. "I thought you kids did everything on the one tablet thing."

"We still need *books*, Mum," Livvy would counter with an eye-roll and the worldly-wise, patronising tone of voice the young reserve for the old and decrepit.

Donna put the finishing touches to her make-up in the mirror. It was a long time since she'd been to a solicitor's office, so she wasn't sure what you were supposed to wear to them nowadays or what the protocol was. Did you shake hands with the solicitor, or call her by her first name or what?

"You're not going to tea in the Phoenix Park with the President, Mum," Livvy had giggled when she'd seen her mother frantically rummaging through her wardrobe the night before the big appointment.

"That's not till next week, silly," Donna had deadpanned back, quick as a flash. She mostly wore tracksuits and old T-shirts to her work as a cleaner (anything else would get destroyed), but she had a few decent tops, skirts and pairs of trousers. The trouble was picking things that would go well together.

"Can you wear trousers to a solicitor's office?" she'd asked Livvy.

Livvy had laughed at that. "Mum, you can wear anything you want to a solicitor's office. You can wear a clown's outfit with giant shoes and a red-rubber nose, or you can waltz in there in the nip if you want!"

Ah, the confidence of youth! The kids of today had none of the niggling fears and insecurities their parents had had. They didn't kow-tow to people like solicitors or teachers or priests or even the Guards, the people who'd once had all the power in the community back in the bad old days. And maybe that was a good thing, Donna thought. Maybe it didn't do to give a small number of individuals all the power. Too much power corrupted, that was the problem. And shure, weren't priests and nuns the same as all the rest of us when it came down to it? They all had to wee and poo too, just like everyone else, and eat and drink and take baths and go to sleep. They were *human*, just like everyone else. Whether or not they *acted* as if they were, that was another matter altogether.

In the end, Donna had settled on a black top and trousers which could be worn with a little blue jacket she really liked. She sprayed on some perfume and picked up her handbag, the battered black one she always carried. There was so much stuff in it that transferring its contents to another, less knackered, bag was out of the question. Better to just keep everything together in this one. If Madam Solicitor didn't like it, she would just have to lump it. The bag was non-negotiable.

When she was finally ready, she locked up the house and left. Across the close, the party house from the night before was quiet and empty-looking. A few deflating balloons tied to a tree were bobbing about tiredly in the light breeze, as if they'd seen enough action the night before and now simply couldn't be arsed doing whatever was expected of them today. A few cans littered the damp grass. All the curtains were still closed. Donna looked curiously across and wondered if the party people were inside and still sleeping off the booze, or if they had all stumbled hungover down to the Luas and gone to work. Today was a workday, after all, even if it *was* a Friday, a day which a lot of Irish people chose to regard as optional, or at least a take-it-easy-here-comes-the-weekend kind of day. The Irish loved their weekends, especially their Bank Holiday ones.

What had happened at the house the night before was so strange. That beautiful young woman, all tearful and rain-sodden, being shouted at by that tosser in the pinstripe trousers. Neither Donna nor her husband Mick, who'd been unpacking their groceries from a late-night Thursday supermarket run, had any time for bullies like him. Mick, who had worked for nearly thirty years as a bouncer in various pubs and clubs, was well able to handle himself. He'd intervened at one point, asking the girl if she needed help. Mick could have taken on that blustering wally in the pinstripes without breaking a sweat. But the girl had said no, as girls in her situation often did, and Mick had left it. You rarely got thanks for intervening between a warring couple, and sometimes you even got a smack in the chops yourself for your trouble. Donna knew that.

They had gone inside then, Mick and Donna, but despite Mick's advice to leave well enough alone, Donna had raced upstairs to the open bathroom window, where she'd had a ringside seat for the final act. Livvy had wandered in from her bedroom, curious about all the palaver, and watched alongside her mother as the man, who was called Nathan, begged his girlfriend, Orla (they could hear everything perfectly well), to come back to him. A baby seemed to be the main bone of contention between them, although Donna reckoned personally that the man's temper was the real issue they should be looking at. Orla had screamed across the close at the man: "*I want a baby!*" Then the man, who'd looked flabbergasted at first, had seemed to be saying, okay, yes, we can have one if you want, if it's that big a deal to you. As if they were talking about buying a new couch from IKEA or something.

Orla had stood outside by herself in the rain while the

man had gone back into the party house for their jackets. The party people, who by this stage were clustered in the dripping garden watching the little drama play out, mock-booed and hissed at him for making such a dog's dinner of the whole thing as he stormed past them. He slammed the front door behind him, which only served to occasion more mirth and merriment from the watchers. A few minutes later, he came out of the house carrying the two jackets. He wrapped his soaking wet girlfriend in her coat and the pair walked off together in the rain, holding hands, in the direction of the Luas. *Well.* Only when Donna was certain that there was no more to be seen did she close the bathroom window and go back downstairs to put away the shopping.

"Talk about being a nosey neighbour, Mum," Livvy had teased her good-naturedly then.

"I didn't see *you* minding your own business either," Donna pointed out, at which her daughter merely grinned like the mischievous imp she was.

"I was just keeping you company, Mum, that's all."

Donna had been genuinely worried about the girl, Orla, though. Having a baby with a man like that Nathan fella, who'd been bullying her publicly and shouting at her, and who'd even started threatening Mick, a total stranger (Mick would have mopped the floor with him), would be the ruination of her, surely. A baby tying her down to that lump of a brute was the last thing she needed. At least the night before she'd been able to run away, even if she'd come back almost immediately afterwards. There'd be no running away with a baby. Donna sincerely hoped that the girl would see sense before it was too late and run far enough away so that Pinstripes would be unable to find her. Donna had never had that kind of trouble herself with Mick. Mick was what they called a gentle giant. He was six foot two, burly and broad-built, with hands like two shovels, but he'd never hurt anyone who hadn't hurt him first.

He could separate a bunch of drunken men brawling outside a pub or club without turning a hair (well, his head was actually shaved), but he'd never once laid a hand on Donna or on any of their three kids. Never even raised his voice, really, unless Donna screeched at him first, which happened occasionally. They weren't perfect – what couples were? – but Mick loved his family. They were very lucky to have him. He worshipped Donna and his only daughter Olivia, and he loved his two sons, James and Adam. He'd make shite of anyone who looked crooked at any one of them, and they all knew that and were secure in the knowledge that, at least while Mick was around, they were safe and nothing could harm them. But Donna sometimes worried about her husband. She was worrying about him now as she boarded the Luas at Balally that would take her to Dundrum to meet him. From there, they would go on together to the solicitor's office. He took so much on himself. That was the main problem with Mick. He carried the weight of his whole family on his broad shoulders and sometimes Donna worried that it might be too much for him, especially because he wasn't one to ever really talk about his feelings.

"*Please move down the tram,*" said the automated female voice now over the tannoy.

James and Adam were exactly like Mick. They never talked about their feelings either, which drove her mad. But you could expect that with teenage boys or lads in their early twenties, or so her friends were always telling her. Boys were secretive – they kept a lot of things inside. Adam though, their middle child, was a real worry. He was in his second year of music college now and Donna genuinely couldn't remember the last time they'd had a proper conversation about anything other than mealtimes, dirty washing or course fees. He'd been staying over with a college friend since Tuesday night and, as far as she knew, he hadn't even bothered to text any of them, never mind phone. And he hadn't smiled or seemed happy in God knows how long, either. But on the rare occasions when he did smile, to Donna it felt like the sun suddenly shining through the clouds. She loved all her children but, if she was being honest, she'd always had a soft spot for Adam, her gentle, quiet middle child. Livvy at least was an open book, thank God. You always knew what Livvy was thinking or feeling because she told you out straight. Donna loved that about her, even though there were times when she wished that her daughter would keep more stuff to herself.

Donna was yanked abruptly from her thoughts when she saw that Mick was waiting for her at the Luas stop, bless him.

"Where'd you park the car?" she asked after she'd hugged him and given him a peck on the cheek.

"In the car park up the street. It's only a few minutes' walk to Avondale Road."

"Are you sure you want to do this?" she asked him, thinking how well he looked in his dark leather jacket and good black trousers. Under the jacket, he was even wearing a proper dark shirt with long sleeves, instead of his old Metallica T-shirt. She had shined his black shoes for him herself and they were positively gleaming.

Mick shrugged his giant shoulders. "What choice do I have?" he said simply. Then, to change the subject, he asked, "Any sign of life from the party house?"

Donna shook her head and rolled her eyes in a *would-you-look-at-the-state-of-them* kind of way.

"The garden is in bits but there's been nobody about all morning, so either they've all fecked off to work, dragging their hangovers behind them, or they're all still in bed dying." Then she blurted out, "I hope that girl's okay, Mick, that poor Orla one from last night. I honest to God hope she won't get back with that . . . that *prat* in the suit. The state of him, threatening you like that."

"I think she probably already has. Didn't you tell me that they both went off together in the rain? Holding hands, no less. Very romantic. He must've promised her the sun, the moon *and* the stars, anyway, to get her to go off with him meekly like that."

"Well, please God she has the common sense to get away from him for good," said Donna. "That kind of thing just worries me, you know? It makes me think of our Olivia and what might happen if she ever ended up in an abusive relationship like that one."

"Any man who lays a hand on our Livvy will wish he'd never been born," Mick said grimly.

"I know, love, I know." Donna squeezed his arm. "But what parents really have to do is to teach girls that the kind of man they deserve is the man who treats them well. Still, most girls are supposed to go for guys that remind them of their dads. Livvy won't go far wrong if she picks a lad who reminds her of you."

They chatted on about the kids and the job of furniture-moving that Mick had been doing for a friend in

Dundrum that morning – hence his meeting her there with the car – and then, suddenly, they were standing outside the solicitor's office which formed part of the parade of shops on Avondale Road. To Donna's relief, it looked more understated and shabby than she'd been expecting. I'm more than good enough to be here, she told herself firmly as she mounted the narrow staircase behind Mick. I own and run my own business, an office-cleaning company with two employees besides myself.

But she needn't have worried. The solicitor was lovely. For one thing, she was much younger than either of them had anticipated.

"Hi, I'm Aideen Quinlan and it's really nice to meet you both," she said warmly in a lilting Donegal accent, coming towards them with an outstretched hand. "Won't you sit down and make yourselves comfortable? Would either of you like tea or coffee?"

Mick said no at the same time as Donna said yes. Then Mick said yes while Donna said no. The solicitor laughed and said that they'd *all* have tea or coffee, herself included.

When they were all three of them sitting comfortably with the hot drinks and a plate of biscuits in front of them, Aideen, a personable and bright young woman with big fashionable glasses and chestnut-coloured hair drawn back off her face into a messy bun, picked up a blue folder off her desk.

"Well, as we discussed on the phone," she said, "Margaret Bowen passed away peacefully in her sleep five days ago. What money she had has gone to an animal charity. Apparently, Miss Bowen was very fond of animals, especially cats." She paused and looked over at Mick. "The part that concerns you, Mr. McKenna, is right here in this folder."

She extracted a sheaf of papers and shuffled them, then cleared her throat.

"Miss Bowen specified that I read her story to you personally, here in this office. I suppose she just wanted to make one hundred-per-cent-sure that she was heard. Afterwards, when you leave, the papers are yours to do with as you wish. Is that all right with you?"

Mick nodded and gripped Donna's hand.

"Right, well then, we'll begin." She cleared her throat again and began to read. "'*I was born in Cork in 1940 . . .*'"

She must be well used to this type of thing, Donna thought admiringly, because she doesn't sound a bit self-conscious or nervous.

"'*My people were farmers, poor but not dirt-poor, like some others we knew. I was the eldest of seven children, a small enough family for the time. Some families we knew at the time had eleven, twelve, even thirteen children in them, so seven was nothing unusual. My father was a cold, hard, austere man. You could never talk to him about anything except the farm, not like the way children talk to their parents nowadays. Nowadays it's all about the talking but back then it was different. He never drank a drop of alcohol (his parents had both been alcoholics) and he was deeply religious. We went to Mass every Sunday of course and we were made to go every morning in Lent, and woe betide us if we misbehaved in the church or tried to get out of going. We were also made say prayers every morning and evening and there were pictures of the Sacred Heart in nearly every room in the house. The one in the kitchen was the most important one because it had the light underneath it. My mother was always saying things like 'Imagine talking like that in front of the Sacred Heart!' or 'I only hope and pray the Sacred Heart can't see you now, coming home in that state in front of Him!'*

The priest was the most important person in the town and, if you met him on the street, you'd have to step aside to let him pass and say 'Good morning, Father' or 'Good evening, Father'. If you were a child, sometimes the priest mightn't even acknowledge that you'd spoken, they were that high-up in the scheme of things. If you were to ask me today was religion shoved down our throats when we were younger, I would have to say yes. All the things that happened to me later in life have caused me to stop believing in the Catholic Church. I no longer go to Mass or take the Sacrament.

It's harder to stop saying my prayers, because I've said my prayers every day of my life, even when I was in the place. Those prayers were to ask God to set me free but He never did. Maybe He only answers the prayers of the higher-ups, the rich and powerful, because when I was downtrodden and laid low in the place, He never spoke to me.

My mother, in her own way, was as distant and unloving as my father. The main thing I remember her constantly saying was that she'd never wanted children. If she had her time over again, she was always telling us, she'd go away and become a nun because nuns had no children and they lived to be a hundred because of it. It was because they had no stress, you see, and their bodies never had to bear the burden of children. Looking back, I suppose it wasn't very flattering that she said this to us so often, but back then we just accepted it. I remember also the way my mother would sit out in the back garden every evening after dinner and have a smoke of her pipe (her own mother, my grandmother, had always smoked a pipe too), the chickens clucking away around her feet and the old donkey coming over for a nose. She'd sit for hours just thinking, smoking her foul-smelling pipe and staring into space, and we weren't allowed to come near her because this was her private time for regretting the choices she'd made. She'd tell us that straight out, in case we were ever in any doubt. I loved my mother, despite how cold she was and how often she pushed me away. As the eldest, I think I was a disappointment to her. There were definitely other kids in the family she preferred to me. It always cut me to the quick when I saw her favouring others, which happened frequently. Even though she had a hard life – having to cook, clean and wash for a husband and seven children all very close to one another in age is no joke – I can't feel sorry for her because of what she let happen to me later.

When a baby sister came along who was years younger than me – nearly ten years younger – I finally felt like I had someone to love. I lavished all my love and care on this one tiny little human being. My mother didn't mind at all that I monopolised the new baby because she had no time to mind her herself. She didn't want to either. I think now that maybe she resented the new baby because it was taking her back to square one. She'd thought that she was finished with all that, the nappies and the bottles and the sleepless nights, but now she was having to start again from scratch and she was disgusted. She could hardly stand to look at the child. It just represented more housework and drudgery to her.

I suppose that a psychologist today would say that I was so starved of love that I focused all my attention on this new baby sister. Now, all these years later, she doesn't know anything about my existence. That's how good and thorough a job they did of erasing me from the family tree. That's one thing I can never forgive my parents for. They denied me and my sister the chance of a proper relationship, a friendship. My little sister will never know how much I loved her, or even that I existed.'

Mick was gripping Donna's hand so hard now that she was wincing.

Aideen Quinlan paused for a minute, cleared her throat and gave a little cough before taking a sip from a glass of water that sat on her desk.

"'*When I met Danny in 1957,*'" she went on, "'*I suppose that what happened was almost inevitable. He was so handsome, so charming and funny that I was probably in love with him by the end of our first meeting at a local dance. I'd literally never met anyone like him in my entire life which, up to that point, had been extremely sheltered. My parents hadn't wanted me to go this dance and, if they'd known what was going to happen as a result of my going there, they'd have stopped me from attending. I think I got pregnant during our first sexual encounter. I knew about babies from things I'd seen on the farm and heard from friends at school, who always seemed to know much more than me about that kind of thing. I knew how they got in (the babies, I mean), and I knew how they were supposed to get out, although that thought in particular terrified me. After all, how could something as big and solid as a baby pass through an opening as small as, well, as a woman's front bits? I had seen calves and piglets born on the farm, but I was a human being. Surely it was different for human females than for animals? Anyway, I couldn't understand how this part of the process was going to work at all. I suppose I was an awful eejit, really, and as green as the grass.*

Time passed, anyway, and Danny went back to England, where he was working as a roofer and making good money out of it. He'd only been back in Ireland on a sort of extended holiday, which lasted one whole summer. He was as Irish as I was, only he left Cork to go to England when he finished school because he'd heard that there were good pickings there. London was still rebuilding itself after the war and labourers could make a fortune amongst the ruins and the rubble. I'd been too afraid to tell Danny – or anyone – about the baby, so I let him go off all happy because we'd had such a wonderful time together and he had lots of lovely memories to look back on.

Bully for him, I hear you say, and you're right. My biggest regret in this whole thing is that I didn't tell him in person that I was in trouble while he was still in Ireland. God knows how things might have turned out then. He might have married me, and I could have kept my baby and maybe we could even have had one or two more, who knows? But there's no point in dwelling on the 'what ifs'. Life is full of them and they never get you anywhere. Anyway, it only upsets me to think about what-might-have-been. I try not to do it too often but I'm only human after all.

A letter came for me from London about a month after Danny had left. I've kept it till this day, although now it's so crumpled from the constant readings and re-readings that you can hardly see the words on it any more. It's newsy and chatty and full of all the things he'd been doing and the places and people he'd been seeing, and I was so jealous of him being over there, meeting new people, happy and busy and without me, that I wanted to die.

Instead, I was stuck at home in Cork, growing more and more miserable by the day. When I wasn't helping out on the farm, I'd go for long walks by the river and think about my Danny and cry. If it was raining, my tears would mingle with the rain until I felt like I was all water. I even thought about drowning myself a time or two, but I couldn't bring myself to do it. I was too afraid of what it would be like. Anyway, killing yourself is the worst sin you can commit. The thought of being locked away from the face of God for all eternity was too much, too big for a young girl of my age to contemplate. I wasn't yet twenty, much too young to die.

And the baby inside me continued to grow. The first two or three months, nothing much happened to me except that I felt noticeably more tired than usual and I seemed to have lost my appetite. After the third month, however, things changed considerably. I was putting on weight which I tried to hide by wearing big jumpers. I remember I had a green one, scratchy and with a huge cowl-neck that wasn't fashionable at all (the kids today wouldn't be seen dead in it), but at least it hid the bump. There was also a brown one I liked. I had more energy during this time, had a huge appetite and constantly craved citrussy-tasting things like oranges or orange-and-lemon sucky sweets.

Was I worried about what would happen when the baby was due to come out? Yes and no. During the day, I seemed to have huge quantities of denial at my fingertips that I could comfortably hide in but, in the night, lying in my narrow bunk bed with my four younger sisters in the same room with me, was when I feared the future. I'd lie awake terrified, thinking about it, dreading the day of reckoning and panicking that every little twinge I felt was the onset of early labour. I longed for Danny but he seemed to be very far away from me now, almost as if he'd never happened. He was like a dream I'd had, but the baby inside me was no dream. I managed to keep my pregnancy concealed for more than eight months. How can they not notice, I asked myself every day, how can they not see what should be obvious to everyone? Are they that blind, that oblivious, that uncaring? My mother said afterwards that she'd noticed, that she'd known, but that she was just waiting the whole time for me to 'get the boat to England' and do away with the baby like another girl in the town was supposed to have done. Abortion wouldn't be legalised in England for another decade or two but there were certain people you could go to if you were in trouble. All you needed was an introduction from someone else and a few quid. I wouldn't have had a clue myself how to go about such a thing, even if I'd wanted to. I felt sick when my mother said what she said. You'd have been waiting a long time, I wanted to scream at her, for me to do that.

I only told them in the end because things were happening in my body and it was clear that something even bigger was going to happen soon. In the end, it was literally only the fear of that 'something bigger' that forced me to reveal my carefully guarded secret. My one consolation was that it was much too late in the pregnancy for them to make me take that dreaded 'boat to England' themselves. Maybe that, as well as the sick fear of telling such cold, puritanical angry people about something so personal, so intimate, something created out of love, was the reason I had hugged my secret to myself for so long. In any case, once the genie was out of the bottle, there was no squashing it back in. Why were they always so angry, my parents? It was a question I often asked myself. I understood that their lives – in particular my mother's – hadn't worked out the way they'd expected them to, but did that give them the right to take it out for ever after on their children? Back then, of course, children weren't valued as individuals the way they are today – they were only more mouths to feed. They got the family doctor, a sharp-faced, old-womanish little man with a thin, reedy, high-pitched voice, to come to the house and confirm that there was indeed a baby. Even as he was roughly handling my abdomen, part of me was still genuinely expecting him to say that it was all rubbish, nonsense, all in my imagination, there was nothing there at all. But it was much too late for that. My mother did what she always did during a family crisis and, after a few cutting remarks as to my character and what she said about 'the boat to England', she disappeared off upstairs, pleading one of her sudden conveniently timed 'indispositions'. She left me alone with my father, something I find it hard to forgive her for because she knew full well what he was like. I think she didn't care, as long as he was directing his anger at us kids and not at her. He shot hard, cold nasty questions at me, such as who the father was and when and where did it happen and all that. As soon as I could, I escaped off to bed, relieved that he hadn't shown me the expected violence. He could have battered me, but he must have been too shocked to react in his usual way. Believe me when I say I got off lightly that night. Climbing into my bunk bed in the bitter cold of a January night, I fell into a dead sleep.

When I awoke the following morning, it was to a

vastly different world to the one I remembered. It might sound clichéd to say that nothing was ever the same again, but that's really how it was.

It was after ten o'clock, for one thing. I'd slept in! I would normally have been up and about doing my jobs on the farm hours before. I wondered why the rest of them hadn't called me. Not only that but, when I dressed and went downstairs, I noticed two things immediately. There was a brown suitcase standing packed by the front door, and my younger siblings were nowhere to be seen. My parents wouldn't tell me where they'd all vanished to, or whose the suitcase was. They just told me to eat my breakfast, which I did. I was filled with trepidation, but I still didn't realise the seriousness and extent of my predicament. If I had, I might have given suicide a second hearing.

When I'd finished eating my porridge, all lumpy now from having been sitting on the hob since seven o'clock that morning when my mother had made it, there was a knock on the door. It was the parish priest, who was a great friend of the doctor who'd called to the house the night before.

'Hurry up now and get your hat and coat on,' my mother urged me, as she bustled round making tea for the priest.

'Where are we going?' I asked her, frantic now, but she ignored me.

When I was dressed in my coat and hat, my father came in from the farm and had a quick muttered exchange with the priest. My father put the brown packed suitcase in the back of the priest's car. And that was it. Without a word of love, encouragement or even goodbye, without a word even about when we might see each other again, my mother pushed me into the passenger seat of the priest's car and shut the door. The priest got in and started the car. It rolled away down the driveway.

I was too afraid to look back at my parents. What if they weren't waving? Somehow I knew they wouldn't be. What if they weren't even still there at all but had gone back about their business? I'd be even more crushed than I was at present. I didn't chance it in the end. I was too afraid of what I would or wouldn't see.

I asked the priest a few times where we were going but he kept absolutely silent for the whole journey so, eventually, I fell silent too. After about two hours of driving, he stopped at a café and bought two sandwiches and two cups of tea in plastic cups. He wordlessly gave me one of the sandwiches and one of the teas. The sandwich was just plain ham and a bit chewy but I was hungry so it hit the spot, and I was very glad of the hot sweet tea.

When we started driving again, I noticed that more and more of the road signs were saying 'Dublin.' Were we going to Dublin? I knew by now that my parents were sending me somewhere and that it was to do with me telling them about the baby, but I still had no idea where it was or what it would entail for me and my child. I wouldn't be long finding out. About five hours after we'd left Cork and we'd driven through what was unmistakably Dublin because of all the signposts, the priest's car made its way up the long winding driveway of a huge, imposing red-brick building, standing in its own private grounds, which I knew instinctively was an institution of some kind. The moment I saw it looming over me like something out of a nightmare will be imprinted on my mind for ever. The priest indicated to me with a jerk of his head that I should get out. I did so and took my suitcase from him when he handed it to me. Nervously, I followed him up the steps to the huge brown front door that had been waxed to within an inch of its life. The heavy knocker too was gleaming with polish. Even outside in the fresh air you could smell the wax polish.

A nun in a long black habit, complete with one of the old-fashioned wimples, came to the door in answer to the priest's knock. She and the priest had a whispered conversation, clearly not intended for my ears. Then, to my astonishment, the priest descended the steps, got back into his car and drove off without so much as a word to me or even a glance in my direction. He'd been cold and distant towards me and hadn't spoken a single solitary syllable to me during the long journey, but he was my last link with my home and my family and I felt the panic rising up in my throat. Where was I? Would I be staying in this place with the huge brown door and the polished knocker? Were there more nuns here like this one who was looking me over coldly now like I was something unpleasant she'd stepped in?

From the moment I'd told my parents about the baby, my fate had been sealed. The nun told me sharply to follow her inside and, when that heavy brown door banged shut behind me, even without knowing yet what this strange place was and what it would come to mean for me, the noise it made already sounded to me like the clanging shut of a prison door.

Dear Michael, you will already have guessed that this place to which I'd been sent was a Magdalene laundry, a place of so-called 'atonement' for one of the worst sins of all, the sin of being a 'fallen woman'. Much has been written in recent years about such places and I hope most people today understand how wrong it was of the nuns to imprison women in such a way for years and years when they hadn't even done anything wrong. These laundries were places where the nuns abused and exploited the so-called 'penitents' and profited greatly from the women's labour.

When I arrived first, my blonde curly hair was cut and I was given the shapeless, sexless grey uniform and underwear that all the 'penitents' were forced to wear. Then I was made to sign my admission papers in the presence of a hard-faced, cold-voiced Reverend Mother. Because I was so near my time, I was put straight to bed in the infirmary and, three weeks later, I gave birth to a baby girl who was taken from me at the moment of birth and never returned. I heard her first cries but nothing else. 'It's better that way, so you don't get attached to it,' the civilian nurse told me briskly but it didn't feel 'better' to me. I was given something to dry up my milk and, four weeks after the birth, I was put to work in the laundry, a fate that had been marked down for me since I had first passed through the doors of this place. They were only waiting to get the baby out of me and away from me so they could own me properly. I asked the nuns many times what had become of my baby, who I hadn't even had a chance to name, and the answer was always the same. 'She's gone to a good home, better than you could ever give her, so be thankful.' Thankful? I felt murderous for those awful first few months, then all the fight went out of me and the pain settled down into a dull ache that became my constant companion, every day and night for the rest of my life.

My family never came to see me. They never wrote to me either, although when I'd been in the place six months I received a letter addressed to me in my mother's handwriting. My heart leapt. Were they coming to take me away from this terrible place now that the baby, the source of all the 'trouble', as they saw it, was gone? I opened the letter and saw only Danny's face smiling up at me from a newspaper cutting. It was his obituary. He'd died in London, falling off a roof in a tragedy at his work, and his body had been brought home to Cork to be laid to rest. It was a fine obituary, all about Danny's cheerful personality and the sports he'd loved and the teams he'd played for when he'd lived in Cork. He was leaving behind his parents, three brothers, two sisters and a dog called Rocket, or Rocky for short. There was no mention of his baby daughter or the woman (me) he'd once said he loved who'd given birth to his child on her own, with the father miles away across the Irish Sea. So far away he might as well have been on Mars. I felt like I didn't exist, neither me nor my daughter. I cursed my mother for sending me something so coldly dreadful as that death notice without a word of comfort attached. There wasn't even a note from her inside. What a spiteful woman she was, and how glad she must have been that Danny was dead. All hope died in me then. I had nothing to live for. My precious baby daughter was gone for ever, my beloved Danny too, and my family wanted nothing to do with me. The Reverend Mother told me that my parents had given her their permission to keep me there with the nuns after the baby was born. It's a terrible thing to be told that your family don't love you, don't want you. I decided there and then that I didn't care what happened to me after that.

I stayed in the laundry until it closed down in 1992. Thirty-five years of my life was given to that awful place. Even then, though, I didn't want to leave. Quite honestly,

I was afraid to. I had nothing and no one. Where would I live? What would I do? A social worker helped me to find a room in a halfway house and I did cleaning jobs or worked in launderettes in Dublin because it was all I knew. I spoke to no one, not until recently, about my experiences as a so-called 'penitent' behind those high convent walls. A chance meeting in a coffee shop with a very kind lady called Rosita, who'd been through the same experience, led to her putting me in touch with an agency that searches for long-lost relatives of people like me.

I hope that you won't mind me writing to you and casting a shadow over your life with my sad story, Michael. I promise you that that is not my intention. I would like for someone in what remains of my family to know what happened to me because I think it's important. My parents cut me out of their lives when they heard about my baby. In order to do this, they must have told lies about me to my siblings and friends and to our neighbours. Someone can't just disappear out of people's lives like that without lies having to be told and excuses made. My mother, in particular, was a past master at twisting the truth to suit her own ends, so she was most likely the one who came up with the cover story. My personal guess is that they told everyone that I ran away to England with some young fella and simply never bothered to contact them again. They may even have pretended to some of my younger siblings at some point that I'd died or had never even existed. The little baby sister I cared for so much might have had some vague shadowy memories of someone in her baby days loving her to the moon and back, but she wouldn't remember who it was. This cuts me like a knife wound, but it's only one of the crosses I've had to bear.

Michael, I know that you have children yourself now, two sons and a daughter. Love them all, Michael, but especially your daughter. She is a very precious gift that you have been given and you must mind her well. If she ever comes to you in the same situation in which I found myself in 1957, I beg of you and your wife to be there for her and not to desert her. Thankfully, I know that times have changed and that to be expecting a baby outside of marriage nowadays is no longer regarded as the big sin it used to be, and women are no longer shunned or scorned because of it. Women can even make choices about this kind of thing now. I would thank God for this every day but God no longer exists for me. He ceased to exist the moment the convent doors banged shut behind me in that place. Ironically, though the convent was full of crosses and holy pictures and it was run by nuns, there was no God in that place, and he certainly wasn't present in the laundry, where I slaved alongside other women like me for thirty-five years. Religion is no longer part of my life. How can it be, when God let such things happen to me, and others like me, behind those convent walls? I cross the road when I see a church now. I shudder when I see a nun or a priest because they remind me of what was taken from me. I was never able to find out what happened to my beautiful baby daughter. I only hope that she lived to see happier days than I ever saw myself. I think of her and of my baby sister – she'll always be a baby to me – and of you and your family as I lie here. Everything I never had myself I wish for you all.'"

Aideen paused and took a soft breath before reading the final words.

"'*Yours with all best wishes, Margaret Bowen.*'"

Aideen shuffled the papers back into the folder. Then

she tactfully pushed the tissue box on her desk towards Donna who was crying openly. Mick was blinking and swallowing hard. "There are some notebooks and papers and a few wee photos that came with this letter," Aideen said quietly.

"Thank you," Mick said gruffly, his voice thick with what Donna recognised as unshed tears.

He reached out and took the folder from the solicitor's outstretched hand along with the little packet of papers.

"And there's no doubt, is there, that my mother was Margaret Bowen's youngest sister – the baby sister she talks about in her letter?"

"No doubt whatsoever, Mr. McKenna," the solicitor said gently.

Donna squeezed Mick's hand tightly. Olive, Mick's mother (they'd named Olivia after her), had died of breast cancer only the year before, a relatively young woman still in her sixties. As Donna knew as well as Mick did, Olive had never mentioned having an older sister called Margaret. Her sister Maureen was the eldest sister of the family as far as Mick and Donna had always been aware, and maybe Olive too for all they knew.

Mick held it together until they reached the car, then he broke down and sobbed as openly as Donna had, sitting in the driver's seat with his head in his hands and the blue cardboard folder containing the letter and the little packet of papers on the back seat.

"Let it all out, love," Donna said soothingly as she gently stroked his arm and shoulder.

When he'd composed himself, he blew his nose on a bunch of tissues Donna handed him, then, embarrassed, he started up the engine and drove them both back to

Balally. Donna, knowing her husband very well, nearly as well as she knew herself, tactfully chose not to break the silence on the way home. There would be plenty of time to talk later, over a hot cup of tea.

When they reached the house, they were surprised to see their oldest child, James, standing waiting for them at the front door. He was supposed to be in college today, where he was studying computer science. It was Friday, so he was on a half-day but, still, he was supposed to be there, wasn't he, and not here, waiting for them?

"Is everything okay, son?" Donna asked him anxiously, ushering him and a red-eyed Mick inside the house to the hall. "Is Olivia okay?"

"It's not Olivia, Mum," he said grimly. "It's Adam."

"What about Adam?" Donna's legs suddenly felt weak.

"Mark's texted me," James said.

Mark was Adam's college pal, living in Ranelagh, with whom Adam had been staying since Tuesday after college.

"He was looking for Adam," James went on, a hint of panic in his voice. "Apparently, Adam left Mark's gaff on Wednesday morning and no one's seen him since."

Donna clung to Mick for support as her legs went from under her.

STOP 6: WINDY ARBOUR

Maroon, Vicky and Graeme

Maroon boarded the Luas at St. Stephen's Green, having bought a return ticket to Windy Arbour, a place she'd only ever known as a stop on the way to Dundrum Shopping Centre and had never been to. From the size of the place, she didn't think she was missing out on too much.

As the tram trundled up to the stop known as Charlemont, stopping for a minute to disgorge and pick up more fares, she saw the Garda frogmen dragging the canal for that young college student who had gone missing the week before, that Adam Somebody. He was on the front of that morning's paper – it was a lovely photo, he was certainly a handsome lad – and she'd heard a brief report on the local radio's news bulletin that morning as well. A couple of auld ones at the Luas stop at St. Stephen's Green had been discussing the story animatedly while waiting for their tram. It reminded them vividly, they'd been saying, of that other lovely-looking young fella who'd gone missing in 2010 in the Victoria Street area on the night of the taxi drivers' strike. The auld ones blamed the taxi drivers for going on strike. If that poor young lad had been able to get a taxi home that night, he might have been alive today, God rest him. Anyway, both auld ones were equally certain that this new young man Adam Somebody's disappearance was down to suicide. It was all the pressures on young people nowadays, they maintained, which made them snap and decide that they just couldn't cope with life any more.

Maroon shuddered and averted her eyes from the grisly sight of the frogmen. The whole thing was horrible. It made her think of Andrew. You had to keep a careful eye on boys. You just never knew what was going on behind the impassive, monosyllabic façade they insisted on constantly maintaining and, with some lads, it was like pulling teeth to get a civil word out of them, never mind a straight answer to a straight bloody question.

Maroon took out her make-up compact and checked her face. In her fake leopard-print coat, her skin-tight leggings and metallic-blue high heels, she'd been attracting looks from men since she'd left her flat. There was one sitting across from her now on the train who was eyeing her up covertly while pretending to scroll down on his phone. Every now and then, he'd look up from his scrolling and try to catch her eye but she'd just blank him. Today, at any rate, he had no chance, although he was good-looking enough with his long dark coat and dark slicked-back hair. Today, Maroon had work to do and was all business. Satisfied that she looked all right, she clicked her compact shut and put it away in her handbag. She uncrossed and then re-crossed her legs for comfort, drawing a broad grin from her admirer in the opposite seat. Oh, fuck off, loser, she thought. Just because you've seen *Basic Instinct* doesn't mean you can ogle *me* like I'm Sharon fucking Stone. He got off at Beechwood with a backwards leer in her direction, leaving Maroon to gather her thoughts before her own destination. She was surprised that he hadn't tried to press his phone number on her before he'd left. Guys were always doing that to her. Sometimes she phoned them, mostly she didn't. It all depended on what impression they'd made on her. She decided just as the tram was pulling into Windy Arbour that she wouldn't have called *that* guy. She knew his type of old: sleazy, demanding, kinky, disrespectful of women, wanting the stuff his wife or girlfriend wouldn't do for him, and then he'd drop you the second he'd had his way with you. Almost certainly married or otherwise attached and would give you a fake name and number if you pushed him for a contact detail. His fake name would invariably be Steve, Dave, Mark, or Jack, because Irish guys had very little imagination. A name containing two syllables was seemingly beyond their capabilities. To hell with him, anyway.

"*Please move down the tram*," said the automated female voice over the PA system. Everyone usually ignored her baffling instruction. Like, which way was *down* anyway? And why did it matter? Anyway, *showtime*, Maroon told herself when she got off the tram at Windy Arbour.

A man approached her immediately.

"*Um*, are you Miss, *erm*, Maroon?" he said politely. "I saw your photo on the website."

Maroon nodded. "Then you're Graeme Groves?" She offered him her hand. Her long fake nails were metallic-blue, like her shoes. She wore rings on three fingers of her right hand, and four on her left. (She'd never put much faith in the maxim that less was more. Going the whole hog was much more her style.) None of them were made with real stones. The man took the proffered hand and pumped it vigorously while nodding confirmation. At least his handshake was dry and firm. Guys with limp, sweaty palms often had other limp, sweaty things that turned Maroon's stomach.

"Do you mind a short walk?" he asked her then, eyeing her high heels dubiously. "I didn't bring the car because it's literally just a short walk, like I told your boss on the phone." He spoke in a strangely formal, inflectionless kind of way that vaguely rang bells with her.

"A short walk is fine," Maroon said, faintly amused by his earnest manner. She fell into step beside him.

He was very tall, almost unusually tall for an Irish guy, but he seemed to be matching his steps to suit hers, which she appreciated because it wasn't as easy to walk in four-inch heels as she made it look. Her heels and toes were already pinching quite a bit, but she was well used to it. It was all part of the job.

"And you're definitely not a serial killer, anyway?" she said, more to make conversation than anything else. She stifled a yawn while waiting for his answer.

The man shook his head. "Oh no," he said in all seriousness. "Your boss asked me the exact same question on the phone but I told her no, definitely not. I wouldn't have the time for that kind of thing. And even if I were that way inclined, which I'm most certainly not, I'd be much too afraid of the Guards coming after me. This one time," he went on, looking straight ahead as he talked, "I found out that a shop assistant had given me an extra tenner in change. I felt like a criminal, like I should be on the Guards' Ten Most Wanted List or something. I had such a bad panic attack that I ended up in A & E for the night. No, the whole serial killer business wouldn't be for me. You can take my word for it, one million per cent."

"That sounds, *erm*, stressful," she ventured, not really knowing what to say to this bizarre anecdote. "The whole A & E thing, I mean."

"You'd better believe it was. I thought every siren outside on the street was the Guards coming to get me. Of course, the next day I tried to give the money back but Hassan from the Londis wouldn't take it. He said he didn't know anything about it, and that he wouldn't be able to account for it when he was doing the till at the end of the day, which was fair enough. I wouldn't have wanted him to get into trouble on my account. He told me to give it to a homeless person if I really didn't want to hold on to it myself."

"And did you? Give it to a homeless person?"

"Well, yes. There's a man who sits outside the shop every day begging. He said if I added another tenner to it, he'd be able to buy himself a half-decent bottle of whiskey."

"The nerve! I hope you told him where to go."

"Oh no. I didn't need to. He knew fine well where to go himself, seeing as the off-licence is just straight down the back of the shop, between the deli and Household Cleaning. He was off like a light when I gave him that second tenner. Left his blind-stick behind him and everything."

Maroon looked up at his profile curiously. Was he joking or what, she wondered, but there wasn't the trace of a smile on his earnest face. He really was an incredibly good-looking guy, and even though he was dressed down in a sweatshirt and jeans, you could tell that they were freshly laundered and had been meticulously pressed. Not all men took such care over their appearance. At least he'd be clean, she thought idly as she kept pace with him down a long, tree-lined avenue.

Near the end of it he paused and said: "Well, *um*, here we are. I hope it's okay for you."

Maroon murmured something non-committal as he took her elbow and escorted her up the front path of a big house with a well-kept garden, strewn with fallen leaves in glorious colours of red, gold, orange and burnished brown. There were bushes with bright red berries on them and even a birdhouse in which a lone bird – a thrush, maybe? – was pecking energetically at something that looked to Maroon like a muesli power bar on a string.

"Nice place you've got here," she said, looking up at it and wondering, as she did every time, is this it, then, the place where my luck finally runs out and this guy kills me and chops up my body in his bathroom so that he can fit me into a suitcase and chuck me in the canal? It was a risk she ran every time she did a job, even though the agency had all the guys' addresses and credit-card details so that they could be identified quickly if anything happened. A fat lot of good that would do her if some guy had already gone all Norman Bates on her, Maroon always thought, but those were the risks you took in a job like this. At least she was being paid extra for it. The money would come in very handy.

In the sitting-room, a spacious book-lined room containing a desk with a laptop on it in one corner, Maroon took off her leopard-print coat and dropped it on one arm of the couch. A fat marmalade cat sat curled up cosily in one corner of the couch. Maroon loved cats but Andrew wasn't keen on them, so she wasn't able to have one in the house. She reached out a hand to the orange-coloured moggy, who purred extravagantly.

"She must like you," Graeme Groves said in surprise. "That hardly ever happens. Lady Simone doesn't like anyone usually."

"Except you, I suppose." Maroon sat down on the couch near the cat.

"Oh no. She hates me most of all. She never has anything to do with me if she can help it, except at feeding-time. Then she can't get enough of me."

Maroon looked at him curiously again for any sign that would indicate that he'd been making a joke, but his face was totally deadpan.

"Would you like tea or coffee?" he asked politely then.

"Um, a black coffee, please. No sugar."

"Okay. No sugar."

He left and she heard him clattering about in a room across the hall from the sitting-room which she assumed was the kitchen. There was the distinct sound of a crash and a muted but still recognisable swear word.

She was surprised but quite pleased at the offer of coffee. She sometimes got offered an alcoholic beverage but mostly they just wanted to get down to business. In a way, Maroon preferred that. The sooner they got down to it, the sooner she could get out of there and go home to Andrew. No money would change hands. The men paid by credit card through the website, and the payment included a service charge. If she had no physical money on her, no actual notes or coins, then she couldn't be robbed. You met all sorts in this job. This man seemed different, not the kind to rob a defenceless woman. You never could tell, though, just the same.

When he returned, he was carrying two mugs of coffee – one black, one with milk – on a small tray. He set the tray on the coffee table beside the couch and sat down in an armchair opposite Maroon. Immediately, though, he leaped to his feet, crying "*The biscuits! I forgot the biscuits!*"

He rushed out of the room, returning seconds later with a packet of plain digestives and a plate.

"Damn, damn, *damn!*" he muttered to himself. "I screwed up at the last minute. I'm always doing that. I fall down at the last hurdle. I nearly manage it but then I mess it up. That's typical of me." He looked as if he was about to cry.

"It's all right," said Maroon, who was beginning to see the light. "I don't need any biscuits, thank you. The coffee's fine on its own. I had a big breakfast earlier."

"That's not the point," Graeme replied stubbornly. "A good host always offers a guest a biscuit to go with their coffee."

"You *are* a good host." Maroon picked up her coffee and took a sip of it, even though it was still much too hot. "This is really decent coffee. See, I'm enjoying it."

"Are you really?" He brightened a little. He stared hard at her for a minute or two, then he said, "Are you really called Maroon?"

She laughed and shook her head. "No, of course not. Who's called *Maroon*?"

"Well, I thought it might be your real name because you have those lovely purplish streaks in your hair," he said shyly.

She fingered her long purplish-brown ponytail. "You like them?"

"Oh yes. Very much."

"I wasn't sure about them at first, but now I think I'll keep them in for a bit."

He nodded vigorously, then said, "May I be allowed to know your real name?"

"Of course, if you like. It's Vicky."

"Vicky!" he repeated. "Vicky. *Vicky*. Yes, I like it. I like it very much. It suits you."

"Thanks. Now, can I ask *you* something personal?"

"It's rude to ask personal questions," he said, but he said it nicely.

"Yes, you're right. It is. I won't ask it so."

"Ah no, go on. I don't mind *you* asking."

"Well, if you're sure," she said.

He nodded vigorously, sitting up all straight and formal and waiting for the question, as if he were on *Who Wants to Be a Millionaire* and there was a lot of money riding on the answer.

She crossed her legs and looked at him curiously, wishing that she could smoke a cigarette with her coffee. "Are you autistic, Graeme?"

He blushed to the roots of his hair. After a while, he nodded. "How did you know?"

She shrugged. The purple top she wore slipped down off her shoulders a little bit. "A lucky guess."

"How long have you known?" he said then.

"Since he was a baby," she said automatically, then stopped and bit her lip. Why had she said that? She hadn't meant to say that. It had just slipped out because Andrew was on her mind, and now Graeme Groves was looking at her in confusion. "Sorry, look, forget I said that. Listen, do you want to get down to it or what?"

"You mean the sex?"

She nodded, hiding a smile at the serious way he said 'the sex'. "It's what I'm here for. Isn't it? Well, isn't it?"

"Couldn't we just talk for a bit instead?" he pleaded. He sounded like a little boy begging for an ice cream.

"It's your money. What would you like to talk about?"

She wasn't entirely surprised by his request. Guys often requested her services and it turned out that all they wanted was a woman to lend them a sympathetic ear for an hour or two. Sometimes they still wanted quick sex afterwards, but sometimes too it would never come to that. All they genuinely wanted was just a chat with a woman who'd be pleasant to them. Vicky could do that. Some men were lonely. That was okay. There were lots of lonely people in the world.

"Who's the baby you talked about just now?" Graeme said. "When I asked you how long you'd known I was autistic, you said 'since he was a baby'. Who's the 'he'? I mean, if you don't mind me asking?"

"Do you mind if I smoke in here?' she said, unable to contain the longing for a second more.

Graeme looked a bit disapproving, then he said, "If I get you an ashtray, then will you tell me who the '*he*' is?"

"I swear." She made the Boy Scouts' sign with a half-grin.

Seconds later, the sounds of mad clattering from the kitchen reached the sitting-room.

"I can't find any ashtrays!" Graeme wailed. "I don't think I have any! You see, I'm not a smoker myself. It's such a disgusting habit. It turns my stomach."

"Don't worry about it," she called back, wincing. That had certainly told her, anyway. Most people weren't so brutally upfront about their dislike of cigarettes. They usually just made a face or wafted their fingers about passive-aggressively for a bit to dispel the smoke. "An ordinary saucer or a side-plate will do."

When she was at home, she often stubbed out her fags in her coffee cups but somehow she didn't think that that would go down too well here, in this pristine and neatly organised house. Even Andrew said that smoking was a disgusting thing to do.

Eventually Graeme returned with a saucer in his hand.

"Here it is!" he said triumphantly. "I chose this one because it's got a chip in it, so it's not a good one exactly, but don't worry, it's still perfectly clean."

"Okay, thanks," she said, thoroughly bemused by all his flapping about.

"So now will you tell me who the 'he' is?" he repeated, seating himself on the armchair opposite her once more.

"Are you sitting comfortably?" she said wryly, wanting to smile at the sight of this tall, lanky guy settling himself more comfortably on the couch just because she'd suggested it. He held a cushion to himself the way Andrew did when he was watching television. "Then we'll begin . . ."

Andrew was her baby boy, her sixteen-year-old son who she'd brought up on her own because his father was a no-good jailbird. She'd met Andrew's father when she was only sixteen herself, the age Andrew was now. His name was Tommy Keeley. Still was, unless he'd changed it and, knowing Tommy the way she did – he was so damned slippery – it literally wouldn't have surprised her in the slightest. He'd been exactly the kind of guy to sweep a silly, naïve schoolgirl off her feet. (It was her own fault for falling for a guy called Tommy, the archetypal rebel's name. Sometimes Vicky wondered if she'd have fared any better with a Terence or a Malcolm. As it was, she might just as well have teamed up with a Jimmy, a Johnny or a Danny, the ultimate rebel-without-a-cause names.) Tommy had been out of school for ages himself, he told her proudly, since he was twelve or thirteen, and he now tore around the streets of Dublin on his motorcycle every day until it was time to go and collect his dole and spend it all on fags and booze and petrol for the bike. Vicky thought that all that stuff he talked about doing sounded incredibly romantic and rebellious. She wished that she herself were half so grown-up and daring. She was stuck in school for another two years and she was already wishing that she could leave. She'd done her Junior Cert and hadn't fared too badly in it, but she was dreading the poxy Leaving Cert. Everyone knew it was way harder than the Junior Cert, and the thought of those additional two years of gruelling study was filling her with despair. She wasn't altogether sorry, then, when she discovered she was pregnant with Andrew. She'd be able to leave school and she and Tommy could set up home together with their baby. They wouldn't be able to live with Vicky's parents. Her mother had remarried after the death of her husband from a sudden heart attack, and Vicky's stepfather was a despot who went ballistic when he heard about the baby. He called Vicky every name under the sun and even belted her one in the face so that, when she fled round to Tommy's place with a suitcase, she had the beginnings of a lovely shiner.

Tommy's mother was dead and his father was well on the way to becoming an alcoholic. The flat was littered with empty beer cans, and takeaway boxes, their leftover contents long since congealed, cluttered every surface. So many times Vicky nearly puked, with the baby in her stomach and all, trying to clean the place up for Tommy and his old man.

Even when it was clean, Vicky decided that she didn't want to live somewhere where the spectre of alcoholism constantly hovered, waiting patiently to carry Tommy's father away. Old Man Jeff, as Tommy called him, made the most depressing sight, slumped in his armchair in front of the telly from one end of the day to the next, the pile of empties on the floor around him growing ever bigger. He never went out, except to collect his dole and go to the boozer. It was horrible.

"Don't you want to help him?" she'd once asked her boyfriend curiously, but Tommy merely shrugged.

"It's his choice. What he does is nothing to do with me."

No love lost there, Vicky decided. She said no more about it.

Eventually, the pair of teenagers went to stay with Vicky's Aunty June, her mother's sister, for a bit. June was motherly and sensible and she went down to Dublin City Council, or Dublin Corporation as it was known back then, on Fishamble Street and more or less demanded that they give her pregnant niece and her boyfriend a flat, which, much to Vicky and Tommy's surprise, they did. The flat on Thomas Street was where Vicky and Andrew were still living today.

They hadn't been living in it long, however, before Tommy started filling it up with boxes of stuff he got from 'friends'. When Vicky asked him what was in them, he wouldn't tell her, only that he was 'holding them for a friend'. When the cops came and raided their flat, Tommy went to prison for a year. He started his first sentence not long after Vicky had given birth to their son in the Coombe with only her Aunty June for company. Tommy was out with his mates during the labour, flashing his cash about and playing the big man. When he came out of prison after only serving six months – "Time off for good behaviour, Vicks," he'd said with a grin – the flat began to fill up with boxes of stuff again. Vicky went berserk and chucked him out, boxes and all. He went back to his dad's flat for a bit, but living in squalor no longer appealed to Tommy, not since he'd become used to having Vicky cook and clean for him. Even the prison was cleaner and more inviting than his dad's place. He went back to Vicky with flowers stolen from outside a petrol station and a drawer-full of promises that he wasn't long breaking.

Vicky had to face facts. She was a teenage mum with a petty thief for a boyfriend. Over the years that followed, Tommy was in and out of prison for theft, breaking and entering, lying to the dole people, receiving stolen goods (a favourite pastime) and other petty crimes. When he eventually got sent down for a long stretch after an innocent householder, an elderly woman, was hit on the head with a tire-iron during a burglary (Tommy wasn't the aggressor, but he'd been there and witnessed it and had done nothing to help the old dear), Vicky decided she'd had enough of his shit. She kicked him out for the last time. She brought his remaining belongings round to his dad's flat, where Jeff Keeley was still pickling himself to death with booze. She changed the locks of the flat in Thomas Street and tore up the visiting orders that Tommy sent her from the prison. It was hard but she did it.

"I just didn't want Andrew growing up around that kind of thing," she told Graeme now. He nodded as if he knew exactly what she meant. Easing off her high heels and slipping her bare feet up under her on the huge comfy couch, she lit another cigarette and continued with her story.

She'd brought Andrew up herself from then on, with little or no help from anyone. She lived on social welfare allowances and did cleaning and child-minding jobs and even dog-walking jobs, and she put Andrew in school when he was old enough. She hadn't given a flying fuck about her own education but, oddly enough, she cared very much about Andrew's, and about his future too. The school confirmed her own early suspicions that there was something very different about Andrew. He was exceptionally bright in some ways but slow almost to the point of backwardness in others. He could do sums in his head that the guys who made up the entrance exams for NASA would have wrestled with but putting on his own socks and doing up the laces of his trainers defeated him completely. He also was on the go from morning till night, and had real difficulty relating to kids his own age and people in general. Strangers made him nervous, hostile and even openly rude. A change of plan and the sudden appearance of an uninvited visitor could trigger a meltdown.

As a child, he'd had terrible tantrums that Vicky at first assumed were par for the course with toddlers and developing children. As he'd grown older, however, these 'tantrums' turned into bouts of violent rage as Andrew tried to make sense of the world around him with the limited tools at his disposal. Angry at the absence of a father without being able to find the right words with which to articulate his thoughts, he lashed out at everyone around him, with Vicky who was always there getting the worst of it time after time. He saw other kids around him with fathers and devoted grandparents and he hit out at Vicky because she had failed, as he saw it, to provide him with either. He became more and more aggressive in his behaviour towards her and others until the mainstream school in which he'd initially been enrolled suggested it might be best if Vicky found him a 'special' school, because he was clearly suffering from psychological problems and his temper was out of control. The other kids in the school were terrified of him and so was Vicky by this stage, much as she still loved him with all her heart. The head teacher, another motherly and understanding woman not unlike Vicky's Aunty June, had put a distraught Vicky in touch with the local School-Age team of psychologists, speech-and-language therapists and occupational therapists. Attached to the Health Service Executive, they were like a group of professional troubleshooters specially trained to help kids with the most complex emotional, psychological and even physical problems. They had saved Vicky's bacon, anyway, and she didn't care who knew it.

Some painfully intense therapy sessions, with a child psychologist who was very good at her job, followed for both mother and son. A diagnosis of Autism and Attention Deficit Hyperactivity Disorder for Andrew didn't faze Vicky at all. She welcomed it with open arms. It was comforting and reassuring, in fact, to know that there were legitimate reasons for Andrew's strange and aggressive behaviour. Not that having autism made you violent, the child psychologist was quick to point out, but frustrations arising out of not being able to express yourself adequately to the people around you frequently did. Vicky was mainly relieved to learn that the violent outbursts stemmed mostly from his two medical conditions and not specifically from having an absentee jailbird for a father. That *must* have affected him too, though, she was always thinking. She lay awake at night consumed with guilt over the whole thing. She loved her son dearly but why did she have to saddle him with a petty criminal for a father? She had never really stopped beating herself up about her inability to provide Andrew with the normal family situation he saw around him every day. Luckily, in the last few years the idea of the traditional nuclear family had taken a bit of a battering and now, of course, families came in all shapes and sizes. That had helped to ease the pressure on Vicky a little, but she still needed to keep taking the anti-depressants and sleeping tablets her doctor had prescribed for her during the worst of their black days.

Andrew was doing well now anyway, thank God. He was in a wonderful special school that catered for his emotional, physical and intellectual needs as best they could, but places like that cost money, even if they weren't fee-paying. There was money for equipment and money for outings and money for all the extra activities they did which Vicky knew would contribute greatly towards helping Andrew to live an independent life some day. The school was worth its weight in gold for what the teachers there had done and were still doing for Andrew. For that reason, Vicky didn't mind putting up with the escort work. Well, it was called 'escort' work but everyone knew that there was more to it than that. If she had ever 'escorted' anyone somewhere even once, other than back to their place for the quickie for which she was being paid, she certainly couldn't remember it. But the escort work paid well, much better than the cleaning, and it was worth it if it meant that she could continue contributing towards Andrew's education and his future for as long as he needed her to. She put every cent she could into a bank account for Andrew's future. He was still her baby and always would be. She would do whatever she had to do to keep him safe and happy.

"How did you get into this . . . *erm*, this line of work?" Graeme asked her now. "I mean, if you don't mind me asking?"

To Vicky's surprise, he'd looked like he was blinking back tears as she'd talked about her and Andrew going through such tough times together with nobody to help them. She couldn't really talk or think about that time herself without getting a lump in her throat. Those had been difficult years, even harder than when Andrew was a baby and Tommy was banged up for receiving stolen goods. And they weren't even out of the woods yet. Autism, like puppies, wasn't just for Christmas: it was for life. Vicky lit another cigarette and said: "Well, Graeme, I don't mind you asking at all. It was like this . . ."

She had been at work one day, cleaning an office block with another woman, a thirty-something native of Poland called Irina. With her sculpted cheekbones and marvellous figure, Irina somehow managed to look like a top model while capably manoeuvring the big awkward floor-buffer from one storey to another in the building that was eerily quiet now after the hubbub of the day.

When they were cleaning one of the bathrooms, Irina suddenly stopped what she was doing and surveyed Vicky critically.

"You know," she said in her sexy Polish accent that Vicky loved to listen to, "you could be really beautiful if you made an effort."

"Thanks," said Vicky drily. "That's just what I want to

hear when I'm scrubbing someone else's shite off a toilet seat."

"How would you like to make some *real* money?" Irina said then. "I have a friend who runs escort agency. She is looking for girls. Is all on the level. Nice clean place, good money."

"Escort agency?" said Vicky, her eyebrows raised. "Isn't that just another way of saying prostitution?"

Irina shrugged gracefully, a toilet brush in her hand. "Is good money. You could book yourself holiday, get some sun on that pale face of yours."

It was true that Vicky desperately needed a holiday, but there was something else she needed money for even more at the moment. In the spring, Andrew's class was going on a trip to a farm in the West of Ireland, where the kids would be supervised, well fed and entertained for seven whole days. They'd be out in the fresh air from morning till night, there were ponies for them to ride, a lovely safe little beach for sea-bathing, and sheep, pigs and cows to look at and even to help mind. It would teach the kids to be independent, taking care of the animals *and* themselves for a few days, plus it was a great chance of a break for the parents. The forms had to be filled out and sent back into the school soon and all monies fully paid in advance. Andrew was dying to go on the trip but the cost was prohibitively expensive. Vicky would have to clean many more toilets to be able to afford it.

"How much?" she said, her heart pounding.

Irina named a sum that made Vicky's eyebrows disappear upwards into her hairline.

"If it's that good, how come you don't do it yourself?" she asked Irina.

"Oh, I do," Irina replied with a grin. "This week I just cover here for Paulina while she is in the hospital having her gallstones removed. Paulina is my mother's cousin from Poland."

"I see," said Vicky slowly.

"Come with me when we finish here. I will introduce you to Magda, my friend who has the agency. You will like her, I promise you."

Vicky took a deep breath. She pictured Andrew on a farm in the West of Ireland, riding a little pony in a green field with the wind in his hair and a bit of colour in his cheeks for once, the kind you didn't get when you were living in the city and breathing in the polluted air.

"Okay," she said. "It can't hurt to meet her."

Magda had been friendly but business-like. She looked Vicky up and down and nodded approvingly. "You will do good here," she said. "You, the men will like."

"See?" said Irina, nudging Vicky and smirking triumphantly. "What did I tell you?"

The premises was down a laneway just a few minutes' walk from Connolly Station. It consisted of the top floor of a rundown-looking building that had a launderette on the ground floor and a scruffy-looking tattoo parlour on the first. In the shabby reception area of 'Stilettos Kiss-a-Gram Agency and Massage Parlour' (the massage end of things was the official business of the agency, their 'front') sat a gigantic Polish man called Piotr, who read his newspaper and smoked a foul-smelling brand of tobacco while the business of the agency went on around him.

"Piotr is our muscle," said Irina, planting a kiss on his huge shaved head. "He is my little brother," she added by way of explanation to Vicky, whose eyes widened at the thought of this Colossus ever being described as anyone's 'little' anything. "No one ever misbehave while Piotr is here."

Vicky could well believe it. There were four bedrooms beyond the reception area, all neat and clean, with old but serviceable furnishings. In one of them were the massage tables and scented oils that served as the agency's *'cover'* and, in another, stood the kind of clothes rail you'd see in a department store.

"All the costumes you will need are here," said Magda.

Vicky's eyes widened again at the sight of the nurse's outfit, the French maid's costume, the sexy nun's attire, the teacher's gown and mortar board, the Ban-Garda uniform, the Bunny Girl's leotard, the sexy witch's cloak, the Little Mermaid costume, complete with sweeping fish tail, the traditional hooker's outfit and the ballerina tutu, plus many more, all lined up side-by-side on the rack. There was even a Tinkerbell outfit, complete with the kind of fairy wand that Vicky would have adored to get for Christmas when she was a nipper. What was this place anyway, a knocking-shop or the fucking Disney store? There were also all kinds of props, from a teacher's cane to what looked like a proper hospital drip, and all the tubes and bags necessary to give a patient an enema. *Christ on a bike, what have I got myself into this time, and does no one just have normal sex any more? What the hell is with all these props and extras?* Vicky repressed a shudder but managed to keep her cool.

"Mostly you will stay here in one of these rooms," Magda was explaining now as the three women headed back to the reception area. "Sometimes, although not very often, you will go to man's home. For this you get paid extra. We have some disabled customers, including man in wheelchair, who prefer the home visit. If anything happens to you, we have man's address and credit card details to give to police, although we prefer to keep police out of our business if we can. Any questions?"

"You're not getting me into a fucking tutu," said Vicky.

Behind his newspaper, Piotr snickered.

"How do you do it?" Graeme asked her now. "How do you manage to . . . you know, have sex with all those strange men without going crazy?"

"I just think of Andrew."

"You think of your son when you're having sex with your clients?"

Vicky burst out laughing. "No, you idiot," she said, but she said it nicely. "I mean, I try to make myself think of all the things I can do for Andrew with the money I'm making."

"Oh, I see. Does Andrew know about the work you do?"

Vicky shook her head vigorously, her purple-streaked ponytail swinging in tandem with her movements. Graeme watched it, enchanted.

"He thinks I'm doing office work or cleaning jobs on a temping basis, which helps to explain the odd hours. But mostly it happens during the day, when he's at school."

"Isn't it a strain on you having to keep it all a secret from him?"

"Yes," she said simply. "But what else can I do? I need the money. *We* need the money."

"When he's older, he'll be able to work out for himself what you've been doing. He's pretty much at that age now."

"That's a risk I'll have to take," she said stubbornly. "I can't just pack it in, can I?"

"Well, why not?" Graeme was looking at her intently now. "Why *not* just pack it in?"

Vicky laughed and lit another cigarette. "And what'll I do for money? Who'll pay my bills? You?"

"I could," Graeme said, in what she was beginning to think of as his deadpan voice.

"Excuse me? What are you on about? I don't let anyone *keep* me, if that's what you're getting at. I'm nobody's property. Is that what you're suggesting?"

"Not at all. Just hear me out, will you, Vicky? I've got a proposition for you. A proper business proposition, I mean. Not the kind you're thinking of."

"Oh yeah?" she said sceptically.

"Your hackles are up. Just like Lady Simone's when someone gets her back up."

"Stop comparing me to your cat and tell me what you're on about, will you?" Vicky said crossly.

"Do you see that big pile of stuff on the desk over there?"

Vicky looked to where he was pointing. Of course, she'd noticed the desk with the laptop on it when she came in. It was piled high with loose papers and cardboard folders that looked as if they too were stuffed with papers. Some of the papers had spilled over onto the floor. Was he going to suggest that he pay her to be his cleaner or something and tidy that little lot up? He was getting a clip on the ear if that was his big plan.

"My dad and my brother Carl are financing me in setting up my own graphic-design business. I already do freelance work for a few different companies, but now I want to run my own business and go after more, and bigger, clients. Maybe even employ a few people in the fullness of time. '*Graeme Groves: Graphic Design*' – it's got quite a nice ring to it, don't you think? Carl's looking at some business premises for me next week or the week after in town, although I'd be working from home – from here, I mean – for a bit at first. They worry about me because I'm the youngest in the family and also because I have special needs, see?"

He said it so matter-of-factly that Vicky was surprised. It didn't sound like being 'special' had particularly ruined Graeme's life or even affected it negatively too much, not like it had Andrew's.

"But the point is," Graeme went on, coming to sit on the couch beside Vicky, much to the annoyance of Lady Simone, who'd been licking herself comfortably on the plump cushions and enjoying all the extra space, "if I'm setting up my own graphic-design business with Carl and Dad's backing, then I'm going to need a secretary, a personal assistant. We've been talking about it quite a bit, but we don't have anyone particular in mind yet or anything. Do you have basic computer skills?"

"I can do emails and Facebook," Vicky said doubtfully.

It had been Andrew who'd taught her how to use their computer, Andrew who'd practically bullied her into learning the basics because "You need to know this stuff, Mum, for if I'm ever not here". Much as she'd been horrified at the thought of Andrew not being there with her at some point in the future, she'd been happy enough to finally learn the mysteries of what people called 'emails' and 'Facebook'.

"That's perfect!" Graeme said happily. "I'd need someone to send and answer emails and set up and run the Facebook page. That's all you'd need, basic skills. That, and sending out invoices. I'm good at the graphic design end of things but not at the sending out of bills thing. I'd be bankrupt in a month if I was left to myself. That's what my dad and Carl both say."

"It sounds too good to be true, that you'd just want me to come in here and send out a few bills for you."

"Oh, and you'd make the coffee too," deadpanned Graeme. "You'd have to make it good and strong, the way I like it."

"Oh, would I now?" said Vicki with a half-smile.

"Oh yes, you'd have to do that," he said, half-smiling too. "That would be one of your most important duties."

"How long have you known you were autistic?" Vicky asked him suddenly. "You're clearly high-functioning. You're like Andrew in that way. He's very high-functioning too, in some aspects."

"I was diagnosed with what they used to call Asperger's Syndrome back when I was in college," Graeme said. "I'm thirty now. Now they just call it ASD, or Autism Spectrum Disorder. But you know that already, because of Andrew. They're lumping us all in together now under the same umbrella, to make it easier. I don't really mind. I never liked the word 'Asperger's' much anyway. Too many people still pronounce it as 'Ass Burgers'. I can still live a perfectly normal life with the help of my parents and my brother Carl, but – *erm* – I do find it hard to talk to girls. Women. The – *erm* – opposite sex. *Um*, ladies."

She did. "Is that why you called the escort agency yesterday?" Vicky tried to sound tactful about it. "Because you haven't had – *erm* – a woman in a while?"

He nodded, flushing slightly. "I thought I needed sex, but the minute I saw you I realised that what I really wanted was to talk to someone."

"Thanks a lot," said Vicky, mock-offended. "Am I that hideous? Should I just put a bag over my head, then, so you won't have to look at me?"

"But I like to look at you."

He said it softly, with what Vicky somehow understood was utter honesty. Andrew was the same. He couldn't tell a lie to save his life, not even to get himself out of trouble. It was partially an autism thing.

"You're beautiful," he said. "You're actually the most beautiful woman I've ever seen in my life."

"You're not so bad yourself," she said, looking at him critically for the first time.

He was tall and well-built, with dark-brown hair that needed cutting and dark eyes. At thirty, he was two years younger than her, but she felt years and years older than she was. This was always happening. She felt older than most of the guys she met. She knew it was because she'd been pregnant at sixteen by her jailbird boyfriend and had been caring for a differently abled child on her own ever since, not knowing till a few years before that there was a name and treatment, though not a cure, never a cure, for Andrew's disability. You could *manage* your autism so that your life could run relatively smoothly, but you couldn't make it go away.

"So, what about it?" Graeme said. "Will you take the job? I promise you that it's a real job and not a pity job or a made-up one. You can talk to my father and Carl about it if you like. In fact, I insist on it. Anything to prove to you that it's a proper job and not something I dreamed up on the spot, just because I fancy you like crazy and don't want you to walk out of my life after just a couple of hours."

He blushed bright red when he said that last bit. Vicky

had to admit that he sounded one-hundred-per-cent genuine. She also had to admit that she fancied him too, even though she had no intention of taking things any further with him. She was already feeling an urge to mother him that would surely spell trouble for her down the line. He was good-looking, so what? Good-looking, gently spoken, educated and not short of a bob or two. A guy like that wasn't for the likes of her, with her disabled son and a one-time boyfriend who was doing fifteen-to-life now for an armed robbery in which a security guard had been shot in the shoulder.

"I don't know, Graeme . . ." she said hesitantly. "I'd need to make as least as much money with you as I do with my – with my escort work and I'm not sure you can do that."

"How much do you earn now?" he asked her out straight.

She told him, expecting him to turn pale and try to backtrack.

"I could match that," he said with a shrug of his broad shoulders. "With maybe a bit extra on top. Plus," he added, his eyes suddenly bright and his tone excited, "if you weren't working all the hours God sends cleaning or escorting, you could go back to school and do your Leaving Cert! And with that extra qualification under your belt, well, you could do pretty much anything else you wanted to do then."

Vicky stared at him. Leaving school with only her Junior Cert, and a fairly indifferent one at that, to her name had been one of the greatest regrets of her life. Graeme might be autistic, but he'd been bang on the money when he'd managed to cut straight to the heart of her secret longings purely on the basis of the conversation she'd just had with him.

She tried to conceal the excitement she felt bubbling up inside her as she said, "Look, I'm really not sure about this, Graeme. Sure, I'd love to give up being a sex worker . . ." Why pretend any more that that wasn't what she was, when it would be obvious even to a blind man that she had sex with the clients? "But it's a big step you're suggesting. I need to think about it. I mean, why me and not someone else?"

"Because you're not only the most beautiful woman I've ever seen in my life, you're also the bravest and the toughest, and I think it's an absolute disgrace that you've had to go through so much . . . so much *shit* on your own with no one to help you." He sounded like he really meant it too. He was furiously blinking away the tears and running his hands through his dark hair as if he were agitated.

"What are you then, my knight in shining armour?"

"If you want me to be, I will."

There was a silence. Then she said: "Graeme, have you by any chance ever seen the film *Pretty Woman*, with Julia Roberts and Richard Gere?"

He shook his head. "Should I have? Is it any good?"

"Christ, no. Don't bother with it if you ever come across it. It's a . . . it's a load of old bollocks. Not realistic at all."

"I'd better make a note of it so." He looked worried. "To remind myself not to watch it."

To her amusement, he tore a page off a notepad on the coffee-table and wrote on it in giant capital letters: '*PRETTY WOMAN: DO NOT WATCH. RUBBISH!!!*'

"I'll Sellotape that to the television later, just to be on the safe side. Just in case, you know? In the meantime, I'll make some more coffee while you think about my offer."

He got to his feet, stuck the pen he'd been using behind his ear and disappeared into the kitchen with the tray of empty coffee mugs. "Better still," he went on when he returned again a minute or two later without the tray, "why don't you make the coffee for both of us? I can't possibly hire you anyway unless I'm confident that you can make a decent cup of coffee. I take mine very hot and strong, with only a splash of milk and two lumps of sugar. And don't forget the biscuits – from the tin."

"Fine by me," said Vicky, getting up and going into the kitchen, glad of the chance to be alone with her thoughts for a few minutes.

The kitchen was covered in yellow Post-It notes. On one cupboard was a note that said clearly in big bold capital letters, *PLATES,* and on another, *CUPS.* On the cutlery drawer was a note that said *KNIVES, FORKS AND SPOONS.* On the wall above the kettle was a larger Post-It where someone had clearly written down the instructions for making tea, starting with *FILL THE KETTLE WITH WATER, THEN SWITCH IT ON.* Beside this were instructions on how to make coffee in the cafetière which was standing on the counter, also beginning with *FILL THE KETTLE WITH WATER, THEN SWITCH IT ON.* On the counter there was a tin labelled *BISCUITS* and another labelled *CAKE: TO BE EATEN BY THE 19TH AT THE LATEST.*

Vicky swallowed hard as she blinked back the tears that were starting behind her eyes. Andrew wrote notes like this too, or she helped him sometimes by writing them herself. He still had the instructions for tying his shoelaces or, more likely, the laces of his battered trainers, written on a yellow Post-It note stuck to the end of his bed. He didn't need it any more, strictly speaking, but he liked the comfort of knowing it was there. "In case I forget," he'd told her with one of those grins that made her whole being light up with happiness.

She filled the kettle with water and then switched it on. As she rinsed out the mugs and then the cafetière, she thought about Graeme's proposition. Imagine if she did, in fact, become his personal assistant in a thriving little business. Imagine being able to talk openly about her job in front of the other mothers at Andrew's school, without having to tell blatant lies about what she did for a living. Imagine, too, going to night-school, doing her Leaving Cert and actually getting it! She'd felt inferior to other people for so long, simply because she'd left school at sixteen to push a pram and live in a council flat, like people probably expected of her just because she came from a poor family.

She'd been blessed with good looks, which she still had now in her early thirties because she took care of herself, but good looks didn't last for ever. If she had some sort of a qualification, she'd have something to fall back on and at least be able to say that she'd achieved something with her life. Although Andrew was, and always would be, her biggest and brightest achievement.

She spooned a generous amount of coffee into the cafetière, added water, put on the lid and left it to infuse. And wouldn't Andrew be so proud of her! He was always saying he was proud of her anyway for being such a good mother to him, but he knew how much it had affected her to leave school without having done the Leaving Cert. At the time of her pregnancy, she'd practically sprinted out of the school doors with relief and joy that her time there was over. But she'd had plenty of time to reflect over the years that followed, years in which she felt she'd been looked down on by everyone she'd ever met because she was only a single mother whose child's father was in and out of jail for various petty crimes. What she wouldn't give to be able to hold her head up for once. Never to have to be Maroon again but only ever Vicky, just Vicky, Andrew's mum who was studying for her exams!

She was so damn tired, she wasn't thinking straight, that was the trouble. Her life and Andrew's had been one long struggle. What would it feel like to hand over the reins to someone else, she wondered, to let another person take care of *her* for once, even in a small way? She'd thought that Tommy would take care of her and Andrew but that had ended in catastrophe. The way she felt right now, she had a good mind to take Graeme up on his offer. Why did she always have to be so damned independent, doing everything the hard way? Couldn't she let someone give her a helping hand for once? Could she not take a chance for once? Maybe she should be across the hall in that sitting room right now, biting Graeme's hand off in gratitude.

"How's that coffee coming along?" Graeme called out.

"Ready in a jiffy!"

Vicky poured the coffee, chewing on her lower lip, something she always did when she had a decision to make.

The work side of things could all be ironed out easily enough, but what about the romantic side? If she worked side by side with Graeme every day, they'd end up in bed together for sure. They were just too attracted to each other for that not to happen. What would happen to their working relationship then? Would Graeme want her out of his house and his business after they'd done the dirty deed? And imagine if he didn't, and they went on to have a full-on, proper male-female romantic relationship? She'd have an autistic boyfriend as well as an autistic son. And after today, she already kind of felt as if she was destined to be surrounded by autistic males whichever way she turned. How would she cope? How would Andrew cope? He was always saying that he'd like her to meet someone decent, but he probably felt safe saying it because he knew that there was no real chance of its ever happening. How could it? She was never going to meet someone that she'd like enough to want to put him ahead of Andrew. It might be a different matter, though, if she brought home an actual flesh-and-blood male for her son to meet. The whole thing was just messed up. It was better not to change things. It was better to leave them the way they were. Wasn't it?

"Don't forget the biscuits!" Graeme called out. "There might be some ginger ones left!"

"Okay – just coming!"

Vicky opened the tin marked *BISCUITS*. There was a yellow Post-It note inside. She read it, then peeled it off the biscuit package and turned it over and over in her hands thoughtfully. When she eventually brought in the coffee and biscuits on a tray, the crumpled Post-It note was in the pocket of her skin-tight leggings. She was keeping this one.

"I can give you both my answers now," she said.

STOP 7: MILLTOWN

Carl and Tara

Carl got on the Luas at Milltown, after first buying a ticket to Brides' Glen, where he lived. He'd spent a fairly unsatisfactory morning looking at two possible premises for his brother Graeme's graphic-design business, which was still only at the planning stage. And the way he, Carl, felt right now, knackered, irritable and temporarily carless, he had a good mind to tell Graeme to shove the whole thing up his arse and find his own bloody business premises. But, of course, there were reasons why he couldn't – *wouldn't* – ever do that. The Great Autismo (his affectionate nickname for his extraordinarily intelligent sibling, who enjoyed practising his magic act as a way of unwinding) was his little brother. There was nothing he wouldn't do for him. Even now, when Graeme had properly put the cat among the bloody pigeons and no mistake.

"Excuse me," said a large lady with two overfilled shopping bags as she heaved herself into the seat beside Carl.

He forced a polite smile to his face as he squished himself up against the window like a fly, but inwardly he was heaving a huge sigh. Why did the fat ladies always want to box him in like this? It was bad enough that he already had two schoolboys sitting across from him with their long gangly legs and their loud music that he could hear perfectly well even though both boys were wearing earphones. Their fancy designer trainers probably cost more than he earned in a week. *Tsk tsk*, kids today. Carl sighed again, out loud this time. Maybe he was just getting old. Too old for public bloody transport, anyway. The sooner his car was back from the garage, the better. Probably cost him a bleedin' fortune as well, but it'd be worth it not to have to ride this fucking sardine-can on wheels every bloody day. And people were always telling him how great the Luas was! He tried scrolling down his phone to distract himself, but Facebook just wasn't doing it for him today.

"*Please move down the tram*," said the automated female voice whose other more useful function was to inform the passengers of the different stops along the way. What a posh sexy voice she had, Carl thought, wondering briefly if there was a real woman behind the voice and, if so, what she would look like in lingerie with her hair undone, draped artistically over his bed. Jesus! He must be sex-starved indeed if he was fantasising about having it off with an automated voice. Clearly, he was no longer suited to a bachelor existence. Carl Groves, you knobhead!

Disgusted with himself, Carl forced his mind away from Sexy Robot Lady and back to thinking about Graeme's bombshell. They'd all been gathered around the table the other week for Sunday Dinner as usual – Dinner With A Capital 'D' – when Graeme had decided to just lob it into the middle of the table like a fucking unexploded hand-grenade and watch complacently while it went off. Mum and Dad had nearly had heart attacks, especially Mum.

"Oh, by the way, gang, I'm getting married," he'd announced, as casually as if he'd been declaring his intention to change his brand of toothpaste. That was the autism, though. Graeme always announced things, whether catastrophes or triumphs, with the exact same level of deadpan-ness, in the same monotone voice he used for all declarations.

But, as far as his family was concerned, this one was a catastrophe for sure.

There had been a dead silence round the dinner table. Carl's wife Karen (they were separated at the moment but she was still to all intents and purposes his wife) had paused with her wineglass halfway to her mouth, and it took a lot to get Karen to stop drinking at the Sunday Dinner Table.

Dad had asked Graeme worriedly, "Is this a joke, son?" while Mum had paused in the act of cutting up her meat to stare across at Graeme as if he'd suddenly developed stigmata in the middle of his meal. Even the kids – his and Karen's – had shut up for a minute.

"Are you fucking serious?" Carl had demanded, breaking the silence.

"*Fucking fucking fucking!*" echoed six-year-old Lauren, swinging her legs in delight.

"Lauren, stop that!" Karen had expostulated. "Now see what you've done, Carl!"

She was always thrilled to get a chance to score points off him anyway, but she was never happier than when his sub-par parenting was being publicly called to account once more.

He'd pointedly ignored her and said to his brother, who was calmly spearing a bit of broccoli with his fork,

"Well, are you serious or what?" (The broccoli, by the way, was the main reason Carl hadn't been surprised to hear that his younger brother was autistic. Nobody normal ate broccoli. Certainly no one normal who didn't have a gun to their head ate it willingly and, what's more, with every appearance of enjoyment, pronounced it delicious and asked for seconds. Graeme wasn't just autistic. He was fucking nuts, he had to be.)

Graeme nodded, as calm and self-composed as ever.

"I'm deadly serious," he said.

"To a *woman*?" Carl said.

"Yes, of course to a woman." Graeme was not in the least ruffled. "You're only saying that to rattle me. You know perfectly well that I'm as straight as you are."

"Who is she, son?" asked Mr. Groves, looking even more worried now he'd established this wasn't a joke. "Have we met her?"

"I don't think so," said Graeme. "Unless you've ever used the Stilettos Kiss-A-Gram Agency and Massage Parlour, have you, Dad? Their number used to be in all the phone boxes until they took them down. The boxes, I mean. Not the cards. Although I suppose the cards had to come down too when the boxes did. Now they mostly leave their cards in the Chinese takeaways and places like that. I found mine one night I was getting an egg foo yung, actually."

"You're marrying an escort?" Carl had stared at his younger brother in disbelief. "You must be off your trolley. A fucking *prostitute*?"

"Daddy said it again!" squealed Lauren delightedly. "*Fucking fucking fucking!*"

"You've really done it now!" hissed Karen at Carl from across the table.

They'd stopped seating Karen next to Carl at the Sunday Dinner Table since the time she'd stabbed him in the hand with her fork while pretending to be going for the potatoes. He still had the scar to remind him of that happy day.

Now a red-faced Carl turned to face her angrily and said, "Can't you just shut up scoring points off me for a minute? Can't you see that this is serious?"

"What's a Fucking Pwozzy-Tute?" asked five-year-old Georgie innocently.

"It's a woman who has sex for money," snapped back Carl without thinking.

"*Carl!*" expostulated Karen and his mother together.

"He's only five years old!" added his mother.

"Well, then," said Carl testily, knowing he shouldn't but unable to stop himself, Graeme had given him such a shock, "it's about time he learned that life isn't all hugs and kisses and Postman fucking Pat."

"*Fucking fucking fucking!*" echoed Lauren blissfully. "*Fucking fucking fucking! Fucking fucking fucking!*"

"Lauren, please!" begged Karen – then, when Danny, their four-year-old, howled, "Georgie, did you just kick Danny?" Georgie shrugged, as if to say that it was a matter of complete indifference to him what his feet decided to do, under the table and independently of his body.

"Who is she, son?" Mrs. Groves said then, looking at Graeme distraught, as if she'd only just realised that her baby wasn't in nappies any more but was a hulking grown man of nearly thirty-one.

"I'm delighted you asked." Graeme reached across to the potato bowl to help himself to more roasties. "Top-notch spuds today, by the way, Mum. Where'd you buy these?"

"Never mind the fucking spuds," growled Carl. "Who is this tart?"

Graeme's cheeks coloured hotly. "She's not a tart, and I'll thank you not to refer to her as such."

"Well, who is she then?" Carl, feeling distinctly in need of a pick-me-up after the shock of hearing that the little brother he adored was taking a wife none of them had ever met before, had a swig of his wine, draining his glass.

"Her real name is Vicky," Graeme said with a note of pride in his voice. "Her escort name is Maroon because she has these lovely purple stripes in her hair. She's a really interesting person. I think you'd love her like I do, Mum and Dad, if you met her, which I hope you will do."

"How long have you known her?" Carl expertly corkscrewed open the bottle of wine he'd brought with him as a courtesy gift and poured himself a big hefty glass without offering it to anyone else. He knew he was behaving badly but he didn't care. After another shitty boring week at work, Sunday was meant to be his day of rest, goddammit, his day for relaxing and seeing his kids in a normal family environment. This was all too much to take in at once.

"Let's see now," said Graeme, seeming to count back in his mind. "Friday, Saturday, Sunday, yes, three days. We met on Friday."

"Friday just gone?" spluttered Carl.

"Since Friday?" Dad choked on his meat and Mum had to pound him vigorously on the back.

"You've only known this woman *since Friday?*" Carl asked.

"Well, yes, since Friday." Graeme looked surprised himself at all the surprise his family was expressing about the only-having-met-her-on-Friday thing.

"How old is she, Gray?" Karen was staring with open curiosity at her brother-in-law.

"She's about thirty-three." Graeme seemed as happy as Larry to get a chance to answer questions about his fiancée. "She was very young when she had Andrew, about sixteen I think, if I remember what she told me correctly."

"She has a teenage son? Where's his father?" Carl was speaking ominously quietly. He always spoke quietly when he was about to explode. And who could blame him? This situation was fast becoming farcical.

"Well," Graeme said, "he's been in and out of prison since Andrew was born, so he might be there now for all I know. On the other hand, he might not be. I really don't know. I'd have to ask Maroon. I mean, Vicky. I'd have to ask Vicky. I still keep calling her Maroon by accident because that's what I knew her as at first."

"How did you propose, Gray?" Karen asked him, taking a bigger than usual (and that was saying something) swill of her wine.

Carl glared at her. Was she trying to stir the shit or what?

Graeme, however, just smiled, as if remembering something pleasant. "Well, you'll probably think that I'm a hopeless romantic for doing this, Karen. I put a yellow Post-It note with the words '*MARRY ME, VICKY*' on it in the biscuit tin, so that when she went to take out the biscuits to go with our coffee, she saw my note." Then he added proudly, "I took her to buy the ring on Saturday. Yesterday, I mean. It's a really stunning big diamond. I was going for something a bit subtle, myself, but Vicky had her heart set on this really flashy one so we got that one instead."

"So she's a bloody gold-digger," Carl said. "Now I've got it."

"No, she isn't." Graeme was instantly on the defensive. "Don't judge everyone by your own grotty standards."

"What d'you mean by that?" demanded Carl. "How am I judging everyone by my own 'grotty standards', whatever that's supposed to mean?"

"If the cap fits, wear it," said Graeme piously.

"What does that even *mean*?" Carl's face was red with anger. "All you ever do is talk in fucking clichés and riddles that don't even mean anything. I'm gonna punch you in a minute, Gray."

Graeme, the stronger of the two by miles, narrowed his eyes, unperturbed. "You can try."

"Now, now," said Dad, frantically pouring oil on the troubled waters, "no one's punching anyone. We'll work this thing out together as a family, like we always do."

"Is Mummy a Fucking Pwozzy-Tute like Mawoon-Vicky?" Georgie asked his father.

"Well, if the definition is a woman who takes money and presents for sex," Carl said nastily. He could have bitten his tongue off the minute the words were out of his stupid big fat mouth, but it was too late to recall them. Wasn't there a line in the Bible about that kind of thing, a line that said you might as well throw a sack full of feathers off the top of a high mountain in a big wind and then try to catch them all, as attempt to take back hateful words once you'd said them?

Karen stood up and threw the remains of her wine into his face. Well, he couldn't complain. He deserved that.

Carl's mother burst out laughing. She kept on laughing and laughing and laughing until her husband had to come round the table and put his arms around her and ask her if she was all right.

"Of course I'm all right," she choked out between laughs. "Why wouldn't I be all right, Bernard dear? My baby boy's marrying a *hooker*. With a teenage son who has a – a *jailbird* for a father." She screeched with manic laughter until the tears rolled down her face, ruining her carefully applied make-up. "And my other son has grossly insulted his wife and had wine thrown in his face!"

"I want to be a Fucking Prozzy-Tute when I grow up and get presents and money for sex," Lauren decided.

"Are there any more spuds?" Graeme, seemingly oblivious of the bomb he'd dropped, was chewing away happily. "These are *really* tasty."

"Georgie kicked my fucking ankle again!" complained Danny.

"That's because you're a K-U-N-T," spelled out Georgie, swinging his sturdy little legs briskly. "K-U-N-T spells 'kunt'."

Lauren's eyes widened in delight. Another new swear word! Her brothers picked up some really cool language at school. She tried on the new word for size.

"K-U-N-T," she said. It positively rolled off the tongue. "K-U-N-T spells *kunt*. Grandma, what's a kunt?"

Sunday Dinner – Dinner With A Capital D – was over for another week.

Now Carl was on the Luas and it appeared to be Everyone-Trample-On-Carl-Day because everybody who passed him seemed to be stomping on his bloody feet. He missed his car, he was starving with the hunger after having to skip his lunch because of a tardy estate agent's inability to turn up to a property viewing on time, and he was annoyed about the waste of a day. The two premises he'd viewed in Milltown hadn't been suitable for Graeme's new business, the one Graeme was still adamant he was setting up but now with Vicky's help. She was going to send out invoices and final notices and suchlike, and she was even planning to take an evening course in accountancy or book-keeping or something similar so that she could eventually do the company's books. Graeme was ridiculously excited about his new business and his equally new fiancée. He was going to pay her a proper wage to be his personal assistant so that she could quit the escort business and sign up for a night class somewhere. And he was taking his responsibilities as Andrew's new stepfather seriously too, by googling *'how to be a good stepdad'* online and printing off the tips that came up and studying them earnestly whenever he got a minute. He wouldn't be meeting Andrew any time soon, because Vicky was waiting for the right time to tell her teenage son the news that she was engaged, but when they *did* meet, whenever that was, he was determined to be prepared. *'Fail to prepare, prepare to fail'* was his motto, and Graeme never failed to prepare if he could help it.

Carl had met Vicky a few days earlier, but only after Graeme had practically begged him to. He'd had to admit that she wasn't the hard-faced little money-grubber he'd been expecting. On the contrary, she'd seemed very nice, rather shy even, and she was certainly very good-looking. Carl could imagine that she'd been extremely popular as an escort. What had struck him most about her, however, was the way he could tell that she'd had a hard life and a hard time bringing up the kid on her own while his loser of a father was behind bars, but that she'd stuck with it and was doing the best she could with it. He honestly couldn't fault her for that. By the end of their meeting, in fact, he'd nearly wanted to take her away from her shitty life himself and turn her into the princess he thought she probably deserved to be. He could understand totally why Graeme wanted to look after her and save her from more slings and arrows. But if she hurt him, he'd decided grimly, then she'd wish she'd never met anyone in the Groves family. Graeme was his little brother, the Great Autismo, and no woman was going to take his money and break his soft, loving autistic heart. Carl would be Keeping An Eye On Things in a big way and, the minute Graeme needed him, he'd be there. Even before Graeme had his autism diagnosis, Carl Groves had always looked out for his little brother, who was a good three or four inches taller than him now and could pulverize him in an arm-wrestle. (But only because Carl hadn't time to go to the gym these days and was a bit out of practice as a result.) But, for now, it looked as if he was going to have to stand back a bit and let Graeme make his own mistakes, if that was what this marriage to Mawoon-Vicky, as all three of his kids now persisted in calling her, was going to turn out to be. How could it *not* turn out to be a mistake? At the very next opportunity, however, Carl was tying Graeme to a chair and forcing him to watch a DVD of *Pretty Woman* from beginning to end. With any luck, he might learn a few pointers from it. Maybe he could use this awful, awful film to teach Graeme the difference between real life and the fantasy life according to a big-budget Hollywood movie. Only in Hollywod movies could there be a happy ending for the rich bloke and the escort. It never, *ever* happened in real life. This was the point he urgently needed to communicate to Graeme. He thought Karen might have a DVD copy somewhere. He'd ask her the next time it was his turn to have the kids. Boy, wouldn't that give her a laugh? She'd think he was going soft in his old age.

Please move down the tram, repeated the automated female voice everyone usually ignored. "And kindly keep out of the way," muttered a bored Carl to himself, "while I dance the can-can naked with my knickers on my head and a rose between my teeth." Even if she said that, there still wouldn't be a flicker from the travel-anaesthetised public, he was sure. It took a lot to rouse people from their stupor these days. He sighed heavily.

A woman sat down across from him and accidentally bumped off him while crossing her long legs.

"Sorry, sorry," she apologised, putting in her headphones and beginning to scroll down on her phone.

"Not at all, no worries," Carl said, studying the woman appreciatively.

He'd been so lost in thought that he hadn't even noticed the gangly schoolboys getting up to leave before this woman could take their place. She was a looker all right, but not in such a way that she was a clone of a million other women. She was tall, with impossibly long legs in tight black leggings and black suede boots. Her short dark hair was slicked back from a face with great cheekbones and her earrings were dangly and silver and reached nearly down to her shoulders. She had great style, as his mother Ivy would say. There was something oddly familiar about her too. He felt as if he'd seen her before somewhere, but not looking like she did now. Maybe her hair had been different or something. Longer maybe.

He was trying to remember where he knew her from when she suddenly pulled out her earphones, leaned forward and said to him: "Excuse me, but are you Carl Groves?"

"Yes," he answered, bemused. "I thought we knew each other all right. I was literally just trying to figure it out. And you are . . .?"

"Tara. Tara Robinson. We were in school together."

"Of course!" he said, snapping his fingers.

Of course he remembered her now. Tara had been one of the best-looking girls in his class, with long dark hair and great breasts that she'd developed early, if he remembered correctly, and he was sure he did. Great breasts were not something a man tended to forget. She'd been sporty too, very athletic, always in a tracksuit and trainers.

"Weren't you in training for the Olympics at one point or something?" he asked her.

She pulled a wry face. "I *was*. Ankle injury put paid to that." She waggled her left boot at him and he made what he hoped were suitably sympathetic clucking noises.

"So, what do you do now then?" he asked, genuinely interested.

Tara was a real cracker. He remembered now that they'd gone on one disastrous date together when they were in school. He'd ruined things by going for her breasts too soon into a kiss. She'd slapped his face and flounced off home, and that had been the end of that.

"I'm a rep for a pharmaceuticals company." She made another wry face.

"Oh, very good," he said politely. "That sounds interesting."

"It's not at all, I can assure you." She laughed. "I'm

bored brainless with it. What about you, what do you do?"

"I sell life insurance," he said.

They both burst out laughing.

"Are you married then?" she asked him then, indicating his ring.

"Separated." He shrugged in a *what-can-you-do* kind of way. "Six months now. We have three kids. Lauren is six, Georgie is five and Danny is four. They're like the steps on the stairs. One kid a year, three years in a row. Looks like that's it for us now. Three's plenty."

"That's a shame. That you're separated, I mean. Not about the kids. They sound lovely. What happened there? With you and your wife, I mean?"

Carl shrugged again. "We were fine until we got married. Once the rings were on, we just couldn't seem to agree on anything. We argued about literally everything, even stupid things. *Especially* stupid things. The stupid things caused the most bloody trouble."

That was true enough. The row that had proved to be the straw that broke the camel's back had been about hoover bags, of all things. Carl was supposed to pick some up but had forgotten. The ensuing squabble about his thoughtlessness had morphed into World War Three. Karen was screaming at him about how he was a selfish bastard of a husband who put himself before everyone else – he'd shouted back a bit and the next thing he knew, he was a weekend dad back living with his parents at the age of thirty-four, taking his kids to McDonald's and a movie on Saturday afternoons and phoning them from his mobile every evening to say goodnight. He wasn't stupid enough to blame the hoover bags for the separation, but he still gave them a dirty look when he passed them in the Homewares aisle of the supermarket where he had done his depressing shopping-for-one in the beginning. Was there anything more soul-destroying than buying a bland, tasteless dinner for one in a plastic tray? Thank God for his mother's cooking and the fact that she'd pitied him enough to cook for him again. He'd tried to look after himself at first and be an independent single-man-about-town but he just couldn't hack it. Maybe he simply wasn't cut out for the single life any more.

Now it was Tara's turn to cluck sympathetically.

"What about you?" Carl asked her now. "Are you married? Divorced? Other?"

For response, she flapped her left hand at him. There was a rock on her wedding finger the size of a small cat. He was surprised he hadn't noticed it before. He gave a low whistle.

"That must have cost a fortune. Who are you marrying – Bill Gates?"

"In a few weeks' time, I'll be Mrs. Tara Robinson-Devore."

"Devore?" Carl screwed up his eyes as he tried to remember where he'd heard the name before. 'Not . . . not *Ritchie* Devore? From school?"

Tara nodded. "The very same."

Carl remembered Ritchie as a quiet, studious guy, a decent enough skin but not terribly exciting, a bit Tim-Nice-But-Dim. His parents had been moderately wealthy so Ritchie, an only child (Ritchie Rich, the obvious nickname), had always had good clothes and shoes and nice new clean schoolbooks, instead of scribbled-on hand-me-downs with the answers already written in by previous students and such edifying mottoes as *'AMY LUVS DARREN 4EVA'* inscribed within their pages. He hadn't been a prick about it, though, and there'd been many occasions when he'd let a panicked Carl copy his French homework. Carl had been okay at Maths and Sciences but languages weren't his strong suit. They were all Greek to him.

"What's old Ritchie doing now?" he asked, only half-interested in hearing the answer.

"He works in his dad's factory."

Was it Carl's imagination or did talking about Ritchie cast a cloud over Tara's expression? "Oh yeah. What was it they manufactured again?"

"Cutlery," said Tara glumly, and this time there was no mistaking the cloud.

He took a chance. "*Um*, Tara, is everything okay between you and Ritchie?"

Tara bit her lower lip. She didn't need lipstick because her lips were full and red, like Angelina Jolie's. She looked as if she was trying to decide something. Then she seemed to come to a decision because she leaned forward suddenly and said to him conspiratorially: "Can you keep a secret?"

Carl nodded, feeling a frisson of excitement run through him suddenly.

"I'm going to the Dundrum Town Centre to buy a suitcase."

Carl stared at her. "*Wow!*" he said. "That's a doozy all right."

"That's not the secret, silly," she said with a giggle. "That's not it at all." Then, urgently: "Listen, Carl, where are you going?"

"Jesus, Tara, that's a bit existential for a tram-ride home, isn't it? I mean, where are *any* of us going, when you think about it? And will we even know about it when we get there?' To be honest, I've sometimes thought that we all –"

"Dope! I meant where are you going right now? On this Luas?"

"Oh, this very minute, you mean? Just home to Brides' Glen. I'm back living with my folks since the separation. Karen and the kids get to keep the house, obviously. I'm supposed to be looking for a place of my own but every time I start house-hunting for real, Karen starts hinting that she might possibly be on the verge of letting me come back home. I never know if she's serious or if it's just another form of mental torture she's devised for me."

"And do you want to go back home?"

"Yes and no. Of course I want to be back living with my kids and sometimes I even miss Karen, God help me, but we've spent so much time arguing, I don't know if I could go back to that. Life now is boring but at least there's no constant aggro like there used to be when we lived under the same roof."

"Will you get off here at the Dundrum Town Centre with me?" Tara leaned forward and took both his hands in hers as the tram trundled to a halt. "I could really use someone to talk to right now, Carl."

He hesitated. He really shouldn't get involved in someone else's complications – he had enough of his own – and, besides, he was feeling worn out. But … a Thursday evening spent at home with his parents in front of the telly, watching the *Nine O'Clock News* and discussing the next day's weather in tedious detail was all he was in for if he headed on home to Brides' Glen. Tara was good-looking and fun to be with and he was separated, wasn't he, so it wasn't like he was committing any major crimes by going off with her for a couple of hours. He was a grown man, wasn't he? And she was an old schoolfriend. Plus, he didn't need anyone's permission to go off with a beautiful woman for a couple of hours of an evening. He made up his mind, then he nodded.

"Great," Tara said. "We can go for a coffee somewhere – someplace we can talk."

She linked her arm into his once they'd stepped off the tram.

Things were looking up, thought Carl. "Sounds like a plan," he said. "'*Lead on, Macduff!*'"

Tara didn't buy a suitcase that night. She and Carl didn't drink any coffee either. They found a cosy little bar in a small hotel not too far from the Luas stop, and curled up in a nice private corner with two pints of Bulmers and a packet of peanuts each. Carl tried to do the thing where he threw a peanut up in the air and caught it in his mouth, but he failed dismally every time. He didn't mind, though, because his failed attempts sent Tara into paroxysms of laughter and she looked very sexy when she was laughing.

"So what's this big secret, then?" he remembered to ask her, halfway through his second or third pint.

"*Promise you won't tell anyone?*" Her voice was a theatrical whisper.

"Cross my heart and hope to die."

She leaned in closer to whisper in his ear. "*I've won the Lotto.*"

"*What?*" Carl immediately forgot to whisper. "*But that's fantastic, Tara! Are you sure?*"

She nodded, fishing two crumpled pieces of paper out of her bag. One was a Lotto ticket and the other a newspaper cutting with the winning numbers on it, the date and the amount of the prize money. Carl checked the numbers. She was right. They matched exactly.

"Two point four million!" He whistled through his teeth. "Congratulations, Tara! That's fucking amazing. I've never met an actual Lotto millionaire before. Ritchie must be over the moon about this, is he? Or is he still in shock?"

"I haven't told him," Tara said quietly. She bit her lip and lowered her eyes.

Carl stared at her. "Why not?" he said, and then added: "Tara, why were you buying a suitcase?" Silence. "Tara, are you running away?"

No answer at first, then she whispered: "*Yes. Yes, Carl, I am.*"

"But why?" Carl was bemused. "You and Ritchie make a lovely couple, and now you've got all this money. You can both do whatever you want in the world now."

"Don't you get it, Carl? It's Ritchie I'm running away from!"

"But why? He's not . . . he's not abusive to you, is he?"

Tara shook her head vehemently. "Christ, no! If anything, I'm abusive to him. Oh, not physically or anything. I'm just a real bitch to him sometimes. I've often wondered how he puts up with me. He must really love me."

"Then what's the problem?"

"Oh Carl!" she burst out suddenly. "I'm bored sick of him! He's just so bloody boring. He goes to work, comes home, goes to bed, gets up, goes to work again and that's it."

"I don't know whether you're aware of this or not, Tara," Carl said in mock-confidential tones, "but that's what everyone does. It's actually called *life*."

"Oh, don't be such a smart-arse." Tara elbowed him in the side. "You know what I mean. He never wants to go anywhere, have any fun. His idea of a good night in is watching *Winning Streak* with his bedtime cocoa, and his idea of a good night out is to come home early from wherever we've been and watch *Winning Streak* with his bedtime cocoa."

Carl said nothing. Since going back home to live with his parents, he'd watched *Winning Streak* and drunk cocoa going to bed more nights than he cared to count. It was all older people like his parents seemed to want to do. That was the thing about growing older in general, though, he'd noticed. You genuinely didn't want to go out raving all night any more. You were tired from working your arse off all day and you fancied early nights or quiet nights in. Now that he was in his mid-thirties and freewheeling terrifyingly quickly down towards middle age, he fancied the idea of staying in more than he did the idea of going out. Did that make him boring too, he wondered, boring like old Ritchie?

"He never wants to take risks, do anything adventurous, have an adventure!" Tara moaned. "Haven't you ever wanted to have an *adventure*, Carl?"

"Every time I go into work and sit down at my bloody desk," he said wryly.

"Well, there you are then." Her tone was triumphant. "Ritchie doesn't care a jot about adventures. All he wants to do is work in his dad's stupid cutlery factory, then come home to me and the kids. Which we don't have yet, by the way," she added gloomily, "but he wants them. Loads of them. A whole army of them, he's actually said so. He probably wants to raise them to work in their granddad's cutlery factory like little robots, churning out knives, forks and spoons till they die and hand over the reins to *their* children, and their children's children, and their children's children's children."

"I have to say, Tara, that doesn't sound too bad to me." Carl took a long swill of his pint and wiped his mouth. "I mean, that's the kind of thing that everyone wants deep down. A bit of continuity and the knowledge that their name and their family will carry on after them."

"I'm too young for all that," said Tara stubbornly. "I haven't had any real fun yet. I was denied this" – again she waggled the foot that had cost her her Olympic dream at him – "and I haven't had any proper fun yet to compensate me."

Privately thinking that life usually felt under no obligation whatsoever to compensate you for what you considered to be its rank unfairness, Carl said, "Tara, what exactly were you planning to do when I met you today?"

"I told you, I was running away." She sounded sulky now as she ran her fingers through her short, slicked-back dark hair.

Carl thought again that it really suited her this short. She certainly had the face for it, with the sharp sculpted cheekbones and everything.

"I was going to go home with the suitcase and pack it, then I would have gone online and booked a cheap flight somewhere. Well, it doesn't have to be cheap now I'm a millionaire," she added with a laugh. "But I don't have the money yet, not until I go to the Lotto building, which I was going to do tomorrow. Which I *am* going to do tomorrow. I'll tell you what, Carl," she went on, her eyes shining, "why don't you come with me?"

"What, to the Lotto building?" he said, thinking of all the work he had to do the next day before he could bugger off home for the weekend and watch telly and drink cocoa with the folks. Christ, he was really going to have to watch how boring he was becoming. He'd be an old man, in slippers and an old-man cardigan, in no time at all at this rate.

"No, silly! Although of course you can come with me there if you want to. I meant, come with me abroad somewhere for a few weeks. Have a real adventure for once in your life."

Her hand was on his thigh now. Carl was beginning to feel rather hot under the collar as he contemplated Tara's offer. Could he really just drop everything, jack it all in, walk away from all his many commitments to go and lie on a beach somewhere with a beautiful woman for a month or two? On the one hand, he'd be nuts not to go with Tara. She was gorgeous and stylish and her hand on his thigh was beginning to make him feel very horny indeed. If it strayed any higher, she might get her answer sooner than she'd bargained for.

"Same again," he indicated to the barman, who'd already supplied them with three or four refills so far.

Carl was starting to feel pleasantly tipsy, but he still had to consider the downside of his sexy companion's offer. Karen would never forgive him if he just swanned off to Tahiti or wherever else with Tara, and not only would she not forgive him but she'd make sure that the kids didn't either, and the thought of that was something he didn't even want to contemplate. Then there was Graeme, the Great Autismo. Carl loved his brother as much as he loved his kids and there was no way he was going to leave him to the tender mercies of Mawoon-Vicky Who Used To Be a Pwozzy-Tute, even if she did seem kind-hearted and genuine, and even if Graeme was a fully grown man of nearly thirty-one, who just wanted to be left alone to make his own decisions and his own mistakes like so-called 'normal' people.

He looked at Tara curiously. "Are you really going to run off somewhere without telling Ritchie?"

She nodded, starting on her fourth or fifth pint. She was bright red in the face now from the drink, as he knew he was himself, and slurring her words. "That's not all I'm not telling him." She giggled.

"What? What else aren't you telling him? Are you pregnant or something?"

"Christ, no!" Then she started laughing. She laughed until the tears began to stream down her face. "*The ticket's half his!*" she spluttered eventually.

"What do you mean, the ticket's half his?" Carl's brain was starting to feel fuzzy.

"I mean, he paid half and I paid half," she said, still laughing. "That's how we do it every week. We share a ticket. So that means that half the winnings are his by rights."

She wiped the tears from her face with the sleeve of her black top and looked expectantly at Carl, who wasn't really sure what he was expected to say. *Well done, Tara, for pulling the wool over the poor bastard's eyes so thoroughly and diddling him out of his rightful half of two point four million quid which, unless he was completely blotto which he didn't think he was, was one point two million buckaroos, which was still a tidy stash of cash in anyone's language?* He didn't think he could manage this long speech in his current state of inebriation, so instead he just said: "You're a mad bitch, Tara, that's what you are." He air-jabbed at her with his forefinger for emphasis.

Still laughing, she said: "Shall we see if we can get a room here? And a nice bottle of wine to take up with us?"

He was about to say that maybe he ought to be thinking about getting home – the *Nine O'Clock News* was already well under way and the weather girl had been wearing some really cheeky little outfits lately – when she began to kiss him on the mouth like they were already lovers. He was about to say that he had some work to do at home and that he was supposed to call his kids before they went to bed or else they wouldn't sleep, when her hand moved higher on his thigh and then a little bit higher and then . . .

"Yes," he gasped. "Yes, yes, *yes*!"

The sex was a disaster. Tara fell about the room laughing after pulling repeatedly on his willy, which was reacting poorly to her untender ministrations and all the booze. Every time he tried to put it in her, it went soft and she'd scream with laughter again until he'd get annoyed and tell her to put a cork in it. Either it was the booze, he decided, or the guilt he felt that she wasn't Karen. (He hadn't slept with anyone else since the separation and he wasn't sure he wanted to. He liked being in bed with Karen, chatting softly about the kids before they fell asleep, exhausted from the day. He liked the way she spooned up against him when his back was to her, and he liked the way the sound of her even breathing was the last thing he heard as he drifted off to sleep every night.)

Eventually, Carl and Tara both just passed out on the big bed and slept the sleep of the really, really drunk. When they finally woke up, with dry mouths and banging headaches, it was morning. Carl sat up and rubbed the back of his head gingerly. He thought he might have banged it off the bedpost while in the throes of the-passion-that-never-was. It was no fun, crawling around hungover on a strange and possibly dirty floor, looking for bits of your brain.

Tara was beside him, clad in her underwear and clutching her head, groaning.

"You should never have let me drink so much," she said.

"*Let* you?" He was annoyed and showed it. "I'm not your mum."

"Sorry." She leaned over the bed to find her clothes. Both their clothes were everywhere. "I just have this rotten hangover headache."

"You're not the only one," Carl said grimly, and as they dressed he told her: "Tara, *um*, I'm not going abroad with you and your winnings."

"That's okay." She pulled her top down over her head and covered up her breasts, which were every bit as lush as Carl remembered from their schooldays. "I shouldn't have put you on the spot like that. It was unfair of me. None of this is your problem. I shouldn't have dragged you into it. It was just – just seeing you like that on the Luas. I got sort of carried away. Heat of the moment and all that."

"That's okay." Carl grinned. "It was brilliant while it lasted, thinking I could just jack everything in to go and live on a tropical island somewhere with a beautiful woman from my distant past."

"The offer still stands if you want." She looked at him shyly.

He stared at her, wondering if she was serious. "I can't," he said eventually. "I'd miss my kids too much and that's the God's honest truth. I think I might try again with Karen, if only for their sake. I think she'd agree to a reconciliation if it helped the kids. And, to be honest, I miss her too."

It was funny, he thought, how it had taken a night of nearly-passion with another woman to make him realise that.

"It's your loss," Tara said, pulling on her boots.

She sounded miffed now but miffed was okay. Miffed he could handle. He'd had plenty of practice with Karen of handling miffed.

"You're not still thinking of going through with it, are you? Running away from Ritchie, taking the money that's half his, starting again somewhere else without telling him a dickybird about anything, like he's some selfish asshole who's knocked you about or mistreated you in some way?"

Carl was surprised to find as he spoke whose side he was on.

She continued lacing up her boots and didn't look at him. "I don't know, Carl," she said after a silence. "I genuinely don't know."

STOP 8: COWPER

Liz, Gerry and Jean

Liz Grimes only barely made the Luas. It was practically pulling out of the Cowper stop when she came running up, huffing and puffing like an old pair of bellows. Damn and blast Gerry, she thought irritably as she found herself a lovely window seat about halfway down the tram. It was his fault she'd been running late and was now all out of breath, him with his endless demands and stupid questions about petty little things. *Have you seen my glasses? Why have you moved the tea caddy? Where's my newspaper? Have you moved it? Why are you for ever bloody moving everything? What time will you be back? Where's my pen – the one I do the crossword with? No, not that one, the crossword one!* He'd try the patience of St. Peter himself.

Liz was sick and tired of his moaning. Why could he never get up off his arse and look for these supposedly missing items himself? They weren't even really missing anyway. It was nothing that a few seconds of using your God-given eyes wouldn't put right in a jiffy. Liz sighed. That was the great mystery about all husbands, wasn't it? They were big men to the outside world but, once that front door closed on them, they were as helpless as babies.

If Liz hadn't given up her own career as a schoolteacher to support Gerry and his slow climb towards becoming a partner in the accountancy firm where he'd worked all his adult life, he'd probably never even have achieved that.

Liz shook herself mentally, trying to banish all thoughts of Gerry for the time being. These monthly shopping trips and long leisurely lunches with Jean Dennehy were the absolute highlight of her month, the twelve highlights of her endlessly long year. She wasn't having this one ruined just because Gerry had been a pain in the arse as usual this morning. She took several deep breaths, ignoring the funny looks she was getting from the two giggling schoolgirls in the seats opposite. It was the middle of the bloody morning, Liz thought crossly. Either they were very late for school or very early going home, and Liz, frankly, didn't approve of either. She recognised their school uniforms. She had a good mind to ring up their school and complain. No, no, she thought hurriedly. That was the kind of petty thing that Gerry (known privately to his wife as the twin brother of Victor Meldrew from *One Foot in the Grave*) would do. Now that he was retired – they were both in their mid-sixties – and under her feet all day every day, he had nothing better to do with his time than make piddling little complaints to various state bodies about real or imagined grievances. His greatest pleasure these days, seemingly, was to write endlessly to Dublin City Council about potholes in the road, faulty street lights, the illegal dumping of rubbish, and graffiti emblazoned across walls and all over those bloody electricity boxes, or whatever those boxes were that had the mini-murals drawn on them. She'd seen a few quite decent ones but some of the designs were positively baffling. Still, that was modern art for you, she supposed.

She wouldn't mind but Gerry got the same fobbing-off letter back from the council every time without fail.

Dear Mr. Grimes,

We have registered your concerns re whatever it was and please be assured that steps will be taken to rectify same at the earliest possible opportunity. In the meantime, do please try to get yourself a life, you sad pathetic old git, and stop bothering people who actually have *lives with your pettifogging little complaints.*

Yours sincerely,

Someone Considerably More Important Than You

Liz opened her newspaper, deciding that she had time for a quick read before the tram got to St. Stephen's Green. That attractive young couple were on the front page, the couple who'd been on the television news the night before with the story about their big Lotto win. Such a lovely story it was too. They apparently always bought a Lotto ticket together every week, this couple, and finally their patience and perseverance had paid off and they'd won the two point four million, a tidy little sum by anyone's standards. Liz stared at their smiling faces for a long time. Their names were Tara Robinson and Ritchie Devore. The girl Tara was a very striking-looking young woman, and that was an unusual enough name, Devore, thought Liz. She wondered if the young fellow had any connection with the Cork Devores, a family she'd known in her youth. They were engaged, and of course they'd be starting off their married lives on a high now with the two point four million in the bank. Liz wondered if having that amount of cash in the bank at the start of *their* married life would have prevented her and Gerry from drifting apart the way they had. Sadly, she acknowledged that it probably wouldn't have. Personality would always out in the end.

Liz had loved him so much when she'd first known him. She was a country girl up in Dublin in the late seventies to do her teacher-training, and Gerry was a native Dubliner, a trainee accountant in a firm that foresaw good things for the sensible, level-headed young fella. Funny how all the things she'd loved about him at first, like his sensible level-headedness, had ended up being the things she hated about him now. Sensible level-headedness had somehow transmuted over the years into boring, Scrooge-like penny-pinching and a level of caution that probably only very few people possessed. It was a level of caution that stopped him from doing anything that resembled fun and games and kept him at home in his armchair with his newspaper, criticising everything and anything about the world today.

Gerry had nearly had an apoplectic fit when their daughter and only child, Leah, had decided to defer her own teacher-training college for a year and go travelling, something that not many people had been doing in the early 2000s. Afterwards, of course, it had become tremendously popular and then almost the norm, but back then Gerry had completely failed to comprehend why Leah would want to do such an unorthodox, irresponsible thing.

"Travelling?" he'd said as if he'd never heard the word before. "What do you mean, you want to go travelling?"

Leah, a beautiful girl with long light-brown hair and a free-spirited personality that Liz was convinced she couldn't possibly have inherited from her soulless father, had stared back at him in surprise and said: "Travelling, Dad. As in, back-packing through Europe and maybe parts of Asia as well, you know? I'll never get another chance to see a bit of the world, not once I've done my teacher-training and found a job in a school somewhere. A holiday here and there isn't exactly the same thing."

"She's right, Gerry," Liz had put in from the sink where she'd been drying up the breakfast dishes. "Why not let her go now and get it out of her system once and for all? She'll be much more inclined to settle down once she comes back, won't you, lovey?"

Leah could always rely on her mother's support, although Liz had never told her daughter that she'd always regretted giving up her job as a primary schoolteacher to support Gerry's much more important career as an accountant. He'd needed a good, faithful wife in the background to cook lovely dinners for his colleagues so they'd think what a great family man Gerry was, just the kind of man they wanted as a partner in the firm. It had taken years, though, and a great many such dinners, for Gerry to achieve his dream of full partnership. By that time, Liz had long grown disenchanted with the whole concept of marriage, and with sacrificing one's own dreams for the sake of your spouse's. The notion had grown decidedly stale and dull over time.

Together, Liz and Leah had worked on Gerry until eventually – and very reluctantly – he'd agreed to let Leah defer her teacher-training college place for a year to go backpacking on the Continent and across Asia for a year with a friend from school, a girl called Susan. It wouldn't be so bad if their daughter and only child was going with a friend they knew and trusted from Leah's schooldays. What had happened next was something for which Gerry had never forgiven Liz, even though of course it had no more been Liz's fault than the Man in the Moon's. Whilst travelling through Bulgaria, Leah had met and fallen head-over-heels in love with an impoverished artist called Gorka, a handsome fella with an artistic soul and sheer magic in his paintbrush. Leah had actually married this young man within a few weeks of knowing him, and the first her parents had heard of it was when Leah telephoned from a payphone in Sofia to say that she wasn't coming home. She was staying in Bulgaria with this Gorka fella, while her friend Susan was joining up with some people she knew who were touring through Greece.

Gerry had nearly had a heart attack, he'd been so angry and upset. Nothing that Liz could say or do was able to reassure him that it was just a whim of Leah's and she'd be home just as soon as ever she'd tired of the whole marriage lark, for which she was still much too young and immature, surely. It hadn't been a whim, however. Leah really loved this man and, seemingly, he loved her too. Twin boys had been born to them barely ten months after the wedding and that was that. Leah was 'stuck' in Bulgaria with her 'new family,' as Gerry kept putting it. Liz had a strong feeling, though, that Leah was genuinely happy with her new home, her new husband and her beautiful new twin boys, but there was no telling Gerry that.

"This would never have happened if you hadn't pushed her to take that so-called 'gap year', Lizzie," he raged day and night until Liz could recite his complaints by heart. "It's your fault she was out there in the first place, where this Gorka fella could take advantage of her.

I hope you're happy, are you, now that she's stuck in that backward feckin' country, tied down with a husband and two kids who don't even speak English. I hope you're happy, Liz, now that you've got what you wanted. Our daughter, our only child, gone from us for ever because of you, because you could never say 'no' to her."

There had been no reasoning with him. It had been a very hard cross for Liz to bear, knowing that her husband blamed her for their daughter never going to teacher training college and never even coming back to live in the country of her birth. They came home for holidays once a year, Leah, Gorka and the two boys, Jack and John, two gorgeous brown-eyed, dark-haired little lads who were the spitting image of their father. Liz and Gerry had to pay for all their airfares and other expenses because Gorka's parents, with whom the young couple lived, were old and dirt-poor and Gorka was making little or no money yet from his painting. He had to work as a waiter in a local restaurant to pay the bills, but only during busy periods in the summer months when the restaurant was short of staff. The job therefore couldn't be relied on as a steady source of income. Liz had been worried sick at the way that Leah had looked thinner, her blue eyes huge in her tanned face. Were they all eating enough, she wondered? Did they actually have enough to live on out there? She lived for their visits and wished they could afford to bring the four of them over to Ireland more than just once a year.

She and Gerry had gone over to Bulgaria themselves just once. The visit had not been a success. Leah and Gorka had both been overjoyed to see them but Gerry had made the visit a nightmare, making his displeasure and disgust at everything patently obvious to everyone. *Gorka's parents had no English. The twins were allowed to run wild and weren't learning to read or write yet, even though they were four years old. Gorka never sold any paintings. What the feck were they living on, and anyway a man couldn't support his family by drawing pictures, however pretty or interesting they were, could he? The climate was a bloody disaster. There were bugs everywhere. Leah was too thin.* (Even Gerry could see that.) *She'd given up her teacher training for this, a marriage in a strange country with a husband who didn't have two pennies, or whatever they called them out here, to rub together? Are you happy now, Liz? Are you happy now that you've finally seen what all this 'travelling' and 'gap-year' nonsense has led us all to?*

The sarcasm and bitterness in his voice could have stripped the paint off the walls. Liz could have murdered him for his rudeness and discourtesy, which he never bothered to hide from either his daughter, his son-in-law or Gorka's parents. They may not have spoken English but they could tell when someone was slagging them off. Liz had barely spoken to him for weeks after they'd returned to Ireland. They never again went over to Bulgaria themselves – it wasn't worth all the Gerry-aggro, much as Liz would have loved to see them all – but simply paid for Leah and her little family to come over to them in Dublin. Until Leah got sick, that was.

When the twins were twelve, Liz had received a phone call from a distraught Gorka to say that Leah had been diagnosed with stomach cancer. She'd been opened up and the prognosis wasn't good. She wasn't expected to live beyond a few more days. A frantic Liz and Gerry arrived in Bulgaria to find that their beloved daughter had passed away the night before their plane had landed. The funeral had been a nightmare. Gerry had stood on the opposite side of the coffin to Liz, doggedly refusing to address a word to Liz or Gorka or either of Gorka's – and Leah's – two handsome young sons, each of whom was crying quietly to himself. Gorka's parents were both dead by now. They were buried in the ancient churchyard a few gravestones over from Leah's. The sun had blazed down on the little funeral party, to add a macabre touch, and none of it had even seemed real to Liz. She honestly felt like it was one of those horrible surreal dreams that would fade as soon as you opened your eyes in the morning. But it wasn't a dream and going back home to Cowper in Dublin had been even worse. She knew Gerry blamed her for what had happened. He'd made no secret of the fact that he thought Leah would still be alive if she'd lived in Ireland and been treated for her cancer in an Irish hospital instead of in a 'Mickey Mouse First Aid station in the back of beyond', as he so caustically put it.

"I'm only going to say this once so make sure you listen well," Gerry had said when they'd arrived home, in a tone of voice she'd never heard from him before. "I never want to hear any of their names mentioned in this house ever again, and that includes hers. Is that clear?"

He'd gone round the whole house then and put all the photo albums and framed photographs of Leah, Gorka and the children into a box. He put the box in Leah's bedroom and fitted a heavy padlock on the bedroom door. Liz couldn't even go in and sit in her daughter's old room to think about her quietly and mourn. After he'd locked the room, Gerry had been as good as his word and never mentioned any of them again. He said nothing when the odd letter arrived from Bulgaria with photos of the boys inside for Liz and he never forbade her from writing back, but neither did he look at the photos and marvel at how quickly the twins were growing and how there was a distinct look of Leah about them now that they were older. When they'd been babies, they'd looked like chubby little clones of their father but, as they grew, they became so like Leah that it broke Liz's heart to see it. Liz hadn't seen Gorka or her grandsons since Leah died. Gerry had made himself clear on the subject. There would be no money forthcoming for plane tickets for Gorka and the boys to come over to Ireland. Once, Liz had broached the subject of herself going to Bulgaria alone to see them. It was the biggest and most frightening row they'd ever had, and the closest Gerry had ever come to hitting her, as far as she was aware. She had never mentioned the subject again. Years had passed. The boys would be nearly men now. Gorka had remarried a few years after Leah's death, a Bulgarian woman with whom he had a daughter now. It was understandable that Gorka would write to Liz a lot less frequently these days, but she missed his letters and, more than anything else, she missed the photos of the boys. Her grandsons, and Leah's precious sons.

"Please move down the tram," said the automated female voice that everyone ignored.

Liz sighed now as she came back to the present with a gentle jolt. The tram was nearly at the St. Stephen's Green stop and she'd have to start gathering her bits-and-bobs together. She took a last long look at the lovely smiley photo of the Lotto couple, before folding up her newspaper and slipping it into her bag to finish reading on the return journey. They looked so happy together, this Tara Robinson and Ritchie Devore. Liz hoped their happiness would last and, if they ever had children, that they'd make decisions together and each would allow the other person the chance to have his or her say. Couples today were different and so modern, Liz reflected as she zipped her return ticket for the Luas safely into her purse, which went into a secret pocket in her handbag. She'd been holding the ticket in her hand as usual, in readiness for the man (or woman) who checked them. She only used the Luas the odd time when she needed to go into town, but the ticket collectors were a lovely friendly bunch of lads (and ladies!) and Liz enjoyed meeting them. It was a bit of human contact, after all, and human warmth, something she didn't get much of from Gerry.

What was I just thinking about? she asked herself as she disembarked. She'd had a lot of headaches lately and sometimes had difficulty gathering her thoughts because she felt so woolly-headed at times. She hadn't dared mention this to Gerry in case he decided she'd gone senile and needed to be packed off post-haste to an old folks' home. She wouldn't put it past him. He would have the house to himself then, and he could put down his spectacle case and his precious crossword pen anywhere he liked and no one would move them. He was becoming almost fanatical about his possessions being moved or touched in his old age.

Oh yes, couples today, that's what I was thinking about, Liz thought as she crossed the street and made her way to the foyer of the Stephen's Green Shopping Centre, where she and Jean always waited for each other. Couples today were different, and marriage today was different too. No longer did you marry a man for life and allow him to dictate to you what you did, what you wore and how you behaved until the day you died. Hers was probably the last generation that would have that kind of marriage. Women today could divorce a man if he was violent, aggressive or miserly, and the man was made to pay child support by law, whether he wanted to or not, for the children he'd helped bring into the world. Women could bring up children on their own or with the help of friends and family, or they could choose not to have kids at all, if they didn't feel the need to, or if they wanted to concentrate on their careers. It was all so different now.

Even Leah's marriage, the little Liz had seen of it anyway, had seemed happier and stronger than Liz and Gerry's. Gorka had looked at Leah in a way that Gerry had never looked at Liz, even when they'd first started going out together. Gerry had been much too sensible and level-headed for all that romantic nonsense. Gorka, on the other hand, had looked at Leah as if he adored her, like she was the best thing that had ever happened to him and he was the luckiest man alive to have her. What a love they must have had together! Liz had both envied her daughter that and yet wanted it for her too. And, of course, Leah and Gorka had married because they'd wanted to, and not because they had to, or, like Liz and Gerry, because it was expected of them. Liz and Gerry's generation had been expected to grow up, get a trade or a college education, followed by a job-for-life, and none of this chopping-and-changing-jobs-every-five-minutes thing that the kids today seemed to do. Then they were expected to get married, have children and stay together until they died, because this was good holy Catholic Ireland and divorce hadn't yet been introduced. Liz had been awarded her teacher-training degree but she'd been expected to abandon all thoughts of a career of her own when she got married. Gerry's career had been the important one, the one that really mattered. Things were different today, and Liz was thankful they were different. Nowadays, women at least stood a chance in life.

"*Yoo-hoo, Lizzie dear!*" trilled Jean Dennehy's familiar lively tones, breaking into Liz's reverie as she stood in the lobby of the Stephen's Green Shopping Centre, lost in thought. "*I'm not late, am I?*"

Good old Jean. She said the same thing every time they met. She was always flustered, always running a few minutes late, always red in the face from rushing around madly trying to catch up with herself. She and Liz had been friends for years and they loved each other dearly.

Now, when the initial flurry of greetings was finished, Jean looked at her friend curiously and said in hushed tones containing more than a hint of shock: "Lizzie dear, you haven't put your *eyebrows* on!"

"I don't believe you," said Liz, whipping her little compact mirror out of her handbag and checking for herself. Then she said, in the same shocked whisper: "Shit, Jean, I've never done that before, come out without putting them on. That's Gerry's fault now, that is. He held me up over breakfast, demanding this and that and saying he couldn't find his bloody reading glasses. He had the two of us searching high and low for them for ages this morning and he kept getting more and more panicky, like it was the end of the bloody world or something. You know what he's like. Then, of course, it turns out that they were down the back of the cushions on his bloody crossword armchair like they always are. If only one of us had thought to check there in the first place, I mightn't have been so hot and bothered as to forget to put on my bloody eyebrows! I blame Gerry entirely. He got me all worked up, and over nothing as usual."

She was starting to sound dangerously close to tears, so Jean, putting a hand on her friend's arm and leading her towards the escalator, said soothingly, "Never mind about that for now, dear. We'll go on up to the bathrooms and you can put them on there. I need a quick wee anyway, shure."

On the way up to the bathrooms, Liz felt like everyone was staring at the crazy lady who'd forgotten to put her eyebrows on. She'd come all the way from Cowper to the Green (Oh God, had everyone been looking askance at her for the entire journey? Was that what those two silly schoolgirls had been giggling about non-stop, her missing eyebrows?) none the wiser as to the status of her eyebrows, but now she was painfully aware of their absence, as was the way of it. She half-expected to hear an announcement on the public address system drawing everyone's attention to the fact that her eyebrows were missing.

"Attention, shoppers, there is a Crazy Lady currently ascending the escalator to the top floor who has clearly forgotten to put her eyebrows on. Apparently, she was distracted by her fussy, annoying husband who thought his reading glasses were missing when, in fact, they were under his big fat arse the whole time like they always are. Please direct pitying glances towards this Crazy Lady as she is obviously in need of our sympathetic yet disparaging looks in order that she learns her lesson and such an outrage never happens again. Forcing shoppers to look at

women who have not applied their make-up properly is cruel and abusive towards the members of the public who may unwittingly come into contact with such female persons and is now a prosecutable offence. It is particularly undesirable in ladies of the older generation, etc." And so on.

Liz didn't breathe easily until she'd pencilled in both eyebrows as steadily as she could manage it in the women's bathroom. She ran a brush through her short, still-dark curly hair and slicked some of her favourite dark-pink lipstick on her mouth for good measure. Jean made the same lame joke she always made when they used the toilets in the Stephen's Green Shopping Centre, the one about its costing twenty cent to spend a penny. When they emerged from the loos, the Centre was already crowded with lady shoppers, even though it wasn't yet noon.

Liz said: "Oh look, there's an exhibition down the way there about the Irish Famine, will we have a look?"

Jean took her friend by the arm and determinedly steered her in the opposite direction. "You must be feckin' joking!" she said with a laugh. "I've come into town to spend Clive's hard-earned cash and get blotto on wine at lunch, not to peer at blurry pictures of feckin' skeletons from over a hundred years ago."

Liz had to laugh. Jean, not always tactful, was as good as a tonic sometimes. "All right." She grinned. "Shops first, then the boozy lunch?"

"Is there any other way?" Jean said.

Jean was a tireless shopper. Sometimes even Liz, a champion shopper herself, had trouble keeping up with her friend. Jean thought nothing of scouring every clothes shop and shoe shop on or near Grafton Street, and that included all the shops in the Stephen's Green Shopping Centre itself, for hours on end until she found the perfect top/belt/scarf/shoes/handbag to go with an outfit she'd bought, and if she sometimes ended up at the end of the day buying something she'd seen in the very first shop she'd been to, well, that was just the way it went sometimes, wasn't it? She drove her husband demented with how long she could deliberate over a certain pair of shoes or a handbag.

"It's a *bag*, woman," Clive would moan. "You're only going to be putting a ton of crap in it anyway, so what does it matter what it looks like, for Christ's sake? I can get you a plastic carrier bag for a few cents if you just want to cart a load of crap around in it."

Clive, naturally, didn't understand the importance of things like shoes and handbags. He was a *man*. These days, he refused point-blank to go shopping with his wife. He said he wouldn't go shopping with her again even if Dublin City Council installed a row of 'husband chairs, complete with built-in Sky Sports,' up and down Grafton Street, and he meant it too. That suited Jean just fine. He only slowed her down anyway. Now she was in her element, loading her arms with items to take into the Brown Thomas changing rooms. She was like a child. Every two minutes she'd be calling Liz over, saying: "Liz, Lizzie, come here, will you look at this!" Liz would '*oooh*' and '*aaaah*' over the blouse or dress or pair of trousers or sandals, while knowing that she couldn't herself afford Brown Thomas's prices.

Jean had her own credit cards which Clive had given her. Clive, who used to have a high-up position in a bank (actually, he'd been a manager for the last twenty years of his working life) was retired now, like Gerry. Liz used to have only the money Gerry gave her for the 'housekeeping' to buy things for herself, until the time she'd rebelled a few years earlier and threatened to leave him unless he gave her a VISA card and put a couple of hundred euro on it for her each month. He'd done it, albeit with a shockingly bad grace, and only because she'd threatened him with a divorce, which she warned him would have been costlier still. Although she never knew from where she'd found the courage, to her surprise Gerry had seen her point. She'd saved every penny of the money for her monthly shopping trips and lunches with Jean, who'd been her best friend in the world since they'd been at teacher training college together. That was one thing Liz would say to the modern girls of today, girls like that young Tara Robinson one, the young woman from the newspaper, one piece of solid gold advice she'd give them. Always have your own money. Don't let some man be doling out a few measly euro to you once a month like a tight-fisted Victorian Papa. Mind you, she reflected now as she waited for Jean to get her items bagged up at one of the Brown Thomas checkouts, that Tara girl from the paper probably wouldn't need any such advice. She had her own money, all one point two million of it, to be precise. Liz sincerely hoped that she wouldn't let the fiancé, the Ritchie fella or whatever his name was, tell her what to do with it. Separate bank accounts from your spouse, that was the way to do it nowadays.

Back out on Grafton Street, Liz caught her breath at the sight of Leah walking ahead of her up the street. But, of course, it wasn't Leah at all, just a young woman with the same long pale-brown hair and the same look of Leah from the back, the same grace and quick light footsteps. That happened to Liz a lot. Since Leah's death, she'd seen her beautiful daughter on nearly every street in Dublin. Sometimes it would be Leah as she'd be now, in her mid-thirties; other times it would be Leah as a schoolgirl, laughing and chatting away happily with her friends from secondary school, with a big heavy bag of books on her back. Then the fog would clear from Liz's eyes and she would see that she'd been mistaken after all, that it wasn't her precious daughter, only someone who resembled her slightly from a distance.

For lunch, the ladies chose a little Italian restaurant off Grafton Street that they often went to on their days out. Jean was a terrible flirt and she'd eye up the handsome young waiters and even make suggestive remarks about them to Liz, who'd laugh and say: "Stop it, Jean, you're an awful woman altogether. He'll hear you!" But Jean never took any notice – she'd just go on laughing and eyeing up the waiters as much as she pleased. You couldn't stop Jean from having a good time and enjoying herself. She was like that. She *expected* it and, if she didn't get it, she'd complain about it loudly, but not in a mean, spiteful way, not like Gerry might.

Now, as she expertly twirled her spaghetti round her fork, she said to Liz: "How's old Gerry, anyway? Still the same as ever, is he?"

This was usually Liz's cue to launch into a long tirade of complaints about Gerry, and there was normally plenty of material to run with. Today, though, she just fingered the rim of her wineglass idly and said: "I really don't know."

Jean swallowed a mouthful of her food and took some wine. "He's not sick, is he?"

"Well, he kind of *is* in a way."

"Well, is he or isn't he?" Jean was now looking curiously at her friend.

"I'm not sure. I'm really not sure."

"Lizzie love, you're talking in riddles," said Jean, a tad impatiently. "What's wrong with your Gerry?"

Liz shrugged. "Nothing really. Except . . . except I think . . . I think he might be dead."

Jean stared, a forkful of spaghetti halfway to her lips. "Whatever do you mean, Lizzie? What do you mean, *he might be dead?*"

"Well," said Liz slowly, as if considering the matter carefully, "I think I might have killed him."

Jean put down her glass and fork and gave her friend her undivided attention. "Lizzie dear, I think you'd better tell me what's happened."

"Well," said Liz, still speaking slowly as if she was thinking over what she was saying, "he was shouting at me again about his glasses case. He made me late by making me search the whole house from top to bottom for the bloody thing. Then, when he reached down the back of his crossword armchair, he said "Ah, here they are!" and he'd made me waste so much time looking for them when the whole time all he'd had to do was just stick his stupid hand down the back of the armchair."

"What happened next, Lizzie?" Jean had grown a little pale.

"I was so angry, Jean. He'd made me so late with his bitching and whining and losing things. I just couldn't take it any more. I . . . We were in the sitting-room. While he was still leaning down the back of the armchair with his hand on the case, I . . . I grabbed up the poker from the fireplace and I hit him on the back of the head with it."

"And then what happened?" Jean whispered.

"Well, nothing really." Liz took a sip of her wine. "He just fell down without a word and lay on the rug perfectly still, just with all this blood coming out of his head. That'll never come out, you know," she added chattily. "It's a lovely cream rug. It'll never come clean again."

"So, are you saying that you didn't stop to check if he was dead or not? You didn't call anyone, you didn't ring for an ambulance, you just came straight in here to meet me?" Jean's voice was trembling now.

Liz shrugged again. "What else could I do? He'd made me so late. Do you think I could get this to go?" she added, poking at her spaghetti bolognaise which was starting to congeal. "It's gone all cold. D'you think I could get a doggy-bag or something?"

Jean stared at her. "I think we should call someone now. To go out to your house and check on Gerry. He could still be alive."

Liz shuddered. "I hope not."

Jean took out her phone. She was in the process of dialling '999' when Liz reached across the table and put her hand over Jean's.

"Don't do that, Jeannie dear, please. What if he's not dead? You'll only get me into trouble."

"But . . . but even if he's not dead, surely he still needs medical attention? I mean, it's been a good three hours now since we met up at the Green. The whole time we've been together he could have been lying there bleeding to death."

"Not Gerry," Liz said sagely. "His head's too hard." She giggled, then the giggle turned into a fit of laughter, drawing curious looks from the other diners.

"You're in shock, Lizzie," Jean said. "That's it. I'm calling someone. You and Gerry both need help."

The laughter stopped abruptly.

"Please don't, Jean. Can't you just come back with me on the Luas to the house? I'm afraid to go back on my own. I swear to you that you can call anyone you want once we get to the house. For all we know, Gerry could be perfectly all right. He could be sitting up drinking a cup of tea and waiting to give out to me when I get in, over all the stuff I bought in town today and all the money I spent."

Jean seriously doubted it based on what she'd heard but, after a slight hesitation, she said: "All right. I'll go back with you. But the minute we find out what the situation is, I'm going to phone for help, okay, Lizzie? Do you understand?"

Liz nodded and smiled like a child who's been promised an ice cream. Jean paid their bill while Liz arranged for the remainder of her food to be put into a doggy-bag.

"It's a shame to waste good food." She was nodding to Jean, who just looked at her oddly.

They gathered up their carrier bags and left the restaurant. Liz seemed much more relaxed now and she chatted away about silly, random things, even mentioning a row that she and Gerry had had during the week over the price of firelighters and where was best to buy them, of all things. When they reached the Stephen's Green Luas stop, Jean bought a return ticket for herself as Liz already had hers from earlier in the day. Liz continued chatting away once they reached their seats and settled themselves in with their bags and baggage.

"We must have you and Clive over for dinner again soon." Liz said it suddenly, as if the idea had just occurred to her. "I know that Gerry's a real bore when it comes to get-togethers. He has no manners, God bless him, and he hates people coming over, invading his space as he calls it, but the bang on the head might have made him more amenable, so we'll see. How about this coming Thursday? Would that suit, do you think?"

Jean was looking at her oddly again but then she nodded. "That's grand, Lizzie. This coming Thursday will be just fine. Should I . . . should I bring anything?"

"Nothing at all, just yourselves," trilled Liz gaily. "Unless you want to bake up a batch of your world-famous peanut-butter cookies for after the meal."

"Yes, of course, I'd be delighted to bake some. That's no problem, Liz."

There was silence for a while, and then Liz said: "There's an awful lot of doughnut shops opening up in Dublin, have you noticed?"

Jean couldn't say she had.

"Oh yes," said Liz knowingly. "So many American companies are setting up doughnut shops over here. I've seen them and some of them *do* look terribly artistic, the doughnuts I mean, not the shops, but you'd be walking around like a heart attack waiting to happen if you were to eat them on a regular basis. It's a wonder the government isn't trying to ban them, the way they're always putting up the price of booze and fags."

Jean said nothing, only nodded.

It didn't take the tram long to reach Cowper. They disembarked, Liz calling out a cheery goodbye to the friendly ticket collector as they left. The sun was still shining and it was a lovely day, even though it was late enough in the year.

"You're as white as a sheet, Jeannie dear," said Liz as they walked up the road to the house. "Do you suffer from travel sickness at all? Because that's what this looks like. You've gone quite green around the gills. I tell you what we'll do. I'll make you a grand hot sweet cup of tea when we get in, with a plain biscuit or a water-cracker. They're great for settling the stomach after you've had the motion sickness. I never get it myself on the Luas. It's so much smoother and less bumpy than the buses. They go up and down like a flippin' roller coaster, making people sick as dogs."

There were no police cars or ambulances in the driveway anyway. The sun was setting for the evening over the top of the house and it looked a picture in the dazzling sunlight.

Liz and Jean walked up the path to the front door with their bulging carrier bags.

"Do you think we need the grass cut?" Liz turned to her friend as if the condition of the front garden was suddenly of vital importance.

Jean looked at it and shrugged helplessly. "I don't know. It looks fine to me."

"I think we can leave it for another week or two. It's just that Gerry always likes to get it sorted before the winter sets in."

Liz unlocked the front door with her key. Inside the hall, she put her carrier bags down and began to take off her coat to hang it on a hook just inside the door.

"*Yoo-hoo, Gerry, I'm home,*" she sing-songed. "*Gerry, are you there? Gerry . . . ?*"

STOP 9: BEECHWOOD

Jamie and Callum

Queer. Faggot. Pervert. Deviant. Fairy. Nancy Boy. Homo. Arse-bandit. Uphill gardener. Shirt-lifter. Pillow-biter. Hershey highwayman. Pansy. Batty-boy. Limp Wrist. Gaylord. Gay-boy. Sissy. Poofter. Had he forgotten any? Probably, and anyway, new ones were still being dreamed up all the time by people who clearly had nothing better to do with themselves. Jamie continued to repeat the words in his mind while he waited for the Luas to chug away from the Parnell Street stop in town and take him back out to Beechwood. They were like the opposite of a positivity mantra, words he repeated in his mind while he waited to get to sleep, waited for an appointment, waited for the kettle to boil, waited for a bus or the Luas to come. He still did it out of habit, even now when life was good, and had been good for quite some time. Maybe he should replace the derogatory words with some more heartening ones. *Love. Lover. Loving. Boyfriend. Commitment. Relationship. Sex. Fun. Laughter. Cooking. Home. House. Engagement. Marriage. Gay Marriage. Civil Partnership. Rings. For ever. Eternity. Happiness. Truth. Openness. Out in the open. No More Hiding, No More Shame, No More Fear.* He was still reciting these to himself experimentally when the tram moved off.

He could see what was clearly another gay couple, a few seats down and across from him. He had a radar for that kind of thing (a *'gaydar,'* even), as he assumed most other gay people did. The couple were two lads on their phones, scrolling away like two separate entities, but every now and then, they'd catch each other's eye and grin in that special way that couples of all persuasions have with each other. It gladdened Jamie's heart to see it.

He took out his own phone and immediately began scrolling, checking first to see if Callum had left him a tweet or a Facebook or Instagram message. No, there was nothing, although there was sufficient evidence to show that Callum had been on Instagram less than an hour before. Ah well, shure, thought Jamie, trying to be mature about it, they weren't joined at the hip, after all. After reading some of his Facebook messages from other people, he couldn't resist leaving Callum a cutesy message that read: **Hey, babes, on the Luas now, be home soon.** He left a smiley face and a row of kisses after his message, then began scrolling idly down through his newsfeed, checking back every few seconds to see if his message had been marked as **'seen'**. Everyone on Facebook was posting those *'Thank God It's Friday'* posts. Jamie knew exactly how they all felt. He'd been counting down the days and even the hours himself this week, but only because this Friday was a special one and he'd asked to have the Saturday and Sunday off work. There wasn't much point in his getting excited about Fridays most other weeks, because he worked in a men's clothing shop in town which was open seven days a week, but this week was special.

"Mind if I sit here?" said a large middle-aged man carrying several plastic bags, breaking in on Jamie's scrolling reverie.

"Not at all. Work away," Jamie said politely, going back to his phone.

"I don't want to squash your flowers."

The bouquet was draped artistically across Jamie's lap. "You're grand. Not a bother." Jamie moved the flowers a bit more to his left towards the window.

"Forgot her birthday, did you?" the man remarked congenially, in the easy, familiar way some Irish people have with one other.

"No, it's just a little . . . private celebration, actually."

Jamie went back to his scrolling, hoping the man would take the hint and pipe down. But the man was settled now, all nice and comfortable with his carrier bags arranged around his feet, and unfortunately disposed to chat. The attractive young couple who'd won the Lotto recently (a cool two point four million between them, if you please) were finally out of the news, and the free local newspaper on the man's lap was open at the page about that old man from Cowper who'd recently died when his wife had bashed him over the head with the poker. There was some talk of the wife possibly being out of her mind, so she'd most likely be sent to a mental hospital, rather than to prison, for her crime. It was shocking what people got up to behind closed doors, Jamie thought, idly scanning the headlines on the other man's paper. He wondered how far the woman, the wife in the story, had been pushed by her husband before she'd felt she had to do what she did. He doubted if she'd done it for fun, or if she'd just woken up with a sudden urge to brain her hubby with the poker. There was usually more to a story than just what you read in the newspaper.

Anyway, the man with the carrier bags and the free local newspaper could obviously tell that the two people across from himself and Jamie, a man and a woman, were closed for business. They were looking at their phones with glazed eyes and headphones in their ears, like most of the other passengers. Terrified to make any kind of contact, whether eye contact or verbal contact, with their fellow travellers. That's the way it was on the Luas nowadays. The protection of being on your phone or listening to music on your earbuds prevented others from trying to interact with you. There was safety, not in numbers, but in whatever bit of technology you happened to be carrying. You saw someone with a book the odd time. There were still people in the world who read books, though they might be becoming an endangered species.

Dammit, thought Jamie, wishing he'd had the cop-on to put in his own earphones a bit quicker. That normally forestalled any attempts at interaction or conversation on the part of the other passengers. In fact, it was almost unheard of for passengers to interact with one other at all, beyond the usual courtesies involved when strangers had to sit together for any length of time. The *excuse me's* and the *mind if I sit here's* and the *sorry, this is my stop here, I'll just get past you's*.

"Is it your girlfriend they're for?" The man in the next seat folded his arms comfortably and nodded towards the flowers.

Jamie thought for a moment. He still hated being asked

that question. He and Callum had decided from the start that they'd both be husbands if they got married. They wouldn't have one husband and one wife – they'd each be husbands. If they had to choose, though, Jamie would almost certainly end up being the husband by virtue of his being the only one of them who was currently earning a wage. He and Callum had joked before about their being a typical fifties' couple, with a breadwinning hubby, Jamie, and a stay-at-home wife in the form of Callum. But Callum wasn't terribly domesticated and, even though he was now unemployed and had all the time in the world on his hands, he left the housework mostly undone and the meals uncooked. Usually, Jamie did everything when he got in from work. He did it without complaining because he loved Callum and he loved that today's society had decreed that they could be together without any fear of retribution from anyone, at least legally. What wouldn't he have given, though, for a hot home-cooked meal to be put in front of him when he got home (even some kind of boil-in-the-bag dish would have been an improvement on what was currently on offer, which was nothing) and a tidy house? Instead, all he got was a grumpy Callum, stiff and cranky from sitting on his arse watching TV box sets all day. It was a wonder his eyes weren't square from goggling at so much telly.

To the man beside him, Jamie said reluctantly, "No, they're for my partner actually." He hated that word too, even more than some of the words for gays. *Partner.* It was so wishy-washy, so non-committal somehow. It was a nothing kind of word. It could mean a male or female or even a business partner. He sometimes wished someone would invent a new word with a bit more 'oomph' to it but, in the meantime, he supposed 'partner' would have to do.

"So she's the romantic type, is she? Likes being given flowers?"

"Yes, I guess – *h* –" He hesitated and then stalled on the 'he'.

The man got it. "A man, is he, then, this *partner* person?" he said with interest.

He turned in his seat to look more fully at Jamie, who blushed to the roots of his close-cropped gingery-blond hair. Thank God the people around them were on their phones and earphones and weren't listening avidly to Jamie's being quizzed so publicly.

"Yes." He knew he sounded embarrassed and hated the way his voice came out in an apologetic-sounding squeak. He cleared his throat and said again in his manliest voice, more forcefully than he intended, "*Yes.*"

Jesus, he thought, why was there never a middle ground to these bloody situations? If he lived to be a hundred, he'd probably still be all awkward and defensive when asked about matters pertaining to his sexual orientation.

"Ah shure, isn't it grand nowadays that we do have all the gays out in the open, and getting married now and everything? What d'ya think of the whole gay marriage thing?"

"Well, obviously I voted for it myself," Jamie replied stiffly. He was being cautious because he didn't yet know if the man was going to turn nasty in a minute, as people sometimes did.

"I would've voted for it myself like a shot," said the man, crossing his long, heavily booted legs, "but I wasn't registered to vote at the time."

A fat lot of good that is to anyone, then, Jamie thought, wisely keeping his own counsel on the matter. Out loud he said, mainly out of politeness and not interest: "And have you registered to vote since then or what?"

The man shrugged as if it were a thing that was, sadly, out of his control. "D'you know something? I've never thought about it since." He said it almost wonderingly, as if it were such a bizarre, unorthodox thought that it wouldn't have occurred to him in a million years. "So, you're gay then?" he asked Jamie, who blushed again and nodded uncomfortably.

The man looked at him almost admiringly, as if he were a particularly well-groomed dog he'd passed on the street, or a lovely vintage car or something. "And how long have you known? About being gay?"

Jamie sighed. Thereby hangs a tale, he thought.

He'd known since he was about twelve or thirteen, around the time that he and his classmates were hitting puberty and starting to take an interest in girls and everything that went with that. Breasts, sex, masturbation, willies, where babies came from and all the rest of it. His classmates in his all-male school, even if they didn't know for sure that he was gay, certainly *acted* as if they knew. *Faggot*, they'd call him with mean sniggers when he passed them in the hallways or in the classroom on the way to his seat. *Poofter, gayboy, queer, nancy boy*. Their vocabulary was maybe more limited than that of the teenagers of today, but they still managed to get their point across succinctly. *Bent as a nine-bob note*, that was another favourite. God only knew where they'd picked that one up. It sounded like something Dirty Den from *EastEnders* might say. In class, feet would be stuck out for Jamie to trip over as he passed by. Sly kicks would be directed at him in football or gym class. He'd be dunked and held under in swimming class until he really thought he might drown, and all behind the lifeguard's back, of course. His homework would be stolen out of his bag and his ruined copybook might turn up later, stuffed down a toilet in the boys' jacks. The one time they'd shoved his actual *head* down the lavatory and flushed it repeatedly, they'd laughed and crowed over their triumph for weeks, calling him '*Shit-Head*' and '*Shit-Face*' on top of all the other names they had for him and commenting on the '*stink*' whenever he entered or left a room. They'd been little shits to him, literally. Jamie's surname – Sweetman – hadn't helped either. It just gave them more fodder for their stupid jokes.

But time had passed and Nature had been kind to Jamie by way of compensation, causing him to bulk up naturally during his adolescence and, as soon as he was old enough, he'd started working out and even taking boxing lessons at a local club and strengthening himself even more. He quickly lost his skinny, almost delicate, frame and became more solid. By the time he'd left school, his former bullies were thinking twice before taking him on. When he left school and immediately found work in the men's clothing shop where he was still employed, he'd straightaway started taking self-defence classes for men, as well as still going to the gym most days after work. He'd had a feeling those classes would come in handy, and they had. Well aware that he wasn't completely immune from gay-bashing or anti-gay violence just because of his size, he at least felt reasonably confident now that he could protect himself and Callum from an unexpected (or wholly *expected*) attack. Gay-bashing was still a popular sport amongst drunken males on a night out. It hadn't gone away just because the majority of the country had voted to bring in gay marriage. Just like racism against black people hadn't died down when black people had been given the vote, or even when Barack Obama had become the President of the United States of America and, by definition, the most powerful ruler on the planet.

Naturally, Jamie gave the stranger on the Luas only a very brief, diluted version of his story. When he'd finished recounting the details of how and when he'd first realised he was gay, the man said: "Fair play to ya anyway, for sticking with it." As if being gay was a college course you were trying to complete, or a series of driving lessons or a jigsaw puzzle or something, Jamie thought. "And what did your ma and da think about all this being gay stuff and everything?"

"Not a lot," Jamie answered wryly.

Their finding out had happened by accident, worse luck, and after Jamie had lain awake in his bedroom at home night after night for years as well, agonising over how to tell them. He'd always known it wouldn't go down well. His father, Jim Sweetman (a misnomer if ever there was one – Jim Sweetman was anything but!), was a real man's man, a former factory worker now on Disability leave, an individual with a drink problem and a short fuse. This combination made him difficult to approach for anything material, like a few quid for schoolbooks or a new pair of trainers, never mind a heart-to-heart chat about something as incendiary as his son's sexuality. Jim had never really loved Jamie, or at least this was how Jamie genuinely felt on the matter. He cared more, or seemed to anyway, about Jamie's two older brothers and his older sister. Jamie was the runt of the litter and had been small and almost frail-looking in his childhood. Also, Jamie liked listening to music and spending hours alone in his room with his CDs, often penning song lyrics of his own or poems, the kind of tortured poetry churned out by angsty teens before they grow up and have no time to write poems any longer because there are bills to pay and work to go to and children to mind. Writing poetry alone in his room instead of playing football with the other lads on their road didn't endear Jamie at all to his disgusted father. He didn't hear the words '*faggot*' and '*queer*' only at school, and he didn't get thumped only at school either.

Jamie's mother, Nora Sweetman, was a quiet little sparrow of a woman who was terrified of her violent husband. She didn't stand up for Jamie any more than she stood up for herself against the brutish, blustering man she'd married. She'd kept well out of things the day her husband found the little stash of gay porn in their youngest son's bedroom while he was looking for cash with which to buy booze. He'd beaten the shit out of his then nineteen-year-old son when Jamie had come home from work, and then he'd thrown him out of the house in the rain. A badly shaken Jamie, blindsided by the attack, had managed to get a friend from work called Matt, a decent friend as he'd turned out to be, to agree to let him bed down on his couch for a while. Jamie had never again gone home, and his parents had never bothered to contact him again, not even his mother. Anything for a quiet life, that was Jamie's mum, even if it meant she never saw her youngest son again.

He stayed in touch, through text or social media, with

his two brothers, Niall and Gerry, and his sister, Marie, who all had growing families of their own now, although his brothers in particular didn't want to know anything or hear a peep out of him about his being gay. It was almost like a condition of their staying in touch. *You can text us and all that, but none of your faggotty-ass stuff or that's the end of it.* Jamie knew the score and played the game by their rules. He had to, if he wanted to keep in touch with them, his own brothers. Marie at least was a bit more liberal and didn't go into a mad panic and start flapping if Jamie accidentally let his gayness slip out for a moment, although you couldn't exactly say that she embraced or encouraged it either. It was through Marie that Jamie learned that their father was dying of alcohol-related complaints, and that their mother was nervier and more timid and self-effacing than ever. Marie's considered opinion was that their mother would have a nervous breakdown and become estranged from the real world altogether if the old man didn't hurry up and die soon, releasing her from her torment. Jamie hated his father for what he'd done to him but, in a way, he hated his mother even more. Fathers were *meant* to be aggressive and violent and impossible to approach about matters like sexuality, weren't they (that was what Jamie had been brought up to believe, anyway), but mothers were meant to protect you, to shield you from the blows. Jamie's mother had simply abandoned him to his fate, like the heartless coward she was. Jamie told himself he couldn't have cared less about what happened to either of them, but they cropped up in his thoughts the odd time just the same. It grieved him badly that they didn't know about Callum, that they hadn't met Callum and that they were unaware that their youngest son had met the love of his life and was happy, was finally living the life he was meant to be living and had longed for nearly his whole life.

"And what kinda fella is yer man anyway, what's-this-his-name-is-again?" said the large man with considerable interest.

Jamie was impressed by his interest, which seemed genuine.

"*Please move down the tram,*" said the automated female voice that everyone routinely ignored.

"Callum," Jamie supplied automatically. Well, he thought, that's a good one. What kind of a man *is* Callum?

They had met two years before when Callum had come into the shop where Jamie worked one lunchtime. They'd clicked instantly, each being young single males who liked their clubbing and pubbing, who were into fashion and good grooming and who openly admitted that they couldn't live without their phones or social media. It had actually been Callum who'd asked Jamie out that very first day. Jamie had said yes immediately. They'd had a fantastic night together and become a couple straightaway. Now they lived together in a lovely rented house in Beechwood. They shared the place with a heterosexual couple called Chris and Julie, who were totally cool about sharing with a gay couple, and an equally relaxed and liberal heterosexual female called Philippa, whose boyfriend Michael didn't live with her officially but he might as well have been living there, the number of nights he stayed over. What was so great about the house was that Jamie and Callum didn't have to pretend they were anything but what they were, a perfectly normal gay couple who had rowdy, noisy sex together sometimes and who took baths together the odd time or used the bathroom together, one in the shower and the other shaving or on the loo. Chris and Julie, and for that matter Philippa and Michael, were all just as sexually active and, since they all paid their rent through the bank, there was no need for a nosey landlord to come over and start making comments about sleeping arrangements or causing trouble for anyone.

At least, that was how it had been in the beginning. Jamie and Callum still had sex in bed nearly every night out of habit, but they didn't do the spontaneous things they used to do any more, like making love in different places or at odd times, or whenever they felt like it. Callum was much less affectionate and physically demonstrative these days too. This falling-off of their sexual routine had seemed to start when Callum was let go from the phone shop where he worked. That was four months ago now, and since then he'd made very little effort to find a new job. He spent a lot of time online, supposedly 'looking for work', but Jamie was pretty sure he was just slobbing about on social media all the time. Which was perfectly fine, of course. He had every right to take some down-time, Jamie told himself sternly whenever he found himself disapproving of Callum's online activities. It just would have been helpful if Callum used some of his free time to hunt for a new job, mainly so they could go back to sharing the expenses and bills equally, like they used to do at first. And it would have been even more helpful if Callum had picked up a dish-brush every once in a while to wash up the remains of their meals, all of which Jamie cooked when he came in, hot and tired, after a day's work. He'd been meaning to talk to Callum about the division of labour regarding the household chores and the bills and stuff, Jamie confided now in the stranger, his travelling companion on the Luas, but the time never seemed to be right for such delicate negotiations. Callum was never in the mood for a heart-to-heart chat these days. "I'm depressed," he'd say plaintively as he sat on the couch in the mornings with the duvet wrapped around him, watching breakfast telly, eating biscuits and crisps and, incidentally, leaving crumbs for Jamie to vacuum up later. And that would be the end of the conversation. And now it would all have to wait again, because Jamie had other stuff he wanted to talk about with his lover tonight. Important stuff. He had something planned that was guaranteed to divert Callum's attention away from his worries and woes.

In the meantime, Jamie didn't mind paying for everything and doing all the cooking and cleaning for the two of them in their part of the house. He had to do the cleaning anyway if Callum was currently not bothering his arse, otherwise they wouldn't be pulling their weight as housemates, and the others in the house might start to object. The last thing Jamie wanted was to antagonise Chris, Julie and Philippa. They were blessed with good housemates and Jamie didn't want to screw things up. If only Callum would snap out of this self-pitying rut he seemed to have burrowed himself into lately, like a small animal preparing for hibernation. Jamie had a strong suspicion that Callum wasn't really depressed but merely lazy. He *liked* lolling around on the couch and letting Jamie take care of him. While Jamie was okay with the way that Callum looked up to him and treated him as big strong Jamie who could handle any problem, he was starting to feel a bit under pressure to constantly take care of them both. At twenty-five, he was only a few months older than Callum, after all.

Maybe it was Callum's background that was to blame. Miraculously, Callum hadn't been bullied in school like Jamie, presumably because he didn't 'look gay', as Jamie felt he himself must have done, and also Callum's father had died when his son was a baby. There hadn't been an angry male parent around to go ballistic when it turned out that Callum was gay, only an adoring mother and sister who loved him so much that even his telling them he was a serial killer of baby lambs couldn't have caused them to withdraw their love for so much as a second. And they'd never let him lift a finger around the house when he was growing up, so that was why Callum wasn't particularly domesticated, unlike Jamie, who'd been keeping house for himself since he was nineteen. Callum had had a much easier time of things. Jamie, on the other hand, had had to fight hard for his place in life, in school, in his family and in his job. He'd spent his whole life fighting, or so it seemed. Callum really had had things that bit easier. After tonight, after he'd sprung his surprise, Jamie was going to try to get Callum to shoulder a bit more of the load. Callum was at heart a sound guy. Jamie was confident that he could get his boyfriend to see sense and offer to halve the burdens.

"Well, this is me here anyway." Jamie gathered up his bouquet of flowers and the little backpack he brought in to work with him every day, containing bottles of water, deodorant, his lunch. "Beechwood. It's been nice talking to you."

He meant it too. It had been weird unburdening

himself to a total stranger like that, but in a strange way it was kind of cathartic as well. Maybe he should sign up for a series of counselling sessions or something. He'd had a lifetime of bottling things up and he felt like he still had a load of things to get off his chest.

"And you," said the large man easily. "My name's Luke, by the way." He extended a huge weathered paw for Jamie to shake.

"And I'm Jamie. Where are you off to yourself?"

"Oh," said Luke, shrugging massive shoulders, "wherever this yoke takes me, I suppose." He saw Jamie looking at him curiously and went on: "I ride this thing all day sometimes. It gets me out and about, meeting people."

"Do you have a ticket?" Jamie asked him, knowing already what the answer would be.

"D'you know something?" said Luke with a grin, yawning and stretching comfortably before resettling himself in the window-seat formerly occupied by Jamie. "I never think about these things."

I bet you don't, you old fare-dodger, you, thought Jamie, grinning to himself as he disembarked and started up the road to Burton Drive.

No smell of cooking wafted his way when Jamie put his key in the lock and opened the front door. Ah well, he thought, no change there then. (Chris and Julie wouldn't be back yet and Philippa, who often wrote her magazine articles from home, was probably saving herself for her usual Friday night dinner out with her boyfriend, Michael. Still, he'd hoped that Callum might have bestirred himself to throw something together as it *was* Friday, the start of the weekend, but why change the habits of a lifetime?) Jamie went straight to the kitchen, knowing that there was zero chance of bumping into Callum there, and filled a vase from under the sink with tap water. He artfully arranged the flowers he'd bought in the vase and placed them on the kitchen table. They looked lovely. Flower-arranging was another little talent of his that his father hadn't appreciated.

"*What are you, lad, a fucking sissy or something, a nancy boy?*" he'd roar whenever he caught Jamie trying to pretty up the place up a bit.

Jamie had never responded. He'd bitten his lip and flushed like mad, but he'd never responded verbally, and even that had got his father's goat big-time.

"*Stand up for yourself, boy!*" he'd bellow while shoving Jamie in the chest till he fell backwards onto the floor. "Don't just sit there on your arse like a fucking big girl's blouse, fucking *do* something, will ya!"

But Jamie, paralysed by fear, had never given his father the response he'd been seeking, and his father had in turn responded to his son's lack of reaction by upping the bullying. By God, but the old man wouldn't tangle with him these days, Jamie often told himself grimly. Jamie was gym-fit now, and bulky and broad-shouldered to boot. The old man wouldn't know what hit him if he went for the Jamie of today. Jamie thought of his father every single time he put flowers in a vase, every time he bought a little painting or an ornament or put soft fluffy cushions on his bed or on the couch. His father's taunts and insults rang resoundingly in his ears at these times. Jamie was a real man. He *was*. Liking things like comfy cushions and flowers that gave off a lovely scent didn't make him any less of a man. How could it?

Jamie dug the takeaway menu out of the drawer and

phoned the number on the brochure. He ordered a Chinese meal for two for half an hour's time. That would give him enough time to shower and change and get ready for the surprise. But first he'd look in on Callum. His boyfriend was predictably sprawled on the couch watching some rubbishy gameshow. The duvet from their bed, the one with the lovely flowery patterned cover on it, was crumpled on the floor beside him. That set Jamie's teeth on edge straightaway. He'd spent good money on that duvet (and the cover!), and here was Callum treating it like an old dishcloth. Still, he reminded himself sternly, things and possessions didn't matter. It was people who mattered. He wasn't going to start a world war over something as inconsequential as a silly flowery old duvet cover. He could always get another one from somewhere if he was that bothered about it.

"How was your day, babes?" Jamie said as brightly as he could.

Callum looked at him and shrugged.

Jamie tried again. "Well, what did you do?"

Again the shrug, the bored look. Callum put out a languid hand (like Oscar Wilde on a bloody chaise-longue, thought Jamie) as if to indicate the television and duvet and say: "What the fuck d'you think I've been doing?"

Jamie hated it when Callum was sarcastic. He had a very cutting tongue on him for one so young. "Well, any joy on the job front?" Jamie made his voice sound as cheerful as possible so that Callum wouldn't think the question was a big deal.

"What do *you* think?" Callum yawned hugely. "Is there anything to eat? I'm bloody starving."

Fighting back his irritation, Jamie said: "I've ordered

us a Chinese takeaway for half an hour's time." And guess who'll be paying for it, as per usual, he wanted to add, but didn't.

"Half an hour?" groaned Callum. "I'm starving now!"

"I suppose it would never occur to you to go in the kitchen and cook something yourself," Jamie snapped, suddenly unable to contain his temper. Then he could have kicked himself when Callum recoiled as if he'd been struck.

"You know I'm no good at that domestic goddess stuff. You know perfectly well that you're better than me at all that kind of thing."

"Well, like I said, I could teach you how to make a few simple dishes," Jamie said placatingly, sitting down beside Callum and putting his arms around him. "It might be fun."

Callum said nothing, just turned up the volume on the TV.

Jamie sighed inwardly, then he got up. "Well, I'm off to have a shower and change, so. Anyone else in the house?"

"Only Philippa, I think." Callum yawned hugely again. "The others aren't home yet."

"Right. Would you listen out for the door then while I'm in the shower? The money's on the table."

"Okay." Callum sighed as if it were too much trouble to even contemplate, but he'd do it if he absolutely had to.

Greatly irritated now, Jamie headed upstairs. He loved Callum so much, but lately he was starting to feel like the harassed parent of Kevin the Teenager from *The Fast Show* rather than a man in his mid-twenties in a relationship with another man in *his* mid-twenties, in an equal partnership in which both men should be bringing something to the table. It had been a while since Callum had brought anything to the table but sulkiness and an unwillingness to face up to any unpleasant realities. And, God, he was so bloody sensitive these days!

Jamie heard the toilet flushing and then the bathroom door opened. It was Philippa. She was wrapped in a towel and her hair was covered turban-style with another towel. They each greeted the other with a 'Hello, stranger' apiece as they hadn't seen much of each other that week.

"We're having a Chinese in a bit," Jamie offered out of politeness. "You're more than welcome to join us if you'd like?"

She demurred, as he'd known she would. "What? And play gooseberry to the two lovebirds all night?" she teased. "Nah, you're all right. Michael's coming round later to take me out to dinner. We've got a table booked at the Taj Mahal for around half-nine."

"Long way to go for a bit of grub," Jamie joked feebly, but Philippa laughed just the same.

"I'll see you guys later," she said. "I'm off to make myself ravishingly beautiful for Michael and to see if I can squeeze in a quick couple of episodes of *Game of Thrones* before he gets here."

"Sounds like a plan," said Jamie.

When they'd parted ways, Jamie rather distractedly took a shower, his mind on Callum. He didn't want to be too hard on the poor guy. Maybe Callum was depressed. Unemployed people got depressed, didn't they? Sometimes they even got suicidal. Maybe he really was just depressed. *Or maybe he's just a lazy, selfish little bollocks who's perfectly happy to laze around the house all day while you go out to work to pay the rent and bills for the two of you,* said the spiteful little voice from somewhere deep down inside him that he tried but failed to ignore.

Certainly Callum had been down in the dumps and impossible to please lately, but Jamie didn't think it was because he'd been let go from his job at the phone shop. Jobs in phone shops were ten-a-penny nowadays. You could always get another one if you really wanted to, probably within a day or two if you shifted your arse. *But Callum doesn't really want to, does he,* went that spiteful little voice again. *And the reason he's so sulky and moody all the time now is because that's his true personality, the one he was hiding from you at first, but now he's hooked you so he doesn't have to try as hard any more.*

Shut up, shut up, shut up, Jamie told his inner voice as he quickly showered and washed his hair. Well, it felt good to be clean again anyway. Working in a men's clothing shop in town was hardly the equivalent of going down a coalmine or up a chimney, but he was still surprised at how grubby he felt at the end of a day. It was probably working in town that did it. Town could be such a filthy place to spend any length of time in. He dressed himself in a dark-blue tracksuit with a clean white T-shirt underneath, towel-dried his short, spiky gingery hair (try being gay *and* ginger-haired in a school like his old one!), which was so short it dried in minutes, and went downstairs, full of the joys again after casting off the grime and dust of the day. Okay, so Callum was being a little difficult, but it was nothing the two of them couldn't work out between them. They loved each other after all, didn't they? His phone rang in the pocket of his tracksuit pants as he reached the hall.

"Hello, I'm outside your house with your food delivery," said an angry foreign voice.

"Why didn't you ring the doorbell?"

"I've been ringing and knocking for ten bloody minutes!"

"For fuck's sake, that's Callum's fault," muttered Jamie as he hurried to answer the door.

Once he had the food set out on plates in the kitchen, he went to the sitting-room where Callum was still lying on the couch, watching his gameshow with the volume on high.

"Didn't you hear the door?" Jamie demanded. "Driver said he'd been knocking and ringing for ages."

Callum shrugged. "I might have heard something, but I thought you or Philippa might get it."

"For fuck's sake, Callum! Philippa's in her bedroom with her door shut and her hairdryer and her telly on." All the irritable feelings from before his shower were bubbling up inside Jamie again. "And I was in the shower. I *told* you to listen out for the door, didn't I? And anyway," he added indignantly, "why should Philippa have to listen out for our delivery guy? It's our food, isn't it? And I specifically asked you to listen out for it."

"What's the big deal?" said Callum. "Food's here now, isn't it? Why don't you bring it in here and we'll have it in front of the telly? It'll be nice and cosy, just the two of us."

Oh, will it now, thought Jamie darkly, but he bit back the retort for the sake of peace, which after all was the only thing that mattered, and went to get the food. They watched *Coronation Street* together and ate their takeaway. The food was surprisingly good after all the fuss, and even Callum seemed to brighten up once he'd eaten every scrap on his plate.

He cuddled up to Jamie after they'd pushed their plates away from them and said: "I'm feeling horny now, what about you?"

Jamie laughed and patted his stomach. "Well, I don't

know about horny, but I'm definitely feeling *fat*, after that little lot."

"Are you sure you're not the least bit horny?" Callum teased, running his fingers up and down Jamie's inner thighs.

"Well, maybe a little bit." Jamie found he was responding, despite himself, to Callum's caresses. He gasped when Callum kissed him full on the mouth while cupping his crotch. He relaxed into the kiss and allowed Callum's clever fingers to work their magic.

"Hey, what's this?" said Callum, his hand on the outside now of Jamie's tracksuit pocket. "Is this a gun in your pocket or are you just pleased to see me?"

"It's just my phone. Don't stop what you were doing there. Keep going."

"I know what your phone feels like," said Callum, giggling, "and this definitely doesn't feel like your phone. Here, what's this?" He shoved his hand deep into Jamie's pocket and pulled out the contents, a small midnight-blue velvet jewellers' box of the kind that normally contains only one thing.

"Don't open that, please, Callum," pleaded Jamie, trying to yank back the box. "It was meant to be a surprise for later. Please, Callum, give it back!"

But Callum had already opened the box and taken out its contents. He stared wide-eyed at the delicate gold ring set with three tiny diamonds. On its inside was inscribed the words: *Marry me, Callum.* He stared at the ring and then at Jamie and then back at the ring again.

"Oh fuck," he said.

STOP 10: RANELAGH

Philippa and Nicola

"Please move down the tram," said the automated female voice and, as usual, no one obliged.

Philippa boarded the Luas at Beechwood with her little weekend bag, paying the fare with her Leap card. She couldn't wait to get to Nicky's and tell her about everything that had gone on in the house the night before. There had been murder in the place. Philippa had never seen anything like it. It was fucking mayhem. She'd been in her room with her glass of Friday-night wine, watching an episode of *Game of Thrones* to pass the time till Michael came to pick her up and take her out to dinner. She was engrossed in her programme when suddenly she became aware of shouting down in the front hall. She muted the sound on her little television and listened. Yes, there was definitely shouting, and it *was* coming from the front hall.

Still in her dressing-gown – she wasn't putting her new top and trousers on until the last minute in case she spilt red wine on them – which had happened before so it wasn't like she was being overly careful – she went to the stairs and peeped down. To her surprise it was Jamie – smiley, easy-going optimistic Jamie – who was doing all the shouting. He was yelling at Chris, who was standing in the hall with his coat on, looking as though he'd just come in. Chris's girlfriend Julie was sitting at the bottom of the stairs crying, while Callum was standing behind Jamie, trying to pull him away from Chris. Philippa furrowed her brow. What the *fuck* was going on here?

She'd hurried down the stairs to join her four housemates, carefully stepping around Julie at the bottom, and said, "What's up, guys? What's all the shouting about?"

"Ask *him*," Jamie replied angrily, shoving Chris in the chest so that he fell backwards against the front door.

"That one's on the house, Jamie mate," Chris warned, "but you're paying for the next one. You're getting a pasting if you try that again."

"For Christ's sake, Jamie," Philippa said, coming to stand between the two men, who were about equally matched in height and size, "what's this all about? What's Chris done?"

"*He's been having it away with Callum behind my back!*" Jamie said, glaring furiously at Chris, who glared back. "Callum's just admitted it to me. And after I've just fucking *proposed* to him and all."

Callum looked down at the ground, shamefaced, saying nothing. For the first time, Philippa noticed the little velvet ring-box in Jamie's left hand. Aghast, her hand flew to her mouth as she looked from one to the other, Jamie to Chris and back again.

"Is this true, Chris?" she asked her housemate, who just shrugged sulkily and looked away, as if it were nothing to do with him.

There was a loud sob from Julie on the stairs. Philippa

turned and looked at her properly. She was in an awful state. Tears and snot streaked her face and she looked as if she'd had the rug properly yanked out from under her. Which she had. *Chris and Callum?* Philippa was appalled. No wonder Julie was in bits. She decided to take charge of the situation.

"Right." She held out a hand to Julie. "I'm taking Julie into the kitchen to make her a hot sweet cup of tea. If you lads want to continue the argy-bargy, at least do it in the sitting-room, okay? If the neighbours hear the two of you shouting blue murder in the hall like that, they'll call the Guards and the landlord will turf us all out, okay?"

"I'm not discussing anything any more," Chris said defiantly. "I'm going upstairs for a shower."

"Oh no, you're not," Jamie said, grabbing at the sleeve of Chris's jacket. "You're staying down here so we can sort this out."

"There's nothing *to* sort out," said Chris, angrily pushing Jamie's hand away. "It only ever happened the once. I don't know why you're making such a big fucking deal out of it."

"*You liar!*" wailed Callum. "It was way more than just the once. You even said you *loved* me."

"*Oh fuck off, you whingy little faggot!*" Chris elbowed his way past the group in the hall and headed for the stairs.

Jamie made as if to pull him back.

"Let him go, Jamie," Philippa said warningly, surprised at how firm and assertive her voice sounded. "Give everyone a chance to cool down. You and Callum take the sitting-room. Go on now, away with the pair of you – *shoo!*"

To her surprise, they did what she said after a moment's hesitation. Chris disappeared off upstairs and almost immediately the little group that had been left downstairs heard the shower running. A devastated-looking Jamie went into the sitting-room, followed by Callum. Philippa closed the door behind them but then decided to leave it slightly ajar, so she could hear them in the case of further emergencies.

"Come on, Julie love," she said then, ushering the sobbing young woman into the kitchen.

She sat Julie down and set about making tea.

"Stupid Question time," Philippa said, when the two of them were sitting at the kitchen table with their hands wrapped round steaming hot mugs of tea, extra sugar lumps for Julie because sugar was what Philippa's nan always said was good for a shock. "How are you feeling?"

Julie shook her head as if in disbelief. "I don't know," she said between gulping sobs. "I just don't know. I can't believe it."

"I take it that, *erm*, you didn't know that Chris was, *um*, possibly bisexual?" Philippa's tone was gentle.

Julie shook her head vigorously, her eyes wide and drenched with tears. "No. How could I? He never mentioned it. I've never seen him so much as look at another man like – like *that*. I didn't have a clue. We were even talking about getting married and having kids together some day."

Phillipa personally thought that it was better for Julie to find these things out *before* the wedding vows were taken but she said nothing. No one, but no one, wanted to hear shit like that at a time like this. Later, much later, she might be glad of it but not now. For now, her world was in ruins and she needed someone to just be there for her and comfort her and (maybe) say what a bastard Chris was to have treated her so shabbily. (She might not be ready for that stage yet, especially if she was still in denial. That usually came a bit later and, when it did, Philippa would be ready with her denunciation of Chris the Bastard. Hell, she was already ready with that one now. She'd never really liked or trusted Chris.)

Philippa pushed the biscuit barrel towards her housemate and urged her to take one. "It's the good shit too, the custard creams," she said with a cajoling grin. "Not just the plain digestives, *haha*!"

Julie managed a watery smile and took one. Philippa took one too (just to be polite, of course), and there was a momentary silence while both women dunked the biscuits in their tea. The silence was broken by the sound of raised voices in the sitting-room.

"I'll go in to them in a minute," Philippa said. "See if poor Jamie's okay. I can't believe he actually proposed to that little weasel Callum. I've never thought Callum was good enough for our Jamie. There's something sly about him, plus he's a total user. Look at the way he's just sat on his lazy arse here for weeks on end while Jamie goes out to work and pays for everything – rent, bills, food, the works. He's even been paying for Callum's phone credit and Internet access. He told me so. Paying for Callum to sit at home wanking to porn, drinking tea and eating biscuits. Poor, poor Jamie."

Julie gulped out another sob. "I blame Callum. He led Chris astray. Chris isn't gay, or even bisexual. He's not! I know he's not. How could he be? He's been with me for four years. How could he be with me for four years and be gay and not love me?"

Maybe he's with you because you're a sweet obliging doormat who lets him wipe his feet on you, Philippa could have said but wisely refrained. It wasn't really any of her business. It was just something she'd observed since they'd all been living together in the same house. She poured more tea for Julie, waving aside the other woman's feeble protests. Irish people turn to cups of tea in a crisis, regardless of age or sex. This was one of the oldest crises in the book. More tea than usual would therefore be required.

"When do you suppose it happened?" Philippa asked as she munched enthusiastically on a custard cream. *Yummy*.

"All those days Chris was supposed to be *working from home*." Julie sounded bitter. "The bastard. He's made a proper fool out of me, hasn't he?"

"You weren't to know." Philippa was firm, hoping to forestall another bout of crying. "How could you have? Poor Julie." She reached across the table and took the other woman's hand in hers. "It must have come as a terrible shock to you."

Julie nodded fervently. "It did. We had literally just walked in the door. We hadn't even had the chance to take off our coats before Jamie came storming out of the sitting-room with Callum behind him, accusing Chris of all sorts."

"Did Chris try to deny it at all?" Philippa helped herself to another biccy. Just to keep Julie company, of course. There was nothing worse than feeling like you were the only person chowing down.

Julie shrugged. "At first, but there wasn't really much point. Jamie had already dragged the whole sorry story out of Callum. There wasn't any point really in Chris's denying anything."

Philippa shook her head in sympathy. "The bastards," she said. "Chris and Callum, I mean, not Jamie. Sorry," she added, realising that she'd just called Chris a bastard in front of Julie.

But Julie only shrugged again. "Well, it's the truth, isn't it? Chris *is* a cruel bastard, for putting me through all this trauma."

The two women sat and drank their tea in silence for a few minutes. Then they heard the sound of feet in heavy boots running down the stairs, followed by the noise immediately afterwards of the front door slamming so hard that the windows in the kitchen rattled.

Julie looked up from her tea in alarm. "*Chris!*" she shrieked. Jumping up from her seat, she bolted out into the front hall, stood there staring for a moment, then ran up the stairs and into the bedroom she shared with Chris, a worried Philippa in hot pursuit. Inside the bedroom, Julie looked around wildly, then flew to the wardrobe, flinging it open to reveal that Chris's half was empty. The same with his drawers in the big old-fashioned dresser and his half of the bedside table. His suitcase was gone from the top of the wardrobe too.

Julie threw herself down on the bed and bawled her eyes out.

"Oh shit," Philippa said.

"What's wrong?" came Jamie's voice from the doorway. He was standing there with Callum's sly little goblin face peeping out from behind him. (*That* was who Callum reminded her of, Philippa realised suddenly – the evil goblins from *Noddy* – Gobbo and Sly!)

"It looks like Chris might have done a runner, the louse." Philippa spoke quietly but Julie still heard every word and howled all the harder.

"The sneaky, cowardly little fuck!" Jamie shook his head in disbelief. "There's your big man," he said then, turning round to face the quivering Callum. "There's your big lover man for you, running away because he's too chickenshit to face up to what he's done. Why don't you run after him then, if you love him so much?"

"I don't want to run after him," Callum said sullenly. "It's *you* I love. It's *you* I want to be with. I only told you all that stuff about Chris because I didn't want there to be any secrets between us. I never had any intention of going off with him, I swear to God."

"Tell it to someone who gives a shit," Jamie said grimly, turning away from Callum in disgust and sitting down on the bed beside Julie. He stroked her long hair, wet with tears, back off her face and talked to her in soothing, gentle tones until her sobbing ceased.

Then the doorbell went and it was Michael coming to pick up Philippa, unaware that he was walking into a madhouse. Philippa flew down the stairs to let him in and quickly tell him about the situation with their friends. Michael was a decent sort of guy and Philippa had no difficulty in persuading him to cancel their dinner plans, so that she could take care of Julie and keep an eye on Jamie as well. Jamie wasn't really impulsive, or the type to do anything dodgy like taking his own life, but Philippa wasn't prepared to take any chances. Jamie had had his dreams of marriage to Callum shattered into a million pieces. She would be up all night on Suicide Watch, and not just for Jamie, either. Poor Julie was utterly crushed by Chris's cowardly absconding. Naturally, Chris's phone was switched off when Julie tried to call him. Philippa could just murder him for causing all this fucking upset, she really could.

"But it's Jamie I feel sorry for really," she told her sister Nicola now, as she sat at Nicola's huge scrubbed-pine kitchen table in her big fancy house in Ranelagh.

It was Saturday lunchtime and they'd just finished eating pizza with Nicola and Shane's kids, Kimmie-short-for-Kimberley and Little Nicky-short-for-Nicholas. The kids were now out in the massive back garden, swinging on the swings, whooping madly and running in and out of Kimmie's Wendy House as if they were being chased by demons.

"I mean, Jamie is such a sweet guy," Philippa went on, nodding in approval as Nicola, also Nicky for short but not *Little* Nicky, topped up their wineglasses. It was the weekend, Nicola's husband Shane was away in Cork on business until Sunday evening and Philippa was staying the night. It was wine o'clock in the house, in other words. "He's had some absolute disasters of relationships before he found Callum, and he really thought that Callum was The One, you know? I mean, Callum was sort of all right when he was working, but since he lost his job, well, he's been positively horrible to Jamie. Slobbing around all day is bad enough but then he was bitching and griping at Jamie as well for leaving him on his own all day. For Christ's sake, like, what the fuck was he expecting Jamie to do, pack in his job so he could sit around on his arse all day in the house keeping Callum company? Talk about unreasonable."

She was interrupted by the tumultuous arrival in the kitchen of Kimmie and Little Nicky, each as black as soot from head to foot after their turn around the garden.

"Aunty Pip, will you come and chase us?" begged seven-year-old Kimmie. She and her little brother, aged six, adored a good game of chasing.

"In a minute, sweetie. I'm just telling your mummy a story."

"Is there a pwincess in it?" Kimmie asked with keen interest.

Philippa thought for a minute. "Not really. Not as such. But it does have a nasty *ogre* in it called Callum, *with lots of big sharp pointy black teeth for eating bad children with!*" She roared and made as if to grab them both.

The two kids ran back out into the garden, screeching in terror mixed with appreciation. They also enjoyed a good scare. Philippa laughed and took another swig of her wine.

"Very nice wine, this is." She licked her lips appreciatively.

"You'll give the kids nightmares," Nicola said in tones of mild reproof.

"Ah, nonsense. Scary stories are all part of the fun of growing up. Anyway, where was I? Oh yes, Jamie. Well, I really, really hope that he kicks that Callum fella to the kerb and isn't daft enough to take the little user back. And the same goes for Julie, to be honest. Chris is super-controlling in subtle ways, so subtle that people on the outside wouldn't necessarily be able to see it but it was always there. I know that this hurts like hell for poor Julie now, but it might actually end up being the best thing that ever happened to her. I would have been afraid to leave her on her own for the weekend, only for the fact that she texted her sister and the sister's coming over this afternoon to stay the weekend with her. Jamie and Callum are still in the house too, but I don't mind telling you that I hope Callum will have packed his bags and be gone by the time I get back tomorrow. Either of his own accord or because Jamie's got the spleen to actually get rid of him. He's an excuse for a human being, that Callum."

"Good to know you're so impartial, Philly dear," Nicola said dryly.

"*Haha*," said Philippa sarcastically. She studied her older sister more carefully then and said: "Nicky, are you okay? You've hardly said a word since I got here. You've just let me prattle on for ages without saying anything, and that's not like you at all. Usually I'm trying to get words in edgeways. Is everything okay with you and Shane?"

"Me and Shane are fine. It's not that."

"*Oh-ho!*" exclaimed Philippa triumphantly. "So there *is* something. I knew it! Come on then, out with it, girl. What is it?"

"You're not to make a big huge deal out of this, Pip," warned Nicola. "I know you. That's what you always do. That's what you're like. But I really don't want you to do that this time. And you can't tell anyone either, not even Michael."

"Not even Michael? But I tell Michael everything!"

"Not this time, Pip. You've got to promise me, otherwise I'm not saying a word, okay?"

"Fine." Philippa heaved a huge dramatic sigh. "I swear, cross my heart and hope to die. So, what is it then?" She stared at her sister expectantly.

Nicola bit her lip for a moment, then she said: "This is kind of hard to talk about, Pip. I mean, it's really not me at all, all this."

"All what?" Philippa was greatly intrigued now.

"It's just . . . I think . . . I think there's someone else in the house with us."

Philippa's eyes widened. "What, you mean like a squatter or someone?"

The house was certainly big enough for a squatter to hide in unnoticed, indefinitely in fact. It was a huge old sprawling red-brick house, built late in the nineteenth century. Set well back from the road in an acre of wild garden, it had been unlived-in for several years before Shane and Nicola had come along six months ago and declared it the perfect place to bring up children. The acre of garden gave the impression of its being in the countryside, but the fact that the house was actually situated in busy little Ranelagh meant that they weren't isolated, as they might have been in the countryside. It was the perfect compromise between city and country, both Shane and Nicola had decided, and it had turned up at exactly the right time, too, just as Shane had been made a full partner in the architectural practice where he worked and so they had a little extra money to play about with. The house had cost them slightly less than they would have expected too, which was a marvellous bonus. Now, Nicola shook her head and bit her lip again.

"I don't mean a squatter. Not the human kind anyway."

Philippa's eyes widened even more. "*No way*," she breathed, awestruck. "You don't mean, like, a supernatural entity or something like that?"

Nicola shrugged. "Maybe. I can't think what else can be happening, anyway."

"*Tell. Me. Everything.*" Philippa pulled her chair up closer to her sister's and poured them each more wine.

"There's not that much to tell," Nicola said quietly. "It's more . . . like, sort of feelings I have, like feeling that there's someone standing right beside me looking over my shoulder or there's someone brushing past me, but when I go to look, there's no one there."

"Go on," Philippa urged, spellbound.

"Once or twice over the summer, not long after we'd first moved in, I actually felt a light touch on my arm when I was on my own in the house and Shane was out with the kids, but there was nobody there. Nothing but the smell of a woman's perfume, something old-fashioned and flowery and light but heavenly, really heavenly, not unpleasant at all."

"*Wow*." Philippa gazed in wonder at her sister. "Was there anything else?"

"Well," Nicola said slowly, "when I walk through the rooms, there's always this feeling of someone else being there with me, watching me. I feel like I hear someone else breathing, or sighing heavily even, as if they were sad. I see shadows where there shouldn't be any shadows and once . . . once I thought I heard someone whispering my name, but there was no one in the house but me at the time."

"Holy *fuck*, Sis!" Philippa nearly choked on her wine. "That's freakin' unbelievable. Have you told Shane?"

"*No!*" Nicola said fiercely. "And you mustn't breathe a word of it to him or to anyone else – you promised, remember?"

"I won't tell a soul, I swear! But why don't you want Shane to know? He's your husband."

"I know who my husband is, thanks," Nicola said dryly. 'But he'd only worry about my mental health, let alone my mental competence levels, if I told him. He'd think I was overdoing it with the kids and trying to get the house all straight and fixed up in time for Christmas and everything. It's only a few weeks away now. And now that he's been made a partner in the business, he needs to be able to concentrate on that for a bit while I do the house-and-kids-and-Christmas thing. We both agreed on that when he got the promotion."

"I get your point. Don't worry. I won't breathe a word to him. But what are you going to do? About your ghost, I mean?"

"So, you *do* think we've got a ghost then?"

"Without a doubt." Philippa could hardly contain her excitement. "I've seen enough horror movies to know how these things work, thank you very much."

"Oh yes," Nicky said with mock-sarcasm. "I forgot how you pretend to like horror films now, specifically to make Michael think you're a big fan of the 'genre', just like him."

"Excuse me, sister dear, but I was only pretending in the *beginning*," Philippa defended herself hotly. "I'm genuinely into them now, I'll have you know. I watch everything that's going. I actually watch more horror than Michael does these days."

"Oh, I just think it's a bit demeaning, that's all," teased Nicola, "pretending to be something you're not, just to get some guy to go out with you."

"Says the woman who faked an interest in architecture to get Shane to propose," countered Philippa. "And anyway, it worked, didn't it? For both of us."

She giggled and, seconds later, both sisters were in hysterics laughing.

When the laughing eventually stopped, Philippa said: "Right, we'd better get back to business, I suppose. What do we do about this ghost?"

"So, you'll help me then?"

"Of course I will. That's what sisters are for." On impulse, Philippa leaned over and gave Nicola a hug.

"You don't know how happy that makes me, Pip. I've felt so alone, carrying all this around with me for the last few months. I was too afraid to tell anyone in case they thought I was a mental case and packed me off to the funny farm or something."

"Well, now you've got me, so don't worry. The first thing to do is to decide what kind of ghost we're dealing with here. It's obvious, firstly, that it's a woman. Are we agreed on that? We are? Right. And she's most likely from the Victorian times, judging from her old-fashioned floral perfume and how old the house is and everything. Let's say 1880s, 1890s, right? Now, what kind of terrible tragedy might have befallen her? Let's see now. Okay, so, she might have been a governess or something who fell in love with the handsome young son of the house. She gets pregnant, he can't marry her because he's already betrothed to a rich countess or something and, anyway, our little governess is only a commoner. The son of the house can't possibly marry her so . . . *erm*, so she goes up into the attic and hangs herself from the rafters. Now she spends all eternity waiting to be reunited with the soul of her lover and their unborn child. Are there any rafters in this house, by the way? Where do people normally keep them, anyway?"

"Wow, Pip, why don't you write gothic romance mysteries instead of a magazine column on modern dating and relationships and shit? You clearly have the mindset for it," Nicola teased again.

"Don't think I haven't thought about it," replied Philippa smugly. "One day, Sis, one day. So, back to our little Victorian governess friend, then. Maybe she's looking for a replacement for the man she loved? Maybe it's Shane she's after!"

"Then why isn't she breathing and sighing on *him*, then? Why am *I* the one she contacts?"

"True, true. Wait a minute, wait a minute now, maybe it's a replacement *child* she's after, to replace the one she had who died when she hanged herself . . . ?"

"Don't even think about it," said Nicola sternly.

"Right, right," Philippa replied hurriedly, too late thinking of her little niece and nephew out in the garden playing. "You're right. it's probably not that at all. I never much cared for *The Woman in Black* anyway. All style and no substance. And it put me right off that it was Harry Potter in the lead role. I kept looking round the whole time for Ron and Hermione. Look, how's about you take me on a tour of the house? There's probably at least a half-a-dozen rooms I haven't properly explored yet. We can look for clues to the mystery."

"Okay, grand." Nicola got up from the table. "Just like we're the Five Find-Outers or the Secret Seven or the Famous Five or one of those." The sisters had cut their reading teeth on Enid Blyton.

"Exactly! And we're not forgetting *you*, Mr. Chardonnay," Philippa said fondly, grabbing up the wine bottle for the tour. We could never forget *you*, my precious darling bottle of life-improving booze."

"Let's start with the cellar," Philippa said. "You *do* have a cellar here, right? All big old houses have got to have a cellar. It's practically the law."

"Well, it's more of a basement room, really."

Nicola led her sister out of the kitchen and across the hall, to the door that opened onto a darkened staircase leading down into the bowels of the house.

"I'll just switch on the light here. This was one of the first things I made Shane do when we moved in: put in a working lightbulb here. No way was I going down into a pitch-black basement to look for the Christmas decorations or the spare portable telly."

"Quite right too," said Philippa approvingly. "Crikey, this place is a bit spooky, isn't it?"

She looked round at the enormous, mostly empty space in which she found herself. Shane and Nicky's boxes and tea-chests of spare stuff, their contents all clearly marked on the outside in felt-tipped marker pens, barely filled up a corner of the huge room. There was tons and tons of room left, to fill with practically anything they wanted.

"You could fit a small country in here, Nic. Are you just going to leave it half-empty like this?"

"Shane is thinking of making it into a sort of a man-cave for himself. Putting in a flatscreen telly and a fridge for cold beers, even a pool table for him and his mates."

"Isn't it well for some?" Philippa laughed. "Why can't *you* have it for a woman-cave, only use the fridge for wine and chocolate and to hell with the pool table?"

"It gives me the creeps down here, that's why," Nicola admitted. "I much prefer the upstairs rooms, where there's lots of light and you can look out into the garden. Down here gives me the shivers. I wouldn't want to feel, I don't know, kind of cut off from the upstairs. Down here makes me feel sort of . . . sort of *entombed*."

"Are you getting any supernatural vibes down here right now?" Philippa refilled her glass from the bottle, then took a long swig of her wine.

Nicola shook her head. "Nothing at all."

"Have you ever felt any supernatural vibes down here before?"

Again, the shaking of the head. "Nothing at all down here. I told you, Philly, I make it my business to come down here as little as possible."

"That's a shame. Basements are normally jammers with supernatural shit. And it's a shame as well that there doesn't appear to be a fruit cellar down here. That's where

Norman Bates keeps his mother, you know, when he doesn't want anyone to know that he's still got her with him. She sits all day down here just rocking, rocking, rocking away in her old rocking chair, with the dim light from the one bare bulb shining straight through her hideously empty eye sockets. *Ow!*" She screeched when Nicola punched her on the arm. "That actually hurt, you evil bitch!"

"It was meant to." Nicola turned to go back up the stairs.

In the huge sitting-room on the ground floor, the sisters stood side by side.

"Is there anyone here?" Philippa called out in what she felt was a suitably otherworldly voice *"Is there anyone there who'd like to make contact with us?* D'you sense anything, Nicky?"

Nicola shook her head. "It might be a case that whoever, or *what*ever it is, won't put in an appearance while there's the two of us here," she suggested. "It might just be me on my own she wants."

"Nonsense." Philippa started briskly pulling open the cupboards that lined the walls but found only the kids' toys, books and other random bits-and-pieces of household detritus. "Ghosts love attention. They're desperate for it, starved for it, even. Wouldn't you be if you'd been haunting a house on your own for, like, a hundred years, and then suddenly a family moved in? You'd be trying to make contact with them in every way possible."

"I suppose."

"*Helloooooooo!*" Philippa hollered, her voice echoing in the spacious room. "*Is there anybody there?*"

But her calls went unanswered.

Out in the hallway, Philippa looked up towards the sweeping staircase triumphantly. "Ah-ha! This must be the staircase where the red rubber ball from *The Changeling* comes bouncing down the stairs one step at a time, *bouncy bouncy bouncy*, to come landing ominously at George C. Scott's feet. And upstairs, one of the baths will be filling up with water of its own accord at this very moment and a secret door covered up by a bookcase or something leads the way to a hidden attic room where a child died a horrible death a hundred years ago tonight. This is probably a gruesome anniversary or something. How utterly delicious!"

She giggled, and Nicola shook her head at her sister as if to say, *Where the fuck are you getting this mad stuff from?* Out loud she said: "Gee, Sis, I hate to burst your bubble but the attic's not hidden at all. There's a perfectly good staircase leading up to it for all to see. A Stira, as a matter of fact, one of those nice handy pully-downy things you see on the telly."

"You've no imagination, you haven't," grumbled Philippa as she ran ahead of her sister up the stairs.

"Just look out the landing window there for me and tell me if the kids are okay!" Nicola called up after her as she followed.

Philippa did as she was asked. Down in the garden, Little Nicky was chasing his older sister with what looked like a big dirty stick or half a tree branch he'd found on the ground. Kimmie was shrieking her lungs out and running away as fast as her legs would carry her.

"They're fine," Philippa said and hurried on.

Up in the attic, which was enormous and just as easy to access as Nicola had said, Philippa poked into all the various corners and nooks and crannies. She shrieked when suddenly she spied the unmistakable black outline of a female figure standing silently by the one small window.

"Ah Jaysis, it's only a mannequin with a sheet over it!" Philippa sighed with relief when she investigated closer.

"For my dressmaking business," Nicola said. "That's if I ever have time to pick it up again."

"These things are as creepy as fuck." Philippa pulled the sheets off no fewer than four mannequins similarly draped in sheets. "Why don't you throw them away, or give them to the local Perverts' Society? I'm sure they'd be glad of them as, you know, sort of instant girlfriends?"

"And what about my dressmaking business?" demanded Nicola.

"What about it? When was the last time you made a dress?"

"When was the last time I had the time?" Nicola sounded cross. "I've been slightly busy, remember, having two very active kids, moving house and supporting my husband's career?"

"Keep your hair on, Nic," Philippa said. "No one's getting at you."

They left the attic floor and went down to the master bedroom on the floor below.

"Now, this is more like it," Philippa said. "I can sense a definite cold spot here."

"Sorry, the window behind you is open," Nicola pointed out.

"So it is." Philippa clucked in disappointment. "Well, let's go and check out the kids' bedrooms then, see if anyone's at least written *'GET OUT'* in bloody capital letters on the walls or sent down an infestation of flies."

"Pip, would you *mind* not talking like that about my kids' bedrooms, please?"

"Right, sorry." Philippa flapped absentmindedly at her sister. "Oh look, one dead fly anyway," she said hopefully, pointing to the deceased insect on the landing windowsill. "The start of an infestation, maybe?"

"One fly does not an infestation make, Pip."

"Spoilsport. Wait a minute. I think I can hear some sort of ghostly music."

"Sorry, that's just my ringtone." Nicola pulled her mobile phone out of the back pocket of her jeans. "Shane loves that song. It's 'Stairway to Heaven' by Led Zeppelin. Hi, sweetheart," she said into her phone then, clearly talking to Shane.

Philippa wandered away to give the couple some privacy to talk. In the first spare room she placed her wineglass and the bottle on a bedside table, then looked through all three spare rooms, opening wardrobes and poking into dresser drawers, all mostly empty except for some rather vintage-looking striped shelf paper, the kind housewives used to love to line their drawers with. *Haha, line their drawers!* She sniggered, the wine gone straight to her head as usual.

After about five minutes, she felt Nicola tap her lightly on the arm from behind.

"Right, Sis – let's see if –" she began, but there was no one there.

The room was empty save for herself, and all was quiet except for the lightest of light sighs, a mere intake of breath really, but Philippa heard it clearly in the silence of the room. Genuinely spooked, she hurried back to the master bedroom, where Nicola was just hanging up after her chat with Shane.

"I think I've just met your ghost," she told her sister in a rush. "Well, at least we haven't been formally introduced but she – if it *is* a she – touched my arm and sighed at me in that spare bedroom over there just now."

Nicola stared at her. "Are you serious? You're absolutely sure?"

Philippa nodded. "I'm as sure as I *can* be," she said grimly. "Someone – or some*thing* – that I thought was you just touched me on the arm back there and breathed on me."

"What are we going to do?"

Philippa shrugged. "This is the point in the plot where we're supposed to high-tail it to the local library and demand to see copies of their old newspapers on microfilm or microfiche or whatever they call it nowadays. Then we'd find out that someone died horribly here in a fire that once burnt the house to the ground back in 1899 or something, and that they've been haunting the place ever since, trying to find peace."

"I kind of wish they'd find peace somewhere else." Nicola sounded decidedly tetchy. "I'm really not sure I like the idea of sharing my new home with a ghost for the rest of my days. And what does it want, anyway? I mean, it's all very well you saying that it wants to find peace, but how does it *get* this peace? And what exactly are we supposed to do to help it?"

"We could hold a séance," Philippa said excitedly. "Have you got a ouija board?"

"Hang on, it's in the kitchen drawer with the Sellotape and the pens with no tops, I'll just get it," replied Nicola sarcastically. "Of *course* I don't have a bloody ouija board, Pip. Why would I? It's not exactly the kind of thing you pick up in the pound shop next to the birthday candles and the baby wipes."

"Ah well. It doesn't really matter anyway, seeing as neither of us is able to use one. Maybe we could hold a séance without one. Like, with just ourselves and a few candles, maybe some spooky music. Once the kids are in bed, of course."

"Speaking of the kids, can you have a look out that window there? See if they're okay? You're nearest."

Philippa craned her neck out the window and had a look. Little Nicky had by now tied his loudly protesting older sister to a tree and was threatening her with the big dirty tree branch. His mouth was open in a soundless whoop of triumph. It was starting to rain and the sky was black and heavy with huge moisture-pregnant clouds.

"I already told you, they're perfectly fine," Philippa said. "Shall we go and look for candles, then? And is there any more wine?"

It was late in the evening now and the rain had been falling steadily for over an hour. The wind was starting to pick up too. *Strictly Come Dancing* was on the television in the sitting room and a dinner of spaghetti bolognese with a side-salad and garlic bread had been cooked by Nicola (with some 'help' from a tipsy Philippa) and wolfed down by everyone.

On the huge comfy sitting-room couch, wineglass in hand, Philippa was saying: "And I love Michael dearly, of course I do. I've known that pretty much from the moment I met him. The thing is, he's not very open or forthcoming about his emotions and I've got this awful feeling that if I tell him outright that I love him, he won't be able to say it back and he'll just say 'thanks' or something horribly non-committal like that and I'll be, like, totally fucking crushed. Like, I'll never be able to lift my stupid fucking head up off the ground again for embarrassment, d'you know what I mean?"

"I know what you mean," replied Kimmie solemnly. "But I think you're not giving Michael enough cwedit here. I think if you talk to him honestly about how you feel, he might supwise you."

"D'you really think so?" Philippa asked her niece hopefully, just as Nicola entered the room with a tray of tea and biscuits for after their meal. "Ah, good woman yourself! I see you've got a ton of candles for later." Philippa gave her sister a knowing wink when she saw what else was on the tray.

"It's not just for the séance, Pip. The weather's turned really bad out there. It's working itself up into a right old storm. It even said on the radio that there might be power cuts in parts of Leinster." Nicola settled herself on the couch and poured the tea from the big teapot. "That's us, by the way," she added, handing Philippa a mug of tea.

"This house wouldn't by any chance be built on an Indian burial ground, would it, Sis?" Philippa asked her sister suddenly. "Because if so, that would explain a lot."

"In Ranelagh, Dublin? I doubt it."

"*Hmm*, I suppose you're right there." Then: "Wait a minute. Would it have been a lunatic asylum at any point, d'you know? Or a prison or even a workhouse or a fanny-waxing salon? Anywhere there might once have been tremendous suffering, you know?"

"I don't know the history of the house, Pip."

"Yes, sadly, that's where the library's old newspapers would come in handy, if we had access to them, that is." Philippa stroked an imaginary beard thoughtfully, much to Kimmie's amusement. "Is the local library still open?"

"At ten to eight on a Saturday night? Not a chance."

"No harm. I'm sure the power of our own imaginations will work just as well. We can *imagine* what might've happened here, can't we?"

"Would you mind not imagining it in front of the kids?" Nicola heaved a sleepy Little Nicky, surprisingly hefty for a six-year-old, up on to her lap. "Remember, little pitchers have big ears." She nodded in Kimmie's direction. "And, speaking of which, would you please watch your language around the kids? They're picking up all sorts of filth from their Auntie Pip, who's supposed to be setting a good example to them."

"Yeah, yeah, sorry," said Philippa, flapping her hand in assent with her mouth full of biscuit.

"I dwew some little pitchers in school yesterday," Kimmie said, her mouth also full of biscuit, "but none of them had ears."

"What was in your pitchers?" Philippa asked her keenly, before adding in an excited aside to Nicola: "We could be on to something here, Sis. Kids in horror films are always drawing pictures of the ghosts that are intruding on their families."

"I'll go and get them," said Kimmie happily.

A minute later she skipped back into the sitting-room, clutching a sheaf of papers which she handed to Philippa, who was already wearing her Proud Aunty Pip face in readiness.

"Aw, aren't these marvellous?" she cooed as she quickly

leafed through them. "We must stick all these lovely dwawings, *erm*, I mean *drawings,* up on the fridge . . ."

Then suddenly her expression changed in mid-leaf.

"Who the fuck's the guy in this pitcher?" she demanded of her niece.

"*Language, Pip!*" Nicola expostulated, shaking her head in disapproval.

"That's Michael, of course," said Kimmie. "*Your* Michael."

"I can see *that*. You've written his name over his head there. But what's this he's doing? And who's that beside him?"

"He's getting married to that girl," Kimmie said, as if it were obvious.

"And why am I not in this pitcher?" Philippa said.

"You *are*," Kimmie insisted. "That's you crying in the corner there."

"What the fuck?" Philippa glared at her sister. "Have you ever known her to be psychic?"

Nicola shrugged. "Not especially. Although, there was this one time . . ."

"What one time?" Philippa looked alarmed.

"Well," said Nicola slowly, as if trying to remember, "there was this one time when I lost my purse with quite a lot of money in it. Shane thought I'd spent the money, but I hadn't. I was really upset with him for thinking that. I turned our old house upside-down looking for it. I'd pretty much given up on it when Kimmie just walks into my bedroom where I'm sitting on the bed crying about it and she tells me that it's up on top of the wardrobe. And, sure enough, it is. I'd put it there for safe-keeping and forgotten about it. And high up enough and far back enough so that neither she nor Little Nicky would have been able to climb up to see it there – and why would they do that anyway? She wasn't able to remember how she knew where the purse was, so we had to just let it go."

"Sister dear," said Philippa through gritted teeth, holding out one of the Little Pitchers to Nicola, "this is a pitcher – a picture – of my boyfriend Michael, *my* Michael, getting married to someone else. Excuse me if I'd like to know where Kimmie got the idea from. I mean, has Michael been talking to you, or to Kimmie, or what?"

"Of course he hasn't. We've never even seen him except for the times you've been with him, like the times you've brought him over here."

"Then why the feck is she drawing pitchers of him and some woman? What's been putting that in her head?"

"Mawia told me," Kimmie said complacently.

"Mawia? Who's Mawia?" said Philippa.

"She means 'Maria'." Nicola leaned forward to put a protective hand on Kimmie's shoulder.

"Well then, who's Mawia? *Erm*, I mean Maria?" Philippa directed her question at Kimmie.

"She's the woman who lives in our first-floor bathwoom," said Kimmie.

"Are you absolutely positive we should be doing this?" stage-whispered Nicola.

It was nearly eleven o'clock. The storm was in full spate outside. The lights had been flickering on and off all over the house the whole evening. Nicola and Philippa had amassed a little collection of candles, matches and a couple of flashlights in case of the power-failure which now seemed likely, if not inevitable.

The kids had insisted on not being put to bed until

after the *X Factor* live show, even though they were both fast asleep on the couch before the fourth act – a middle-aged *'Overs'* lady of stout proportions, murdering Cilla Black's 'Anyone Who Had a Heart', much to the audience's amusement. (The older ladies were always the first to go home, Philippa thought. Society had no use for them, except for advertising anti-ageing creams, and seemingly television talent shows hadn't either.) The kiddies were in bed now, clutching teddies and deep in Dreamland. Philippa had been inclined to quiz Little Kimmie at greater length and in infinitely more detail about this 'Mawia' person and why she had told Kimmie to draw Philippa's boyfriend marrying another woman, a woman with very short hair like a boy's who definitely wasn't Philippa. Michael didn't even like short hair on women. Philippa was absolutely certain of that. He was always running his fingers through her long luxuriant chestnut locks and saying how gorgeous they looked and felt to the touch and how much he loved women with really long hair like hers. But Nicola, ever the protective mother, had put the kybosh on any further quizzing of Kimmie, who in any case had answered Philippa's frantic questions with only a maddeningly enigmatic smile and a shrug of her shoulders.

Now the two women were installed upstairs in the first-floor bathroom, ready to hold their séance, the séance to which Nicola hadn't yet quite reconciled herself.

"Some things it's better not to know, surely?" she kept insisting.

She hadn't even wanted to go into the big old bathroom on the first floor where the kids had their baths every night. There was a bathroom on each of the four floors of the house, and en suites in the master bedroom and in two of the guest bedrooms. Shane and Nicola had the en suites installed themselves for convenience and comfort. Tonight, Philippa had to enter the first-floor bathroom by herself first, just to make sure that this 'Mawia' person was nowhere to be seen. Only then would the nervous Nicola agree to go in herself and help Philippa set up for the séance.

Now Nicola said: "Would you still be doing this if Kimmie hadn't shown you that picture she dwew – I mean, drew – of Michael marrying that other woman?"

"Of course I would," said Philippa staunchly. "You asked me to help you with your ghost, and séances are the only proper way to flush out a ghost. If you'll excuse the bathroom pun."

She laughed but it wasn't a laugh of amusement, it was too forced for that. Nicola reached out and put her hand on her sister's, squeezing it a little in what she hoped was a comforting way. Nicola knew that Philippa adored Michael and was now terribly worried about Kimmie's drawing, although she was trying to hide it behind a front of bravado. Before Michael, she'd been single for a whopping four years while she tried to get over a break-up with a guy who she'd also adored, but he'd been a cheating rat bastard who'd made shite of Philippa's loving heart which, in Nicola's opinion, she gave too fast and too freely, leaving herself open to being hurt, which happened pretty much every time. Nicola desperately didn't want the same thing to happen now with Philippa and Michael. She knew how much Philippa loved him and, in fairness to the guy, he'd always struck Nicola as a decent sort, friendly, generous and good-looking, but not so good-looking that you'd worry about leaving him alone with other females. That was very important in a boyfriend.

"You shouldn't set too much store by Kimmie's drawing," Nicola said now. "Shure, for God's sake, she once drew me and Shane as spider people, with eight hairy legs each and a load of googly eyes, and that never happened, did it? We never turned into spider people, scuttling around the place scaring people like the guys in those D-movies you're always watching to impress Michael."

"B-movies," Philippa corrected automatically. "And I don't only watch them to impress Michael. I actually enjoy them for themselves now."

She was never too downhearted to correct someone if they were wrong about something.

Nicola, who'd made the little mistake accidentally-on-purpose to rouse her sister to something like her usual animation, breathed an inner sigh of relief.

Then Philippa piped up: "Yes, well, maybe, but then there was that time she drew a pair of tits on the postman and a few weeks later he knocked in to say he was going off for a sex-change and you'd be getting a new guy for a few weeks, and when he came back to work he was Lucille instead of Larry, or whatever his name was. We were both surprised, you and me, that the Post Office apparently had such an enlightened take on modern sexuality, remember? I've only just remembered it myself."

"I'll give you that," conceded Nicola reluctantly. "But just to add that she's wrong as often as she's right, so you'd be better off not paying any attention to that silly drawing and just getting on with your life as usual, as if you'd never seen it."

"That's easy for you to say. But it's not *Shane* in the

picture buggering off and marrying a woman with short hair which, by the way, I know for a fact Michael doesn't like." She knew she'd said this already but it was important, wasn't it? Well, wasn't it? Right now, it felt like all she had to hold on to.

"Well, there you are then." Nicola's tones of fake heartiness sounded hollow even to her own ears. "It can't be right, so. Just forget about it for now and put it behind you. Let's just get on with what we've come up here to do, will we? What are we meant to be doing, anyway?"

Nicola was well used to employing distraction as a technique to prevent her kids from killing each other on rainy days. She was pleased to see now that it worked successfully on adult sisters as well. Philippa seemed to give herself a mental shake and to perk up a bit.

They were both sitting cross-legged on the bathroom floor, with the blinds tightly drawn against the storm, the main light on and about two dozen fat *and* skinny candles lit and scattered around the place, mostly standing in empty jam-jars that Nicola, typical little housewife that she was, would clean and keep after use in case they ever 'came in handy' for anything. And now look at them, coming in handy all over the shop! They had their wine with them too, of course. It was always wine o'clock when the two sisters got together. Philippa, the 'expert' on séances because she'd seen more horror films than Nicola, had drawn a circle on the floor with chalk nicked from the kids' toybox. Inside the circle she'd drawn one of those pentagram thingies. Nicola didn't know what it meant but it looked really authentic and impressive and occult-y. Both of them were seated inside the circle because they'd be safe that way, Philippa had said. The circle would protect them from any harm or evil that might threaten to befall them. Nicola didn't know who (or what) might be wishing harm on them but she was glad of the safety of the circle, nonetheless, and of her sister's close proximity.

Now, Philippa said in her sort of solemn, otherworldly voice: "*Is there anyone there? Can anyone hear me? Do you wish to communicate at all? Speak to us if you're there?*"

Nicola spoiled the effect somewhat by sniggering.

Philippa glared at her before going on, in the same otherworldly type of voice: "*We wish you no harm, spirit, if you're there, okay? We just want to get to know you, that's all. Are you there, spirit? Give us a sign if you are. Any sign will do. We're not fussy. Flush the toilet if you like or run one of the bath taps. Or even blow out the candles.*"

Nicola snorted with laughter.

"Oh, well, if you're not taking this seriously –" Philippa began.

The overhead light went out and they both screamed.

"It's just a power cut, Nic, nothing to worry about."

Philippa's voice was awfully shaky in the semi-darkness. It sounded to her sister as if she didn't really mean what she'd said.

"But what if it's the sign you were asking for?" Nicola started to get to her feet. "I'd better go check on the kids, see if the lights are out all over the house."

"You can't leave the sanctity of the circle! It will mean terrible danger for both of us! You could even get us both killed!"

"I'll only be a minute."

She disappeared for a few moments.

When she returned, she said, "The kids are fine, but the lights are out all over the house. It's a power cut all right."

"Of course it's a power cut, because of the storm," said Philippa crossly. "Now can you please get back in the sanctity of the circle so that we can continue with the bloody séance?"

Nicola giggled as she lowered herself awkwardly back into the circle with her wineglass.

"*Spirit, we know you have suffered –*" began Philippa earnestly again.

"How do we know that?" Nicola sounded intrigued. "How do we know she's suffered?"

"Well, she's a ghost, isn't she?" snapped Philippa. "It stands to reason that she must have suffered something in her lifetime. At the very least, she's suffered death, hasn't she? That's a form of suffering, isn't it?"

"She might have died peacefully in her sleep, mightn't she?" Nicola was becoming argumentative now. It often happened that way when she was drinking. She'd argue the toss about everything and anything. "That's the way I'd like to go, not knowing anything about it."

"If she died peacefully in her sleep," an exasperated Philippa said loudly, "then would you mind telling me why she's haunting your upstairs jacks a hundred-plus years later?"

Nicola had no answer to this.

Philippa made a 'humph' sound and then continued in her otherworldly voice: "*Spirit, we come in peace! We bring you wondrous offerings of, erm, soap and shower-gel and, erm, some lovely face-flannels and loo roll if you will only reveal yourself to us and tell us your terrible story of suffering and pain.*"

"I'm not sure I want to hear a terrible story of suffering and pain while I'm sitting in this awkward bloody cross-legged position," Nicola grumbled. "My legs are feckin' killing me. I'm too old for sitting on floors. Couldn't you just ask her for the abridged version? Or maybe we could hear the story in instalments?"

Philippa pointedly ignored her sister's interjection. *"Spirit, I ask you again, will you reveal yourself to us? We promise you that no harm will come to you if you will only give us a sign that you hear us. Give us a sign, oh spirit! Don't be shy. Ah, go on, please! We'll be your friends!"*

The candles guttered and went out, but not before they'd revealed a huge black shape, which definitely hadn't been there before, in the open doorway of the first-floor bathroom.

Both women screamed.

STOP 11: CHARLEMONT

Michael and Melissa

Michael jumped on the Luas in town. Charlemont was his destination today but, if there was time afterwards, and it was a big if, he might just take the Luas to Beechtown, to the house Philippa shared with her friends. He needed to spend some quality time with her and, as soon as the funeral was out of the way, he intended to do just that.

He watched as a tall, dark-haired guy seated across from him tried to pick up a good-looking Spanish or perhaps Brazilian woman who was sitting beside him. The girl was laughing, obviously flattered by the man's intentions but not really taking the dark-haired sleazebag in the long dark coat seriously, maybe because she could clearly see the wedding ring on one of his long, tanned fingers. Michael certainly could, anyway. It stood out a mile. The guy was nuts if he didn't think that other people could see it too. What a jerk, decided Michael idly, his thoughts immediately dismissing the other man and sliding back to the night before last when he'd stopped off at Philippa's sister's huge old house in Ranelagh during the storm, and had scared the living shite out of them by suddenly appearing in the darkened bathroom doorway unannounced.

It had been a desperately stormy night and, on his way home from the hospice, he'd decided to call in at the house to check on the two women, who he'd known were alone there with the children for the weekend. Nicola's husband Shane had gone off to Cork for two days on business, which apparently he did fairly often, and Philippa would frequently go and stay with her sister and her little niece and nephew to keep them company at these times.

Michael still wasn't sure what exactly had been going on in the house when he'd reached it and found the lights off all over the big, sprawling building. That much he'd been kind of expecting anyway, the bit about the lights being off, because there were power cuts all over the city because of the storm, which had been quite a significant one, enough to warrant its being given a woman's name anyway. There were numerous trees down in the city and the Electric Ireland lads were still working around the clock trying to restore power to all the places that had lost it. After knocking on the front door and ringing the bell for several minutes and getting nowhere, he'd tried one of the front sitting-room windows, not really expecting it to be unlocked, and then climbed inside the house sharpish, out of the storm, when he'd found that it was. What the feck were Nicola and Philippa thinking of, to leave it unlocked like that? They must have been distracted indeed to commit such a dangerous oversight. It was lucky that it had been just himself trying to gain access to the place at eleven o'clock at night, in the middle of a raging storm, and not some mad axeman from a horror movie or something.

The big old house had been as spooky as hell in the dark, straight out of a horror film with the thunder crashing and the lightning flashing outside, and enough rain to nearly wash the whole place away in a mudslide. Michael had wandered through the downstairs of the house, calling out the two women's names, but there'd been no answer. Up he'd gone then to the first floor where he'd found them in a bathroom of all places, both squiffy and huddled together on the floor surrounded by candles. After shrieking with horror when he'd first appeared silently in the open doorway, they'd both flung themselves at him and begged him to stay the night, or at least until the lights came back on, which they hadn't done for some hours. They'd been rather close-mouthed, the pair of them, regarding exactly what they'd been doing on the bathroom floor in the middle of the night, surrounded by candles and sitting in what had looked to him suspiciously like a pentagram. He'd seen enough of them in the horror films he loved to know what they looked like and what they were generally used for, and he knew that Philippa did too. When he asked them if they'd been holding a séance and why, they said they were doing it for a laugh. They weren't laughing, though – in fact they looked terrified. He felt there was a good bit more than that to it. Maybe it was better not to know. At any rate, he wasn't in the headspace just then to go there. If Philippa wanted to tell him of her own accord at some stage, well then, that was fair enough.

He'd gone to bed with Philippa then in one of the guest bedrooms, after first making sure that the house was properly locked up and that Nicola and the kids were safe and tucked up for the night, and they'd made fast, urgent love which had been good (oh, so good!) for both of them. He'd fallen into a dead sleep after that, the strain of the last few days beginning to tell on him at last.

The morning after, he'd headed off pretty much straight after breakfast, promising to call Philippa when he had the chance. She and Nicola had been giggling and whispering together like schoolgirls and seemingly they hadn't at all minded his nipping off early. Clearly they had stuff to talk about that didn't concern him, which was fair enough. After all, he had some business of his own to take care of.

Michael had gone straight back across town to the hospice, only to find that Melissa had died in the night, barely an hour or two after he'd left her, in fact. They hadn't called him because they'd known he was going home to sleep and they hadn't wanted to disturb him. The single roar of pain he'd let out at the bitter irony of this piece of spectacular mistiming said it all. For the last two or three weeks, he'd spent every moment he could at Melissa's bedside. He'd taken special leave from work 'on compassionate grounds' and he'd messed Philippa about a fair bit too, seeing her for only a few hours at a time but not being able to explain to her the real reason *why*. He'd pleaded tiredness, stress, pressure of work, everything he could think of, just to keep on juggling his relationship with Philippa on top of everything else, and so far it seemed to be working. She'd noticed he was absent more, that he was distracted and constantly yawning, and once, to his eternal shame, he'd been so tired and emotional he'd even become tearful. He'd had to lie through his teeth that time and say he had a toothache. He'd been ashamed about having to tell her an outright lie, but what was he supposed to do? Tell her the truth? He couldn't do that. He couldn't just sit down beside her and take her hand in his and say, '*Oh, by the way, Philippa honey, the reason*

I've been missing so much over the last few days is because Melissa, the real love of my life and I really do mean that, has come home to Ireland to die of cervical cancer and I've got to be there for her as much as I can because I let her down once and I can't ever do that again.' Oh yeah. That would go down really well with Philippa. Wouldn't it just.

He sat on the Luas now and wondered what Philippa would say if she knew that three days before, he, Michael Redmond, had married Melissa Creighton while she lay in her bed in the hospice, a brightly coloured scarf wrapped round her delicate naked head. The priest, to give him his due, had performed the service quickly and efficiently so as not to overtax the patient and, even though Melissa had drifted off to sleep towards the end of it, she had done so with Michael's ring finally on her finger and a quiet smile on her face. She'd looked happy and, to Michael, that was worth the price of a thousand wedding rings. He'd been glad he'd asked her to marry him, and that he'd finally done the right thing after all these years. It made the situation somewhat more bearable, that at least she'd died as his wife. But why, oh why, had he left her the other night to go and check on Philippa? Because he'd felt sure that Melissa had a few more days left, that's why, he reflected bitterly now. And he'd been wrong, as he'd been wrong about so many things before. Well, he was a gobshite, that much he'd always known. He'd been a gobshite even as far back as those days with Melissa, when he'd refused to marry her because he was a stupid cowardly prick who was afraid of commitment. He'd give anything now for the chance to commit to her for life. Strange that he wanted that now, when all chances of achieving it were long past. Life was funny like that. Yeah, he thought angrily now, it was funny like a hole in the head was funny.

"*Please move down the tram,*" said the automated female voice.

He closed his eyes as the Luas chugged softly onwards and thought back to the time it had all first gone wrong for them.

They'd been together only about a year when Melissa told him that she was pregnant. They already both knew they loved each other and so it wasn't a problem. In fact, at the time it was the icing on the cake. Together, they moved into a grotty little flat in Rathmines where they had to share a bathroom with another couple who lived across the hall. It wasn't ideal, but they were young, fresh out of college, and they made the best of it. The landlord had specifically stated that no children or pets were allowed, so they kept Melissa's pregnancy from him when he called in for the rent. Michael would arrange to be there to give him the money or Melissa, if she had no choice but to meet him on rent-day, would wear a big heavy jumper to conceal her burgeoning bump. Michael had an internship at an advertising agency, the exact way he'd been hoping to start his career in advertising, and Melissa worked as an illustrator for a small but extremely popular and busy publisher of children's books. They were both doing what they wanted to do, they were in love and they were having a baby together. The world was theirs for the taking.

"What will we call her?" Melissa had said to him one night, when they were snuggled up in bed together after a frugal couples-starting-out-together dinner of instant noodles cooked on the hotplate and a few straggly-looking green vegetables, purchased at half-price because they were past their best.

"I think you mean what will we call *him*, surely?" Michael replied with a smug grin.

"Well, him *or* her. I have a name in mind if it's a girl, but only if you like it too, of course."

"Come on, then, out with it." He stroked her bump under her peach-coloured nightie. "What is it? Let me have it."

"It's not a bomb, silly! It's a name for a baby," Melissa giggled. "If you must know, it's Eugenia. After my grandmother who died when I was four. You know, my mum's mum?"

Michael considered it for a minute. "Eugenia Redmond, I like it. Of course, you *do* know that the other kids in school will knock seven shades of shite out of her for having such a posh fancy name?"

But Melissa was staring at him now. "You said Eugenia *Redmond*," she said quietly.

"Did I?" Michael sounded surprised. "I don't remember."

"That's *your* name," Melissa said. "Does that mean that you want her to have your name?"

Michael, in a hole now and playing for time, stretched, pretended to yawn and idly scratched his armpits. "Well, I don't mind what name she has," he said casually. "What does it matter whether it's Redmond or Creighton on the birth certificate? That's only a piece of paper, isn't it? We'll know she's ours and that's all that matters. And anyway," he added lightly, "we don't even know what sex it is yet. It could be a boy for all we know, and then where would you be with your Eugenia, *huh?* *Huh?* Where would you be then, *huh?*"

He tickled her under her arms because he knew that that was where she was the most ticklish. She giggled as a natural reflex, but he could sense the disappointment washing off her in waves. She wanted the baby to have Michael's name and, by extension, she wanted to have it for herself too. Michael wasn't thick. He'd known what she meant all right. She wanted them to get married. An awkward silence ensued after the giggling and tickling, during which Michael yawned theatrically, stretched again and turned over, mumbling something about having an early start in the morning.

"Night-night then, honey," he said with his back to her, in a jollier tone than he was feeling. In fact, he felt like a total heel but he also knew that he was unwilling to do anything to rectify the situation. In that case, what was left to do but go to sleep?

After a short hesitation, she whispered in the dark: "Goodnight, then."

And that had been that, for the moment at least.

The baby was born, and it was a girl, so they called her Eugenia. She was a beautiful, happy sunny-tempered baby, seeming to combine the best of her two parents' personality traits. They moved in with Melissa's mother, May, because they could no longer hide from their landlord the fact that they were parents. Melissa's mother, a widow, was glad of the company. Melissa gave up her job at the publisher's to look after Eugenia full-time, but when the child was about six months old she began accepting commissions from them to work on book illustrations from home. Michael, who was himself busy at that time Getting Ahead In Advertising, said he didn't mind her taking on the work if she thought she could manage it. Melissa said she was sure that she could manage it as well as all the baby stuff and so that was what happened. When Eugenia was two-going-on-three and it was time to start putting her name down for various schools in the area of Dublin where they lived, the subject of marriage came up again. Both parents had put their names down on the child's birth certificate but, since they weren't married, Eugenia had her mother's surname.

"I feel awkward about the two of us, you and me, having different surnames on these school application forms," Melissa said carefully one night. "It looks, well, kind of bad."

Both Eugenia and Melissa's mother had gone up to bed, and Melissa and Michael were alone in the kitchen drinking steaming mugs of hot chocolate before going up to bed themselves. Michael was working on an advertising campaign for a brand of washing powder and he had a few pages of scribbled notes, which he was inclined to dismiss as rubbish, laid out in front of him on the kitchen table. Melissa was standing at the ironing board, pressing his work shirts and a few little things of Eugenia's.

"What do you mean, it looks bad?" Michael barely looked up from his scribbling. The warning bells were ringing in his head loud and clear. He knew that she could tell by his voice and the way his hackles had seemed to rise suddenly, like a cat's, that he was on his guard, on the defensive. He always was when this subject came up. It made her tentative around him, the way she was being now. It made her tiptoe around him like he could go off at any moment, like an explosion waiting to happen. Though he knew he was possibly being unreasonable, this irritated the hell out of him.

"I just mean, it looks like Eugenia, well, it kind of

looks like she doesn't come from a . . . a proper family."

"A proper family?" echoed Michael, annoyed. "What do you mean by that? She's got a mother and a father and three grandparents who love her. If that's not a proper family, I don't know what is."

"I don't mean she's not loved. Of course I don't mean that," Melissa said, flustered. "I just mean that . . . that it would be so much easier, all this school stuff, if . . . if we all had the same name. That's all I mean."

"Easier for whom?" Michael really sounded cross now and he could see that Melissa was nervous. This was such a touchy subject with him.

"For, well, for Eugenia when she goes to school," she said lightly.

"How is it going to make a difference to a four-year-old what her last name is?"

"I don't know," said Melissa, close to tears. "I just mean it would be handier from . . . from the point of view of all these school application forms if we . . . if we all had the same surname."

"Look, Melissa," he said wearily, running his fingers through his hair until it stood on end, "my parents got married and had the same name, and now they're split up and my mother's back to calling herself by her bloody maiden name. Your parents were married and now your dad's dead and your mum's on her own. How has it made a blind bit of difference to any one of them what their bloody last names are? How will it make a blind bit of difference to Eugenia?"

"It . . . it won't, I suppose," whispered Melissa, her face wet with tears.

"Exactly," snapped Michael. "Now, if you don't mind,

I've got a logo and a slogan to come up with by tomorrow for a stupid fucking washing powder that'll probably make people come out in fucking hives when they wash their clothes in it, and your constant wittering on is doing my head in. Call Eugenia whatever you want on those bloody forms. Call her Redmond, Creighton or fucking McGillycuddy's Reeks-Supercalifragilisticexpialidocious for all I care, but just leave me out of it and give me five minutes of bloody peace and quiet to work in, will you?"

Melissa unplugged the iron, picked up her little bundle of clothes and fled.

When Eugenia Creighton was four years old, two or three months before she was due to start at the local primary school, Michael received a rare phone call from his child's mother in work.

"I think it's your, *erm* – Melissa," said the secretary he shared with four other advertising executives. She transferred the call to Michael's line. "I think she's upset or something," she added, before turning back to her work.

Michael picked up his phone. "Honey?" he said, his mind still on the account he was currently working on. There was only a noise that sounded like crying on the line. "Honey?" he said again. "Melissa, is that you? Lissy?"

He could only make out the words 'Eugenia', 'rash' and 'hospital'.

"Hospital? For a *rash*? Don't be ridiculous, Lissy. You don't take a kid to hospital just because she has a *rash*. What are you talking about? Slow down now. I can't make you out properly. What is it? What exactly's happened?"

Then she said a word that made his blood run cold.

He listened intently for a moment or two, then he said,

"Right. I'm leaving now. I'll be there as soon as I can, okay?"

He put the phone down, had a quick word with his colleague at the desk next to him and left the office. He arrived at the hospital to find his daughter critically ill with meningitis. Melissa was in a state of shock, her widowed mother May in tears beside her, holding her hand.

When Eugenia died the next day, Melissa went into hysterics and had to be sedated. The days before the funeral were the worst of Michael's life. Friends and family came and went and even stayed overnight at Melissa's mother's house, but nothing any of them said or did could ease the feeling that he was wading through a nightmare. Melissa refused point-blank to speak to him, but then she was zoned out on the sedatives they were giving her, so he couldn't blame her for that. On the day of the funeral, she stood on the opposite side of the grave from Michael, heavily drugged and propped up on either side by two of her mother's sisters, small bird-like women who were the spitting image of May Creighton, with twin expressions of grim determination on their faces. He was glad that they were there for Melissa and her mother, since he realised he had little enough to offer them himself at the moment. When his eyes met Melissa's across their daughter's newly dug grave, she looked right through him as if he wasn't there. It gave him a weird feeling, but he still put it down to the fact that she was medicated up to the eyeballs. She wasn't herself; not that anyone was likely to be themselves after what had happened. Their beautiful good-natured little daughter dead of a dreadful disease, just weeks before she was due to embark on the first leg of her school journey? It made no sense to Michael. How could it? It was wrong, a terrible mistake, a wrong thing that wasn't meant to happen, that shouldn't have happened. No, it was no wonder that Melissa wasn't herself, that she was looking at him, looking *through* him, like he wasn't even there.

But, a week or two after the funeral, a horrible couple of weeks of strained or non-existent conversations, during which he'd felt uncomfortably unwelcome in the house, he arrived home from work to find Melissa packing her things in the bedroom she shared with him. He couldn't have been more surprised if he'd found her packing *his* things.

"What's going on, Lissy?" he asked nervously.

"What does it look like?" she said in a tone of artificial brightness.

"*Erm*, it looks like you're packing your, *erm*, things."

"Got it in one, Michael *Redmond*." There was no mistaking the savage sarcasm in her voice. "Go to the top of the class. Give that man a fucking medal."

"Lissy, what's wrong?" She glared at him. "Apart from the obvious," he added hurriedly.

"Nothing's wrong, Michael *Redmond*." She continued to haphazardly cram her clothes, books and bits-and-bobs into a suitcase. "What could possibly be wrong? Our daughter, yours and mine, Eugenia *Creighton*, is dead and buried and nothing will bring her back. Oh, and guess what?" she went on, still with the same manic, rather frightening brightness to her tone.

"What?" he whispered, his heart sinking.

"Our daughter's headstone is ready." She beamed at him. "And guess what else? And this is the really brilliant part. Guess what's going to be engraved on it for all eternity?"

Michael stood stock-still, scarcely daring to breathe, waiting for what he now knew was to come.

"That's right," went on Melissa, just as if he'd spoken. "'*Eugenia Creighton, beloved daughter of Melissa Creighton! Till we meet again in Heaven.*' That's it now for all eternity. Doesn't it have a lovely ring to it?"

"You – you left my name off the headstone?" His hands were beginning to shake uncontrollably.

"Well, of course, Michael *Redmond*." She still had that terrifying grin plastered on her face, the grin that frightened Michael and made him wish he'd done certain things differently. "I mean, you didn't want our baby daughter to have your name when she was *alive,* so naturally I assumed you wouldn't want her to have it when she was *dead* either. After all, you're dead a long time, Michael, aren't you? Of course you wouldn't have wanted your precious *name* on our daughter's headstone for all to see for all eternity. That would be *way* too much of a commitment for the ever-cautious Michael *Redmond*."

Her manic grin was almost a snarl now. He wouldn't have been surprised if she'd jumped over the bed like a wolf to bite him right through his jugular. Michael went cold all over. He felt his former fear of commitment coming back now to boot him viciously on the arse. It was his own fault. He'd had this coming, hadn't he? He'd refused to marry Lissy because he was afraid, like a pathetic spineless coward, of taking that last step, that final step on the road to commitment, just because his own parents' marriage hadn't worked out. He had deliberately kept an escape route open for himself, just in case the strain of having a girlfriend and a child ever became too much for him. He'd been a wimp, a gutless wonder. Instead of manning up and meeting his responsibilities head-on, he'd done a half-assed job. It would almost have been better not to have been there at all, rather than being present in that inexcusable one-foot-on-the-running-board way he'd been there. No wonder Lissy felt angry now, and embittered. He didn't blame her. She had every right to feel like this, to have a great big fat go at him. Christ alone knew he deserved it. He'd let down both her and Eugenia.

"But you don't have to go, Lissy." Crossing to her side of the bed, he took hold of her shoulders. "I know I've been a total prat, but we can fix this. I can marry you now, if you still want me to. Just name the day."

She let fly suddenly and walloped him across the face. His eyes widened in shock and surprise and he let go of her shoulders.

"*Fuck you!*" She was almost spitting the words at him. "*Fuck you and your precious name! How dare you offer it to me now, when it's too late?*"

"But it needn't be." Eagerly, he tried to take hold of her by her shoulders again. "That's what I'm saying to you. We'll get married and have another baby, do things properly this time."

"*How dare you!*" she screamed. "*Another baby? Replace Eugenia? That would fix it?*"

"No! I didn't mean –"

"*Don't you get it?* I couldn't marry you now even if I wanted to. It's too late for Eugenia. Nothing you do or say now can fix that. She knows you didn't want her to have your name while she was alive. How can *I* take it now that she's dead? I can't. I told you, I couldn't do it now even if I wanted to. It would be disloyal to Eugenia and I won't be that. Whatever else I am, I won't be that."

Her voice had softened towards the end of her speech and that was when Michael understood finally that no amount of cajoling on his part would make any difference now. Defeated, he sat down on the bed, crushing a pile of her underwear that was ready to go in the suitcase.

"But you don't have to be the one to leave." His voice was flat and dull. "This is *your* mother's house. I should be the one to leave. I'll move out tonight, and you can stay here."

She shook her head emphatically. "No. I need to get away completely, or I'll never get through this. You can stay here if you want. Mum won't put you out on the streets, but she might have to start charging you rent."

He stared at her, aghast. "So you're really leaving me? Leaving here?" His eyes began to fill up with tears.

She nodded. "It's for the best. Oh, and Michael?" she added softly.

"What?" he said hopefully.

"Don't try to find me. I don't ever want to see you again after today."

"Tickets, please," said the Luas ticket man.

"Right, sorry, yeah, here," said Michael, blinking like someone coming out of a dream, or a coma.

"*Please move down the tram*," said the automated female voice. She was on fire today. That was twice now this journey he'd heard her robotic but strangely soothing tones.

He put his ticket back in his wallet and the ticket man moved on.

The sleazy, dark-haired Casanova was still seated across from Michael, but the Brazilian or Spanish woman was gone and had been replaced by an attractive Irishwoman, with long brown hair loosely piled on top of her head, glasses and a light sprinkling of freckles. The dude was hitting on *her* now and this time he wasn't wearing his wedding ring. The twat must have finally remembered to take the bloody thing off before he started chatting up women he met on the Luas.

Michael's thoughts slid back to when Melissa had left him. She'd gone to England to stay with an old schoolfriend until she could find a job and a place of her own. Quickly enough, she'd found a job in a publishing house and had gone back to doing the illustrations for children's books, a job she loved. A flat of her own soon followed and she began to seriously put down roots in England. She'd come home for Christmas at first but had stopped that when her mother died. The house had been sold and the proceeds divided equally three ways between Melissa and her mother's two sisters. Melissa had never really been that close to her aunts, so she'd stopped returning to Ireland when her mother passed away, which had been a good few years ago now. She'd had a few relationships since Michael, nothing serious, and she'd had no more children. She'd just about come around to thinking that she might at last be able to cope with having another child (although at that time she'd had no particular father in mind) when a routine cervical smear test had come back flagged as problematic.

Funny how you could spend a lifetime in some place, Michael thought now, but when you learned you were going to die, you wanted to do it at home, in the country of your birth. After her chemo had failed and she was riddled with the cancer that would kill her, Melissa had come back to Dublin to die, in a clean comfortable hospice that tried its utmost to make the dire process somewhat bearable. She hadn't wanted to die without being reconciled with the father of the only child she'd ever had. Michael, despite being devastated about Melissa's cancer, had never been so happy in his whole life to hear from someone. He was glad and grateful beyond measure that he had seen Melissa again, and that she'd agreed to marry him and let him put things right at last after so many years.

The funeral would be in a day or two. Melissa would be buried with Eugenia, who would have been fourteen years old now if she'd lived. Melissa would be buried under Michael's surname of Redmond and, almost best of all, she'd given permission for the surname on Eugenia's headstone to be changed from Creighton to Redmond.

"Can I join you both, you and Eugenia, when it's *my* time to go?" Michael had asked Melissa as she lay in her bed in the hospice one day.

He'd kept his tone light just in case she took it the wrong way and he'd have to pretend he was only joking, but she'd nodded weakly and smiled and said yes, that she wouldn't have wanted it any other way. He'd been glad, oh so immeasurably glad, that he had her blessing to lie in the ground beside them both when his turn came. Some people might have considered that to be a morbid thought, but he was relieved beyond measure to have finally erased his shame. In the meantime, he was still alive and hopefully would be for a long time to come. Seeing his once vibrant and beautiful Melissa wasting away in front of his shocked eyes had somehow renewed his interest in life. *'In the midst of death we are in life'*, wasn't that how that old quotation went? Or was it the other way around? Either way, he thought he knew what it meant now.

He wanted to live what was left of his life to the fullest. He was tired to death of the cut-throat nature of the medical advertising business. And it didn't make him feel as if he was *achieving* anything – designing logos and coming up with yet another annoying slogan or jingle for laxatives, support stockings or flu remedies. He wanted to leave something behind him that would last, and somehow he didn't think that any of the advertising campaigns he'd worked so hard on would cut it in that way. What he really wanted to do was to *write*. He had a dozen ideas kicking around in his head for a short horror novel or even a filmscript for a horror movie, and what he dearly wanted was the time and energy to commit his ideas to paper. He wasn't saying that he'd be the next Stephen King or James Herbert (his heroes) or anything like that, but what he desired most was the chance to try, to really try, just to see if he had it in him. If he failed, well shure, what harm? At least he'd have had a go at it. Nothing ventured, nothing gained, right?

And then there was Philippa. Oh God, and then there was Philippa. He had yet to tell her about Melissa, that she'd been the one big love of his life whom he'd never forgotten, that he'd had his one and only child with her and that now they were both dead – oh, and he was looking forward to lying beside them both in the soft earth when it was his own turn to bite the big one. He knew that it wouldn't go down well with Philippa, however modern-minded and easy-going she tried to be. What woman wanted to be told that she was competing with not one but *two* ghosts for her man's affections? Wouldn't most women say 'to hell with that' and walk away? He wouldn't blame Philippa if that was exactly what she did say when she heard his story. He somehow didn't think she *would* leave him, though. Yes, Philippa was every inch the modern woman with her numerous social-media accounts and her fancy job on a glossy magazine writing about modern relationships, but he had a strong feeling that she was just a regular woman underneath her polished exterior, an ordinary woman who wanted nothing more than a home, a husband and babies. Especially now that she was nearly in her mid-thirties like Michael, and her biological clock was probably ticking loud enough to wake the dead.

Michael was beginning to think that he would like to settle down with Philippa, to maybe even marry her and have a child with her, but he was also inclined to believe that he'd had his one shot at happiness with Melissa and Eugenia. He could try, of course he could, but he was scared. Scared of what Philippa might say when she found out that he'd kept something so huge from her. He had a dead wife and a dead child to his name and his wife, who he'd only just married, had just died and he'd never mentioned a word about any of it to Philippa. What the hell was she supposed to make of that? And then there was the fact that, when he died, regardless of whatever woman he was with, if he *was* in a relationship with a woman when he passed away, he fully intended to be buried with Eugenia and Melissa. How much of a turn-off would that be for Philippa or for any woman? It was a good job that Philippa liked him so much, Michael thought now as he got off the Luas at Charlemont, or their relationship wouldn't stand a snowball's chance in hell of surviving this major blow.

He began to walk along the canal up to Portobello,

carrying Melissa's package in his work briefcase. He'd be putting in an appearance at work later on today, after he'd delivered the package as per her instructions. He was on compassionate leave from the agency at the moment, which was just as well because, if his colleagues hadn't known the real reason for his absence, he'd probably have been hearing sarcastic remarks from his co-workers any time now along the lines of: "*Soooooo* nice of you to drop in," and "Oh, now, don't tell me, I recognise the face but I just can't think of the name!" Advertising may not have been what he wanted to do for the rest of his life, but for the moment he had no other options lined up and he needed the regular pay cheques and the bonuses.

It was a decent enough day, if a bit chilly, and he sat down on a bench by the canal for five minutes, his briefcase with the package in it carefully tucked under his arm. All around him, life was going on. A mother duck was gliding gracefully down the canal, followed by no fewer than six of her offspring. Michael smiled and remembered that the four-year-old Eugenia had liked nothing better than a trip to the park or canal to feed a bag of stale bread to the grateful ducks. *The Grateful Ducks*, good name for a band, that, he thought. A couple of cyclists whizzed past him on the pedestrian path *(Bloody cyclists! Use the fucking road like you're meant to!)*, followed more sedately by a sweating jogger. A lady dog-walker went by with several small yappy dogs on leashes, and two elderly ladies trundled by with their shopping trollies, gossiping nineteen to the dozen without once stopping for breath. *My God, didn't that Bridget one have some brass neck on her!*

Michael's mind returned to the first time he'd met

Philippa. The magazine she worked for had held a Christmas party a couple of years before for their staff and all their advertisers, of which Michael's agency was one, and he'd gone because he was hungry and fed-up after a long, frustrating day at the drawing-board. Might as well let someone else feed him for a change, and if there was booze there, well, so much the better. He'd seen a gorgeous girl on her own in a corner with a huge glass of wine in one hand and her phone in the other. She was wearing a short black leather skirt and a sort of loose-fitting blouse thing that had the exact same chestnutty glints in it as her mane of long, gloriously coloured hair. He'd found himself a drink, commandeered a plate of peanuts and gone over to casually offer her some before he lost his nerve.

"Peanut?" he'd said politely, instantly appreciating how she was even better-looking at close quarters.

"Smooth move, Romeo," she'd said with a giggle, and that one giggle had been his undoing.

"I'm sorry, but it's my best line," he said solemnly, hoping that she would giggle once more so that he could hear it again, and she did.

He was lost. He never left her side for the rest of the party and, when the revelries were all winding down for the night, he took her home to Beechwood in a taxi, stifling the urge to jump on her once he realised that she was falling asleep with all the wine she'd drunk. He'd walked her to her front door, kissed her chastely on her forehead while slipping his phone number into her handbag and waited in the taxi until he saw a light go on upstairs in the darkened house. She'd texted him the very next day to thank him for minding her and seeing her home without 'trying anything' (her words), and they'd been an item ever since.

Michael got to his feet now, stretched and yawned and recommenced walking slowly up the canal towards Portobello, the parcel's destination. Now he knew so much more about Philippa than he'd done at the beginning, and it only made him like her all the more. He'd learned that she was confident and polished on the outside but an insecure bag of nerves on the inside. He'd learned that she was passionate about animal welfare and that she added the chestnutty glints to her naturally mousy-brown hair herself. It had taken him a while to find out that last secret thing of hers about her hair, and even then she'd sworn him to silence about it. On pain of death, she'd said with another of those giggles he loved, and naturally he'd promised to keep her secret till his dying day. He thought he'd reached the root – no pun intended – of Philippa's insecurity. It started at home (didn't everything?), with cold-fish parents who never praised her or gave her any encouragement. The fact that they'd emotionally neglected their four daughters equally didn't really cut any ice with Philippa. She was possibly the most conscious of all four siblings of having been cheated in the parental love department. Her sister Nicola had found love and babies and a smashing big old house with a pleasant enough guy called Shane, but Philippa and her two other sisters, Coco (christened Christine) and Geraldine, were still laboriously negotiating the dating wilderness.

Michael was aware that, with those four little words '*Will you marry me?*' he could make Philippa happy and whole again in her own eyes, into a complete (and complet*ed*) woman and fully functioning human being. She seemed to need it badly, and he'd been nearly inclined to give in to the impulse he was feeling to just bite the bullet and propose marriage to her, when Melissa had contacted him literally out of the blue. Now he was going to have to wait and see how Philippa reacted to the news about Melissa dying as his legal wife before he could do anything crazy like propose marriage to her. She'd probably point out to him angrily that he was already married, wasn't he, so how the feck could he marry her, Philippa, and what could he say to that but that he was now widowed and, after a decent interval had elapsed, he'd be honoured if she would wear his ring and consent to be his wife? All he could do now was wait and see. Life was so bloody complicated.

Michael reached the main shopping street of Portobello. Well, there were only a few shops but enough to qualify as a shopping street, if a minor one. The swans on this part of the Grand Canal were out in force today, preening themselves and graciously accepting bread and bits of food from enthusiastic passers-by, which Michael wasn't sure was good for them but there was certainly no stopping them, anyway, either the swans *or* the bread donors. (They'd come out with their stale breadcrusts in plastic bags – the donors, that is – and the swans were damn well going to get them, come hell or high water. And the donors were damned well not taking the crusts back home again!) The air was clear and bright and the clock on the college wall was showing the time as a quarter to one, give or take a minute. He might just catch this guy in before everyone buggered off for lunch. He found Linklater's Publishing Company sandwiched (no pun intended) between two takeaways, from which the smell of Chinese food and pizza wafted out tantalisingly, making him realise for the first time in a long while that he was hungry and could, in fact, eat a horse if one were available. He'd definitely be stopping off for lunch in one of these take-out places once he'd safely delivered his package.

He took the package out of his briefcase and looked at it. On the front, it had been addressed in his own hand, at Melissa's dictation, to Mr. Edmund Linklater, Publisher, and on the back was Melissa's name. Michael had put down his own address there as she'd asked him to. There'd be no point in sending anything to her old flat in London. She wouldn't be there. She wouldn't be anywhere any more. This bleak thought made Michael feel as if a knife was twisting in his gut. He stood outside Linklater's for a minute trying to calm his breathing, then he stepped inside the publisher's office and a bell immediately jangled somewhere over his head. It was a bit like stepping back into Dickensian times, coming in here, Michael thought as his eyes registered the big old-fashioned oak reception desk and the two smaller oak desks on either side of it. Michael half-expected to see Kermit the Frog as Bob Cratchit seated shivering at one of the desks, quill in hand and saying meekly, "Yes, Mister Scrooge, sir, but tomorrow's Christmas Day! There won't be anywhere open to do business *with!*" Instead, a pretty young woman with a long light-brown ponytail hopped down from one of the desks – they were ridiculously high-up from the ground, those old heavy wooden desks – and slipped swiftly behind the main reception desk.

"Can I help you, sir?" she said brightly.

"*Erm*, I have a package for Mr. Edmund Linklater. From . . ." Here he paused.

"From whom, sir?" The girl behind the desk was looking at him now with mild interest, just as a stooped-over elderly man with horn-rimmed spectacles on a chain round his neck and a shock of white hair emerged from a back room.

Courteously and with a twinkly smile that made Michael warm to him immediately, he said, "I'm Edmund Linklater. I'm the proprietor here. And may I be so bold as to inquire who is kind enough to send me hand-delivered mail?"

This time Michael was ready. "It's from my wife Melissa." His voice was firm and there was pride in it. "You knew her once as Melissa Creighton. Now she's my wife, Melissa Redmond. The package is from Melissa Redmond."

STOP 12: HARCOURT STREET

Becks and Barry

Becks got on the Luas at Charlemont, making sure first to tap her Leap card against the machine. She'd be getting off at Harcourt Street. She'd fallen into the habit of taking the Luas to Harcourt Street nearly every lunchtime now to meet Barry and have lunch with him. She could have walked (it was nearly quicker), but she loved the Luas. It didn't make her feel queasy like the buses always did. She hated the buses.

"*Please move down the tram*," the automated female voice was saying as Becks boarded the train.

She and Barry had more or less the same lunch hours, which was handy. Even though Becks was one of those people lucky enough to be genuinely happy in their job, she loved having lunch dates with Barry to look forward to every day. He'd missed a couple of those lunchtimes lately, pleading pressure of work, but he'd promised her that he'd definitely be there today. They were going to go to that new coffee-and-paninis place round the corner from the Luas stop, and Becks was planning to tell him all about the unexpected coup that Linklater's Publishing Company had managed to recently score. Becks, fiddling with her long light-brown ponytail like she was always doing ("Can't you ever leave your feckin' hair alone for one minute?" Barry had said to her once in mock-exasperation), thought about that coup now while the Luas sat in traffic at the lights. Traffic was heavy today but then it nearly always *was*, at this time of day and so close to the city centre.

She'd been manning the front office by herself a few days ago, when a man had walked through the doors of Linklater's Publishing Company carrying a parcel wrapped in brown paper. He'd been adamant that he would put the parcel only into the hands of Mr. Linklater himself. Just then old Mr. Edmund had emerged from the back room in person and the stranger had introduced himself as Michael Redmond, the husband of a former employee of Mr. Edmund's from before Becks' time called Melissa, or Melissa Creighton as she'd been back then.

"Of course I remember Melissa," Mr. Edmund had said warmly. "She was always one of my most talented employees. She did the most exquisite illustrations for some of our children's books. Most of them are still in print and still quite popular. We were all sad when she left to have her baby, and then thrilled when she decided to keep up with some of her illustrations at home. And how is dear Melissa, Mr. Redmond?"

That was the sad part. Melissa had died of cervical cancer only a few days before. Her last wish had been that her husband Michael should take a parcel of some of her writings round to Mr. Edmund of Linklater's Publishing Company, and so here Michael was now with the parcel in his two hands, presenting it to old Mr. Edmund as reverently as if it contained the Crown Jewels.

"And you say you have no idea what's inside here?" Mr. Edmund had asked with curiosity, adding when the younger man shook his head: "I must say, I'm intrigued."

Becks, who worked as Linklater's receptionist and first reader after Mr. Edmund, made coffee for the three of them and turned the OPEN sign to CLOSED on the front door of the offices, since it was lunchtime by now anyway. Then she'd taken the coffee into Mr. Edmund's inner sanctum, where he and the man called Michael Redmond were already poring over the pages from the parcel. It was a collection of some fifty or sixty beautiful poems, more than enough for a slim published volume, mostly on the theme of the death of a child ("We were so very sorry to hear about what happened to little Eugenia, such a pretty child," Mr. Edmund had said with genuine tears in his eyes), but also about what it was like to be dying, first slowly and then much more swiftly, too swiftly, of cervical cancer.

"*This won't exactly be the book that people will buy one another as a cheering-up present*," Melissa herself had commented wryly in a note attached to her writings, "*but I'm hoping it might touch the people who have themselves been affected by these things.*" She'd added that the book, if Mr. Edmund saw fit to turn it into such, was to be dedicated to her husband Michael and her daughter Eugenia, now an angel in Heaven. She'd accompanied her collection of writings, entitled *Flowers for Eugenia*, with some of the most gorgeous little illustrations Becks had ever seen. She knew that old Mr. Edmund liked them too, more than liked them, judging by the appraising glint in his eye. He may have been pushing eighty but his eye for what would sell and what wouldn't sell was still unerring. Becks, who'd been with the company for nearly five years now, had nothing but respect for the old man's business sense.

Old Mr. Edmund, as he was affectionately known by his small staff, had been running the family publishing business since the early nineteen seventies when his father, Samuel Linklater, the founder of the company back in the twenties, had retired. Now Mr. Edmund and Michael Redmond were carefully examining the exquisitely delicate illustrations, exclaiming and *ooh*-ing and *aah*-ing over each one individually. After an hour or so of deliberation on Mr. Edmund's part, which Becks strongly suspected weren't entirely necessary because she was fairly certain that he'd already made up his mind, it was decided to put Melissa's subtly emotional writings into print for readers to enjoy and cherish. A book would be published, dedicated to Michael and Eugenia as Melissa had wished it to be, and all the proceeds would be divided equally between Linklater's, a meningitis charity and a cancer charity, as Melissa had also requested. Linklater's would benefit too from the positive publicity and sales. The fact that there were two really worthy charities involved, and that the writer of the book had passed away of a disease that had already taken the lives of hundreds of Irish women, might end up being useful selling points for the book and, if the book sold, the charities, as well as Linklater's, would benefit. It was a situation in which none of them could lose.

"You'll have to do the rounds of the radio programmes and maybe even the telly talk shows," Becks had told Michael.

Mr. Edmund had added enthusiastically, "Yes, the more publicity we get for the book, the better. We might even get you to sign a few copies and let people get their photo taken with you at the bookstores. In the absence of Melissa herself, that might well be the best thing to do. The personal touch always goes down well."

Becks laughed and clapped her hands with approval, but Michael Redmond had coloured a dull beetroot-red and said, "Look, I didn't mind at all delivering this parcel for Lissy but I never reckoned on all this other stuff . . . this *publicity* stuff. It's just not me. I'm sorry, but you'll have to do the rest of this without me."

Mr. Edmund opened his mouth to say something, but Becks herself forestalled him. She leaned forward and took both of Michael's hands in hers.

"Mr. Redmond – Michael, can I call you Michael? – listen, you've had a truly terrible time of it. Both your little girl and your poor, *poor* wife have died of two of the most – the most *insidious* diseases that we have in Ireland today. Diseases that should be wiped off the face of the Earth and, if I had *my* way, they would be. If the three of us together promoting Melissa's book raises awareness or saves even *one* person's life who might otherwise have died, isn't it worth it? Worth putting up with a little bit of embarrassment or people saying for five minutes: 'Oh, there's that guy who was on the telly, gabbing about that book?' Anyway, shure in no time at all you'll be yesterday's news." She released his hands and allowed her words to sink in for a moment.

Then Michael Redmond laughed out loud, turned to Old Mr. Edmund and said, "Wow, she's *good*. You want to hold onto this one, you do."

Mr. Edmund laughed too. "Oh, believe me, I intend to, Michael, I intend to."

Then they all laughed together and suddenly, and partially thanks to Becks – everyone called her that, even Old Mr. Edmund – Project *Flowers for Eugenia* was a go, a real go. And the thing was that Becks was being entirely sincere in the things she'd said to Michael Redmond – she hadn't just been buttering him up and soft-soaping him with the stuff designed to bring him over to Linklater's Publishing Company's point of view.

She couldn't wait to meet Barry now for the first time all week, in person instead of just texting or leaving him a voice message (his phone was never on these days) and to tell him her good news. She hoped he'd be as pleased about the whole thing as she was. She waited impatiently as the packed Luas drew to a smooth halt at the Harcourt Street stop. She looked out the window to see if Barry was waiting for her on the platform, as he sometimes was if he got there early, but there was no sign of him today. Disappointed, she disembarked and threaded her way through the throngs of people who normally got off at this stop.

She reached the coffee-and-paninis place before Barry did and found them a comfy booth by the window overlooking the street. Becks loved to sit by the window in places like this or on the Luas and watch the world go by. She was a real people person. She loved meeting the authors (or potential authors) who frequented Linklater's Publishing Company. Old Mr. Edmund was letting her meet more and more of them lately on her own because she was so good with them, so professional and yet relaxed and friendly, instantly putting them at their ease and thereby making them amenable to accepting any little changes to their books that Mister Edmund as Editor-in-Chief might require of them.

"What can I get you, love?" said the waiter in the coffee place, coming to her table with his notebook at the ready.

"*Erm*, is it okay if I just wait for my boyfriend, please?"

"Okay, no problem." The waiter, an Irish hipster with an aggressively ginger beard and man-bun, shrugged. "But keeping you waiting like that? Some boyfriend. You need to seriously give him the elbow, love, and find yourself someone who can get here on time."

Becks blushed, mortified. *And you need to concentrate on your own business and leave me to look after mine*, she dearly wanted to say to the cheeky waiter's retreating back, but she bit back the retort and pretended to be busy scrolling down her phone. Damn Barry, she thought. He'd been doing this more and more, turning up late for their various dates or missing them altogether, sometimes with the flimsiest of excuses. She hoped with all her heart that he wasn't losing interest. She couldn't bear that, she really couldn't. Becks Jamieson was finally in a good place with her life. She adored her job and dear Old Mr. Edmund too, whom she regarded as sort of a surrogate grandfather. He was so approachable and easy to talk to that you could discuss literally anything with him, and he was surprisingly enlightened for a man of his advanced years.

"It's what happens when you get to my age," he'd laughed when she'd said it to him once. "You realise that life's too short to keep disapproving of all the things that bugged you when you were younger. You become mellower, more tolerant of your fellow man and this funny old world we live in."

So work was going really well for Becks, and her father's drinking had eased up a little bit too, ever since the doctor had told him straight out that he was going to be dead within the year if he carried on the way he was going. He flatly refused to even *consider* paying a visit to Alcoholics Anonymous.

"A load of losers sitting around baring their souls to one another like fools," he'd sneer whenever Becks tentatively brought up the subject. There were meetings in her local community centre every week, but she no longer believed she was capable of getting him to attend any. The pamphlets she'd brought home after her trip to the community centre, well, he'd chucked them in the bin without so much as glancing at them, hadn't he?

The door to the coffee-shop burst open suddenly and Barry came in, all apologies.

"Sorry I'm late," he said breathlessly. "Something cropped up in the office. Printer jammed and the floor was awash with all these reams and reams of fucking white paper. Myself and another lad drew the short straw and had to clean the place up."

Becks tried to smile normally, although she didn't feel like smiling. It was five to fucking one already and she had to be back in Linklater's for half-past. And ten minutes at least of the remaining time would have to be spent waiting for a Luas, then the journey back up to Charlemont Luas stop and then high-tailing it back to Portobello. A short journey, admittedly, but it all took time. It all ate into the precious time the two of them had to spend together.

"Let me get these." Barry strolled up to the counter to order their coffees and paninis. "The usual okay, yeah?"

"Yeah." She was disgruntled but unwilling to express her dissatisfaction verbally in case she pissed him off. She was already worried that he might be losing interest in her, the way he'd missed some of their lunch dates lately or had arrived late, on the run and panting, always with an excuse she couldn't find fault with. Taking a sick co-worker to the company doctor for a sudden virulent bout of food poisoning was something you couldn't exactly argue with. Attending an impromtu emergency all-hands-to-the-pump meeting called suddenly by the company's boss wasn't something you could argue with. The fire alarm going off and no one knowing whether it was a drill or if there was a real fire somewhere in the building wasn't something you could argue with. None of it was stuff you could fucking argue with, so Becks didn't even bother trying any more. If he *was* lying, then he was very bloody good at it. Every excuse he ever offered sounded perfectly plausible.

"Any news?" Barry said breezily, sitting back down at the table.

"Aren't you going to even take your coat off?" Straightaway she was irritated. "You look like you're about to shoot off again at any second, wearing your coat in here like that."

"Of course I'm taking my coat off. Look at me taking it off right now."

He proceeded to do just that, though she knew full well that he would have left it on if she hadn't said anything.

"How's work?" he said when he was done removing the coat.

He looked exceptionally handsome today. The dark-blue suit and brown polished lace-up shoes really suited him, and his thick dark hair was slicked back but not too flat to his head. It had a bit of height to it and that really suited him too. He smelled clean too, as he always did. If she wasn't so annoyed with him, she'd have liked to smell his neck, stroke his stubble and breathe in the scent of his aftershave, some pricey but gorgeous-smelling stuff she'd bought him herself for his birthday.

She bit back her annoyance and began to tell him about *Flowers for Eugenia*. Halfway through her story, she stopped.

"Are you checking your phone?" She knew she should have ignored it but she couldn't help it. He'd been doing that a lot lately.

"No, not at all." His tone immediately told her that he *was*. "I was just checking to see if – if Marty had the printer back up and running or if he needed me."

"And does he?" she said icily.

"Does he what?" He looked puzzled now.

"Does he need you back there?" Christ, he could be exasperating at times!

"Nah, not yet," he said lightly. "I'm all yours, babes. I've got another few minutes anyway."

"I'm truly honoured." She couldn't help the sarcasm. She watched him as he crammed his turkey, stuffing and ham panini into his mouth and took a huge bite.

"Ah, come on, Becks," he cajoled, his mouth full. "I wouldn't give *you* a hard time if you had to go and do work stuff. It's not like either of us would have any choice in the matter, not when it comes to work. You don't say no to your boss."

That was true enough, but Becks was still annoyed at him. "You didn't even listen to my work story." Was there even any point in complaining?

"Sure I did," he said easily. "The kid had meningitis and the wife had fanny cancer and you worthy publishers want all the proceeds to go to the two charities or something. Good selling points, those. You should run with them for all they're worth. Make you all a few bob."

Her eyes widened at his callous terminology. "I wouldn't have put it quite like that. There's – there's quite a lot more to it than that."

"Ah, come on, Becks, lighten up." He was pulling his coat on again now and pushing away the remains of his panini. Just a few crumbs were left. Their cosy lunch together was obviously over. "You've a bloody face on you as long as a wet weekend."

She ignored the jibe. Instead she said: "Are you still coming over to mine tonight?"

"Will your old man be there?" he asked pointedly.

Becks shook her head. No, her old man wouldn't be there because he'd be down the boozer as usual. That was where he was every night of the year, except for Christmas Day and Good Friday, the only two days in the whole of the year when the pubs were shut. His being out most nights suited Barry, a typical millennial. Barry had nowhere of his own where they could go to make love. He still lived at home with his parents and a younger brother and sister because he couldn't afford yet to move out and rent anywhere, let alone *buy* a place. An accommodating girlfriend living in a big old house with a lush of a father who was out boozing every night suited him down to the ground. Stephen Jamieson was not an obstacle to Barry's relationship with Becks. Stephen would roll home after closing-time, stinking drunk and smelling like a brewery, crying the whole time for his wife, Becks' mother. He'd collapse into bed and not show his face until the following day, by which time Becks and Barry would long since have tidied up and left for their respective workplaces.

"Grand, so." Barry drained the last drops in his coffee

cup and stood up. "I'll see you around seven, so, okay? Keep it warm for me," he added with a mischievous grin, bending down to kiss her on the forehead.

And then he was gone, just like that. Becks sat there and wondered whether it meant anything that he'd kissed her on the forehead rather than on the lips. Did she have panini on her mouth or something? She ran her tongue over her lips and was satisfied that nothing icky was adhering to them, inside *or* out. So, what was it then? It couldn't be because he was afraid of Public Displays of Affection. They'd kissed and cuddled way more than that in public places before. Like, a thousand times – it was no biggie these days.

Brooding on it, she got up and left the café, hurrying across the road to the Luas. It was genuinely amazing how many of them sailed blithely away while you were still standing around daydreaming and tapping your bloody Leap card.

It was coming up to six o'clock when Becks let herself into the house in Terenure, her heart pounding and her mouth suddenly dry. She dreaded this time every night, because she never knew what kind of state she'd find her father in. Tonight, it wasn't good exactly, but it was nowhere near as bad as it could have been either, as it *had* been on some nights. Stephen Jamieson was slumped in his armchair in front of the telly. Nothing new there. That was where she found him most evenings when she came in from work. They'd have dinner together and then Stephen would go to the pub. The Angelus was on the TV with its distinctive 'donging' sound and the News would be on in a minute. Two, three, four, *five* empties lay scattered on the floor by

Stephen's chair. One can remained out of the six-pack. It was clutched in Stephen's hand, his elbow resting on the arm of his chair. And this was him supposedly drinking less, since the doctor's recent diagnosis of certain liver failure if he kept at it hell for leather the way he had been.

"Hi, Dad." Becks used the tone of false breeziness she tried to adopt with him every night. "How was your day?"

He grunted something unintelligible in return.

"How was work?" Stephen still had his own carpentry business. "Have you had anything to eat?" She prattled on, still doing the bright 'n' breezy thing. "I've got some nice mince here from the supermarket and some of those taco shells you like. We can have Taco Night again. You like that, don't you?"

"Not hungry," he mumbled.

"Well, see how you feel once you smell this delicious mince frying." She attempted a laugh. To her own ears it sounded hollow, a hollow ghastly thing.

"It's November the second tomorrow," he said to her retreating back, as she headed for the kitchen with her bag of shopping.

She froze in her tracks. How could she have forgotten? November the second was the hardest day of the year for them both. She'd been so caught up with worrying about whether or not Barry still loved her that it had pushed November the second out of her head completely. Now she was wracked with guilt.

"Oh, Dad." She went to sit on the arm of his chair and put her arms around him. "I'm sorry. I forgot! I've just had so much on my mind lately . . ."

"It doesn't matter." Stephen's voice was gruff, but he didn't push her away.

They sat there for a while like that, and then Becks said: "Will you be okay by yourself while I go and make the dinner?"

"Go on, away with you, woman. I'm not a baby."

Poor, poor Dad, she thought as she unpacked the food and began getting the dinner ready. She felt crippled with guilt for not having remembered. It was the anniversary of the day on which Becks' bright, vivacious mother, Joanna, had walked out on her husband and five-year-old daughter, Rebecca, for ever. As Becks busied herself at the cooker with the mince and the taco shells and set the table for dinner, her mind wandered back, as it so often did, to what she remembered of that time twenty-three years earlier.

Becks often suspected that her imagination, always vivid and kept active by reading, both for pleasure and in her job (which was also a pleasure), had added some of the details of her memories over the years. Could she really remember how heavy the raindrops had sat that day on the leaves of the trees in the garden, the trees that hadn't already lost their leaves, that was? The leaves had looked positively bogged down with the weight of the water. The whole garden had been waterlogged after the recent rainfall. It was a dark and gloomy day, perfect for November, and Becks' mother Joanna, a true child of the sun, would have been depressed and restless all morning as usual if there hadn't been something special, something different about that particular day. While Stephen had been at work, she'd paced excitedly up and down the long living-room, the one with the big windows that looked out onto the front *and* back gardens, smoking one cigarette after another. They hadn't had the summerhouse then, the gorgeous little summerhouse which Stephen, a carpenter with his own business, had built after Joanna had left them. It was too wet to go out in the garden that day anyway.

"It gives me something to do," he'd said when he was building the little structure and Becks, as young as she'd been, had thought she understood. "Anyway," he'd added with a catch in his voice, "it'll be a place where . . . where you can go to *remember* her, see? Because she loved the sun and being outside in the garden."

"Will you read me a story, Mummy?" she would have asked her mother on other rainy mornings before the rainy morning of Joanna's last day in the house in Terenure, the one Becks had lived in nearly her whole life.

"Not now, darling," Joanna would reply irritably on those other mornings. "Can't you see that Mummy's depressed?"

Rebecca had always just sighed sadly at these rejections and gone back to reading her book by herself. What else could she do? Mummy was so often depressed these days, and most of all on rainy days. Rebecca wondered if it had anything to do with the fact that she fought with Daddy such a lot. They'd been fighting more than ever lately. Rebecca wasn't entirely sure about what, but she *did* know that Mummy was always telling Daddy how bored she was, stuck in the house on her own with a child while Daddy was off working. Mummy didn't call it working though, she called it something else – what was it again – 'swanning around'. And Daddy always retorted by demanding to know how his working all the hours God sent to build up the business was 'swanning around', how was it 'swanning around' when he had callouses on his hands from working as a carpenter for ten hours a day? They'd had some vicious arguments about that very subject. Mummy would fly at Daddy and flail at him with her little fists and Daddy would try to restrain her by pinning her arms to her sides while repeating "For Christ's sake, Joanna, think of the child!" at her over and over.

When it became clear that Daddy wasn't able to take any time off work to 'entertain' Mummy, as he put it, that was when five-year-old Rebecca, accustomed to always being quiet and watchful, always trying to gauge her parents' moods, started to notice that men her mother called 'Uncles' would call to the house while her daddy was out at work. The Uncles were nearly always very friendly to Rebecca, giving her a couple of quid (it was pounds back then, not yet euro) to buy sweets or even bringing ones that kids didn't really like but adults did, like liquorice sticks or cough drops. Rebecca liked it when they brought her chocolates or jellies, and there was one Uncle who even bought her comics – *Beano*s and *Dandy*s and *Bunty*s and *Twinkle*s.

Rebecca quickly recognised that one of the Uncles, Uncle Victor he was called or Uncle Vic as he preferred, was rapidly becoming more popular than the others. Soon enough it got to the point where he was pretty much the only Uncle calling to the house in Terenure's Sycamore Drive. He'd call about an hour after her daddy had left for the day, giving Mummy time to have a long luxurious bubble bath and wash her short shiny blonde hair (that Mummy said came out of a little magic squeezy bottle called *'Radiant Blonde'*) and put on make-up. She had such a pretty face. She was always telling Rebecca how lucky she was to have such a pretty mummy, then she'd stroke Rebecca's face lovingly and say that she, Joanna, was really the lucky one to have a daughter as beautiful as Rebecca. No one had ever been able to make Rebecca beam with sheer happiness the way her mother had.

Uncle Vic would ring the front doorbell in the mornings with his arms full of presents, presents that Joanna would have to hide or tell her husband she'd bought herself out of the housekeeping money – little gifts of flowers, chocolates or baskets of bathroom stuff like bubble bath and mini-shampoos and conditioners, and fancy little soaps shaped like hearts or like tiny bottles of champagne. Mummy always used to laugh and ask Uncle Vic what hotel he'd stolen the bath stuff from this time, and Uncle Vic would take the joke in good part and laugh too. He brought presents for Rebecca as well, who wouldn't be going to school for another year. ("There's no rush for stupid old school, is there?" Mummy was always saying. Rebecca sometimes wondered if Mummy was afraid to be left by herself in the house all day. Daddy had protested but he let Mummy have her way as usual.) Vic was the Uncle with the comics, but he also brought toys, like a cuddly teddy bear dressed in blue dungarees with a pair of sunglasses and a little blue pail and spade for the beach (Rebecca had immediately named him Teddy Bucket), and a set of tiny delicate dolls' furniture. Once he'd brought a Baby Doll so precious and beautifully dressed that Rebecca had loved her on sight. She had never again owned a doll so perfect, a doll she loved more than Baby Audrey.

When the flurry of greetings was over and Mummy and Uncle Vic retired for the day to Mummy and Daddy's locked bedroom to do private things that caused them to make a lot of funny noises, Rebecca would be left to her own devices for the rest of the day. She'd sit in front of the TV and watch the kids' cartoon shows, or she'd play with the toys that Uncle Vic had brought. She was allowed to take whatever she wanted to eat or drink out of the fridge. By now, she was able to make herself a sandwich and she would usually just spread strawberry jam on several slices of bread and take them into the big living-room to eat while watching the TV. On the days that Mummy had forgotten to buy jam, Rebecca would eat the bread dry, which wasn't as nice. On the days when Mummy had forgotten to buy bread, she'd eat a yogurt or an apple. On the days when Mummy had forgotten to buy anything at all, Rebecca would just have to wait till Mummy and Uncle Vic came out of the bedroom to eat anything. Even if her tummy was rumbling so loudly that she could hear it, she wasn't allowed to interrupt Mummy and Uncle Vic. She was allowed to interrupt them only if Daddy came home early without them knowing about it. Sometimes she wished he *would* come home early just so that she could get something to eat, but he never did.

Mostly, she curled up in her favourite armchair and read for the day. Mummy had taught her to read almost as soon as she could walk and talk. Mummy said you were never lonely when you had a book. Rebecca was already able to read the books Mummy had read in *her* childhood, books like *What Katy Did*, *The Wind in the Willows*, and Enid Blyton's animal stories, her fairy stories and her school stories like *First Term at Malory Towers* and *Claudine at St. Clare's*. There was an entire shelf of the actual books Mummy had owned in her childhood in the sitting-room, books she'd taken with her when she'd left home because she couldn't bear to part with them.

Rebecca was particularly entranced by the works of Hans Christian Andersen and the Brothers Grimm. Their stories of beautiful princesses, wicked witches and queens, ogres, enchanted castles and magic spells worked their own magic on her. Mummy said that when Rebecca was older, they would read Mummy's battered old copies of classic novels like *Wuthering Heights*, *Jane Eyre* and *Lorna Doone*, books about windswept moors, doomed love affairs and mysteries. "And, of course, one day when you're older, we'll read Daphne du Maurier's famous book about a timid young girl who marries a rich man who owns a fabulous house in the country called Manderley, and he has a dead wife that everyone seems to still love and miss most dreadfully. Oh, if only I could remember her name!" Then Mummy used to tickle Rebecca and Rebecca would giggle and tell Mummy that they both knew perfectly well what the girl's name was. She still had Mummy's copy of that book, with the words *'This book belongs to Joanna Tate'* inscribed on the inside cover in Mummy's lovely flowing handwriting.

Rebecca had particularly enjoyed the days when she and Mummy would curl up on the couch together, each lost in their own reading adventures. These days Mummy read romances and spy stories, anything with a bit of glamour about it to take her mind off her dreary life, she used to say. Sometimes they'd help themselves from a box of chocolates Uncle Vic had brought, because Mummy said you were never too young to know the joy of combining eating chocolate with reading books.

Often, though, Rebecca would spend her days alone sitting quietly at the front window looking out at the road they lived on. In the mornings, it would mostly be quiet because the adults would all be at work and the kids at school, except of course for Rebecca herself. Things would start to get busy again after lunch when the kids began to come home from school. Rebecca loved watching the people as they scurried past, intent on their own business, their own worries, their own destinations. It made her feel less lonely. She loved it even more when it was raining and people had to put up their umbrellas. Rebecca adored the rain. It had such a friendly pitter-patter sound and it decorated the window-pane with such pretty patterns. It made her feel less alone, somehow. Maybe it was company for her. Mummy hated the rain, saying it depressed her.

"I'm a little sunbeam and you're a teensy-weensy raindrop," she would say about their different tastes, making Rebecca giggle.

Once, a horrid social worker had called to the house, saying that she'd had a report about a school-age child being left at home alone every day. Mummy had been magnificent that day, like a lioness fiercely defending her cub. How dared that awful woman in the ill-fitting, drab-coloured suit insinuate such a thing, when she, the child's mother, was clearly in the house with the child the whole time? And as for why a child of five should be at home in the middle of the day in the first place instead of at school, well, if the woman knew even the first thing about the law of the land, then she'd know that the legal age for starting school was *six,* and the woman ought to mind her own business and concentrate on looking out for children who were actually being abused or neglected instead of harassing innocent families.

"We have to investigate every report we get," the woman had said primly as Mummy had ushered her out of the front door, which she then slammed smartly shut behind her.

Mummy had seemed to go crazy with rage once the door had been shut behind the social worker. She screamed and tore at her hair and even threw a few cushions and ornaments across the sitting-room, heaping venomous abuse on the woman's head the whole time.

"How dare they? How bloody *dare* they, the fucking busybodies?" she'd muttered as she'd poured herself a big drink from the whiskey bottle that Uncle Vic had brought with him on his last visit. Her hands trembling, she drank the whiskey back in one and immediately poured herself another before lighting a cigarette.

Rebecca was sworn to secrecy about the social worker's visit. "We can't tell Daddy about it because it would upset him," Mummy had said. "He works so hard and he doesn't deserve to be upset over a silly little thing like this." And so Rebecca had crossed her heart and hoped to die, as Mummy had requested. That made *two* secrets that Rebecca was supposed to be keeping from Daddy. The one about the Uncles in general and Uncle Vic in particular (you could nearly say that that was actually two secrets and not just the one), and now the new one about the social worker coming round.

Rebecca loved her daddy and she felt guilty about keeping secrets from him, but she loved her mother more. She *adored* her mother, with her soft creamy skin and her hands that were always gentle and never hurt (unlike Daddy's, which were rough and calloused from work, although he couldn't help it), and her shiny blonde hair and her perfume that always smelled to Rebecca like a garden of beautiful wild roses after the rain. Ironic, maybe, because Mummy loved the sun so much. Rebecca wanted to be like her mummy when she grew up. She wanted to *be* Mummy, worshipped by all the men who flocked to her shimmering, vivacious brightness like moths to a flame. So she kept her promises, and Mummy's secrets.

The last day Rebecca saw her mummy was November the second, 1993. It was raining steadily outside but, for once, Mummy wasn't depressed. In fact, quite the opposite. There had been a feeling of excitement in the air from the moment Mummy had come into her bedroom that morning and climbed into bed beside her, warming her cold bare feet on Rebecca's toasty ones. It was a feeling that crackled like electricity in the air and made Mummy's eyes sparkle and shine and her cheeks flush red. The excitement was catching. Rebecca could feel it transmit itself to her before she even knew what the cause of it all was.

"We're going on an adventure," Mummy told her, waiting expectantly for Rebecca's reaction.

"What kind of an adventure?" Rebecca whispered, her eyes wide.

"With Uncle Vic." Mummy's brilliant blue eyes were flashing in anticipation. "You like Uncle Vic, don't you, sweetheart? He's always been so kind to you? Well, the three of us are going away together. You, me and Uncle Vic. We're going to live in Vic's house. It's not as big as this one but it's much nicer, nowhere near as gloomy as this – this old *mausoleum,* and it's near the seaside too. We'll be able to go for long walks on the beach together, the three of us. You'll love that, won't you, my little Becky, my sweet precious little Becka-Boo? We can even go swimming if you'd like."

Rebecca nodded, then she remembered something. "What about Daddy? Is he coming too?"

Her mother hugged her tightly. "Forget about grumpy old Daddy. He'll be just fine here on his own without *us*. Better, in fact. All he cares about is his precious work. Now he can concentrate on it round the clock without having to stop to come home to his family. He probably won't even notice that we're missing."

She laughed gaily and Rebecca did too, all caught up in the merriment.

"But you're definitely taking *me*, Mummy?" Rebecca pressed her head against her mother's chest.

"Of *course* I'm taking you, you silly-billy! I couldn't go anywhere without my precious little Becka-Boo."

Happy and secure in the knowledge that her mother loved her, Rebecca relaxed, smiling, and let herself be hugged and petted. It would be hard to leave Daddy, who wasn't to blame for the fact that he had to work so hard and neglect Mummy but, as long as she was with her mummy, then things would be all right. She began to look forward to the adventure.

"When are we going?"

"Why, today, of course." Mummy stared at Rebecca, as if it were obvious and she was surprised to be asked.

That made sense. Mummy always did everything 'today'. It was as if no other day existed for her but the one she was living right now. Rebecca vowed to be just like her when she was a grown-up, and always do everything 'today'.

While Daddy was at work they packed their things. Mummy sang out of tune at the top of her voice while she carefully packed all of her dresses, shoes, jewellery and cosmetics. She was in a rare high good humour, despite the never-ending rain, and it gladdened Rebecca's heart to see it. Mummy had so many dresses, many of them vintage, carefully sourced from second-hand shops over the years. Some of the dresses were from as far back as the twenties or claimed to be. Mummy simply loved the twenties. She said the fashions then would have suited her tall thin body down to the ground, although the dresses themselves would have barely scraped her knees! (That was one of Mummy's terrible jokes and Rebecca dutifully laughed at it every time she made it.) She even kept her blonde hair short and bobbed like the women back then did and painted her lips in the style of Clara Bow. She was always lying on her back on the couch with her long, bendy legs dangling over one arm, smoking cigarettes and bemoaning the fact that she'd been born in the wrong era. She could just see herself, she'd say, in a silvery flapper dress with matching shoes, silk stockings and a diamanté headband with a feather on it, smoking a cigarette in a long silver holder and flirting with a roomful of *beaux* who would be dazzled beyond measure at how utterly fascinating and bewitching she was. She owned two or three antique candy-striped hatboxes in which she stored bits and pieces of costume jewellery and floaty scarves among other things, and a gorgeous little cream-coloured beaded handbag she said was 'pure vintage twenties'. Rebecca had always loved being allowed to go through the special things Mummy kept in her hatboxes. She was allowed to look at them and even handle them just as long as she was careful. They were very precious to Mummy and so, by extension, to Rebecca. It was like lifting a lid onto another world, a magical world in gracious miniature.

"What about our furniture, our beds and couches and things?" she asked Mummy at one point while they were packing to go to Uncle Vic's.

"We don't need those, silly," Mummy replied gaily. "Uncle Vic has all the furniture we'll need."

Rebecca would be sad to say goodbye to her bedroom, because Mummy had made it so pretty over the years, but she tried not to mind too much. Mummy had already told her that she would have her own little room in Vic's house and that it would soon feel like home because she could bring all her toys, teddies, dolls and books with her.

"Try to be grown-up about it," Mummy had said. "Mummy and Uncle Vic aren't bringing a crabby little *baby* to live with them surely, only a big grown-up girl like you, Becka."

So Rebecca had tried to be grown-up about it and not mind that, by the end of the day, she would be sleeping in a different bed in a different house and Mummy would most likely be sleeping in a big bed with Uncle Vic. All the Uncles had seemed to enjoy being in bed with Mummy. Rebecca had no idea what transpired between them and Mummy in Mummy and Daddy's bedroom, but the Uncles had always left the house later in the day whistling and singing tunelessly, as if they were in a good mood, so whatever had happened upstairs must have been fun for them. Mummy had always been in a wonderful mood afterwards too. She'd call for Rebecca to come up to her, and the two of them would cuddle in the bed together and giggle and Mummy would ask her what she wanted to eat for dinner and, whatever Rebecca wanted, if Mummy had it, she would cook it. The Uncles were all nice, but Rebecca was always glad when they left because then she would have Mummy's undivided attention again and she'd get a hot cooked meal, which was a big improvement on the jam sandwiches. Rebecca's jam sandwiches never tasted as good as the ones Mummy made her, anyway.

"That's because I make mine with a very special secret ingredient," Mummy would say with a knowing smile when Rebecca asked her about why this was.

"What is it?" Rebecca's big blue eyes would be wide with wonder.

"Love," Mummy would reply, while blowing her a kiss.

When Rebecca blew one back, Mummy would pretend to catch it and hold it to her heart.

But now, on the afternoon of November the second, 1993, the rainiest day Rebecca could ever remember, the bags were packed and they were both dressed and nearly ready to go. Mummy had ordered a taxi for them for two o'clock, because Uncle Vic had to meet someone and couldn't take them to his house himself. While they were in the big front room waiting for the taxi to come and drive them to Uncle Vic's house on the other side of Dublin, Mummy asked Rebecca for a sheet of paper and a pencil so that she could write Daddy a goodbye note. She showed Rebecca afterwards what she'd written.

Dear Stephen, I'm leaving you and I'm taking Becka with me because there is no room in your life for a wife and child. Please don't try to find us. All you need to know is that we will be safe and looked after by someone who actually cares about what happens to us, which is more than you ever did. I'm sorry that things between us have to end this way. No hard feelings? Joanna.

Mummy got Rebecca to add the words 'Goodbye Daddy' to the end of the note, and then she left the note on the table in the living-room under the heavy glass ashtray, so it wouldn't blow under the table and get lost. Then she went upstairs to check her face in the bathroom mirror one more time, warning Rebecca to be on 'taxi-watch' in the meantime.

Rebecca dutifully climbed up on to the window-seat with Baby Audrey in tow and looked out at the rain-washed street. No way was she packing her favourite doll in the dark cramped luggage, to get scared and squished in the boot of the taxi. Baby Audrey would be sitting right there on her lap with her when she was in the taxi, being driven away from Sycamore Drive in Terenure for ever. Rebecca's eyes widened when she saw the big white van with the words '*STEPHEN JAMIESON CARPENTRY*' printed in big letters on the side of it suddenly pull up to the garden gate where the taxi was soon going to be. She knew that somehow this meant danger for Mummy's lovely plans, the plans that included her daughter Rebecca, whom she loved so dearly.

Rebecca scrambled down off the window-seat, leaving Baby Audrey behind her in her haste. She bolted into the hall and up the stairs, shouting, "*It's Daddy! Mummy, it's Daddy! Daddy's here!*"

Mummy stuck her head out of the bathroom door, a loaded mascara wand in her hand and an expression of annoyance on her face. "What on earth are you yelling about, Rebecca?" she said irritably. "Haven't I told you a thousand times that young ladies don't shout?"

"Daddy's home." Rebecca was red-faced at being told off by Mummy.

"*What!*" Mummy, by contrast, went chalk-white.

"He's outside the house," said Rebecca. "I saw his van from the window just now."

"*Fuck!*" breathed Mummy, before tearing down the stairs to see for herself. "What the fuck is he doing here in the middle of the day? How does he know? Who told him? He'll spoil everything! He'll spoil *everything!*"

She reached the hall at the same time as Daddy, who'd just put his key in the door. They said nothing as they stood and stared at each other. Daddy took in the little pile of suitcases in the hall, topped by one of Mummy's antique candy-striped hatboxes, bursting at the seams with precious treasures.

"Rebecca, go up to your room," Daddy said in a quiet voice that was somehow scarier than if he'd been shouting.

"But, but, Daddy, Baby Audwey!" Rebecca reverted without realising it to the lisp she'd had when she was younger.

"*Now,* Rebecca." Still in those dangerously quiet tones.

"But, but Daddy –"

"*Now!*" he roared, and with one last pleading glance at Mummy, whose face was pale under her make-up, Rebecca fled.

For a while, it wasn't hard to make out what was going on downstairs. There was an almighty row going on, that much was clear. Mummy was screaming and crying and hurling bitter accusations at Daddy, stuff about him being neglectful and emotionally distant. Rebecca already knew what those words meant because Mummy used them about Daddy all the time. Rebecca knew lots of grown-up words that meant 'bad husband' which she'd learned from Mummy. Mummy was always complaining about Daddy to Rebecca and saying what a bad husband he was, selfish in bed and selfish in other ways as well. Rebecca always felt vaguely guilty about hearing Mummy say such nasty things about Daddy when Daddy wasn't there to defend himself, but she usually managed to dismiss these thoughts because it felt so wonderful to have Mummy confiding in her like she was a fellow adult. In later years, Rebecca would learn that adults weren't supposed to confide in children as if they were fellow adults, especially about sexual things. It was something that adults today called 'inappropriate' but, when she was a child, she'd felt proud and grown-up to be the main repository of Mummy's important secrets.

Downstairs, Daddy was shouting and yelling and doors were being slammed shut and it was horrible. Rebecca climbed into bed and pulled the covers over her head to block out the noise but she could still hear it. She thought of Baby Audrey alone and abandoned in the living room, directly in the line of fire, and she trembled. Poor Baby Audrey! She would never forgive Rebecca for leaving her downstairs all alone like that. At one point, Rebecca thought she could hear a loud banging on the front door and then Daddy shouting even louder than he had been. She wondered if that was the taxi-driver arriving to take Rebecca and Mummy to Uncle Victor's house and then being sent away, amidst much angry yelling, by Daddy.

Then, at some point in the afternoon, everything went quiet downstairs. For some reason, this worried Rebecca more than the shouting. She was too afraid to come out of her room to see what was happening and, as the afternoon progressed, she grew more and more hungry.

At about six o'clock, a full four hours after Mummy and Rebecca's taxi was supposed to take them to Uncle Vic's house, Daddy came to her room with a tray bearing a meal he'd obviously put together himself. There was a cheese sandwich, a packet of crisps, a chocolate bar and an apple, together with a glass of milk in the blue sippy cup Rebecca hadn't used in over a year now. She used a proper big-girl beaker now, the one that had the teddy bears on it. Daddy mustn't have known this. He clearly didn't know either that Rebecca loathed cheese sandwiches and preferred jam ones. If Mummy had made up the tray, she would have done everything perfectly. Thinking about Mummy suddenly made Rebecca afraid.

After Daddy had put the tray down on the bedside table and turned to go without saying anything, Rebecca said shrilly, "Where's Mummy?"

Daddy seemed to hesitate, then he said, his voice tired and flat: "She's gone."

"Gone? Gone where?"

"Just gone, Becka. Now eat your dinner like a good girl and don't make a fuss, okay?"

"*Where's Mummy?*" Rebecca's voice rose dangerously high. Daddy sighed heavily and sat down on the bed beside her, taking both her small hands in one of his own big, work-calloused ones. "She's gone away with . . . with one of her men." He looked like it hurt him to say it.

"With . . . with Uncle Victor?" gulped Rebecca. If Daddy already knew about Uncle Victor, then it was obviously okay to mention him. He mustn't be a secret any more.

Daddy winced as if she'd cut him. "Yes, with Uncle Victor," he said dully.

"W-without me?" Rebecca's eyes were filling with tears.

"It looks like it," Daddy said. "Now, won't you eat something?"

"But . . . but thee would never go without me!" The tears spilled over and down her face and the lisp worsened. "Thee thwore thee wouldn't. I'm her – her pwecious widdle Becka-Boo."

"Well, I guess you didn't know exactly what kind of a manipulative, lying cheating bitch you had for a mother." Daddy was getting up off the bed now and making for the door. "Now eat your dinner and get yourself to bed, okay? I've got some work to do."

Rebecca cried for *hours*. She cried until her eyes were red and sore and her throat felt raw. Mummy couldn't be gone. She couldn't have left the house without her baby girl, her best friend and her little confidante, as she was always calling her. It just didn't make any sense. Daddy could say what he liked, but Mummy wouldn't have left without her precious daughter. She was always telling Rebecca that she was much more Mummy's child than Daddy's anyway. They liked all the same things, like girly chats about fashion, jewellery and make-up and Mummy's ideas about how she might like to design her own jewellery some day. She was even going to call her home business '*RJ's Jewels*,' the initials of each of their names, an '*R*' for Rebecca and a '*J*' for Joanna. Rebecca couldn't bear to think that now they mightn't be able to do Mummy's idea for her own business some day. After sobbing until she was exhausted, she fell into a fretful sleep that didn't make her feel rested when she woke, only hoarse, with a croak like a frog's and with terribly sore, heavy eyelids.

When she woke, it was pitch dark after the heavy rain that had fallen all day. Daddy hadn't bothered to plug in her nightlight so, with trembling fingers, she did it herself, feeling relieved when at least part of the huge room flooded with light. Starving now, she wolfed down the packet of crisps, the chocolate bar and the apple, leaving the cheese sandwich untouched (it was curling up at the edges, *yuk!*) and declining with a wrinkle of her nose the milk that was now warmish and no longer fresh and cold from the refrigerator the way she liked it. After finishing her small repast, she tiptoed to the door, realising now that she really needed the toilet. To her surprise, the door wouldn't open. Had Daddy . . . had Daddy locked her in? But why? And where *was* he? If Mummy was really gone, then Rebecca at least needed her daddy to be there in Mummy's place.

A horrible thought came unbidden into Rebecca's head that made icy fingers of fear claw their way down her spine. What if Daddy was gone too? What if he'd just decided he'd had enough of the nonsense – the bullshit, Mummy had called it – that came with being married with a kid and he'd just packed up and driven off in his van? What if she were all alone now in this big, echoey old house, with Mummy gone off to Uncle Victor's house for ever and Daddy disappeared God knows where in his van, and Baby Audrey, poor poor Baby Audrey, still down in the cold darkened living-room on her own?

Who would look after Rebecca now? Mummy didn't have any relatives. She'd told Rebecca that she'd split from them years before because they were too stuffy and old-fashioned to appreciate her more modern outlook on life and what they'd called her 'flighty' personality. They'd called her 'unstable', she'd told Rebecca indignantly once. Daddy's parents were dead and he didn't get on with his remaining relatives either. So Rebecca didn't really have grandparents, therefore, or the aunts and uncles that she'd read about in storybooks and knew other families had. The Uncles who'd called to the house to visit Mummy wouldn't, of course, have any reason to call there any more, not now that Mummy had left. If both her parents were gone, there would be no relatives to take Rebecca in, no family members to look after her. She'd be all alone in this big scary house for ever, jumping at shadows and the slightest little noise.

Unable to hold it in any longer, her bladder relaxed and let go and she wee-d where she stood, shivering violently with cold and fear by the bedroom door. She started to cry with the shame and fright of having wet herself. She was nearly six years old, much too old to be having this kind of 'accident'. She'd get in trouble for it for sure. There was a big stinky patch of wee by the door now. She went to her dresser where her mummy put her clean nightdresses and lifted one out. When she was dressed once more in a clean nightdress, something made her turn and peek out the window. Her bedroom window overlooked the long grassy back garden lined with trees on two sides and on the third one with a big brick wall. Mummy loved – *had* loved, Rebecca corrected herself miserably – the fact that you couldn't be overlooked by the other houses on Sycamore Street when you were out in the back garden. Mummy had taken advantage of this on numerous occasions to sunbathe naked while Daddy was at work. Rebecca wasn't supposed to tell Daddy that Mummy did this, because Daddy was a – what was it again – a big boring old fuddy-duddy who just wanted Mummy to stay at home knitting socks all day or something like that, and he thought Mummy was too much of a bloody exha – exhib – exhiba

–? Rebecca couldn't remember the long word Daddy had once angrily used to describe Mummy.

The back garden certainly wasn't sunny and bright right now, a place where butterflies chased one another around the treetops and a grey squirrel or two (rodents, Daddy called them, though Rebecca thought they looked adorable and not at all like rats, who were the real rodents) sometimes climbed down from the trees for a curious look-see at the crazy humans. It was dark and still raining, though not as heavily as earlier in the day, and Daddy was standing stock-still on the wet grass, on the place where he later built the summerhouse, staring up at the black moonless sky. He looked like himself, but he looked strange too, and different. Rain drenched his hair, his beard and his glasses and he wasn't wearing a coat, but he didn't seem to mind that he was all soaking wet and Catching His Death Of Cold, as Mummy was always saying to him when he came home from a job all wet and mucky. A shovel lay on the ground at his feet. What was he looking at, wondered Rebecca, because there was no moon tonight and only more rain to see? As Rebecca stared down at him, careful not to be seen by him because somehow she felt that he wouldn't want that, she saw him shudder, as if he were giving himself a shake or something, and snap suddenly out of his trance-like state. She watched as he bent to pick up the shovel, then turned himself around and headed towards the house, out of the rain. Rebecca stayed at the window for several more minutes, looking out at the deserted, rain-washed garden. Only when she was satisfied, or as satisfied as she *could* be, that her daddy wasn't returning to the back garden to stand once more looking up at the black sky in the rain, did she scurry, cold and uneasy, back to her bed.

She was woken in the middle of the night by a steady tap-tap-tapping sound at the window of her third-floor bedroom. Rebecca sat up in bed, bleary-eyed, her heart beating fast. She slipped out of bed and padded noiselessly across the carpeted floor to the window, from where the rhythmic tap-tap-tapping was getting louder and more insistent.

"Mummy?" she said, confused and frightened. "What are you doing out there?"

"Let me in, Becka-Boo," said Mummy from the other side of the glass, her eyes huge and pleading in her chalk-white face. "It's freezing out here."

"But what are you doing outside in the rain?" Rebecca asked her, her own eyes wide.

"Daddy locked me out, just to be spiteful," Mummy said. "See? That's the kind of man you have for a father. Come on, Becka sweetheart, you don't want Mummy to freeze to death out here, do you? Open the window!"

"I'm afwaid, Mummy!"

"Of what, for Christ's sake? There's nothing to be afraid of, Becka darling, it's only me, Mummy! Now open the window before I start to get cross!"

Trembling with cold and fear, Rebecca slipped the catch and pushed the window ajar a little. Immediately, Mummy grabbed at Rebecca's hand and began to pull her roughly through the window, but the hand that ensnared Rebecca's wasn't Mummy's hand at all but a misshapen claw. Rebecca looked into her mother's face and screamed.

The next day there was no sign of Mummy anywhere, or of Mummy's things. In the sitting-room, her goodbye note was gone from under the heavy glass ashtray on the coffee table. Even the heavy glass ashtray itself was gone. Rebecca thought that either Mummy or Daddy – more likely to be Mummy, she was the one who usually threw things – might have flung the ashtray at the other in a fit of temper and then swept up the pieces when it broke. Rebecca peeped in the bin but the pieces weren't there. Strange, but no stranger than some of the things that had happened around here lately.

Life went on. Although Rebecca never stopped missing her mother and wishing that she would one day come back (after all, Uncle Vic's house at the seaside couldn't be that far away, could it?), she adjusted to the new order of things, as kids do. She was sent to school and that occupied the best part of her time, and Daddy hired a stout, middle-aged woman called Mrs. Beech to mind Rebecca after school. Daddy still worked long hours, and when he came home he would eat the dinner that Mrs. Beech put before him, and then he'd spend the rest of the evening in front of the telly with a six-pack of beer from the fridge.

Not an unattractive man when he made an effort, Stephen had had a few girlfriends over the years, but none of them ever lasted long. Rebecca grew into a teenager and decided she just wanted to be known as 'Becks' from now on. She called Stephen 'Dad' now, having decided that she was too old for the 'Daddy' of her childhood years. She experienced the agonising pangs and pains of first love and wished her mother was still around to talk to her about periods and crushes and what boys really meant when they said they loved you and would still respect you in the morning. (She now knew that that was a big fat lie.) Joanna never got in touch, though. Becks always just assumed that she was terrified of being dragged home to live with her boring, grumpy workobsessed husband and tiresome daughter, and was heartbroken about it.

Now Rebecca was twenty-eight years old, she had a good job that she loved and a boyfriend, Barry, who she really felt might be The One. From time to time, though, usually when she was stressed or anxious about something, she still had the nightmare about Joanna tapping at her bedroom window. Every time was as bad as that first time, leaving her sweating, with pounding heart and a scream of blind terror frozen in her throat. Stephen Jamieson, still only in his fifties, had clearly given up on trying to find love and just spent his days working and his evenings boozing, either in the pub or at home in front of the telly. He now had a fully fledged liver problem and the doctor had told him emphatically that if he kept on drinking the way he was doing, he'd be dead within the year. Becks talked to him about his drinking but the seed that had been planted that day long ago, the day that Joanna took off to go and live with Uncle Victor for ever, had grown powerful, far-reaching roots. Stephen seemed resigned to his grim fate. He didn't act as if he cared all that much that he was going to die if he didn't curb his drinking, and Becks couldn't seem to reach him. Sure, he'd 'cut down' a bit when both Becks and his doctor had started getting heavy with him, but how serious he'd been about it was debatable. It even occurred to Becks that he might have been only pretending to drink less and just paying lip service to their concerns. The man he'd been when Joanna was still with them was now long gone, buried underneath layers and layers of protective coatings that stank of stale booze and self-pity. If Joanna hadn't left them, things would be different today.

Becks had regularly checked for a Joanna Jamieson on social media, because she could imagine that Joanna would love nothing more than taking picture after picture of herself in glamorous poses and chic little outfits and then posting the pictures online for all the world to see and admire, but she never found the Joanna she was searching for. For one thing, her mother almost certainly didn't call herself Jamieson any more. She probably used Uncle Vic's surname but Becks had never known what that was. It wasn't even beyond the bounds of possibility that Joanna no longer even called herself Joanna. She might have changed her Christian name to avoid being tracked down by her husband. There was nothing bleaker or more depressing, Becks decided, than scouring the Internet and social media for someone whose full name you didn't know. It was a bit like going to visit an old friend after a long absence and finding that their house, in which you'd played together as children, had been demolished. Becks reflected sadly too that she didn't even know what her mother looked like now. Was Joanna still bleached-blonde and flapper-thin with short hair, or had she grown out her hair and put on weight? Had she had any more children? It would have devastated Becks if she'd ever found out that Joanna had had another child after her or even children. She especially hoped that Joanna had never given birth to another baby girl, a little girl she might have cuddled and called 'her bestest girl', and tucked into bed at night with songs and kisses and promises to stay close by in case her baby girl needed her. It would just be too hard to find out that she, Becks, was no longer

Joanna's only precious baby daughter.

And what if Joanna was no longer even alive? Technically, she could have died at any time over the last twenty-three years. Becks tried hard to suppress this thought whenever it reared its head. It was just too depressing.

Barry O'Donnell, you prick, you're late again!

It was twenty to nine and Barry was meant to have been at her house since seven o'clock. Becks had already bathed and was dressed in new silky pink pyjamas from Victoria's Secret, which she wouldn't have dreamed of wearing if she was by herself and spending the evening lounging around in front of the telly. These pyjamas were to be worn strictly for boyfriends. Under the pyjamas were new silky knickers, also pink, and a pink push-up bra that was as uncomfortable as fuck to wear. Anyone who thought that women dressed like this to please themselves was either nuts or a liar. Or a *man*. And if Barry O'Donnell didn't turn up in the next ten minutes, she was changing back into her regular tartan pyjamas and the big comfy undies that didn't cut into the soft skin under her boobs, and Barry O'Donnell could go and feck himself. No matter how hard he pleaded, she'd be closed for business for the whole night and he'd have only himself to blame.

Typically, just as she'd decided this, he rang the front doorbell. She didn't rush to answer it, although she felt the familiar rush of excitement when she peeked through the spyhole and saw his big bulky shape filling up the space the way it did.

"You're an hour and three-quarters late," she said stiffly as she let him in.

"Sorry," he apologised, taking off his coat and putting it on a chair. "Rob from work was having a romantic crisis. I had to take him for a pint so he could cry on my shoulder."

"You've been with Rob-from-work since five o'clock?" Her voice clearly expressed the scepticism she felt but Barry merely shrugged.

"You know what it's like between him and Mel." He was using that special tone of his that implied that, once more, she was being a tad unreasonable. "They have more ups and downs than a – well, I can't think of something else that has a load of ups and downs, but you know what I mean, don't you?"

Reluctantly, Becks nodded.

"Any chance of a coffee?" He clearly considered the mini-crisis to be over. "And a bit of grub? I'm starving. I've had about five pints and no food and I'm getting light-headed."

"I'm not cooking you anything in *these* pyjamas." Becks could have murdered him for his thoughtlessness. "It'll have to be a sandwich. Why didn't you get some hot bloody bar food?"

"I didn't think of it." He sounded maddeningly unconcerned as he followed her into the kitchen, hands stuffed casually in pockets.

Becks was furious with him. She hadn't got all dressed up like a bloody dog's dinner just to be his skivvy in the kitchen. She hadn't put on this torture device the marketing people optimistically called a *bra* just to butter slices of bread and slap a few hunks of ham and cheese between them. Even now, it felt like her poor boobs were being garrotted in the expensive garment. The pain would have been worth it though, if only Barry would notice how upright and perky her breasts were. She'd put these pyjamas on to be loved in, pampered, adored, worshipped, not to be hustled into the kitchen to make bloody food. She could make food any time. Tonight was meant to be about love-making, about reaffirming their supposed love for each other.

"Your old man down in Dessie's?" Barry asked, grinning, then he sat himself at the kitchen table and opened her dad's newspaper, much to Becks' annoyance.

Now she had to compete with the news of the day as well? This was too much. She nodded.

"He'll be back around half-eleven." She hated herself for sounding whingy, but she couldn't seem to help it. "If you'd got here when you were bloody well meant to, we might have had more time to have the whole house to ourselves." Stephen would indeed be back from the pub at around half-eleven or twelve. He'd walk home, because he wouldn't be able to drink if he brought the car and he *needed* to be able to drink (that was the whole point of the exercise), and anyway the pub was only a short walk away. He'd hang his coat uncaringly on the hook next to Barry's, and then he'd go to bed and be still asleep when Becks and Barry got up early the next day, tiptoeing around the place so as not to wake him. In the mornings, he would get up for work when he was ready, usually after Becks and Barry had already left for their own jobs. He wouldn't go near Becks when Barry was with her but Becks still felt inhibited sometimes, knowing her dad was sleeping just across the landing from them while she was making love with Barry. That was a bit intense. She much preferred it with Barry when Stephen was out of the house altogether, and she knew that Barry did too.

"I know, I know." Barry's mouth was full of the bread

and ham she'd thrown together without any ceremony. "Blame me. I get the blame for everything anyway, so I might as well be blamed for this too."

"Well, who else around here turned up nearly two hours late for our date?" Becks handed him his coffee and didn't care that a few drops slopped onto his expensive shirt. Actually, she'd been kind of hoping that they would.

"I explained that. I told you I couldn't help it." He took a swig of his coffee and said "*Fuck!*" when it burnt the tongue off him.

"It's just that I've hardly seen you lately." To Becks' horror, she could feel the tears welling up and hear them in her wobbly voice. The last thing she wanted was to show weakness in front of Barry. It made her feel like such a typical little woman.

"I know, I know," soothed Barry, putting down his cup and stroking her face. "Look, I'm finished here now. What say we leave this lot here and just go up, yeah?"

The face-stroking continued. Becks felt her anger at him – justified though it was – melting away. Dammit, he was way too good at getting back on her good side. They kissed and hugged at the kitchen table and then Becks led him upstairs to her bedroom, where she'd changed the bedsheets and tidied her bundle of ironing out of sight and sprayed an air freshener around the place to infuse it with the smell of violets, a flower (and fragrance) that Joanna had loved and that Becks loved too. They undressed each other (thank *God,* Becks thought as the hated bra was cast off and flung to the four winds, but not before the effect had been suitably observed by Barry) and made love on the newly made bed. Afterwards, Barry fell fast asleep straightaway, much to Becks' disappointment. He always had a little nap after sex anyway, which Becks didn't begrudge him because everyone agreed that it was an actual physical thing that men needed to do, but it looked now like he was down for the night. And after all her bloody effort too! She was looking gorgeous, her long light-brown hair was down and freshly washed and she'd waxed and oiled places where she hadn't even known she *had* places, and for what? For Barry to just roll over and fall asleep? She poked and tugged at him for a minute, but he just turned over, with his back to her, and began to snore loudly. Becks stared at his broad bare back as if she was seeing it for the first time. On his left shoulder blade was something she had definitely never seen before. A *tattoo*. A fucking *tattoo*! Barry hadn't been tattooed there, or anywhere else about his person, for that matter, when she'd last seen him naked, which had been about a week before, give or take a day or two. It was a pretty ordinary, bog-standard tattoo of a snake entwined about a rose. Hardly original, and kind of an odd place to put it, but all that was beside the point. When had he acquired this tattoo and, more to the point, *why* had he acquired it in the first place? It clearly wasn't to impress Becks, because he hadn't even bothered to show it to her properly. He'd let her discover it by accident. Then for whom had he had it put there? And, as far as Becks knew, Barry O'Donnell was afraid of needles. He'd have to have a pretty special reason for overcoming his fear and getting a tattoo. Or maybe a special some*one?* Filled with dread, she poked him hard in the back.

"What's the big idea, Becks?" he grumbled, half-asleep. "That bloody hurt."

"It was meant to," said Becks tightly. "Barry, since when the fuck do you have a tattoo?"

"Tattoo?" He was bleary-eyed. Then the fog behind his eyes cleared and he sat upright, yawning and scratching under his arms. "Tattoo, yes." He said it as if he were only just remembering. "I *did* get a tattoo the other week, now you come to mention it."

"You never told me you were getting one." Becks was gritting her teeth. She had a dull headache coming – she could feel it behind her eyes.

"I didn't know myself. It was kind of a spur-of-the-moment thing."

"You got a tattoo on the spur of the moment?" Becks' tone was positively glacial.

"What can I say? I'm full of surprises!" He had a self-satisfied grin on his chops that made Becks want to slap him, hard.

"*Who* did you get it for, Barry?"

"What d'you mean, *who*?" He sounded puzzled. "I got it for myself, didn't I? And, *erm*, for you, of course."

"Then how come I'm only finding out about it now, if it was supposedly meant for me?"

"I had every intention of telling you tonight." His face was turning a dull brick-red like it always did when they argued. "I would've told you, if I hadn't nodded off there for a minute." He was the kind of man who would have high blood pressure by the time he was forty because of job stress, too much booze and all the steak-house dinners with his work colleagues. Already he had an unnaturally high colour for a man in his late twenties.

Now he was running his hands through his hair, something he did when he was playing for time. Becks had noticed this habit of his before.

"Barry, are you seeing someone else behind my back?" she asked him straight out. Straight out was always best. You got nowhere pussyfooting around things as if they were made of bloody china.

In the split second before Barry answered her direct question, she saw a fleeting glimpse of something in his eyes that told her that she was right. He *was* seeing someone else. Becks felt like she'd been punched in the stomach, as if the air had all gone out of her. If his next words were '*What makes you think that?*' then she'd have it confirmed for her. Guys who were cheating always said '*What makes you think that?*' when you confronted them about it. It was a way of stalling for time, sure, but it was also because they were genuinely curious about what had given them away, the sneaky bastards, so they could know for next time what *not to do*. Well, she was damned if she was telling him.

"What makes you think that?" The injured tones were all present and correct.

"Get out, Barry," she said evenly, picking up his boxers and flinging them in his face.

"What's got into you, Becks?" He crawled out of the bed and came to sit beside her on the edge. "This isn't like you at all."

"Oh, I'm so sorry," she said sarcastically. "Am I not behaving the way someone who's been cheated on is supposed to behave? Am I not being distressed enough? Well, here, try this on for size, knobhead."

She burst into noisy, messy sobs that sooner or later would require the services of a tissue.

Barry looked on, helplessly, before pulling on his boxers. Presumably, he felt safer with them on than off.

Better on than just floating around Becks' bed, leaving him wholly unprotected in the crotch department.

"Who is she? Is she someone I know? Someone from your work?"

"It doesn't matter, does it?" Barry looked all sheepish now.

"Why do men always say that?" Before he had a chance to attempt to answer her rhetorical question, she added, "It matters to me! Tell me who it is, Barry, you utter shit, if you ever want to bloody well see me again after tonight."

Barry hesitated. He looked like he was struggling with something. He opened his mouth to speak just as Becks realised that there was someone downstairs, someone who was banging fairly persistently on the front door. She suddenly felt like the noise had been going on for some time but she'd chosen to block it out.

"Dad's forgotten his key again," she said. "Hold that thought. I'll be back in two seconds."

Wrapping her dressing-gown tightly around her, she ran down the stairs and opened the door.

It wasn't her father at all, but two Guards, one male and one female. Their Garda hats were off and in their hands, and their faces were serious. Becks felt like her heart was pounding in her mouth instead of in her chest.

"Are you Rebecca Jamieson?" the male Guard said.

Rebecca started to laugh out loud. "*When the Guard is sad, the news is bad!*" she exclaimed, parroting a silly jingle she'd heard once on a television sketch show. Still laughing, she repeated: "*When the Guard is sad, the news is bad! When the Guard is sad, the news is bad!*" She turned and yelled up the stairs "*Hey, you, fuckface!*"

Barry came rushing down the stairs in just his boxers with his shirt covering up the stupid tattoo.

"Come on down here and hear the news! *When the Guard is sad, the news is bad! When the Guard is sad, the news is bad! When the Guard is sad, the news is bad!*"

Barefoot, she began to dance a little jig around the hall.

"All right, Becks, all right," said Barry firmly, stopping her in mid-jig and taking hold of her hands. To the Guards he said: "I'm sorry about this, Guards, I think she's a little hysterical. We've just been having, *erm*, a small disagreement about, *erm*, something and nothing, and I think she's a little bit, *um*, upset, shall we say. I'm Barry O'Donnell, her boyfriend. What's wrong? Has there been an accident or something?"

"It's about her father, Stephen Jamieson," said the female Guard gently.

Barry caught Becks before she hit the floor.

STOP 13: ST. STEPHEN'S GREEN

Laura again

Laura got on the Luas at the St. Stephen's Green stop, near her flat, and prepared to take plenty of selfies. She'd gone to a lot of trouble to get ready for work that morning. She went to a lot of trouble to get ready for work *every* morning, she thought with a sigh, and where had it got her? Precisely nowhere, or at least not where she really wanted to be. Sure, she got the attention of every pervert and sleazebag on public transport, like the guy in the black coat who was eyeing her up a little too attentively right now from two seats down, but she didn't care two flying fucks for these losers. The only guy whose attention she'd ever really wanted was Paul Sheridan's, and that was hard enough to get these days. That asshole Barry O'Donnell had dumped her by text a few days ago too. His girlfriend's father, a raging alcoholic according to Barry, had been knocked down by a hit-and-run driver on his way home from the pub. He was in hospital and wasn't expected to live.

"I've got to be there for Becks," he'd whined at her in his texts. "You *do* see that, don't you, Laura, babes?"

"Oh, just fuck off, Barry, will you?" she'd texted back,

annoyed at the blow to her pride – *she* did the dumping, not some jerk-off of a guy she'd met only for sex a handful of times. Otherwise, she was not too bothered. Barry had been a stop-gap, that was all, nothing more. He was good-looking but a bit too vain and self-centred for her liking. Laura, as a vain, self-centred person herself, recognised the trait instantly in another. She didn't think a relationship between two similarly selfish people was a good bet – too much jostling for mirror space in the morning – but, for a while, his thick black hair and sturdy, gym-honed body had taken her mind temporarily off her troubles.

She'd met him one day at the Harcourt Street Luas stop. He'd been waiting for this Becks person to beetle down from Charlemont, and Laura had had a few minutes to kill before her journey to work, so she'd walked up to the Harcourt Street stop rather than get on at the Stephen's Green one as usual, enjoying the fresh air as she walked. They'd started talking at the Luas stop and Barry had given her many admiring glances, which had pleased her and flattered her after all the bullshit with Paul. They'd swapped numbers and he'd called her the minute she got out of work. She'd invited him over to her flat and he'd accepted like a shot. They both knew what he was coming over for.

After breaking up with Paul, it had felt so good to have a nice hefty male body in her arms and in her bed again. Barry was an uncomplicated lover who seemed to want only to climb on top of a woman and mate vigorously. After Paul's complex needs and all his mad kinky stuff, it had been a blessed relief to have just plain sex and nothing else with Barry. Several times he'd come round to her flat off Stephen's Green after his work and her own job had finished for the day. He worked in an office on Harcourt Street, which was nice and convenient for her flat. He'd make some lame but plausible excuse to his girlfriend Becks (Laura had seen pictures of her on Barry's phone – she was a looker all right but appeared a bit on the sappy side and too goody-goody for Laura's liking) and end up staying half the night at Laura's place. He seemed to be perfectly okay with just having regular sex and the occasional blowjob, which made a nice change from Paul, who was *never* content with ordinary lovemaking. Maybe the truth was that Paul couldn't get aroused unless there was some element of kinkiness, domination and sado-masochism involved. She'd heard of people like that. Either they needed extensive therapy to 'fix' themselves and wean themselves off their fixations or, in this modern day-and-age of 'anything goes', they just had to learn to live with their obsessions and be comfortable with them and open up about them to others, as if it was no big deal that you needed a household appliance shoved up your hole in order to be able to have an orgasm. Even though Laura missed Paul like crazy and wanted him back, she couldn't help feeling relieved that, for now at least, she didn't have to play the bloody dominatrix for him.

Barry O'Donnell loved her collection of kinky underwear and had nearly wet himself with excitement when she wore the stupid purply basque thing she'd worn for Paul. He looked in the mirror a lot though, and he seemed to spend more time and money on his hair than she did on hers, which she didn't like. And he was always *fixing* himself, to the point where she wondered if his hair and clothes were actually the most important things in his life. He seemed kind of shallow to her, and immature, like a little boy rather than a man. He took an awful lot of selfies too, just like Laura did (she couldn't have a go at him for being like that, because she was exactly the same herself), although he was apparently smart enough at cheating to draw the line at uploading to social media the ones he took of himself and Laura at Laura's flat and even in Laura's bed. Those were just for his personal use, he said.

"I don't want Becks finding out about us that way, not when we're just having a bit of fun," he'd said with a grin.

You don't want her to find out about us at all, because I mean less than nothing to you, Laura wanted to say but she didn't.

She was annoyed that he was always calling her 'a bit of fun'. That stung a bit, the way guys were always saying that about her. She was always the 'bit on the side', never the main course, only the starter or the dessert. Always the girlfriend or the mistress, but never the bride, never the wife. That was increasingly how Paul had made her feel in the final weeks of their relationship, and now Barry was trying to do it too. So she'd fought back, against all the lucky women she resented who had their claws into some guy and thought that meant they owned him. She persuaded Barry to stay overnight at her flat, which she knew would get him in trouble with Becks, and it did. She also persuaded him (and this was an absolute hoot) to get a tattoo on his back, a snake entwined around a rose on his left shoulder blade. She knew that Becks, as a fellow woman, so to speak, would go nuts when she saw it and wonder endlessly who he'd done it for. She was right on both counts. Becks gave Barry merry hell about it and then Barry in turn had given Laura merry hell about that.

Shit rolled down, didn't it? Then there was all the trouble with Becks' lush of an old man (it was okay for Laura to refer to him as such, because her own mother had a drink problem too, and it would have been hypocritical of her not to admit this), and Barry had had to call a halt to the whole thing, and by text too, the prick. Laura genuinely didn't care though, or at least so she told herself. It was only her ego that had been bruised, nothing else. Barry had really only been a diversion, a distraction from all the pain and suffering involved in being dumped by a married man who, for better or worse, was still the love of her life. All she'd had on her mind for so long was her big campaign to Get Paul Back. She'd put too much time and effort into that relationship to have it snatched away from her, and yet it was gone nonetheless. How could that be? Still, no one had ever said that life was meant to be fair, had they? And if they had, they'd have been lying, with bells on.

"*Please move down the tram*," said the automated female voice.

Laura sighed. Every day was the bloody same. Nothing ever changed.

The first few days without him had been terrible. She'd phoned Barbara, Paul's wife, at their family home (Laura hated that phrase – she hadn't had one of those herself growing up, not really, so how dared anyone else live so comfortably and cosily in theirs?) in Stillorgan, just like she'd threatened to, and spilled the beans about herself and Paul. It was Paul's own fault for running out on her like the coward he was and she, Laura, had felt entirely justified in acting as she had. She was only doing what she said she'd do if he left her that day. It hadn't gone the way she'd intended, though, and it was a toss-up as to who had felt worst after it, herself or Barbara.

"Hello?" she'd said into the phone that day.

"Hello?" a little girl's voice had replied.

Oh shit, one of the kids. "Can I speak to your mummy, please?" Laura's voice was trembling, much to her annoyance. She wanted, needed, to do this right now, while she was all high on adrenalin and righteous fury and indignation. Any delays, and she might lose her nerve.

"Just a minute," said the little girl.

There was the sound of the phone being put down, then voices and background noise. Laura thought she could hear the sound of cartoons on the television, and picturing the cosy family scene made her feel like Glenn Close's character in *Fatal Attraction*, in the bit where she's looking in the window at her lover with his wife and child and their brand-new rabbit, all curled up nice and warm in front of the fire. Glenn Close's character is so upset and revolted (and feels so excluded) by the scene that she runs round the side of the house to vomit her guts up. Laura thought it was the one scene in the film that made the woman look human, a sympathetic character instead of just a raving lunatic.

"Hello?" said a woman's voice.

Laura recognised it because she'd rung the house once or twice before, out of sheer curiosity, just to hear what her lover's wife, her love rival, sounded like. On each occasion, she'd sounded older than Laura, and tired. On each occasion, Laura had put the phone down without speaking after Barbara picked up.

"Hello?" The woman sounded impatient now. "This is Barbara Sheridan speaking. Who's this?" She sounded so confident and sure of herself, so goddamn fucking *entitled*, that Laura felt her own nerve coming back.

"This is Laura Brennan," she said coolly. "I work at Phelan's with your husband."

"Is Paul all right?" the woman said, suddenly sounding panicky.

"He's fine." Laura took a deep breath before adding, "I'm just phoning to tell you that I've been having sex with Paul for the last two years."

Her heart was pounding like the clappers, now that she'd actually done it. There was a silence, then the other woman said curtly: "Hold on a minute."

The phone was put down again, then there was the sound of the television being turned off and children being ushered complainingly out of the room. A minute later the woman was back. Laura could hear the sound of her puffing furiously on a cigarette.

"Has he dumped you then?" Barbara Sheridan said coldly. "That's the only reason you're calling here, isn't it? He's dumped you, and you're getting your revenge by phoning me."

"He-he'll be back." Laura's confidence was somewhat shaken by the other woman's accurate representation of the situation, as if such a situation had occurred before and she was used to it.

"You don't fondly suppose, do you," said Barbara Sheridan bitterly, puffing away on her fag, "that you're the first great love of Paul's life? Granted, you might have lasted a bit longer than the others, but you still got dumped in the end, didn't you?"

"The . . . the others?" whispered Laura. "There were . . . others?"

Barbara Sheridan laughed, a cold, angry sound with no laughter in it. "Of course there've been others, you sad, dozy bitch. You're not even the first to call here, for fuck's sake. If you believed him when he said that this time was the only time he'd ever broken his marital vows, and he's only broken them for you because you're so special, then you deserve all the shit you get from him. For Christ's sake, there've been two others from Phelan's alone. Remember Diana? She got the sack in the end. And so did that mouthy one with the streaks of pink in her hair – Debbie Somebody."

Laura listened in shock. Those had been girls who'd left Phelan's in the last two years, since she'd been there herself. Diana was the woman whose job Laura had applied for when Diana handed in her notice, and Debbie Crosby had been working in Phelan's when Laura had joined the company two years ago, but she was gone now too. Laura had never known why they'd left. Jesus Christ Almighty. Had they both been shagging Paul? Debbie with the pink hair had only left about six months ago, while Laura had been seeing Paul. Had he been two-timing her with Debbie? It was incredible, impossible – it didn't bear thinking about. Barbara must be lying. Or maybe she'd seen some things, heard some things and misinterpreted them, put two and two together and made five.

"I don't believe you," Laura said, her voice now a lot less confident than she would have liked.

"Believe what you like," snapped Barbara. "Why don't you ask him? Or are you afraid to? You'll not get the truth, mind. He's a compulsive liar. One of these days I'll work up the courage to leave him. And then, after I get what I'm owed, you little office scrubbers can divide up the rest for all I care."

"He . . . Paul doesn't love you." Laura was desperate to regain the upper hand, along with some of her previous composure.

Barbara laughed again. "Do you honestly think I give a flying fuck?" She took another long drag on her fag. "Because, if you do, then you're even dumber than you sound. Good luck to you, *Laura Brennan*. You're going to need it."

Sensing that the other woman was about to hang up, Laura hastily jumped in with, "I'm pregnant too, by the way, *Mrs*. Barbara Sheridan, and it's your precious husband's child. So, how'd you like that, then, Mrs. High-and-Mighty?"

There was a silence, then Barbara hung up with a smart click, leaving Laura to stare, dumbfounded, at the phone.

The few weeks following that phone conversation had been awful, almost unbearable. In Phelan's, Paul studiously ignored her and, if he absolutely had to interact with her, he was coolly professional, calling her Miss Brennan in tones so frosty that they practically had icicles adhering to them. Laura personally thought that he was drawing much more attention to the issue by being so ridiculously distant and formal towards her publicly, and she didn't like the sniggers she was sure she could hear coming from the other girls in the typing pool. She was convinced now that they all knew about her and Paul and that he'd dumped her. She was a fucking laughing-stock. When she walked into the office bathroom, the women gathered gossiping around the mirrors would pointedly stop talking and concentrate assiduously on doing themselves up. When she passed any of the men who worked in Phelan's, they'd eye her up speculatively as if

Paul had told them what she was like in bed, or what her body was like under her clothes. It made her more uncomfortable than she'd have ever believed it would. When she and Paul were together, she'd been dying for everyone to know about them. Now that he'd dropped her like a hot spud, the reality was different. They were glad she'd been dumped, she felt sure. They probably saw it as that snotty bitch Laura, the one who was way too much into her looks, being taken down a peg or two and finally getting her come-uppance. The idea that they no doubt were thinking that mortified Laura.

She thought of handing in her resignation and looking for another job, as Paul had so nastily suggested to her on the night he'd dumped her, but why should she? Why should *she* be the one to have her life disrupted? No way was she looking for a new job just to suit *him*. She liked her job. Well, okay, so it bored the arse off her – she couldn't exactly say that she *liked* it, but it wasn't too difficult and it paid well. Let *him* look for a new job if he was so bothered. She couldn't believe he hadn't been fired before, anyway, for messing about with the female staff. Had those two girls really left (or been fired) because they'd been screwing Paul and it had all gone tits-up? In that case, why not just get rid of Paul? It wasn't as if he was indispensable at his job or anything. No one was. He was only a junior manager. More likely it was just because he was the man and they, as women, were the sluts, the office scrubbers as Barbara Sheridan had called them, so they were the dispensable ones. Sexism and an anti-woman bias were obviously alive and well in the workplace, anyway.

There was, however, another reason why Laura hadn't wanted to give up her job at first. At least she still got to see Paul every day. Out of sight, out of mind, wasn't that what they said? Unless she was right in his eyeline every day from Monday to Friday, he'd forget about her. That was what men did, wasn't it? This way, at least there was still a chance that she and Paul might get back together. If she was in another job, she wouldn't have a hope in hell of getting him to come back to her. He'd ignored all her texts and calls for the first couple of weeks after they'd split up. He'd been screening her calls, of course, but even when she'd put her number on private, he still hadn't been caught out. She'd felt like she'd simply ceased to exist for him. It wasn't a nice feeling, being so completely and utterly sidelined like that by someone who she'd thought loved her.

After about two weeks, she'd changed tack. She'd stopped whinging about loving him to the ends of the earth and back, and instead had started talking his, Paul's, language. She'd accompanied a phone photo of her unclothed breasts with the words: "**Miss you so much. Am sooooo fucking horny!!!**" and sent it to his phone.

Five minutes later, he'd texted back.

"**Are u touching urself?**".

"**Yes,**" texted back Laura immediately, although she wasn't.

Of course she bloody wasn't. Women were mostly lying when they said they were, and men were stupid if they believed it. It was a Saturday afternoon. She was slumped on the couch in sweatpants in front of the telly and had never felt less like having sex in her life, but she talked such a good game that her reward was a phone photo of Paul's erect willy in mid-excitement. It didn't turn her on in the slightest but that wasn't the point. The point was that, if she could still turn *him* on, he might miss the sex they'd had and come back to her. A few more messages later, and he was sending her his very own money shot. Laura smiled to herself in grim satisfaction. Operation Get Paul Back was off to a good start.

She redoubled her efforts to look good in work, which was exhausting because she always went to great lengths to look good for work anyway, and had usually uploaded about a dozen glamorous selfies to social media each morning before most people had crawled out from under the duvet. Upping her game still further in the looks department was hard, mostly thankless work. The one day she'd tried the hardest, so hard she'd nearly killed herself, he'd been out sick, the bloody bastard. When he *wasn't* off sick and she had to go into his office for something or other, she always had a couple of buttons undone on her blouse so that he could look down her top and admire whatever lacy, push-up bra she had on.

The week after the phone sex (or the sexting, as it was now called), she'd sexted him again on a Thursday night, a night on which she'd been accustomed to having him come round to her flat, so she was hoping he'd be at a loose end.

"**So horny**," she'd texted. "**Need u in me now. Can u come over?**"

An agonising half-hour passed with no response. Then her phone rang. She pounced on it.

"I'm on my way over," he'd said curtly. "Keep it hot for me, okay?"

"Okay," she'd breathed. "See you soon."

Then she'd rushed around the flat, frantically opening windows and spraying air freshener everywhere to cover up the fact that she'd been smoking like a chimney ever since the break-up. Her own appearance was picture-perfect. Stockings and suspenders, high-heeled silver glittery hooker shoes and a lovely new black bra-and-knickers combination. Her long blonde hair was straightened to within an inch of its life with the fancy new straightener and her make-up was flawless. They fell on each other like hungry dogs as soon as he was in the door. Laura felt as if she was putting on the performance of a lifetime, slapping him, scolding him and threatening him, even tying his hands to the bedpost with some black-velvet ribbons she normally used for her hair, ordering him to call her 'Mistress' and making him delay his orgasm for as long as he could. From her position on top of him, she was certain that she looked to Paul like the Queen of All She Surveyed, and it made him good and hard and it made the sex last for a long, long time. When he *did* come, when his 'Mistress' eventually 'permitted' him to come, he groaned long and loud before collapsing back against the sheets, his hands still bound to the bed with the black ribbons.

"Untie these, will you?" he said, and Laura's heart sank.

He wasn't going already, was he? She hadn't expected him to stay for dinner or anything, although she'd bought a few nice snackables anyway, just in case he was peckish after all the sex she'd been hoping they'd have, but surely he wasn't going to just bang her and bugger off straightaway, back to What's-Her-Face? She untied his bonds and lay back down beside him hopefully.

"Um, so how are things at home?" she chanced.

He sat up on the edge of the bed away from her and

ran his hands through his thick dark hair until it was all ruffled. "How do you *think* they are, Laura?" he said tiredly. "They're fucking shite, that's what they are. You really dropped me in it when you phoned Barbara."

He pulled on his socks and got to his feet to put on his underwear.

"I'm sorry," she said quietly. "I really am."

"Well, I hope you're happy with the results." He picked his trousers up from the floor.

By the sound of it, he'd deposited all his loose coins on her bedroom floor again. Some things clearly never changed.

He slipped on his trousers and reached for his discarded shirt. "Barbara's on my case twenty-four-seven now. She thinks I'm out doing late-night shopping right now for Christmas. I'll have to stop at the supermarket on the way home and buy something Christmassy we don't need just to prove I was doing what I said I was doing. She gives me no peace now. My time's not my own any more. And as for telling her that you were up the spout! Well, that was a pretty low blow, especially since you know that Barbara's pregnant now too. She could have lost the baby with the shock of that bloody phone call."

"I'm sorry, Paul," Laura said again, though from what she'd heard of Barbara that day on the phone, she genuinely thought that the lady was made of sterner stuff than that. "I only did it because I was so angry and hurt at being dumped like that."

He sat down on the bed again to pull on his socks and shoes.

"Well, *I'm* the one who got dumped in it, right up to my balls." There was so much *bitterness* in his voice. "Barbara will never let me live this down. And she'll never let me go either, not now we're having Baby Number Three."

"How far along is she?" Laura tried not to sound jealous but it was very hard. If only it were her having Paul's baby, a baby that would tie the two of them together for ever! Maybe she should come off the Pill and try to trap him or something. She wished she'd thought of that before tonight – she could even now be pregnant with his child. He surely couldn't leave her if she was having his child.

"Five months." He dropped his head in his hands and groaned out loud.

Laura stared at him. Five months ago, it had been summer, one of the best summers she could ever remember. She and Paul had had a wonderful, magical time together. Laura had almost been able to forget that Paul was a married man with kids and responsibilities and, for a while, until Barbara had reminded him, so had Paul. They'd gone to the Barge Pub in Portobello together after work nearly every day of the heatwave, and sat outside on the canal with the rest of the sun-worshippers, drinking in the unaccustomed sunshine and enjoying each other's company and feeling endlessly, *endlessly* horny with the heat. They'd go back to Laura's flat afterwards and make love. Then they would lie entwined on Laura's bed, drenched in sweat with their limbs locked together. The heat and sweat played havoc with Laura's carefully applied make-up and straightened hair, but it was worth the extra effort she'd had to go to. But had Paul really gone home after those wonderfully special evenings and made love to Barbara too? He must have, thought Laura, who was hurt more than she could say by this thought. What a bastard! What a lying, cheating rat! How easily the lies came to his lips!

wasn't the time to ask him about his sex life
ra, not now when she was trying to win him
istead, trying hard to keep her voice light and
said, "Do you know if it's a boy or a girl yet?"
a knows but she won't tell me," Paul said
She says she's not telling me until she's absolutely
I'm not planning to do a runner on her."
would be a fine thing, thought Laura. "Right.

hat did you say to a thing like that? What *could*
a thing like that? She sat up in bed and began
aul's back, his arms and his shoulders, which
and all knotted up with tension under his shirt.
Paul." She forced a sympathy into her voice
in no way felt. Encouraged by the fact that he
o be enjoying her impromptu massage, she
lightly: "It's going to be so hard on you for the
weeks and months, Paul. Don't forget that I'm
re for you if you need me."
iks." He got to his feet. "I might just take you up

's heart momentarily lifted, then it sank again
turned to her and said, "Look, Laura, there's
n this for you any more. What kind of life would
e, constantly waiting for me to have a few free
when I could sneak out and see you? Barbara and
will be wanting more and more of my time and
a over the next few months and I'm going to have
t to them. I could be the kind of shit who keeps
iging on, dangling on the end of a string, always
for those few snatched minutes here and there.
not quite the lowlife bastard that everyone makes

me out to be, and I don't think I could do that to you. It's better for everyone if we just have a clean break from each other."

"But I really don't *mind* all the waiting around," Laura lied brightly. "I don't mind it at all as long as I can just see you sometimes."

"You don't mind that Barbara's having our third baby, and that I'm going to have to be very much around for the pregnancy and birth and all the night feeds and the nappies and shit?"

Laura, aware that she was telling the biggest lie of her life, nodded, smiled. "I don't mind if you don't mind."

"It would only be for the sex," Paul said then. "I'm being brutally honest here but I have to be. There'd be no future in it. You couldn't expect any commitment from me and you'd have to accept that. Could you accept that?"

"Sure," Laura said, as if it were no big thing he was asking her to do. "If that's what you want."

"It's not what I want." His mouth was set in grim lines. "But it's the way things have to be. And if Barbara finds out, it has to end immediately, and permanently, okay?"

Again, Laura nodded, her smile a little less bright this time.

He shrugged on his jacket. "Right then, I'll have to head off." He was openly looking at his watch now. Before, he would have peeped at it discreetly when he thought she wasn't looking. "I still have to get to a supermarket somewhere, remember, and buy something Christmassy before I can even think of going home. I'll text you, but it won't be for a few days, okay?"

She nodded, smiled again and lifted up her face for his goodbye kiss, which barely grazed her cheek.

When he was gone, she went straight to the fridge. There was a full bottle of white wine and half a bottle of red wine there. She always drank a glass or two before Paul came over, to put her in the mood for sex or, more correctly, to fortify her for the kind of sex Paul wanted, the pervy prick. Now she took out the two bottles. She returned with them to the bedroom, then flopped disconsolately down on the bed and began to drink.

The days fell into a kind of pattern after that for a bit. She'd go to work and try to get through the day, being largely ignored by Paul on the one hand and sniggered at by her bitchy female co-workers on the other. Then she'd head home, stop off at the Off-Licence near her flat for a bottle of wine, go home and drink it. She drank at least a bottle of wine a night, sometimes more. She might have something modest to eat, maybe a salad she'd nibble on for a minute or two like a fussy rabbit, but mostly she'd just drink, keeping her phone on in case he called. When he didn't, she'd collapse into bed and sob herself loudly and messily to sleep, only to wake up again a few hours later with a rotten headache, a raging thirst and a frustrating inability to get back to sleep, so that she was always exhausted at work. A few times, she'd even had a glass of wine or two before work, at eight o'clock in the morning. She was a wreck. Three weekends on the bounce, she went to a nightclub on Leeson Street that was infamous for the number of married men who frequented it and pulled without the slightest difficulty. Those places were like fucking meat markets.

When she took the first guy home to her flat, he'd dived naked onto her bed except for his grey socks and his wedding ring, lay on his back with his hands clasped comfortably behind his back and said: "Go on then!"

"Go on, what?" She'd stared at him, puzzled.

"Turn me on, Blondie. Whatcha think?" He'd looked at her as if she were thick or something.

What are you then, the bloody immersion, she wanted to ask him but didn't. While she was soullessly doing what he'd asked, she felt dead inside. It wasn't a fun experience. She was glad beyond measure when he had left without even a proper goodbye.

The next guy was so drunk he couldn't really manage the sex at all, and the third fella made it clear he thought she was a slut for going home with him on less than an hour's acquaintance. That was rich of him, she'd thought at the time. He was doing the exact same thing as she was doing, plus he was married with a child, but it was okay for him because he was a man. It wasn't okay for her — it made her a slut – because she was a woman. The double standard made her feel sick.

After three weeks, Paul still hadn't texted her to meet up, even though she'd sent him a load of texts herself, ranging from the casual and non-threatening to the downright desperate. **Hey you, what u up 2? Hiya, fancy a chat? Hey there, u horny? I could use a chat/a hug/sex/whatever crumbs u feel like throwing in my direction, please txt me back, Paul, I'm dying here** and so on and so on. He finally texted on a Friday night. Barbara and the kids had gone to stay with Barbara's sister Suzanne for the night. Suzanne and her partner Ida were having a party, to celebrate *life*, was how Suzanne had so oddly put it, whatever all that was about. It was probably some mad lesbian thing, according to Paul, or maybe it was a mad Swiss thing, because Ida was from Switzerland. Paul wasn't exactly in favour with either of the sisters at the moment so he wasn't invited. This party was for the women and children only. They were making a huge big deal out of it as well.

Laura was at home by herself nursing a bottle of wine. She'd been feeling too battered by recent experiences to chance going to the nightclub on Leeson Street again. She was feeling particularly sorry for herself and missing Paul desperately when he finally texted – a curt, cold little text message: **Are you available?**

Even though his message made her feel uncomfortably like a prostitute, she'd texted back immediately – **Yes, come on over** – wildly happy again suddenly to be needed, to be *wanted*, by him. She charged around the flat madly, throwing on sexy lingerie and make-up and perfume with hands that shook, and brushing her teeth until her gums bled, to disguise the smell of drink and cigarettes.

When he arrived at her flat, they went straight to bed. Laura, more than a bit pissed, did her dominatrix act as usual but with so much careless vigour that at one point he had to cry out: "*Take it easy, for fuck's sake, will you? I don't want my face to be marked!*" Even though his wife and kids were staying at Barbara's sister's house for the night, he still didn't stay the night with Laura.

He doesn't want me to get any mad ideas about us being properly back together, Laura thought miserably as he sat on the edge of the bed getting dressed with his back to her. I don't think I can stand this. I don't think I can bear it. I love him so much!

He turned suddenly as he was putting on his jacket. "I forgot – I've brought something to show you." He pulled a crumpled piece of paper from his jacket pocket and passed it to her.

Laura, sitting up in bed naked, trying desperately not to cry about the fact that he was going home already rather than opting to stay the night with her as he might once have done (if he could persuade Barbara that he was watching all-night sport at a mate's house), looked at it curiously. What the fuck . . .? It was one of those scan photographs that the midwife gave expectant mothers when they went for their baby-scan, usually around the fifth month of pregnancy. It was a photo of a tiny baby in its mother's womb, a tiny baby with all its limbs, a baby that looked for all the world as if it was sucking its thumb. Jesus Christ!

"This . . . this is your baby?" she said slowly, stunned.

He nodded, grinning like a village idiot. He actually looked as pleased as Punch with himself, the bastard.

"It's a boy." He was grinning like the bloody Cheshire cat now, all over his smug face. "Barbara told me last night. We told the kids together this morning. They're thrilled to bits. We're already planning all kinds of blue things for the new nursery. Our first boy. Can you believe it?"

Was he really that stupid, Laura wondered in amazement – did he really think that a scan photo of his and his wife's beautiful little unborn baby was an appropriate thing to show to her, his discarded mistress? This hurt was more than she could take.

"Get out," she said softly, laying the crumpled photo on the bed.

"What?" Paul stared at her, startled.

"I said get out," repeated Laura. "Take your photo of your baby with you and piss off out of it."

"What's wrong with you? Are you premenstrual or something?"

"*Get out!*" she screamed. "*I'm done with you. I never want to see you again. We're done, over, finished, for good.*"

"What the fuck did I do?" He was standing there staring at her, patting down his pockets methodically for his phone, keys and wallet. Funny how people were conditioned to do that, Laura thought as she watched him, no matter what the ongoing crisis. Earthquake, hurricane or zombie apocalypse, you couldn't cross the road without checking you had your phone, keys and wallet.

"*Get out!*" She picked up a jar of face-cream from her bedside table as if she intended hurling it through the air at him like a missile. "Get out, get out, get *out!*"

"Oh, don't worry, I'm going," he said, before adding nastily, "And this time I won't be back."

"*Good*. That's good, because you're a dirty lying cheating *pig* of a man and you're not good enough for me. I never want to see you again. *Now get out and shut the door after you!*"

When he was gone, she threw herself down on the bed and cried for him for what she sincerely hoped would be the last time.

Now it was a Monday morning, the Monday after that terrible Friday night, and Laura was on the Luas to work. She'd spent all weekend having a truly horrible Long Dark Night of the Soul. As dreadful as it had been, she reckoned it was worth it. She had poured the remaining booze down the sink on the Saturday morning. She was not a lush like her mother. She was determined not to end up a hopeless alcoholic like Eleanor Brennan. There would be no more drinking to help her cope with life's ups and downs. From now on, she would cope with any crises herself, but while dry, clean and sober and not drowning in booze. She was determined that her relationship with Paul was over. No longer could she sit meekly by while Paul played Happy Families and rubbed his new baby photos in her face, showing her like nothing else had that he didn't give a toss about her feelings at all. She was done with Paul, the bastard.

In her stylish black handbag right now sat her resignation from work, a neatly typed letter that had taken her a while to compose and didn't mention a single word about Paul. She'd be giving it to the younger Mr. Phelan later on today. It was effective immediately, although if they wanted her to work out her two weeks' notice, then she'd do that. It would be hard to find another job this side of Christmas, but she had savings that would last her for a while if the worst came to the worst. A clean break from Paul and Phelan's was what she needed. Aside from her financial situation, though, getting through Christmas would be hard with everyone around her either all loved up or playing Happy bloody Families. Even Eleanor, her alcoholic mother, had someone to spend Christmas with. She had a new boyfriend now, an Algerian waiter of twenty-eight (the same age as Laura!) called Ali, who worked in a fast-food restaurant in the Liberties. Laura had nearly died of shock when her mother had broken the news over the phone.

"Have you given him any money, Mum?" was Laura's first question.

"I don't know what you're implying, Laura," Eleanor had sniffed, offended.

On a Disability payment for her panic attacks and chronic anxiety (chronic alcoholism, more like, Laura personally thought), the forty-five-year-old Eleanor was a prime target for conmen, who smelled her desperation and figured that they could somehow swing it to their advantage. Still, Laura wasn't going to worry about Eleanor and her Algerian toy-boy now. That was very definitely a problem for the future.

Laura, more concerned about the here and now for the moment, checked her appearance in her little gold compact mirror, a present from Paul that was too good to throw out or give away to charity just because Paul had given it to her. Finding her make-up to be flawless, as she'd expected it to be, she took a quick selfie with her phone, then another and then another, and quickly uploaded them to social media from her phone with the caption: **'Moi, en route to the daily grind.'** There. Good. She felt better. It was important to keep up external appearances anyway, no matter how shit everything was under the surface. And Paul might just see these pictures and suffer a pang of longing for what he was missing. If there was even the slightest chance of his seeing them, then all the effort she'd gone to would be worth it a thousand times over. She looked up suddenly and caught the eye of the man sitting across from her.

To her surprise, she realised that it was the tall, dark-haired guy in the long black coat, the one she often saw on the Luas and who'd been sitting two or three seats down from her at the start of the journey.

"I like a woman who takes care of herself, like you clearly do," he said, eyeing her up appreciatively.

"Do you now?" She tucked her phone and compact

mirror back into her handbag. She crossed and recrossed her legs deliberately to see the effect it had on him (he stared at her like he was the Big Bad Wolf and she Little Red Hiding Hood crossed with a nice juicy steak, which was exactly the desired effect), and looked him over as discreetly as she could.

He was certainly good-looking – no one could deny him that – about thirty-five or even older. That was the age Laura preferred her men to be. Paul had been an immature thirty-four going on fifteen, the jerk, and Barry O'Donnell was still only in his late twenties. This guy looked older, like he was a man of the world and knew things about life. His long black cashmere coat had clearly cost a bomb. His shoes were undoubtedly designer, and even his dark subtly patterned socks looked as if they'd just strolled casually off a catwalk. The gloves on his lap were black leather and he carried a matching black briefcase. There was a general air of expensiveness about him. He even *smelled* expensive, a scent that appealed greatly to Laura's trained nostrils. What he was doing on the Luas instead of driving his own posh car, she couldn't imagine. Maybe he liked public transport or something. Maybe it was a good place to pick up women.

"I'm Dominic," he said smoothly, offering her his hand.

"Is that a wedding ring?" She suddenly noticed it winking on the hand he hadn't proffered.

"Well, yes," he admitted, "but don't you worry your pretty little head about that. It's a marriage in-name-only."

He leaned forward and she caught a whiff of his outrageously expensive aftershave and it made her go weak at the knees.

Lowering his voice, he said confidentially, "My Wife Doesn't Understand Me."

"I see," said Laura. She looked him up and down slowly. And smiled.

"I'm Laura," she said. "Tell me more."

NOT THE END . . .

FLOWERS FOR EUGENIA
A POEM BY MELISSA CREIGHTON-REDMOND

She loved all flowers
Loved the snowdrops and daffodils
In spring
Made daisy-chains
In summer
Look at me, Mummy,
Look at the pretty!
Am I a princess?
Of course, darling,
The prettiest princess
She cried when they died
The flowers in winter
When will they come back?
In the spring, darling,
Everything comes back
In the spring
Will you and me
Be here in the spring,
Mummy?
Of course we will, darling,
Why wouldn't we be?
Snowdrops and daffodils
Brighten her grave now
Every spring
Tossing their beautiful heads
In the breeze
And in the summer
There'll be daisies

A blanket of daisies
To cushion her sleep
I'll fashion a chain
For her neck
Lay it round her
So gently she doesn't even stir
Not a breath
Another chain for the headstone
Flowers for Eugenia
Crowning the resting-place
Of this little princess
Who loved them in life
Flowers for Eugenia
Look at me, Mummy!
Flowers for Eugenia
Watered by the rain
Warmed by the sun
To everything
There is a season
Flowers for Eugenia
Ashes to ashes
Dust to dust
Flowers for Eugenia

Printed in Great Britain
by Amazon